LONDON IS DEAD

Michael Keenaghan lives in London. This is
his first novel.

LONDON IS DEAD

Michael Keenaghan

Nocturnal

First published Nov 2022

Copyright © 2022 Michael Keenaghan

All rights reserved

Nocturnal Books
London

A CIP catalogue record for this book
is available from the British Library

ISBN 9798354201891

'The past is the present… it's the future too.'
Eugene O'Neill

CONTENTS

Part One: Dagenham v Hackney

Part Two: County Kilburn

Part One

Dagenham v Hackney

1

Something Better Change

Early 2006

Terry Hart sat at the bar staring into the dregs of his fourth pint.

'Still in one piece I see Tel,' Dan said, walking in and pulling a stool next to him. 'Well come on then, show us the war wounds.'

Terry turned to face him, revealing a bruised eye.

'Is that it? On the phone last night I thought they'd half killed you. What else, they stamped on your ribs?'

Terry put a hand to his side and winced. 'Don't remind me.'

Dan ordered two pints. Then he shook his head.

'I don't know what we're going to do with you Tel. You're like a magnet for grief these days.'

'I'm fed up with it mate.'

'I thought you carried a hammer in your cab?'

'I do, but I didn't get a chance to use it, did I.'

'No offence but that's what you said last time.'

'Are you taking the piss? That time they had a machete and there were three of them. Try swinging a hammer when you've got a foot-long blade wrapped round your throat.'

'Here, this will cheer you up.' Their pints arrived and Dan passed his one over. 'Get that down your neck and maybe we'll get a smile out of you before the night's out.'

They drank.

'You said there were two of the fuckers. Where did you pick them up?'

'Hackney.'

'The old manor? You should see our old school now, they've got knife arches and police at the gates. So what happened, they jumped you when you dropped them off?'

Terry nodded. 'Behind the main road there, near the snooker hall.'

'The place where the dealers hang out? We should plot up, sit and watch, wait for the cunts.'

'What's the point, they were hardly local, were they? Anyway, I've got better things to do, like trying to put some money on the table. If it's possible these days that is.'

'Well you know my answer to that one.' Dan leaned in. 'You need to get back to some real work. You've been playing it by the book for how long now and look at where it's got you.'

'Spare me the spiel alright. Save it for some other mug.'

Dan lowered his voice. 'There's some graft coming up, something big. It's just what you need right now.'

'You're like a broken record. I'm past all that caper. It's a young man's game. I can't be getting locked up at my age, it ain't an option.'

'Keep cabbing and keep getting robbed then.' Dan stood up and put a hand on his shoulder. 'And don't forget the pipe and slippers while you're at it. You're a good driver Tel, you're wasting your talents.'

Terry watched him walk over to the slot machine. He thought of his last stretch inside. It was four years back. All for a vanload of cookers. Another of Dan's ideas. They'd nicked them from a warehouse up Romford, and Terry was delivering them to a buyer when he was pulled over. It was a minor nothing job, yet he served over a year. He'd done a lot longer but not since his twenties. He was in his mid-forties now with a wife and two teenage daughters. He had responsibilities. He couldn't put them through all that again.

The pub door swung open and in strolled Andy, still in his plumbing overalls.

'Oi oi, it's the man of the moment,' he said, sounding far too chirpy for Terry's liking. 'Heard you had some aggro last night. Where's the damage?'

He took a look at Terry's face. 'A shiner, is that all? From the way Dan was banging on I thought you'd done twelve rounds with Big Daddy.'

'They stamped on his ribs as well,' Dan called over, slotting more coins in the machine.

'And you didn't smash the fuckers?' Andy said. 'How much did they take?'

'One eighty,' Terry muttered.

'Who did it?'

'Couple of schwarzers,' Dan called.

Terry shook his head. 'One was black, one white.'

'You said if it happened again you'd hammer the cunts, what happened?' Andy asked.

'Nothing happened,' Dan butted in again. 'That's the problem.'

'Exactly. Why carry a tool if you're not going to use it?'

Terry got to his feet. 'Will you two just shut the fuck up?'

He went to the bogs. He was sick of the pair of them.

Standing by the urinal he could hear voices from inside one of the cubicles. A boy and a girl giggling away. Couldn't they have thought of somewhere better than a crappy pub khazi? Then he realised they were snorting up lines. As he washed his hands the trap door opened and the pair stepped sheepishly out. A kid about seventeen and his skinny girlfriend.

'Had a good time in there did you?' Terry met the boy's eyes in the mirror, aware of the lack of mirth in his tone.

The boy's eyes widened in recognition. 'Oh, hello Mr Hart,' he said while his girlfriend slipped out the door.

Terry turned around. He scanned his memory in case he knew him, but nothing came up. 'And who the fuck are you?'

'I'm a friend of your daughter Leah. I was round your house the other day. I thought you recognised me.' The silly bloke looked wired.

Terry remembered him now. Some kid his wife had introduced as Leah's boyfriend just as the racing results were coming in. He'd put thirty quid on a horse so he'd nodded a quick hello, hardly registering him. Afterwards his wife said he'd been rude, but Terry was more pissed off at spunking another wad of cash.

The boy muttered something and made for the door.

'Not so fast young man,' Terry said, stepping forward. 'I do remember you as it goes. A friend of Leah's you say, and you think it's a good idea sniffing drugs, do you? And who was that bird here, another girlfriend of yours?'

'She's just a friend. And we weren't doing drugs. We weren't doing anything like that, I swear.'

'Of course not. She was just holding your todger in there while you had a slash.' He pushed the boy's shoulder. 'Get out of my sight, and if I ever see you with Leah again you're getting your legs broke, do I make myself clear?'

The boy nodded and left. Terry would have to speak to his 17-year-old daughter about the type of people she was choosing to hang around with. Though maybe he'd just tell the missus, let her sort it out. Leah was blanking him at the moment after he'd tried to ground her for staying out all night.

He turned to the mirror, his bruised eye glaring back at him. What was happening to him these days? He was losing his touch. On some kind of downward spiral. Whatever it was, it needed nipping in the bud sharpish. He returned to his stool at the bar and counted out enough change for another pint.

Dan came up and slapped a fold of notes down in front of him.

'There's a ton twenty for you there, Tel. I've just done a whip round. The lads across the way chipped in too. And here's a bit from me.' He counted out sixty quid from his wallet. 'Add this and you haven't lost a penny.'

'No way Dan, I can't take this.'

'You fucking are taking it.'

'I don't know what to say.'

'Thanks would be nice.'

'Yeah course, thanks – but this is a fair bit of cash here.'

'What are mates for? Don't worry about it.' Then Dan leaned in. 'And if you want to make some more, you know where you can get it.' He slapped his back. 'I've got to run. Look after yourself and I'll catch you later.'

Half an hour later Terry stepped out into the mild spring night. Passing Dagenham Heathway tube, groups of youngsters were dolled up for their Friday night out, loud and lively, but things were quieter as he made his way down the side streets towards home. Up ahead a group of boys were outside a house, a mix of black and white. Music rattled from a phone as two of them jostled with each other. As he approached they turned silent, going from laughing kids to moody men. For a moment Terry considered crossing over, but decided not to. He'd never crossed a road to avoid anyone in his life and wasn't going to start now.

'You got a light?' one asked.

Terry ignored him, walked on.

'Yo, bossman, I'm talking to you.'

He fought an urge to turn round and say something, but didn't. Then the bloke muttered a comment and they laughed. Terry felt his blood boil.

Reaching home he closed the front door and put his jacket on the banister. In the living room the TV was blaring, his 14-year-old daughter Megan slumped on the sofa tapping on her phone.

'Where's your mum?' he asked.

'She's gone to Aunt Linda's,' she said without looking up.

'What about Leah?'

'She's out.'

'Where?'

'I dunno. She went out.'

On the box someone was doing a pisstake version of Michael Jackson's Bad.

'Will you turn that racket down?'

'I'm watching it.'

'No you're not, you're glued to your fucking phone.'

'What are you swearing for? You're always telling me not to swear.'

He went to the kitchen and put the kettle on. Then he hunted through the fridge for something to eat. He stood munching on a cold Cornish pasty. It disappeared fast so he got working on another.

'Ugh, you're like a pig,' Megan said, walking in to take a bottle of Diet Coke from the fridge.

'You can talk, look at the size of you,' he said, wiping crumbs from his shirt.

Suddenly she was yelling at him. 'I hate you, you fucking bastard!' She rushed back to the living room, slamming the door behind her.

Terry instantly regretted it. He'd spoken without thinking. Recently Stacey had gone to visit Megan's headteacher after she'd been bullied about her weight. It was nothing too serious, just a few names from one girl mainly, but his wife had warned him to tread carefully as it was a sensitive subject for her.

'Meg, I'm sorry.' He tried to open the door but she held it shut.

'Any weight problems I've got are inherited from you, you fat

14

fucking pig,' she shouted.

She moved from the door and Terry opened up to see her curled on the sofa, crying into a cushion.

'Megs, listen, I'm sorry. I didn't mean what I said – I love you, you know I love you.'

'Get out!' She grabbed the nearest thing to hand, a framed photo and lobbed it at him. He ducked and it smashed against the wall, landing by his feet. He saw the picture behind the broken glass. Him, Stacey and the girls a decade ago, a picnic in Parsloes Park, everyone smiling for the camera.

'Just leave me alone,' she whined and he retreated, closing the door behind him.

He was standing stunned in the hallway when his eldest Leah walked in the front door. She was wearing an opened fur-lined jacket, her chest spilling out of a tight top, and a skirt that if any shorter might have revealed her underwear.

Leah creased her face, pulling her jacket closed. 'What are you looking at?'

'Nothing.'

'Well don't creep me out like that.'

'I'm just worried that's all, I'm your father.'

'Worried about what?'

'You going out dressed in next to nothing with so many scumbags out there who would rape you as quick as look at you.'

'What are you on about? You're sick. And I'm not wearing next to nothing actually. Mum's right, you need your head tested.'

'Did you see that gang down the road just now, did you walk past them?'

'Killshot and Sammy's crowd? I went to school with them. They're harmless.'

'Killshot, are you serious? Is that what one of them calls himself?'

'It's his street name. He's a rapper. It doesn't mean he actually goes around shooting people. Never mind though, you don't get it. You live in another world.'

'I'm telling you to be sensible, that's all.'

'I'm not a little girl you know, I'm an adult and can look after myself.' She walked past him and made for the living room.

'Don't go in there.'

'What have you done now?' She went in. Inside he heard Megan crying and telling all.

Fuck this. Terry headed upstairs for a shower. He hadn't reached the top before Leah was telling him to get down here right now.

'I made a mistake okay. Tell Megan I'm sorry.' He carried on up.

'You wait till Mum hears about this. I'm texting her right now.'

He went into the bathroom to try and wash away his sins. A short spell of respite before Stacey came home and the inevitable bollocking. He got under the warm water. The bruises on his side were darker now, looked more savage.

He thought of last night. Another attempt happened a few months back, but they ran empty-handed when they heard some sirens. This time they got what they wanted and more. He remembered an arm locking around his neck almost choking him, the cunt shouting to hand over his money. Then he was out of the car and getting kicked about on the ground. He recalled them laughing as they walked away. That was worse than the digs. And on his own fucking manor. He'd collected them only a short walk from where he grew up in Hackney and that bothered him too.

He thought of his old house. Out on his travels, if nearby, he would occasionally drive down the backstreets and pull up outside. There was a sadness to the place that cut him deep. His dad had worked on the buses and his mum kept the place spotless. Lee, his older brother by two years, was popular and made everyone laugh and as a family they were happy. Then so quickly it all fell apart. He remembered the cold blustery evening when Lee didn't come home. His mum was fretting, dad telling her not to worry, he'll be home eventually, he always comes home.

Terry got his coat and walked down to the park where Lee hung around with his mates. It was dark and empty, not a soul around. Back on the street he saw Lee's friends Brian and Big Stu coming along and straight away knew something was wrong. Stu had tears in his eyes; both were in shock. They'd been messing about down the railway and Lee had an accident. All Terry remembered then was the police coming round and hearing the words 'high speed train'. His mum never properly recovered and nothing was ever the same. Two years later they moved from Hackney to Dagenham. Both his parents were gone now.

He stepped out of the shower and dried himself. Exhausted he headed for the sack. He slept soundly for a couple of hours until his wife appeared. She threw him a duvet saying to get his arse down to the sofa as he wasn't sleeping upstairs tonight.

Down in the living room she said, 'You don't know how serious this is, do you?'

'I do know,' Terry said. 'In fact, tell you what, I want the address of her bully at school because I think the cow's parents need a talk.'

'It's you who needs a talking to, criticising Megan's weight. Are you trying to torture the poor girl?'

'I wasn't thinking. It was just a silly comment.'

'I can smell the drink off you, you stink of it. That's another thing, I'm going to tell the landlord of that pub not to let you in no more as you can't even pay our bills.'

'Don't embarrass me like that.'

'I'll do worse if you talk to Megs like that again, I promise you. She's sensitive. And Leah's got her problems too - she's having boyfriend trouble at the moment, so tread carefully and don't get involved.'

Terry remembered the boy in the pub, but thought it wise not to mention it now. He lay on the sofa.

Stacey softened a little. 'How's your eye?'

'It's nothing, it'll heal.'

'You need to look after yourself Terry.'

'Yeah well, under the circumstances it was a bit difficult.'

'So you reckon.'

He looked at her. 'You saying you don't believe I was robbed?'

'I don't know what to believe with you anymore. For all I know you probably just had a punch-up in the pub.'

'I wish.'

She made for the door, then turned. 'Another thing, I've told Aunt Linda that you'll be round in the morning to cut her tree down. The one you looked at before. She's worried if a storm blows it down it could kill someone.'

'I told you, my chainsaw's broken.'

'You've got an axe, haven't you?'

'An axe on a tree that size?'

'What are you, man or mouse? Just do it. First thing.'

2

Twisted Freestyle

Jay was behind the wheel of his black GTi, Bigz riding shotgun and Slim behind as they cruised the Hackney streets. They were looking for somewhere to hit. A shop, take-away joint, anything was fair game, but it was one of those nights when nowhere felt quite right.

'This ain't happening,' Jay shook his head. 'Let's just head down the Palace Pavilion. There'll be nuff nice girls on the pull there tonight.'

Bigz and Slim ignored him, their eyes scanning for action.

'You hear me? Let's leave the work for some other time. It's ladies-free night. I was there last week, pure honeys wall to wall.'

'Listen to this guy,' Bigz tutted. 'All you ever think about is pussy. I need paper man, I've got bills to pay. Adult responsibilities. We ain't all like you, still living with your rents.'

'Big independent man of the world now, yeah?' Jay laughed. 'Until two months ago you were still kipping at your mum's. You're just in a sulk because you're not getting three square meals and your dirty smalls washed no more.'

Bigz took out the matchstick he was chewing and slowly turned to him. 'I'll fucking lick up your face for chatting like that.'

Slim leaned forward between the seats to ease the tension. 'Come on, allow it, the both of you. We're losing focus here. I know a place up Tottenham, near Spurs. An off-licence run by an old black guy. An ancient. He's been done before so he keeps a rusty old machete under the counter. That's all we've got to watch for.'

'I ain't scared of no grandad. If it's a payday then count me in.' Then Bigz stopped to consider the logistics. 'Thing is though, if he wants to play then things could get messy. You know these stubborn old types. I prefer to keep things clean.'

'We could chance it,' Slim shrugged, 'but really you want to hit somewhere you know is loaded. No point playing for pennies.'

'Tell you the truth, right now I ain't too fussy.'

'I'm hungry,' Slim said. 'How about we go Mickey D's?'

'Let's hit somewhere up first. An in-and-out job. Cash in pocket. Then we go Mickey D's.'

'There's this Polish place up Wood Green we could try. Usually just one man there. Thing is, last time I might've heard some barking from round the back.'

'Uh-uh,' Bigz said. 'I don't play with dogs, no way.'

'Well what about one of those 24-hour Turkish shops? Find a quiet one.'

'You stupid? You want the Turkish mafia gunning after you? Nobody goes near those places.'

'Then maybe try the offy up Totty then.'

Bigz pondered it. 'Go on then, fuck it, let's do it.'

Jay swung the car north for N17. Destination enemy territory.

Slim popped a Red Bull. 'Jeez, I'm still knackered from last night you know. I was up Dagenham with my cousin Darren, he lives out there. He's a nutcase. Crazy shit happens every time I meet up with him.'

'What's it like out that way?' Bigz asked.

'Less mandem, but it's still pretty rough.'

'I bet it's all pussies.'

'You'd be surprised. You've still got your old crime families and that. Some heavy crims.'

'Don't care. We've got London on lock. We're fucking running tings.'

'But Dagenham ain't London though, it's Essex.'

'What's the London Borough of Barking and Dagenham then?' Jay cut in, turning from the wheel.

'Fuck knows. But ask anyone who lives round there and they'll tell you it's Essex.'

'Even so,' Bigz said. 'We're spreading out. Mandem are everywhere now.'

'That might be so,' Slim said. 'But we're still mostly operating low-level.'

'No way.'

'It's true. We've got the street, but who brings in all the weaponry and big drug importations? You've got the Pakis and Turks shipping in the H, but a lot of the guns, coke and pill shipments are the whites. They just don't make a show of it. Then there's the East Europeans and they're proper organised too.'

'Fuck that. You're just bigging up the white man because you're half-white yourself.'

Slim shook his head. 'All I'm saying is out Essex way you've got the families that know the game inside out. Fathers and sons who've done hard time. And my cousin's a bit like that. He's a psycho, just like his old man. Darren's done even more time than you,' he laughed. 'And you've spent more years caged up than on the out.'

Bigz kissed his teeth. 'I did fourteen months in Feltham, then a year in Aylesbury. Rest of the time I've been full-time active on the road. You got a problem with that?'

'You've been in Aylesbury twice,' Jay interjected. 'And

Feltham twice.'

'See what I mean?' Slim laughed. 'You spent your best years inside. Now you've hit twenty-one you better watch out bro. Big man's prison.'

'Fuck you.'

'Anyway, I was out with Darren. Mad shit. We got a cab up to his manor and Daz starts looking at me funny, nodding at the driver. The cabbie's a proper cockney, all England tattoos and I'm thinking, no way Daz, you're not. Then we pull in and he grabs the guy round the neck, choking him half to death. Then he yanks him out and starts kicking fuck out of him on the road.'

'How much Ps you make?'

'Two hundred. Then we hit this all-night snooker hall. We blew most of it on these two women in the end. It was daylight by then and we were behind these garages, balling them in the open air. Even the bitches down that way are nuts.'

'I wouldn't go near pussy like that,' Bigz frowned. 'Used goods. You've probably got Aids now.'

'We were strapped up. We're hardly going to ride bareback with slappers on the game, are we?'

'I wouldn't play with anyone on the game full stop.'

'You would if they looked like these two.'

'If they were so hot they wouldn't need to sell it, would they? You two were so coked-up you thought you were sampling quality when you were boning two knackered old junkies craving their next fix.'

'I wasn't that out of it.'

'I bet you were.'

'But I'm telling you I wasn't.'

'You know you were.'

'I said I fucking wasn't, you deaf?'

'Shut your teeth, dickhead,' Bigz turned round trying to swipe him.

'Will you clowns give it a rest?' Jay said. 'You're like children in the fricking playground.'

Near Spurs they toured the backstreets looking for the offy. They found a small line of shops. Only one was open, but it turned out to be a barbershop. Slim was shocked, wondering where it had gone.

Bigz shook his head. 'Typical.'

'I don't get it, it makes no sense.'

'Old timer probably croaked it six months ago. Your intel is useless.'

'Keep driving Jay,' Slim tutted. 'Next corner shop I see I'm hitting it, serious.'

'Let's just get out of here,' Bigz said. 'I fucking hate Tottenham.'

Driving off they passed a lone roadman strutting along in a red puffa. Clocking them he quickly turned away.

'You see that?' Slim said, perking up.

Bigz nodded, looking eager. 'I smell money.'

'What do you reckon, want to give it a go?'

'Let's do the Tottenham pussy. Yo Jay, pull over and keep the engine on.'

They flew out of the car and the guy legged it. They chased him down an alley but lost him behind some low-level flats.

They stopped in a small empty car-parking area, bushes at one side, a builder's skip at the other. The place was a dead end, enclosed by a tall wire fence.

'He must've jumped over,' Bigz said, getting his breath back.

'You never know. I'll check the bushes here, you check by the skip.'

Bigz went for a cursory look but there was no sign. He returned to where Slim was poking the bushes with a stick. 'This is bullshit, he's gone. Let's head back to the car.'

They were setting off when a sound came from the bushes.

'That's him,' Slim said, eyes lighting up. 'Stay here, B. I'll flush him out. If he runs, grab him.' He approached the foliage and out scurried a fox, dashing across the car park.

'Jesus fuck,' Bigz said as it raced past him. 'That thing just scared the shit out of me.'

Slim was bent with laughter. 'Your face.' Then he straightened up. 'Come on, we're done. It's only us and the night creatures out here tonight.'

They started walking when again a noise sounded, louder this time, from over by the skip. 'That ain't no night creature.'

They rushed over and their man jumped out, scrambling up the fence. Slim was there first, grabbing his foot, the guy kicking out until Slim gripped his leg and they both tumbled down.

Slim was on top of him punching until he submitted. Then he stood up, dusting himself down.

'Prick ripped my jacket, you see this?' He pointed out a small tear. 'This is Avirex man, you know how much this shit cost? We should fucking shank him up.'

'Nah, let's see what he's got for us.' Bigz crouched down. 'What jacket you wearing here blud, fucking Primark?'

'This ain't Primark,' the guy tutted.

Bigz slapped him. 'Did I ask for backchat? What's in your pockets, what you got for me?' He found a lock knife. 'Big wannabe with a blade. What ends you from?'

'Tottenham.'

'You being funny - what bits?'

'Park Lane.'

'Who you run with, Northumberland Park?'

'I don't run with anyone. I ain't into all that. The shank's for protection, you know how it is.'

Bigz pulled out his wallet. It was empty but for a child's bus pass. 'Jeez, how old are you?'

'Fourteen. I'm just a child innit so leave me alone.'

'A six-foot-three fucking child? They upping the steroids in the chicken these days?'

Slim stepped forward. 'Were you just a kid when you tried

kicking me in the face up there and ripping my jacket?'

'Leave him,' Bigz said. 'I ain't violating no little boy. Listen pussy, you've been warned. Don't fuck with Hackney. We're the dons in this town, the frontmen, you hear me?'

'Wait, I want his phone. Check his back pocket.'

The boy was reluctant but Bigz whacked his hands away. 'What you hiding?' He dipped in, pulled out a fold of cash and a bag of rocks.

'Rah.'

'I knew it - he's a lying little shotta.'

Suddenly the boy sprung up, tried to make a run for it. Slim tackled and soon floored him. Then he grabbed a steel bar from the skip and bashed it over his head. The guy lay clutching his scalp, fingers bloody. 'You think you can run from us, pussy?'

'Hey, yo.' They turned to see Jay pacing towards them. 'What the fuck are you two doing? It ain't safe out here. Let's go.'

Bigz agreed, but Slim was stalling.

'I said let's move,' Jay tugged him. 'We're in hostile territory out here.'

'Get your hands off my Avirex, man.'

'It ain't real Avirex, you told me that yourself. It's a sixty quid special from Ridley Road market, remember?'

'So what?' Slim rolled his shoulders. 'It's the principle.'

'Yeah, right. Let's get out of here.'

They walked back, checking for prying eyes, but thankfully the whole area seemed dead. As they climbed into the whip a cop car approached from the far end of the road, sirens screaming. 'Shit.' They ducked down, holding their breath as the flashing blue lights blazed closer. The car sped past them and turned in towards the flats.

'That was fricking close,' said Bigz. 'Hit the floor Jay, let's roll.'

'How much we make back there?' Slim asked as they drove towards the McDonald's drive-in on Green Lanes.

'Haven't checked.' Bigz pulled out the cash and rocks, but kept patting his pockets. 'Hang on, where's my wallet gone?'

Slim came forward and grabbed the goods from his hand. 'Forget your wallet, you already told us you were skint. Now let's divvy this up.' The total was two hundred and ten. Seventy quid each. He passed it three ways.

'Nice,' Jay smiled, pocketing his share. 'As for the rocks, you two crackheads can enjoy it cos I don't touch that shit.'

'Nor do I,' Slim laughed. 'But Bigz, he'd smoke anything.'

Bigz was still searching for his wallet, getting worried now. 'I better not have dropped it back there.'

'You probably left it at home,' Slim said. 'Wouldn't be the first time, would it?'

Considering that, Bigz eased up. 'Yeah, maybe you're right.'

'Remember the time we drove out to Watford to deliver that stash of weed? We were rolling up the M1 thinking it was in the boot but you'd left it back at your mum's.'

'Gotta admit, that was fucked up.'

'Tell me about it. We were almost there before you went: hang about, did I load the shit?'

'No way,' Jay shook his head. 'That's comedy stuff. Don't ever run your own business B, you'd be bankrupt before you made your first sale.'

Bigz turned to him. 'We went back to collect it and I made a nice profit that time. A big fucking profit.'

'Okay, if you say so, big man.'

They pulled in and ordered a monster load of food, parked in and got munching.

'I'm definitely going clubbing after this,' Jay said. 'Whether you two are coming is your own business.'

'I ain't nightclubbing with seventy measly quid in my pocket,' Bigz said, polishing off his second Big Mac. 'And I've already lost some of that to Ronnie McDonald. I'd only roll into a rave packing a ton and a half at least.'

'What do you care about being loaded in a club for?' Jay said. 'You hardly even drink.'

'I still like to buy a bottle of bubbly though, spray it about and that. I've got a reputation to maintain. I party lavish, you get me?'

'Sure you do,' Jay laughed. 'You're so tight-arsed you hardly want to buy a Pepsi at the bar. Last time up Stratford Rex you were complaining how a can was five times dearer than Tesco.'

'Fuck you man,' Bigz said, dropping his trash out the window and wiping his hands. 'Anyway, talking of money, I say we can still make a stack tonight.'

Slim checked his watch. 'You're right, we've still got time. What about that chicken shop down Homerton?'

'Place we looked at earlier?'

'Yeah, it'll be quieter now. I did there once before on my own. Jumped over the counter and the guy couldn't wait to get rid of me. The till was so loaded I could hardly get it all in my pockets.'

'Sounds good to me.'

'Not to me it don't,' Jay said. 'Sounds like a lot of hassle I don't need.' He tossed his drink and put up his window. 'I'm up for Palace P. Last week it was 80/20 ladies to men I swear. You two need to chill once in a while. It can't be all work and no play, you know.' He started the engine. 'Now come on. Club time. Agreed?'

'I'm easy,' Slim shrugged. 'What do you reckon B? Your call.'

'Only when I've got a decent roll in my pocket - which will be within the hour once we've done the chicken shop.'

'I ain't feeling it,' Jay said, pulling out onto the road.

'Course you're not,' Bigz said. 'The man who earned seventy notes tonight by sitting on his arse.'

Jay had no comeback for that, and they drove past Manor House, cutting through Stoke Newington and Lower Clapton to the arse end of Hackney: dark and dismal Homerton.

All eyes, they cruised slowly past the shop. They turned and parked in across the road. Things were quiet, not too many passing cars.

'Looks like there's only one man working there now,' Slim observed. 'But even if another pops up it don't matter. Surprise, max aggression and you can't go wrong. There's no customers either.'

'Exactly,' Jay tutted. 'Means there's probably all of two quid in the till.'

'Bullshit,' Bigz said. 'These joints are feeding people morning till night. They're stacking pure paper. That guy probably drives home in a Merc.'

'Waits for the bus more like,' Jay said. 'They're all migrants in these places, probably illegals on a quid an hour.'

'You think these people come here to work for pennies? They could do that back home. They're minting it. It's time for some wealth distribution, serious. They're piling it up in the bank while we've got fuck all.'

'I ain't got fuck all,' Slim said, not too fond of the pauper tag.

'Nor me,' Jay said. 'Right now I've got a roll that'll cover club entrance and drinks all night long. You'll still be out trying to earn pennies while I've got a curvy honey on my lap shoving her boobies in my face.'

'You're dreaming,' Bigz said, concentrating on the shop. 'Now enough of this shit. It's time to go to work. Let's earn some bread tonight.'

He reached under the seat for a bat and handed it to Slim. 'Smash the CCTV cos times like this I'm a little camera shy.' Then he produced a plastic bottle. 'Me, I've got this bad boy.'

'Is that acid?' Slim said, while Jay shook his head.

'Relax, it's just a bit of squirt. Ammonia. Most it'll do is put his sight out for a bit.'

'No way, I don't want you chucking acid around, it could end up in the wrong place.'

'It's a last resort in case things go to shit. Most likely I won't

28

need it.'

'Leave it in the car,' Jay added. 'Or better still, chuck it down the nearest drain. You don't know what you're messing with. My cousin's mate up Milton Keynes got burnt up badly with that stuff. He was dealing in the wrong area and a crew chased and lobbed it at him. His back looks like Freddie Krueger now.'

'You two are such pussies it's unreal. I'm bringing it just in case. And besides, I've got this.' He showed his Rambo knife.

'Blades are fine,' Slim said. 'But acid I don't like.'

'Nor will the guy in the shop if he fucks with me. Now I'm done debating. Let's get this shit on the road. Both of you, out of the car now.'

'Me too?' Jay asked.

'Yeah you. Stand outside and keep watch. It's time you did some work for your money tonight.'

They hooded up and headed over. Jay loitered in the shadows while Bigz and Slim stormed through the door. Slim smashed the camera while Bigz clambered over the counter, blade in hand, making for the shocked lone employee.

'Give me the money or I'll slice you up.'

Panicking the man tried to open the till but it wouldn't budge. Bigz whipped out the bottle. 'This is acid so don't vex me man.' The till popped open and Bigz placed it aside, stuffing the cash in his pockets.

'Watch out!' Slim yelled as another man appeared, wide and stocky, lunging for Bigz. Too late: his arm was around Bigz's neck, choking him. Bigz was trying to thrust his knife behind him, while the smaller guy grabbed the bottle. His cohort ducked and the liquid splashed directly into Bigz's face. The men vanished as Bigz flailed and screamed.

Slim stood in shock for a moment. Then he kicked the side door open and shuffled Bigz out of the shop.

'What happened?' Jay asked.

'What does it fucking look like?'

Two minutes later they were parked outside Homerton Hospital.

'I'm not going in there,' Bigz gasped, his face in severe pain. 'There'll be feds everywhere. I ain't doing bird for this, no way.'

'But your skin,' Slim urged. 'It's peeling off you, look.'

Bigz tried to focus at the mirror, his face blurring in and out. 'I can hardly fucking see!'

'You've been sizzled blud, serious,' Jay said. 'You've got to get some help on that.'

Police cars wailed along the main road as Bigz raced for a solution.

'Take me to Dreadman's yard. His woman's a nurse. She fixed me up last time I was stabbed. Go.'

Big Lucy was at the helm, taking care of things. She'd washed his eyes out and was carefully applying emollient to his skin. Bigz was a little groggy from the opiates she'd administered but was relatively pain-free now. His eyesight still wasn't perfect but at least he could see. Beats pumped from a house party across the street as Dreadman stood smiling by the mantelpiece telling Slim and Jay how he'd earlier supplied the place. It was all posh kids and he made a packet.

Slim and Jay were on the sofa, Slim only half-listening, Jay not listening at all. Jay was on edge. He'd just phoned a guy in the know, and word was the police were hunting left and right, taking this one serious. Apparently Bigz had stabbed one of the shop guys.

'If we get snitched,' Jay said, interrupting the Rasta in mid-flow, 'we'll have to sort out an alibi. Like maybe say we were here all night. We could say Bigz popped out to the shop and got attacked on the street at random.'

'No problem,' Dreadman smiled, pulling on a king-size zoot. 'You youths have been here with me all night. Ain't that right

Luce?'

'All evening,' she nodded, working away.

'Thanks Lucy,' Bigz said. 'I can't repay you enough for this.'

'You've got to start behaving out there boy,' Lucy tutted. 'Because in the morgue I won't be much help to you.'

Bigz nodded, then winced as the pain returned.

'Go easy on him Luce,' Dreadman said. 'I was a young buck once myself. That's what it's like at that age, you're firing on all cylinders.'

'I'll be firing something else when I get my hands on the fucker who did this, I swear,' Bigz said. 'He'll be a dead man crying.'

'Don't worry about all that,' Lucy said. 'It's not important right now. We've got to get you mended up.'

'Hey Bigz, what's the names of these two fine soldiers?' Dreads asked, looking down at Slim and Jay. 'They your two proteges then?'

'I wish, man,' Bigz said, giving them the evil eye. 'Fucking acid being thrown around tonight and where were they? Standing round playing with their dicks.'

'That's not true,' Slim said. 'I told you not to bring that shit in.'

'So did I,' Jay said.

'Shut the fuck up Jay, you're a fucking pussy. At least Slim was in the shop with me - you were hiding as usual doing diddly squat.'

'I was outside keeping watch. Someone had to.'

'Fat lot of good it did. All you wanted was to run off and go raving tonight. I'm getting pissed off with you. Seriously wondering where your loyalties lie.'

'Now come on,' Lucy said firmly, appealing for calm. 'Now's not the time for squabbles. You came to me tonight so you did the right thing. Now let's be positive.'

'Thanks Lucy,' Bigz said, his anger abating. 'It's much

appreciated, I mean it.'

'Anyone for some refreshment?' Dreadman asked. 'Beer, lemonade, ginger ale?'

Nobody answered so he went to the kitchen for a Dragon Stout. By the fridge he exhaled. Bigz bringing trouble to his door again was the last thing he needed. But he owed him. Back in the day Dreadman had run with Bigz's brother Cliff, twenty years Bigz's senior, and as a boy Bigz looked up to them as father figures. They'd regale him with tales from the street – knife fights, gunplay, battles with the police - all to see the wonder on the young boy's face. But now he knew they'd helped create something ugly. Cliff eventually did time for beating a policeman on the Sandringham Road frontline and the inflated status went to his head. He was like Bigz now, a time bomb ticking away. At a party Cliff fought a guy and came out worse, so he grabbed a knife which ended up impaled through his own neck. The *Hackney Gazette* headline read: *BLOODBATH AT PACKED BLUES PARTY.* Bigz was eleven at the time, but from that day on he was trouble. Now he was rolling up to Dreadman's yard covered in acid while he and Lucy's children slept upstairs. But what could he do? He owed him after Bigz saved his life from Hot Iron Mike.

Six months ago Dreadman had been poaching drug customers and unwittingly stepped on the toes of a top Hackney don. Tied to a chair, Hot Iron Mike approached him with his customary branding iron. 'You've messed with the wrong motherfucker Mr Dreads.' Just then Mike's mobile sounded and he paused to answer it. It was Bigz trying to save his skin as Mike owed him a favour. Dreadman had a lucky reprieve. But would his debt to Bigz ever be settled? Only a month back he'd knocked to say his TV wasn't working, could he borrow his one? And often on the street he'd ask to borrow money or some weed. It was a liberty, and Lucy was tiring of it too. He saw no happy ending. He returned to the room with his drink.

'Where have you been for so long?' Lucy asked. 'Where's the refreshments? Go back and get these young men some drinks. Bring some of that nice ginger cake I baked as well.' She kissed her lips. 'Men, no manners at all,' she said, raising a chuckle from the boys.

In the kitchen Dreadman quietly cursed her. Any other woman would expect a swift back-hand the second the guests left for pulling a stunt like that. But Big Lucy had taught him early on that she wasn't that kind of woman. He'd only ever slapped her once and she'd hit him back a lot harder, putting a lid on the matter. But at his age a woman like Lucy was good for him. Too many men he knew were serving long sentences because they'd had no woman looking after them.

He brought in a loaded tray. Suddenly the door bell sounded. The boys panicked thinking it was the police.

'Relax,' he laughed. 'That's just the kids from over the road wanting more supplies. Everyone chill.'

The boys took a peek from the curtain. Outside stood two black men in leather coats. These guys weren't from the party, no way. It was time to roll. They rushed to the back garden to hop the fences.

Dreadman shook his head and made for the door, but Lucy said, 'I'll get it, you've sold those partygoers enough tonight. It's time we put an end to this nonsense and went to bed.'

Expecting the callow students of earlier she was confronted by the two men.

'Where's Bigz?' one demanded.

She looked him up and down. 'Who are you coming to my door with your questions?'

'Just get Bigz and there won't be any problems.'

'There's nobody with that name here. Now be gone from my doorstep before I lose my patience.'

Dreadman sidled up to check them out. One looked like 50 Cent, the other wiry with braids like Snoop Dogg.

'I'm afraid you've got the wrong address brothers so we'll have to say goodnight,' he smiled. He was closing the door when they pushed it back and charged in past them. Their livid complaints were silenced when in the room 50 shoved a revolver in Lucy's face.

'Bigz was here tonight, so I'll ask you politely, where the fuck is he?'

These men weren't messing, but snitching on a hothead like Bigz wasn't a clever idea. 'The only Bigz round here is me,' she said boldly. 'They call me Big Lucy. We know of no other Bigz so you're mistaken.'

The men turned to each other and laughed. Then the gunman whipped her across the face. She toppled to the floor unconscious.

'Rarse clart,' Dreadman yelled, but as the gun turned his way he shut his mouth. He put up his hands. 'I'm sorry.'

'You better be. Now sit down.'

'Eyes,' 50 addressed his sidekick. 'I'll check upstairs. You keep a watch on Bob Marley here.'

As he headed up Dreadman said, 'My kids are up there. Please don't wake them.'

Eyes stood smirking over him, his eyes staring in two directions. 'Your locks are going a bit grey there G. How old are you?'

'Too old for this kind of thing, I tell you.'

Eyes reached into his coat and produced a chunky yellow stun gun.

'I've never used one of these things, you know,' he said, inspecting it. 'A hundred thousand volts they reckon. You want to be my first guinea pig?'

Dreadman shook his head and Eyes issued a sinister laugh.

50 returned to the room. 'There's only kids up there asleep. He must've left in the last half hour.' Then he turned to Dreadman, 'So where's Bigz staying, yardie?'

'I don't know, honest. I hardly even know him these days.'

'Your own cousin and you don't know where he lives?'

'He's not my real cousin, that's just talk. Why are you gunning for him anyway?'

'He's been messing with Hot Iron Mike's chicken shops. They pay Mike good protection which is why nobody fucks with them. As a Hackney boy Bigz must have shit for brains.'

'I agree with you there. I'm done with the bumbaclart's bullshit.'

50 stepped forward. 'We're sick of your bullshit too. You've been harbouring the fucker, letting your bitch patch up his war wounds and it ain't the first time either. Now I want his current address.'

'I swear, I don't know it...'

50 shoved the gun hard into his cheek. 'Stop lying or I'll waste you here and now.'

'Okay, it's somewhere in Dalston, near the junction, that's all he's ever told me.'

50 observed him with a sceptical eye. Then he said, 'You're lying to me.' Turning to Eyes he pointed down at Big Lucy. 'Drag that bitch up onto the sofa.' He began undoing his belt and flies. 'I'm gonna bang this ho right in front of him.'

Eyes laughed as he hefted Lucy's unconscious body.

'That's good.' 50 dropped his jeans to his knees. 'Now strip her down. I want to see some flesh on display round here.' With his hand down his briefs, he turned to Dreadman. 'Watch and learn, star. This is how a real man does this shit.'

Dreadman could bear no more. 'Okay!'

'Ah, you suddenly remember?'

'Kingsland Road, just below the junction. His flat's above the barbershop. First floor, Flat 2.'

'What a shame. I was just about to get to work on this ho. Plenty meat there too.' Then he quickly pulled up his jeans and turned away. 'But I ain't fucking no dead bitch that's for sure,' and the pair cracked up.

They left and Dreadman closed the door behind them. He returned to the room a defeated man. Lucy was returning to consciousness. 'What happened, what time is it, where am I?' she said, one eye swollen shut.

3

Lost Art of Murder

Four a.m. and Terry was considering one more fare before he'd call it a night. He was back in Dagenham, approaching the shops, the main drag empty. Then up ahead by the snooker club he saw a group of men fighting. Some were wrestling, others kicking at a figure on the ground. One bloke was swinging a scaffolding pole, until someone jumped on his back and it clanged to the pavement like a church bell. Terry drove by shaking his head. Dan was right about that place. It was about time they closed it down.

He passed through the lights, the road lined with houses now. He noticed a bloke hurrying along on his own. White, twenty something, cap and tracksuit. Maybe he'd been involved in the ruckus, had made an early getaway. Something made Terry keep staring. Did he know him from somewhere? Then drawing level he clocked his face and recognised him instantly. It was one of the men who'd robbed him the other night.

The man turned down a side street and disappeared. Terry pulled the car over and sat holding the wheel, his mind racing. For a moment he was unsure what to do. Then something clicked in his head and on auto-pilot he stepped out of the car and went around to the boot. He saw his axe. It was still there after he'd done that bit of work for Stacey's aunt. He gloved up, pocketed a rubble sack and placed the tool beneath his leather jacket. Checking the coast was clear, he put up his sweatshirt hood and headed down the side street after him.

Spotting the man up ahead, he increased his pace. Mist hung under the street lights, breath fogging the air as he went. Terry was in the zone, one hundred percent focus. The man swung a right and Terry upped his speed. He was back in sight now. Then the bloke took a left and Terry knew he needed to bridge the gap. He rounded the corner but suddenly the pavement was empty. He checked up and down, both sides. No joy. The man had gone. He must've already entered a house. Bollocks, he'd actually lost the cunt. He felt like kicking himself. But at least he knew the vicinity of where the fucker lived now, so that was something. But just in case, he continued on to the end of the street.

Passing an alley that ran between the houses he stopped. A dozen yards in stood his man, pissing up against the wall. Terry's adrenaline surged. The game was on but he kept his cool. Hands in pockets he turned towards the alley, casual as you like, a local on an earlier-than-usual constitutional.

The bloke stood whistling to himself. He seemed stoned or drunk. At Terry's approach he turned his head, wary at first, but sensing no threat he relaxed.

'Alright bruv,' he nodded, still pissing away, showing no recognition of their last meet.

'Fine thanks mate,' Terry replied cheerfully. He recalled the shave marks in one eyebrow, crafty-looking eyes. He flashed to the bloke kicking him on the ground, his mate snatching his wallet, the pair of them laughing as they strolled away.

The man shook himself and as Terry passed behind he pulled out the axe. The blade crashed into his shoulder and threw him to the ground. He screamed, eyes terrified, one arm aloft as again the blade came down. It embedded into his chest, silencing him. Terry wrenched the blade free. He rose it high to deliver a final blow, bringing it down with force, skull splattering blood and brain matter up the wall.

Terry stepped back. He stood breathing, gazing at the scene, a grisly freeze-frame that stunned him. He felt light-headed, as if at any moment his legs might give way. But he had to pull himself together, get a fucking move on. He fumbled in his pocket for the sack, hands shaking as he inserted the axe and gloves, zipping the lot beneath his jacket. The alley was empty, no life, no sound, only the rush of blood in his ears, a train screaming through his skull. It was time to move. Head-down he turned onto the street. Drizzle fell, turning to rain as he wended his way back to the main road. Reaching the car he put the sack in the boot, noticed blood on his jacket and dumped that in too. With a can of water he gave his face and hands a clean. Then he got in the motor and drove.

The rain was lashing now, windscreen wipers moving left and right as he powered along. He joined the dual carriageway, moving with the flow, his mind in a trance. He was back on the Hackney streets of his youth. Crumbling houses, corrugated iron fences, towerblocks in the sky. He was walking out past the factories, and down through the bushes to the railway lines. Multiple tracks stretching to the distance. On the line stood a boy, arms in cruciform, staring towards an oncoming train. Terry's screams went unheard as the train thundered in, carriages flashing by, then suddenly it was gone. He ran to the scene but there was no body, no blood. He looked at his hands and they were dripping red. He tore back up the embankment, on through the foliage until he tripped and fell, face first to the earth. Bones were embedded in the soil. Limbs poking out from shallow graves. Boys and girls who went out for a lark but never came home. He got up and ran, out past the factories and on through the deserted streets, a fucking ghost town. Back to the terraced house his mum kept spotless. But as he approached it looked neglected, paint cracked, bricks blackened with age. He walked through the door. The hallway smelled damp, wallpaper peeling. In the living room his parents sat staring into space, TV showing static, flames creeping up the walls.

The radio crackled to life and Terry snapped out of the nightmare. The controller asked if he fancied a Stansted Airport run. He was on the A13, the rain had stopped, clock showing forty minutes had passed. He answered to say yes, he'd take it. He took the details and turned around at the next junction.

Terry was wide awake now, back in the swing. Dawn was breaking, a new day ahead and he was moving forward, the nightmare behind him. The past was history, unimportant now, his only thoughts on the task in hand, to pick up a Stanley Dawson from Woodford Green.

He made for the North Circ and reaching Woodford it was broad daylight. He stopped outside the house, a decent semi on a nice street. He gave the fare a beep and out he came, an old boy pulling a suitcase. Terry got out of the car to take it off him.

'Cheers guvnor. My back ain't what it used to be, I tell you.'

'No problem at all.'

Terry brought it round to the boot. Then clocking the axe-bag and his bloody jacket he slammed it back down and put the suitcase by the back seat.

'No room in the boot, no?' Stanley asked.

'It's the missus, she's shoved all the kids' stuff in there.'

'Women, eh,' he smiled.

'Can't live with them, can't live without them.'

They hit the road, Stanley sitting up front. He was a proper old cockney boy, a real talker. His usual driver hadn't been available today, but the bloke was a miserable sod anyway and he preferred Terry already. Next time he'd ask for him personally.

'The more work that comes my way the more I'm a happy

man.'

'Hope you don't mind me asking,' Stanley grinned, 'but how did you get the shiner?'

The bruise was healing up nicely and Terry was surprised he'd noticed it.

'I'd like to say the other bloke looked worse, but there was no other bloke. I was cutting down a tree for an in-law. A branch snapped back and whipped me right in the face.'

'Sure it wasn't one of the in-laws?'

'No chance.'

They rolled up the M11 chatting away. Stanley was off to visit his daughter in Marbella. He took the trip three or four times a year. Like Terry he was an original Hackney boy, Haggerston to be precise, but when he got married he moved to Manor Park where his kids grew up, then later on to Woodford. One of his sons worked in the City and had a six-bedroom house in Brentwood. The other was inside for a failed bullion robbery near Heathrow. His said his only real crime was getting caught because the City was full of crooks too. Terry agreed.

Stanley puckered his nose and put down his window. 'No offence Tel, but is it me or does it smell like a butcher shop in here?'

Terry thought fast. 'I did have some butchers in the car as it goes, right before you. Three of them, straight from Smithfield. I dropped them off at Romford.'

'I see. Don't worry about it. I smell everything. It's like a curse to be honest. Talking of Romford, that's where my son lived before he got himself banged up. Now he's in Belmarsh.'

Terry was mute about his own past blagging exploits, but mentioned his missus' old man who had quite some history behind him. 'He must be the same age as you. He used to mind some of the jewellers in Hatton Garden, knew all the old faces from back in the day. He did a stretch inside when my wife was a kid. She hardly seen him growing up. Stratford he's from originally.'

Stanley thought for a moment. 'His name's not Benny Katz, is it?'

'Christ, that's him, that's my father-in-law. You know him?'

'I used to know Benny well. We shared a flat at one point. Stoke Newington that was, back in the sixties. He married Mary Kerrigan, a girl from a big Irish family down my way.'

'Mary? Unbelievable. That's my mother-in-law. Well, she's gone now, but Benny's still knocking about. He can't walk too well now, his leg gives him gyp, but you still don't want to get on the wrong side of him. I have unfortunately, several times,' Terry laughed.

'He had a temper on him on occasion, I'll give him that. I saw him use a duster on a fella once, damaged him pretty bad. The bloke had just beaten up a woman. Broke her jaw I think. That was down in Soho when he was working for Bernie Silver. Right old dodgy game down there. But Benny was a decent bloke, he'd always help you out. Once I got married I knocked that life on the head, settled down. I've met Benny since, he came to my daughter's wedding and was generous with the present too. Must've been twenty years ago now.'

At the airport Terry took Stanley's suitcase and walked him to the terminal. He'd enjoyed their chat and they shook hands, Stanley saying he looked forward to seeing him again. He eyed Terry's collar area. 'Here, did you cut yourself shaving?'

Terry's insides turned to ice. 'Yeah, I must have. Mind you, with the hours I've been putting in lately I'm not surprised. I've been out in the car since yesterday afternoon.'

'Long shift, eh?'

'Too long.'

Stan looked Terry in the face. The old sod was razor sharp, didn't miss a trick. 'Everything okay, Terry?'

'Just tired mate.' He patted his arm. 'But I've got a date with a nice warm bed so I'll have to let you go. Have a nice holiday.

Enjoy yourself.'

Terry headed for the gents. In the mirror he saw a line of blood across the right side of his neck. There were also tiny spots around his eyes that he hadn't quite washed off earlier. He should've gone home to clean up properly. Or even better, not done the job at all. What was he thinking? He should've just followed the bloke, noted where he lived and sat on it, planned something properly. Used his head. Instead he'd jumped straight in without a second thought. He washed up, the enormity of what he'd done only now hitting him.

He returned to the car and took the motorway back to London. A life term in prison was something he couldn't handle. His kids would no longer have a father and his wife would go off with another man. It didn't bear thinking about. Anything more than two or three years would send him round the bend. He'd rather top himself than be an institutionalised wreck, his mind in tatters. He thought of his mum. After Lee died she was sent away for a while. It wasn't prison but wasn't too far off. He remembered coming back from school one day and his dad sitting there white with shock, saying his mother had had a breakdown. Plates and cups were smashed all over the kitchen and there was blood from where she'd cut herself. They visited her in Claybury Hospital. She was clutching rosary beads, his dad later saying that as a baby she'd been baptised a Catholic, her family being that way on her mother's side. Terry hadn't known that. When she returned home she started going to Sunday Mass in the big church on Ballance Road, and on dark evenings Terry accompanied her.

Terry remembered the priest's sermon at her funeral. Eternal life, how death wasn't a sad but a joyous event, because now she was to meet Jesus Christ her saviour. Terry's dad hadn't thought much of that speech but Terry found it comforting, his mum and brother's deaths given an optimistic perspective. Those times at Mass with his mum he never took much in, but after she died he considered learning more, continuing from where his mum left off, remembering how the priest had said that anyone of any denomination was welcome to come in and pray, that the house of God should be a comfort to everyone. Maybe that something extra was what Terry needed in his life. But time passed and it never happened, and later he put it down to just feeling over-emotional at the time.

But now Terry felt like driving back to that church and talking to that very priest. The funeral was thirteen years ago and he wondered if he'd still be in the parish, or had retired by now. Perhaps he wasn't even alive. But Terry could knock on the door, he had nothing to lose. He saw himself sitting in the priest's house next door with a cup of tea and opening up, talking about his life. Then he pictured himself breaking down, prostrate on his knees as he clutched onto the priest's legs confessing that he'd just killed a man. He'd done other things too, all throughout his life, things he shouldn't have done, things only evil people would do. But Terry was getting carried away, his marbles speeding away into the distance.

He took a deep breath. Terry wasn't a bad man. He wasn't a psychopath. Look at the real nutjobs out there. He'd simply acted on instinct to right a wrong. An eye for an eye with a caved-in head thrown in. The same values humanity abided by for aeons. He remembered his mum gave him a Bible once. She put it next to his bed saying to read a little bit every day, or just turn to it for comfort if he needed it. It was after she'd found blood on his trainers one night. She was worried he was out fighting, getting up to bad things, and she was right. One day in his room he took her up on it. He dipped into the gospels. The part where Jesus talks about turning the other cheek left an impression. It confused him. One minute Jesus was whipping the moneymen out of the temple, the next he was preaching submission to your enemies. It couldn't be right. Then Terry had a think about it and realised it wasn't literal. It was more an act of defiance. Go ahead, hit me, fuck you. You can't touch me. Not the real me. The Bible was clever like that, all about inner strength. If that's what it meant.

But Terry had to consider the here and now. The imperatives. If the Old Bill pulled him it would be game over. Forget about priests and the Bible, he had to dispose of the evidence or he'd be thrown in the bin for life all for a few moments of madness. Coming into London he stopped off at Leytonstone Primark for a new set of clothes, then he headed for the gangster's graveyard of Epping Forest.

He parked in on a quiet lane. Walking through the woods he saw a few people in the distance riding horses, but mostly he was on his own. He found a remote spot and started a fire. The smoke was a tad conspicuous, but his clothes burned down quickly enough, then he let the flames singe the claret off the axe. He dug a hole and buried the lot. As he covered the site with leaves a German Shepherd came bounding towards him. It stopped short, barking away.

'Cindy, get over here,' a man yelled. The dog eyed Terry suspiciously for a few moments, let out a final bark then obeyed its master's call and ran back. The man put the dog on a leash.

'Sorry about that,' his wife called over, the pair of them in Barbour coats and Wellingtons. 'She's a bit funny sometimes about men on their own.'

'She's right,' Terry laughed. 'Never up to no good, are they?'

'What's with the shovel?' the man enquired, no smile.

'Treasure hunting,' Terry said. 'I was out with the kids and a metal detector yesterday. It was beeping like mad. Thought we'd stumbled across some ancient riches but we couldn't find anything. I thought I'd come back for a second look and just dug up a rusty old padlock.' He held it up.

'Better luck next time,' the woman smiled.

The dog was straining for a sniff of the dig site, but thankfully they pulled it along and kept going.

Close fucking call. Terry walked hastily back to the motor. He was glad to be getting out of there.

Arriving home Stacey looked at him.

'You've got a new jacket?'

He looked down. 'Yeah. Bought it from Primark. Good price.'

'What happened to your old one?'

'It was old.'

'So what did you do with it?'

'Chucked it in the bin. Isn't that what you do with old clothes that are falling apart?'

'You threw out a good leather jacket for that?'

'It wasn't good. The lining was torn and it was worn into the ground.'

'So you went to Primark?'

'I went to Primark.'

She raised her eyebrows. 'Okay.'

'Something else,' he said cheerily, changing the subject. 'I met an old friend of your dad's. Took him from Woodford to Stansted. He was reminiscing all the way.'

'Not one of his old gangster friends,' she said, rolling her eyes. 'I don't want to know.'

'Next time you speak tell him I was talking to Stanley Dawson out of Haggerston. They shared digs together back in the day.'

'Don't think I'll bother.'

Terry went out to wash the car. He went to town on both the inside and out and gave the boot a good old scrub with disinfectant. His motor pristine, he had a sandwich and fell asleep in front of the telly for a bit. He woke to Stacey saying she and Megan were going down the shops. Leah was out somewhere too, so Terry fired up the laptop to check the London news.

'A man in his 20s has been stabbed to death in Dagenham. His body was discovered in an alleyway at 5.45am. It is not yet known if police are linking the murder to a non-fatal stabbing

that occurred during a brawl at a nearby snooker hall. Five men are being questioned.'

4

Rideout to N17

Bigz had spent several days chilling at his girl's place in Archway. It was good to have had a break from Hackney for a bit, at least while his face cleared up, and luckily it was healing up nicely. Good job it hadn't been a stronger solution or he'd be walking round looking like a freak forever. He wouldn't be including squirt in his arsenal again, that's for sure.

He took a cab back home to Dalston, keyed open his street door and walked up the stairs. Reaching his flat he noticed the lock had been forced – he'd been fucking burgled. He walked in and the place was a mess. His sofa had a big damp stain on it - piss no doubt - and they'd trashed the TV he'd got from Dreadman. Thankfully the flat was mostly bare, his valuables round his mum's. Then he turned to see a spray-painted message on the wall: YOU ARE DEAD MEAT.

That was it. No way was he sleeping here tonight. After fitting a padlock on the door, he grabbed his bag and headed back to Leona's.

In the cab he phoned Dreadman, enquiring about the two goons who'd knocked round at his door the other night, in case there might be a connection.

'Nah, that was nothing to do with you at all,' the Rasta assured him. 'I just owed them a little money and settled it there and then, no big ting you know.'

Bigz mulled on it. Would Dreadman lie to him? Not after Bigz saved his arse from Hot Iron Mike that time, no way. Then he belled Slim and there was some news.

'Brace yourself for this Bigz cos it ain't good. You know the guy we chased in Tottenham the other night? He's the little brother of a player called Tyson, one of the top Northumberland Park boys.'

'You mean Tyson Brown from Park Lane?' Bigz said, recognising the name and shrugging it off. 'I know that guy. He ain't a top boy, he's just a wannabe dickhead. So it was his brother we done? You telling me that fool found out where I lived and trashed my flat?'

'Apparently you left your wallet behind.'

'You what?'

'You must've dropped it in the car park that night and they got it.'

Bigz grimaced in shame. Leaving ID at a crime scene was something only a clown would do.

'Tyson's bro was found unconscious,' Slim continued. 'He spent three days in hospital. It ain't good. We must've got carried away the other night.'

'You got carried away more like,' Bigz snapped. 'It was you who smashed him over the head with a steel bar. Now look at what's happened.'

'I'm not going to argue B so calm down. We've both fucked up here. All I know is things with Tottenham are tense enough without starting a major war right now. Maybe we can get someone to mediate, get the beef squashed.'

'Have you turned into Jay or something? Tyson's not a badman, I'm not frightened of that pussy. You violate my property, you violate me. I'm being taken the piss out of here.'

'What about his little brother? It's just that, maybe we shouldn't have done him. I mean, how can we defend it? There were two of us and he was just walking through his own ends.'

'How many Hackney men have Tottenham attacked in their own ends? And there wasn't only two of us either. Jay drove us there, played a part in this and don't you forget that.'

'Yeah, but...'

'No buts Slim. We've got to take action. You want to sit waiting for them to take us by surprise? We've got to strike before they do. Show we're not to be fucked with so they back off. It's the only hand we can play now.'

'I'll have to think about this. I want to find out more about this Tyson Brown, I don't know him.'

'Well I do. We were in the same football team a few years back. In this big match against Haringey I was in goal and he slams the ball in our own net. I almost punched him out for that. He's a joker. I say we strike tonight. I'll make some calls, find out where the prick's staying. Then we storm the place.'

'Yeah well, we'll see,' Slim said, sounding none too eager. 'Speak to you later.'

Bigz re-entered his girl's flat. It was empty, Leona still at work. In frustration he threw down his bag and almost punched the wall. Slim's lack of commitment sickened him. Where was dedicated back-up when you needed it? Everyone was loud with the wordplay but a fucking bitch when it came to the crunch.

He texted Leona about returning to her place for his own safety. Then he needed to de-stress so he sat and tried watching TV. A woman with long dark hair was showing a couple around a property in the sun. He pictured a fit body under her summer dress and massaged his crotch for a bit. But he wasn't feeling it. He gave up and went to the fridge for something to eat.

He put some frozen burgers and chips in the oven, then went back and half-dozed until the fire alarm started beeping. He pulled out the smoking food, edges burnt black. It was salvageable; to magic up some flavour he smothered the lot in sauce. He sat and watched daytime TV while eating a very crappy meal. Afterwards he pushed his plate away and lit a blunt. He leaned back and exhaled. What a shitty day.

He must have dropped off because when he woke it was dark outside and his phone was ringing. It was Slim. Putting it to his ear he noticed a burn mark on the sofa chair that must've been from his spliff when he'd fallen asleep. Shit. Leona had only just bought the thing, warning him to smoke out the window in case he damaged it. It would take some explaining.

'The fuck do you want?' he said.

'I want to do him B. I want to obliterate the fucker.'

Bigz sat up, intrigued. 'What's happened?'

'Tyson Brown. He destroyed my fucking moped. I go outside and it's gone. Then I get a text saying: Look down the alley pussy. I do and it's burnt to a fucking crisp. Then I get a message going AAAAHAHAHAHA. Can you believe this shit?'

'It's bad news Slim. But we've got to show we're not taking this or it'll never end. You with me now?'

'Damn right I am. I'm going to bell Jay to pick us up. Sooner we take this show on the road the better. Otherwise we'll be laughed out of the hood. I've already got people asking what I'm going to do about it.'

'Let's go straight at him. Do him right where he lays his head. Full on brutality, no half measures.'

Hanging up Bigz felt a whole lot better. He made some phone calls. One was to arrange a decent weapon, the other was to a Tottenham snitch who owed him a favour. He now had Tyson's current address, the flat where he was staying with his baby mum. The mission was on.

The boys were outside beeping up. Leona was due home and he wanted to be gone before she saw her chair. A riot in his ear was the last thing he needed. He hurried down to the street and climbed in the front next to Jay. He banged him a spud, then turned and did the same to Slim.

Bigz waited until they were riding along to tell them the news.

'Listen up guys. I'm bringing something special tonight. We've got to make a stop-off at Finsbury Park. I'm picking up a Big Mac.'

'A spray and pray?' Slim said, impressed.

'That's right fam. A Mac-10 submachine gun capable of firing 130 rounds of hot lead per minute. How's that sound? My man has it all prepared for me, ready to go.'

'Rah, that's fucking banging Bigz.'

'Don't I know it. Only heavy-duty hardware for an occasion like this. This N4 guy is the go-to man. They call him the Quartermaster. He can talk about guns for hours, but the technical side of things don't interest me. I just like the end product in my hand, preferably holding it between some pussy's eyes.'

Slim was laughing, but Jay wasn't in the mood for this shit tonight. He'd been all ready to meet a hot girl he'd swapped numbers with the night before, all to have to drop everything to go out stoking up the fires with Tottenham. It was madness. Untold lives had been taken in the long-running beef between the two manors. Things had eased in recent times, but here they were trying to ignite a new war.

Perhaps it wouldn't come to all that, but still, it was an inconvenient time. He remembered the phone call from Mia earlier, all the delights she'd promised him. Things that would probably never be granted, because when he'd called back to postpone she'd told him to go fuck himself.

Tonight he'd felt like telling them to shove their mission where the sun don't shine. But realistically it wasn't an option. He'd known them for years, and falling out with long-term friends wouldn't be good for his rep. His close connection ensured nobody messed with him, which was convenient because not only could he live his days unhassled, it gave him open selection to bed all the girls who wanted a bona fide bad boy, which was a fair number of them.

But things were getting too wild. They were in their early-twenties now and Jay wanted to ease down on the mayhem, explore some other options, broaden his horizons, maybe make some real money, but they were still running round scrapping like two rowdy young bucks.

At Finsbury Park they pulled into the Seven Acres Estate. Bigz got out and headed into one of the blocks. He was only gone a few minutes before he returned to the car. He had no bag on him, looked empty-handed.

'What happened, didn't you get it?' Slim asked.

Bigz shook his head. 'Nah, no joy.'

'Shit man, that's a shame.'

'Yeah I know,' Bigz said sadly. Then he whipped out the submachine gun and spun around. 'Bram bram bram, motherfucker!'

'Jeez,' Slim laughed. 'Wow, you got it.'

'Course I did. That's how I roll.'

They continued towards Tottenham. Passing Manor House Bigz answered his phone without thinking and suddenly Leona was yelling in his ear. He owed her a shitload of money for a new sofa chair. How many times did he need to be told to smoke out the fucking window? Can't you be left alone without destroying things like a child? No wonder men are pissed off with you. Your whole life you've had your mum or the system catering for your needs and now you're like some idiot who can't adapt to the real world. I want cash on the table for a replacement chair fucking quicktime, you hear me?

He told her to cool down, they'd chat later in private. No way, she said, they were finished. The front door was getting bolted tonight and he'd have to piss off back to his own pad and hopefully the men looking for him would give him a licking because it was all he deserved right now.

Bigz hung up and turned off his phone. He sat breathing through his nostrils.

Jay glanced at him, holding back a laugh. 'Your woman didn't sound too happy with you there B.'

'Yeah, just a little bit,' Slim added before they both cracked up.

Bigz spun around, lashing with his fists. 'You want to die pussy, you want to fucking die!'

Slim cowered, holding his arms up in protection.

'Whoa B, calm down,' Jay urged, taking a hand off the wheel to coax him back. 'Come on, chill.'

Bigz sat back in his seat, breathing heavily.

'You're out of order,' Slim said. 'What did I do? What did I fucking say?'

Bigz didn't reply. He took out the Mac-10 and checked the ammo. 'I'm using this tonight, I swear it. Tyson's family better be making funeral arrangements. Nobody treats me like that.'

Jay knew tactful diplomacy was needed if they didn't want to end up in custody tonight. A punishment was one thing, but charges of joint pre-meditated murder because Bigz had woman trouble was another.

'Listen B,' Jay said gently. 'Let's not lose our heads and do anything we might regret tonight. Maybe we should be counter-intuitive, hear Tyson's side of things first. Talk before we go jumping in full throttle, potentially turning things ugly.'

'Uh-uh,' Bigz said. 'No fucking way.'

'All I'm saying is we need to look at this logically. You hurt his brother so he trashed your flat and burned Slim's moped. That's an eye for an eye. You could even say things are even now, so why take it further? All I'm saying is, we've got options. We can settle this like grown adults.'

Bigz slammed his fist down on the dashboard and Jay heard something crack. No way. If Bigz thought he could damage his prized car it was no fucking joke.

'You're a dick, Jay. No way am I letting this drop. Tyson sealed his own fate when he and his men entered my pad. One of them pissed on my fucking sofa. If I let this go my name will be mud.'

'He's gotta pay,' Slim agreed, leaning forward. 'But I'm not doing hard time for him. Let's not waste the fucker, just torture him. Maybe in his flat, maybe somewhere else. Tie him up, get him in the car and bring him somewhere for a night of pain. Treat someone like that and they'll be praying for death anyway. Let's be clever with this.'

Finally Bigz exhaled and nodded. He put the gun away. 'Yeah, maybe that's an idea. Torture the prick. We'll fuck him up so bad he'll be too scared to show his face again. I like that.'

Jay was relieved. At least now he wouldn't be facing a murder rap. But whatever happened he wanted to stay peripheral. Unlike the other two he hadn't been targeted, so was likely considered unimportant, which was just how he liked it.

'Anyway,' Bigz said. 'Let's play it by ear. Go there and see what happens.'

Reaching the estate they pulled into the car park. Engine off they stared over at the two six-storey flats, old-school and grimy.

'So this is where he's staying,' mused Slim.

'Place is a right dump,' Jay said.

'This is the slums of yesteryear,' Bigz smirked. 'Tottenham ain't moved into the new century yet.'

The coast looked clear. Bigz inserted a matchstick between his teeth and checked his Mac-10. 'Time to get this party started.'

They stepped out of the car. Bigz went round to tap on Jay's window. 'You leaving it all to us again, Jay? Get your arse out of the whip.'

Jay tutted and got out. Bigz rooted through the boot. 'You still got my slugger, the one with the embedded nail?' He found the bat and handed it to Jay. 'Guy steps out of line, pound some of that into his skull.' Laughing as he slammed down the boot.

He turned to Slim. 'Yo, what you carrying?'

Slim opened his jacket, revealing a machete strapped into a shoulder holster.

'Now that's nice.'

They set off towards the block. Bass beats reverberated as they climbed the concrete stairs. At the top floor they walked along the open walkway to the furthest flat. Bigz pressed the bell, Slim and Jay standing behind him.

A light-skinned black girl opened the door. He asked for Tyson and she said he wasn't in.

Bigz heard a TV and looked over her shoulder. 'You sure about that?'

'I'm sure.' She made to close the door, but Bigz pushed it back and they stormed in wielding their weaponry. They checked each room but he wasn't there. The girl was shrieking at them, and with Leona's insults still fresh in his ears, Bigz pushed her up against the wall.

'Shut up and tell me where your man's at.'

'Get out of here or you'll be sorry. You think Tyson's gonna let you get away with this?'

He gripped her by the hair. 'I said, where the fuck is he?'

'Get off my hair you piece of shit!'

'I'll pull your hair right off, how about that?'

Suddenly she switched, lashing and scratching and Bigz was struggling. He shouted for the boys to get this mad cow off him. They yanked her off and held her at bay.

Bigz stood for a moment gathering his senses. She'd taken him unawares. He touched the already-delicate skin of his cheek, fingers coming away red. Incensed he launched at her, beating her to the floor.

'Jesus Bigz, she's had enough,' Jay said, pulling him away.

Bigz stood there breathing, eyes fixed on her as she lay groaning.

'What should we do?' Slim asked him. 'Should we wait for Tyson or go?'

'I ain't going anywhere. We'll wait.'

'Help!' The girl started banging her feet. 'Help!'

Bigz pulled her up. 'You better shut your fucking mouth.'

'When my man gets back you're gonna die for this boy, you're dead.'

'Am I now?' He pulled the gun from his waist and held it to her cheek. 'I'll blow your brains all over the wall and do the same to Ty when he walks in. Now I'll ask you one final time, where is the pussy?'

With the gun in her face she said, 'He went out on business, said he wouldn't be back till midnight, that's all I know.'

Bigz glared at her. He lowered the gun and put it away. 'Okay.' He dragged her into the bedroom, threw her down on the bed and undid his flies. 'You're gonna suck my dick bitch.'

'Please, I've told you all I know.'

'Leave it B,' Jay urged. 'Now ain't the time.'

'Yeah listen,' Slim agreed, 'maybe we should just come back later.'

'I don't give a shit.' Bigz pulled the girl towards him by the hair. 'I don't like the attitude of this bitch. She's a fucking ho and I'm getting me some, right here right now.'

'Listen to your friends,' the girl pleaded. 'Go, please...'

'Uh-uh,' he smirked, standing before her. 'Now get on that ting – and you two, avert your eyes. I want some privacy round here.'

Slim kissed his teeth and left the room. Jay followed. They headed to the living room, Slim checking the adjoining kitchen for munchies.

Jay sat down, shaking his head. 'He's going too far in there. This is crazy.'

'Nothing I can do,' Slim shrugged. 'You can tell him but he won't listen. The guy does whatever he wants.'

Slim came in with a pile of sweets and crisps. He turned up the TV and settled in. In the background they could hear the girl pleading, then it sounded like Bigz was knocking her about again.

'We're not going to come good out of this,' Jay said. 'I've got a feeling.'

'Chill,' Slim said. 'Being with Tyson that girl's well used to being treated rough. I asked around and Ty's been done for all sorts. The bitch is his property so fuck her too.'

Jay shook his head. This was the side of the road life he didn't like. His own sister was almost raped one night walking home from work. She was passing by a park when a guy tried chatting to her. Next thing he was pulling her into the bushes and she had to fight him off. Luckily a car started beeping which scared him away, but it left her nervous and now she carried a can of mace.

'You remember that time up Frampton?' Slim said, slumped low, one hand down his pants, the other stuffing his face. 'You know, when a load of us linked those two girls?'

Jay didn't want to think about that night. He'd made a concerted effort to forget it. It was years ago and he was young and immature back then. He stared at the TV. Cowboy builders getting doorstepped and questioned, denying everything.

'I know they tried to get us in the shit afterwards,' Slim went on, 'but some girls are into that sort of thing. Maybe they feel dirty afterwards so they try playing victim, but most of these skanks are just liars. They're whipping off their G-strings for untold men so it's a bit silly suddenly crying about it.'

Jay remembered being pulled in and questioned. He was fourteen and had only joined in reluctantly. It was late at night and he was high. It did seem like the girls wanted it, but he remembered one of them crying afterwards, saying they'd gone too far and she hadn't asked for that. Some white boy slapped her, called her a slag. Jay never got involved in anything like that again and the police soon dropped it. Nobody else seemed to give a toss about being pulled in, like the accusations were too stupid to take seriously, but Jay was shitting himself. He was no rapist.

'There's nothing on.' Slim settled on a crime documentary. Police preparing for a dawn raid. As they filed into a housing estate Slim almost spat out his Haribo. 'That's my old flats. I don't believe it.' They watched the cops storm through a front door. A teenager was woken from his sleep, expletives bleeped as he struggled into his joggers, a squad of feds crowding his bedroom. After a search the camera zoomed in to reveal their find.

'All that over a bag of weed?' Slim laughed. 'Jeez, is that all they found?'

'How come they never show any big raids on these programmes?' Jay wondered. 'Like twenty key of H, an arsenal of Uzis – how come it's always just minor stuff?'

'It's to send out a message of fear. Smoke a spliff in your bedroom and one day we just might come for you. It's government policy. Control by fear. Big brother is watching. It's the same as all these programmes about dole cheats. It's psychological, to keep everyone in line.'

Jay was ruminating on that when they heard a noise in the hallway. They jumped up thinking Tyson had come home early, but it was just Bigz. He walked into the room tucking himself in.

'Right, Jay,' he pointed. 'You're next. Get in there and work that bitch.'

He headed for the fridge and selected a carton of orange juice. 'Me, I need some refreshment after that.' He took a lug, wiped his mouth. 'She gives good, every which way. So go on Jay, what you waiting for? Get in there and slam that ho. And here,' he tossed him a pack of rubbers. 'Don't want to be leaving no mess behind, you get me,' he winked. He took another lug of juice. 'She fucking loved it, serious. Wants a balling from the both of you.'

'Look,' Jay stood up. 'Tyson's not here so let's just hit the fucking road.'

Bigz slowly approached him. 'You know, I'm getting stressed with you. You're really starting to vex me.' He took out his gun. 'Now I'm done with your shit tonight.' He pointed it at him. 'Get the fuck in there.'

'Don't point that thing at me Bigz.'

'I'll do more than point it, believe me.'

Jay looked at him and wondered if Bigz was crazy enough to do it. The guy was supposed to be his friend but was more like an enemy these days. Fuck knows what he was capable of. Shupsing his teeth Jay relented and walked towards the bedroom.

'And Jay,' Bigz laughed, taking a seat. 'She's all waiting and prepared for you blud. Dressed to impress. You're going to love it.'

Jay walked in and the girl was standing in stockings and suspenders, trembling in fear. She wiped her bloody nose.

'Shit, what's that idiot done to you? Listen, cover up, I'm not going to touch you.'

'Your friend said if I don't please you he'll kill me. He said he knows where my mum lives, and my children are round there. He's a psycho, he'll kill them.'

'Don't worry about him, he's full of shit.' Jay sat down, put his head in his hands. 'I didn't want to come here tonight. I don't even know this Tyson Brown guy.'

Her eyes shot to him, staring wide. After a few seconds she said slowly, 'Tyson Brown doesn't live here. He lives at the top of the next block.'

'What do you mean?'

'Tyson Barrington lives here.'

'I don't get it.'

She approached him, seething now. 'Are you telling me you got the wrong flat and I've been put through all this for nothing?'

He stood up. 'Now whoa, listen...'

Back in the living room Bigz said, 'Listen to all that tumbling about in there. I'm impressed. Maybe I was wrong about that dude.'

Slim was chuckling along when suddenly Jay flew into the room. 'Let's get out of here now.'

'What you chatting about, dog?' Bigz smiled. 'Better be some left for my bredda here, ain't that right Slimzy?'

'You've brought us to the wrong flat. Someone called Tyson Barrington lives here - Tyson Brown's in the next block. Whoever supplied your info needs a fucking shanking.'

Bigz froze. 'Tyson Barrington?'

'That's right. I've had to tie that girl in bedsheets in there, gag her and everything. She went ballistic.'

Bigz and Slim looked at each other. Both jumped up. 'We gotta go.'

'Who is this guy?' Jay asked, following fast behind.

'You don't want to know. Let's just move.'

Back behind the wheel and driving fast, Jay turned to Bigz. 'Right, you can tell me who the fucker is now.'

Bigz stared at the road ahead. He'd got way carried away back there. What had he gone and done?

'Well come on then,' Jay insisted. 'Who the fuck is he?'

'You heard of an elder they call Lucifer? He got off a double murder charge down South London recently?'

'One of the original Farm boys? Tied two men to their beds, set them alight?'

Bigz nodded.

'No way. Lucifer's one of the Tottenham dons. He's a maniac.' Jay slammed the wheel. 'How could you get the wrong address? You've just signed our fucking death warrants.'

Slim came forward. 'Let's just deny it, say it was some other brothers who burst in. Blame it on men from South. There must be untold men gunning for Lucifer after he got off those killings. Those Brixton crews are hardcore, they're not gonna let him get away with that. Just insist it had nothing to do with us.'

'Exactly, let's do that,' Bigz nodded. 'But what about bashing up Tyson Brown's little bro, how do we explain our way out of that one?'

'We'll have to own up to that. Say we got it wrong, thought he was somebody who'd robbed one of our boys.'

'You mean say sorry?' Bigz frowned.

'Not exactly, just admit it was a mistake.'

'I don't know, we could end up looking like pussies.'

'But we're in serious shit now. We've got to compromise. Because I don't know about you, but I don't fancy burning in my bed.'

5

Heavy Metal

Lunchtime and Terry sat parked near the cab office eating saveloy and chips and reading the *Standard*. Since Saturday night he'd been going through the motions, not letting what happened in the alleyway bother him. If anything, he felt numb. Stacey had had to shake him last night as he was having nightmares, but he couldn't remember a thing. If tremors were rumbling beneath the surface at the minute it was hardly surprising, but why inspect a can of worms? It was best to not dwell on it, let time pass. Things usually righted themselves in the end. And besides, another worry on his plate was something he didn't need.

He browsed the paper. Headlines spoke of London's increasing gang problems, the teenage murder rate up by fifty percent so far on last year. Then he saw: *AXE MURDER IN DAGENHAM.*

A violent brawl in a snooker club has left one man dead, one with knife wounds and another with serious head injuries. Darren Westbrook, 25, is believed to have stabbed a man inside the club before he was discovered dead in an alley a mile away. Police say his injuries were consistent with those from an axe or machete and described the killing as 'particularly brutal'. A man from Romford has been charged with his murder.

Terry read that last sentence over and over. Did this mean he was off the hook? He put the paper down, let it sink in. Could it really be true? An energy rose within him, his system jolting to life after two days of mental torpor. A mugshot of the dead man accompanied the article, but he'd seen that scumbag's face enough. He was more interested in the bloke taking the rap, but there was no name, no picture.

He got out of the car and entered a nearby internet café. He tapped in the details and sure enough found an update.

Billy Shaw, 29, from Romford, had been charged with the murder. The gist was that Darren Westbrook had slashed one of Shaw's mates in a group fight in the snooker hall before making a getaway. The brawl continued without him, spilled down to the street and Shaw followed Westbrook and murdered him with a heavy blade.

Terry searched for anything else about this Billy Shaw character. Sure enough he found a year-old report in the *Romford Recorder* about an armed robbery he'd been involved in. Shaw was acquitted, the others got twelve years each. It all made sense now. After getting off scot free the police had obviously been gunning for him, itching to lock him up for anything they could. They were either fitting him up or hoping to nail him on circumstantial evidence. Shaw's mugshot showed a man with shorn hair, a broad neck and a confident glint in his eye; your archetypal professional blagger who looked like he could do a term of bird standing on his head.

Then he searched out Darren Westbrook, the scum who'd robbed him. He found an old *Barking and Dagenham Post* article. A mugshot showed a bony-looking face staring down the camera. Three years ago he'd been part of a gang who attacked an elderly couple in Basildon, ransacking their home. The police suspected they were responsible for several similar aggravated burglaries across Essex. The bastard got four years. He would've served half. Two years bird for targeting the elderly. Terry shook his head in disgust. An axing couldn't have happened to a nicer bloke.

Billy Shaw was a different story. At present he was on remand for a crime he didn't commit and with his previous and some fabricated police evidence the jury would likely convict him. He obviously wasn't a happy bunny right now, but he was hardly a law-abiding citizen so the shit end of the stick is always a toss-up. You win some you lose some. Waving 12-bores around in post offices doesn't earn you karma points. Maybe there'd be extenuating circumstances and he'd get only a few years. Maybe he had other skeletons in the closet, past sins, and was now paying for them. Who knows. It wasn't Terry's problem. More importantly Terry was in the clear, on the receiving end of some good luck for a change, and back on the street he felt elated.

He got into his motor and drove. This called for a celebration. He decided to bunk off work for the day and hit the pub.

Terry was on his sixth pint. He'd downed a few chasers too. It was still relatively early, the pub quiet, but the spell of solitude had allowed for some philosophical thinking. In his head everything was balanced now, sitting well. Sometimes a few hours of contemplation was just what the doctor ordered. Terry's conscience was clear. He'd encountered a problem, a weight on his shoulders that would've ground him down until he was half the man, so he'd taken the naughty but necessary measures to remedy the matter. It was either that or forever put up and remain silent, which wasn't going to happen. Not with him. All his life he'd never been shy of dishing out violence when the occasion saw fit, so settling for the role of common or garden victim was a no-no from the start. If he'd let the attack in his cab go, put it down to age, bad luck, just one of those things, how many more kickings would be coming his way from now on?

Give the new blood an inch and they'd dance all over you.

The score was settled and Terry was satisfied with the result. He felt no guilt whatsoever. Everyone deserves a break in life, a reprieve once in a while, Terry included. His losing streak hadn't been funny and he couldn't have taken much more of it. He'd hit a rough patch, doubted himself, but it was over now and he could hold his head up again. He flashed back to driving the axe into Westbrook's skull, remembered the splash up the wall, the bloke lying there dead as a dodo. But it didn't seem so horrific now. Just a murky scene from a cheap slasher flick. Draining his jar Terry even allowed himself a chuckle about it.

'Oi oi.' Dan walked in and sat at the bar next to him. 'What are you so happy about?'

'Alright mate. Nothing really. Just having a think.'

Dan looked at him. 'You're lagging. How long have you been in?'

'Fuck knows. I fancied a few.'

'Looks like it.'

Dan took a couple of inches off his pint. He'd just come back from Brentwood after visiting the Marriott brothers. They were putting together a team for some upcoming graft, but still needed a driver. Dan had been assuring them for weeks that he knew just the man. You know Terry, he was one of the best wheelmen in the East End. Saying he'd get him aboard no problem. But quietly he was having his doubts. Why? Because Terry was a stubborn bastard, that's why.

Dan turned to him. 'So what you been up to Tel? Any exciting dispatches from the cabbing world?'

Terry took a lug of his pint. 'There was quite a big dispatch as it goes,' he muttered.

'You what?'

Terry shook his head. 'Nothing mate.'

Dan stared ahead. He needed Tel to agree to the job. It was a hurdle that was holding things back. If this bit of work got pulled off Dan would be one happy fucker, and so would Terry, that's for sure. Cash was running short lately and what's more, two men Dan had done bits and pieces with for years had just received ten years each for ferrying over a shipment of weed from Amsterdam. Their absence meant a drop in Dan's income. But thank fuck he hadn't been involved in the job they'd been done for, because they had asked him. Charlie and Pete had pulled off the run so many times they got slack, left some of the arrangements to a man they trusted but didn't properly know. Oldest mistake in the book. The bloke would be out on the town with them, boozing and chatting up women, shoving more coke up his snout than the pair of them, but it turned out he was an undercover Customs agent and got them bang to rights. The boys weren't taking it on the chin this time. They wanted to nail the bastard. They said they'd found out where he lived. Somewhere near Chelmsford. Dan said he didn't want to hear any more. He was out to make money, live a better life. None of that mad thirty-five years for murder lark. Get into the execution stuff and all the fun goes out the window. It's not fucking Mexico. But then again, betrayed and handed a ten-stretch maybe he'd feel the same way.

'Did you hear me?' Terry said.

'No, what?'

'I said I wouldn't kick that out of bed.' Terry nodded to barmaid Faye, leaning over in tight jeans talking to a punter. 'What do you reckon?'

'Shapely,' Dan agreed, amused at how pissed Terry was today.

A load of police sirens wailed past outside and Dan remembered the amount of plod vehicles on his old girl's road the other day. It was blocked off and they weren't letting anyone in or out. Some bloke had been stabbed to death in the alley there. No loss because the victim was apparently a scumbag. Some druggie who used to go round snatching people's phones. Someone else said he'd done time for breaking into old people's houses. That could've been talk, but odds on his absence was no loss. The council had hosed the claret off the concrete and the wall, but stains still remained because the scene had been a bloodbath.

Dan remembered he'd got off with a woman down that alley once. It was years back, around when he'd moved to the area, a teenager. Popping out to the corner shop he got chatting to a woman two decades older. He walked her home and she pulled him into the alley, getting down to unzip his flies. It was over quickly. She wanted him to come round for coffee, take things further, but he'd had his fun so what was the point. When he told his mates, a couple had similar tales to tell, saying the woman was a lonely nympho whose old man spent days away driving a lorry. When Dan saw the size of the bloke, a bearded monster in a donkey jacket, he was thankful he hadn't gone back for seconds.

'Did you hear what happened the other night?' he asked. 'The stabbing near where my old girl lives.'

Terry took out a local paper and turned to page seven. He placed it on the bar. 'You mean this?'

The mugshot showed a mouthy-looking prick, lines cut through his eyebrows.

Terry said, 'Looks like a silly cunt, doesn't he?'

'The bloke was auditioning for a Vanilla Ice tribute act and got jumped for crimes against fashion.'

Terry spluttered into this pint, had to control himself.

Dan laughed too. 'Weren't that funny Tel.'

'Fucking was.'

Then Dan's phone rang. Terry listened as he chatted to a bloke called Bob, larking about putting on a Jamaican accent. At one point he sang Red Red Wine.

'You mean right now?... yeah okay, I can do that... no problem, will do... yes of course I'll return the favour, don't I always... Nice one.'

'Who was that?'

'A black fella I know. A Hackney boy as it goes. I met him in the nick years back. I call him Bob Marley, he calls me Ali Campbell.'

Dan finished his pint and pocketed his phone. He had to run. Then he had an idea. He turned to Terry.

'You want to earn five hundred smackers for a simple ride up the road? We won't be longer than an hour. It's harmless, just a little scam.'

Tarquin Jones woke up on the sofa of his Dalston flat. Drug paraphernalia covered his coffee table, beer cans littered the floor, and his TV lay smashed from the time two crackheads had tried to kill each other, leaving bloody hand prints that remained on the wall. An acoustic guitar stood in the corner as a memento of more creative days, but it too had succumbed to hard times, a large crack up its side rendering it unplayable. Two years ago when Tarq moved in, the place was pristine, but a lot had happened since then.

Moving from Bournemouth to the edgy delights of East London, Tarq had it all. He had an aspiring model girlfriend and fronted a band that was making waves. They opened a few times for the Libertines, earned interest from labels and the music press and went on to sign to a major. Tarq's manager convinced him he was a star in the making so it was time to think big. Europe, America, Japan. He had all the ingredients: looks, songwriting skills, charisma; invest full trust in yours truly and a life of fame and fortune will be yours for the taking.

Tarq wondered how many times the man had recited those same lines to other gullible young musos while they signed everything away. Tarq's ego was running riot and it was the ultimate ruin of him. He was partying nightly, living the rock 'n' roll lifestyle before his band had even completed the recording of their first album. Add hard drugs into the mix and in the studio he was arguing with the producer and throwing strops like a diva. Word got back to the label that the group was too difficult to work with and they were dropped.

It was a blow, but the band soldiered on, still getting the odd support slot here and there. The momentum had passed but the partying continued. He was good friends with Pete Doherty, bringing crowds back to his flat for afters. But all was not well. As the up-and-coming bands around him went off touring and releasing music to acclaim, all he did was sleep all day and take drugs all night. Envy set in. Back at school he'd played rugby, loved a good scrum, and now on the scene he was becoming a troublemaker, starting fights, making a nuisance of himself. His girlfriend left him one night after a public row in Hoxton Square, and that same weekend he and Doherty were arrested after Tarq glassed a man's arm during a fight at a party. Pete missed an important gig over that and began to distance himself because he was in enough shit with the police as it was. The charges were eventually dropped, but by then things were different.

Tarquin's friends fell away. Meeting them on the street they'd chat for a few moments, but always have to go. Some skipped the niceties and ignored him completely. By now his band had fallen apart and he was full-time reliant on heroin and the crack pipe. He gained a new set of acquaintances, people he met in local drug dens, those who shared his primary interest: spending every single penny he could get on drugs.

His parents begged him to come home. Finally he agreed to go to rehab. Visiting him at the Priory they were delighted to see him back to his old self. But returning to his Dalston flat he decided on one final blow-out. Two days later when he woke from his binge the first thing he did was phone his dealer.

In the end his parents decided he'd have to learn the hard way. They reduced his allowance, but he simply turned to shoplifting and phone snatching. He burgled houses, broke into cars, but no cash was ever enough to cover his increasing drug tab. Once after nicking some tools from a van he decided to rob a corner shop. Scarved and equipped with a hammer he grabbed the old guy and told him to empty the till or he'd smash him into hospital. A hundred quid for a minute's work. He was onto something here.

Seeing some youths hide a machete in a bush one day, he took it for himself. That night by an ATM he targeted a man who looked like he worked in fashion. At bladepoint he forced him to max his card. Hackney was full of these trendies; they were everywhere, blow-ins from the home counties slumming it in the East End. Having been one himself he knew most wouldn't fight back, so it was easy work and paid his tab without having to creep around in people's houses all day. Hackney was so full of crime and the police so stretched it seemed you could get away with anything.

But the more you take the more you want, so money was still a problem. One day it finally came to him. He needed to up his game, start targeting betting shops, maybe even banks. It would mean higher payouts but less overall risk because he wouldn't have to graft so often. It was a big jump, but he was confident he could pull it off. But for such work you need a gun.

He was living in the borough of Hackney, the gun crime capital of London, so how difficult could it be? He asked around. Most people laughed him off, didn't trust him or were too low on the food chain, but a few claimed that for a small fee they could arrange something. He found himself searching for a pub in Bermondsey that was boarded up, another in Canning Town that didn't exist. Then he spoke to his dealer who told him to meet a guy in a Stoke Newington cafe.

Tarq spotted the seated man in a leather hat and dreads as soon as he walked in.

'Hi, I'm Tarq,' he said, sitting in opposite.

The man regarded him sceptically. 'So you're the boy who wants to do some business.'

The waitress came to take Tarq's order. Noticing the man's toast and Ribena he ordered the same.

'You sure you're not working for the beastman,' the Rasta leaned in. 'Because I'm a serious operator here. I only do business with those I can trust. Men who cross me have been known to end up scattered about in pieces, an arm here, a head there, you reading me?'

'Fly sent me. He can vouch for me. I'm local, I live just up the road.'

The man grinned. 'Any friend of Fly's a friend of mine.' Then his smile disappeared and he glanced left and right. 'I hear you're looking for a piece.'

'That's right.'

'You know they don't come cheap nowadays?

'I know.'

'Babylon catch you packing firepower and it ain't no slap on the wrist.'

'I'm aware of that.'

'Okay then. If you've got the notes I can get what you're looking for. But as I say, It'll cost you. We're talking one grand two hundred. That's for one fully-functioning piece with ammo, guaranteed.'

'I want it.'

'And - a one hundred quid handler's fee.'

'Okay.'

'And last but not least,' he put up a finger, 'an arrangement fee. Because now I've got to phone some very heavy people to get the ball rolling, which is the hottest part. The authorities have eyes and ears everywhere these days, so you've got to tread carefully in this game.'

'How much is the arrangement fee?'

'Two hundred notes, my man, putting the final total at a

grand and a half. You get the goods in your hand same day and a bona fide guarantee.'

'It's a deal. When do I pay?'

'I'll take half now, the rest you'll give to the guy I'm about to phone.'

Tarq passed over the readies and Dreadman shoved it down his crotch.

'Right, wait outside while I make this call. I'll give you a shout when I'm done.'

Tarq paced about outside. He was thrilled. This was it. He'd soon be pulling in big money. Without a worry in the world. Maybe he'd even get back into music. He could get a new guitar, start writing songs again. Fulfil what he'd been set to achieve last time round. The possibilities were endless. The man indicated for him to come back in.

'Okay, this guy's the real deal. He'll give you whatever you want.' He checked his watch. 'Could you get to Dagenham in an hour? He'll pick you up by Parsloes Park, corner entrance near Becontree tube. His name's Steve.'

He scribbled it down.

'So, our deal's done and I'm putting you in his hands now. You got a problem, you talk to Steve about it. You happy with that?'

Tarq thanked him and put out his hand but the Rasta made a fist. They tapped.

'Don't be late.' Then he pointed a finger. 'And remember, you don't know me.'

Tarquin took a cab to the London/Essex working-class suburbs, an area he'd never visited before. He stood by the park gates, the sky heavy overhead, distant thunder rumbling. Steve was late, and looking at the uniform two-storey houses that formed Britain's first and largest council estate, Tarq felt restless. A couple with a pram passed him having a row, then a burly middle-aged guy walked by with a Rottweiler. Either the man disapproved of Tarq's presence or he had a naturally sour face. The only people he'd ever met from Dagenham were a couple who used to shoplift around Dalston and came back to his flat occasionally to smoke crack. Both were dead now. The woman overdosed after a month in Holloway getting used to weak prison H, and the man was kicked to death one night in Tottenham after brawling with some Polish alkies.

A white van pulled up. Inside were two builder types, the driver thumbing him to get in the back. Tarq opened the sliding door, sat in among the bags of sand and cement and off they went. It was dark, no windows, and he wondered where they were going. Soon it felt they were on a dual carriageway or motorway and he was getting nervous. What if they were taking him somewhere to rob him? Fifteen minutes later the road sounded gritty and they pulled in. The door opened, the two men standing arms-folded to a backdrop of pylons and industrial units.

'Come on then, out you come.'

They were by the Thames in what looked like a derelict dock. Nearby stood an enormous old warehouse. Tarq wondered if he should forget the whole thing and run for it.

'I'm Steve, he's Norman,' the driver said.

'Tarquin.' He put his hand out but the man just looked at it, turning to Norman who cracked a cold smile. These were bruisers with an edge, a real menace about them.

'Tarquin, eh?' Steve looked him up and down. 'So Bob sent you up from Hackney. You from that manor then?'

'Yeah, I live there.'

'You don't sound like an East Ender, where you from originally?'

'Bournemouth.'

'Dorset? You're a carrot cruncher then?'

They were taking the piss and Tarq felt it was time to assert himself. 'I'm not here to talk about me, I'm here to do business.'

'Is that right? Steve leaned in. 'You sure you're not a fucking policeman?'

'Course not. I'm here to buy a gun. Let's just do the deal so I can go.'

Steve pushed him back against the van. Tarq smelled beer and saw a tattoo on his neck: ENGLAND.

'You sound to me like a dirty filthy copper.'

'No way, I swear it.'

'Well you've got some fucking mouth, ain't you?'

'I'm not police, I promise you.'

'You better not be.' Slowly he let him go.

Tarq noticed the other guy Norman laughing hard.

'Right, get over to the warehouse,' Steve said.

Looking over at the old building Tarq had second thoughts. 'I don't know about this guys. I might've made a mistake here.'

Norman spoke now. 'We're not going to strap you to a chair and cut your ear off, if that's what you're worried about.' Despite Steve being the obvious leader, Tarq would put money on Norman being the most psychotic.

'I've got a better idea,' Steve said. 'If you've made a mistake, the deal's off. In that case you can just hand us our cash and we'll go.'

The pair leaned moodily in, leaving no space to run.

'Okay,' Tarq said. 'We'll do the deal.'

'Well get your arse over to the warehouse then because I don't know about you, but I like to conduct this kind of thing in private.'

Tarq entered the empty hangar. Stray bits of machinery lay about, oily pools across the concrete floor. The shutters closed behind him. Norman patted him down.

'He's clean.'

'Good, saves us having to throw him in the drink. I was just about to mix up some cement. Make him some boots.'

They laughed and Steve slapped his back. 'You're alright son, we ain't gonna kill you.'

Tarq finally relaxed, smiling along. 'I'm glad to hear that.'

'So what exactly are you looking for? A handgun, sawn off - how about a Mac 10?'

'A handgun would be nice.'

'Automatic? Six shooter?'

'Er...'

'We've got Lugers, Berettas, Smith and Wessons, the choice is yours. But you know what,' he paused, 'you look like a bit of a Glock man to me.'

'Do I?'

'Yeah, you young 'uns love your nine-mills don't you? They're easy to use and feel good in the hand. When you're carrying a Glock you know you're really packing some meat.'

'Sounds good. So is it, like, scary-looking?'

'It would frighten the knickers off your granny mate. We've just got a new batch in from the Balkans. They're selling like hot cakes. And what's more, I can get one into your hand not tomorrow, not next week, but today. Bob told you the price yeah? A grand.'

'Hang on, he said it was a grand and a half but he's already taken seven fifty.'

'Greedy bastard. Let's call it nine fifty then. This is a Glock 17 we're talking about, proper metalwork mate.'

'I've only got eight fifty.'

Steve held his chin to consider it. 'Go on then, fuck it, it's a deal. As I say, you won't be disappointed.'

They shook hands and walked back to the van. 'Okay Tarquin, this is how it happens. We'll drop you at the park and return in twenty minutes with the hardware. Happy?'

'More than.'

'Though bear in mind, this is the dangerous part. There's undercover filth about eyeballing vans just like mine, so I can't stress enough how cautious we've got to be. When we make the exchange we've got to be quick, no fucking about.'

'Yeah, course.'

'Good man.'

They dropped him back by the park gates and Tarq stood waiting. It began to rain, softly at first, then slamming down, but he was too excited to care. After a bit the van pulled in. Steve let down his window, put out his hand.

'Money.'

Tarq passed it over and Steve thumbed behind him. 'Past the next corner there's an alcove full of fly-tipped rubbish. A sports bag is on top. You better run in case someone snatches it.'

The van pulled away and Tarq sprinted through the rain. He found the holdall and carried it into the park. Feeling the weight inside he could hardly hold himself back. He stopped under a tree, the park empty in the downpour, and zipped it open. Inside was a taped-up shoebox. He tore it open and found a single lump of scrap metal. A note attached read: NICE DOING BUSINESS WITH YOU CUNT.

Terry and Dan climbed onto their barstools laughing away. They'd hardly been gone any time and had earned themselves four hundred and twenty-five smackers each.

'This is just like the old days,' Terry said, slapping a note down on the bar. 'Ducking and diving. Bringing home the dough.'

'Nothing has changed Terry. You need waking from hibernation. This is just a taster. There's big things happening out there. Weeks from now you could be sporting a nice Range Rover or a Jag. Bringing the family on a luxury holiday. Money in the hand Tel – if you're willing to work for it, that is.'

'What have you two dodgy geezers been up to?' laughed Faye as she placed down their pints. 'You look like a couple of crooks whispering like that.'

'I'm Capone, he's Dillinger,' Dan said.

'Gangsters? Of course, should've known,' she smiled, walking away.

'Steve and Norman more like,' Terry said. 'Norman? Christ, couldn't you have thought of a better name for me?'

'What's wrong with Norman? You've got Norman Wisdom, Norman Tebbit, Norman Bates...'

'Exactly.'

They sat having the craic, laughing about how things had panned out. Ripping off some scruffy posh kid who should've known better. He'd learn. It was a rite of passage, part of the growing process, boy to man. Tel had gone all Reservoir Dogs at one point and Dan had said something about packing meat – it's heat, ain't it? The two mates having a right old giggle.

'What was the bloke's name again?'

'It's Tarquin my dear boy,' Dan said, plumming it up and they split their sides.

Another pint and Terry was thinking of Dan's upcoming bit of work. Maybe it was the drink, but somehow it didn't seem such a bad proposition now. Perhaps it was time Terry brought home some proper money to the table. Brought a bit of joy into his household for a change. Just like when the kids were younger.

Sure enough Dan started talking about the job. Telling him it was planned by the Marriott brothers. Big dough. Those boys don't mess about. Eddie's just bought a vineyard in Spain and Vic's got a massive gaff in Portugal. They're rolling in it.

Terry was getting tempted. He was having to bite his tongue to stay quiet. He didn't want to confirm it for definite but he could feel that old excitement rising again. Stepping outside the system. No longer a cog in a half-knackered machine. Pushing the boat out. Doing something for yourself for a change. Reaping the rewards.

Dan was smiling at him. 'You're coming round, aren't you Tel?'

But no, he was getting carried away. He was drunk. There's no way he'd share the same frame of mind in the morning. It was just the drink messing up his thinking. And the lump of easy money in his pocket. No way on earth was he going back to his old habits. He'd been there, done that and paid the price. He'd have his pint and be off.

Dan turned back to his drink and said no more; he didn't want to push it. He knew Terry well. He'd come round. All in good time.

6

King of the Slums

Word came from Tottenham that Bigz and Slim were dead men walking. Not only had they mashed up Tyson Brown's little brother on the street, but now there were rumours they'd raped one of Lucifer's baby mums in her own bed. If the first charge wasn't serious enough, the second was akin to a declaration of war because Lucifer wasn't just street, he was gangsta elite corps.

Bigz was still over at Leona's place, while Slim was lying low at a friend's in Harringay. Even Jay had got out of Hackney, kipping at his cousin's gaff in Wood Green until the waters calmed. Because at present things were tense. The other night a crew of Tottenham boys linked to Tyson had driven down to Bigz's old estate looking for him. Nobody was around so they cruised the streets to pick on the first roadman they saw. Jumping out they asked a lone 16-year-old what ends he was from. He said Walthamstow but still they stabbed him repeatedly, shouting: 'Don't fuck with Tottenham.' The boy died in hospital and hadn't been lying about E17. He was a straight-goer who'd been visiting his aunt on her birthday.

Bigz was slumped on his jacks watching daytime TV. His phone went, Slim chatting some random shit in his ear. Then he heard the words 'He was cut down with an axe' and he sat up, turned down the TV.

'Who's been cut down with an axe?'

'My cousin,' Slim said, sounding near to tears. 'You know Darren who I was telling you about recently? He's dead B, fucking dead. They found him in an alleyway all hacked up in a pool of blood. It's a headfuck and a half. I was only out with him and then this happens.'

Bigz's mind was ticking away. 'Do you think Tyson Brown did this? To get revenge for us attacking his brother?'

'It's nothing to do with that crowd. It was my cousin's own fault. He stabbed a man in a snooker hall in Dagenham, then one of the guy's friends followed him and took an axe to his head. I'm distraught here bruv, I'm suffering. I just can't believe this. My mum and sister are crying their eyes out.'

Bigz felt a wave of relief. The killing was unrelated, nothing to do with Tottenham, or him. Slim continued harping on about it and Bigz was soon bored so he said, 'Sorry for your loss brother, it's a sick world out there.' Finally Slim said he'd better go, his family needed him right now.

Bigz heated up some left-over pizza and smoked a blunt, making sure to smoke it out the window. Then he continued watching TV and drifted off.

Sometime later he woke, his phone ringing. Leona was back from work, in the kitchen singing some Beyoncé shit. Again it was Slim, but if he planned to bore him about his cousin again he could go crying somewhere else.

'You're not going to like this Bigz. Hot Iron Mike has called us in. He wants to see us.'

Bigz sat up. 'Hot Iron Mike, you're joking me?'

'You think I'd joke about something that ain't funny? He wants a meet with us pronto.'

'Shit. It must be about Tottenham. Listen, we've got to play this carefully. Remember, Tyson's bro was a mishap, but

Lucifer's baby mum, that's lies, just enemies trying to get us in the shit. Let's just pray he buys it.'

'But what if he lets his hot iron do the talking?'

'Don't say that. Just stick to the script. Who do you think Mike's going to believe, fellow Hackney men or fucking Tottenham?'

'I hope so B, that's all I can say. Listen, I gotta roll. Jay's picking me up now. We'll collect you in twenty.'

Bigz tried to think things through. His last dealings with Hot Iron Mike had been on good terms. A stash of Mike's product went missing from a car. Bigz heard it was a couple of London Fields boys, so he did the dirty and let Mike know. Anything to get in the don's good books because with Mike onside people were less likely to fuck with him. Mike was grateful, paid a nice sum and offered him a favour for when need be – which was used on saving Dreadman. Thing is, did a spent favour mean Bigz's credits with the guy were zero now? Mike could be a callous fuck, and wildly unpredictable, so it was impossible to tell.

Slim texted him; they were outside. Leona walked in with a candle and dimmed the lights. 'It's just you and me tonight B. I'm preparing a nice curry and I've bought some wine.'

Bigz stood up and grabbed his jacket. 'No can do. I've got business tonight.'

She stood in his way. 'You better be kidding me. We agreed we'd have a romantic meal tonight and watch a DVD.'

After days spent winning her over, here he was letting her down again, but there was nothing he could do.

'I'm sorry Lee, but it's important. It's work.'

She creased her face in anger. 'What you do isn't work, it's running round playing gangsta with your mates. You think you're still in the school playground. You're a joke. Where do I come in all this?'

'I don't want to argue. Just get out of my way, I've got to go.'

'Piss off then and don't come back. I'm gonna get me a man who gives me some attention once in a while. You think I don't get offers?'

That stung. Bigz tried to speak but Leona said, 'Save it. I've had it up to here with you putting your stupid friends first. Just go, get out.'

Bigz headed down to the street, kicking aside an empty beer can before climbing into the car. He was getting nothing but hassle these days. During the drive to Hackney Slim was banging on about his murdered cousin again, and Bigz felt like telling him to shut up because he couldn't give a crap about his cousin, he had problems of his own right now.

On Lea Bridge Road they turned into the industrial estate that housed Mike's recording studio, one of several strings to his bow. A sign in neon read: MIKE'S RED HOT RECORDS.

Pulling up in the car park all three were silent, growing nervy now. Mike had said eight sharp, so they sat it out for a few minutes. They'd been here a few months ago for the outdoor shoot of a local rapper's video, splashing bubbly about and spitting along, Bigz earning a long menacing face shot in the final edit, but nobody mentioned that memorable day now. A group of youngers, sixteen, seventeen, hung by the studio's entrance, one of them constantly cackling out loud. The sound of fun and laughter wasn't helping Bigz relax. He jumped out of the car.

'Where you going?' Slim asked.

'I can't sit around no more. Let's get this shit done.'

Passing the group, the youths opted for a respectful silence, but Bigz grabbed a spliff from one of them. 'Gimme that ting.' He took a puff and exhaled in disgust.

'What's this weak shit you're smoking? Whoever sold you that needs bullets up the arse.' He tossed it at the youth's feet.

Another boy laughed and Bigz turned to him, swiping the cap from his head. 'Something funny, you little shit? You want me to take that smirk off your face with something sharp?' The boy shook his head, looked down.

Slim and Jay left Bigz to it and walked in the door, neither in the mood for childish games right now.

'Listen to that clown,' Jay said as they headed up the stairs. 'You can't bring him anywhere.' The sound of grimy beats thudded through the walls.

Bigz ran up behind them. 'Hold up, wait for me.' He seemed in a better mood now. 'You see them lot shitting their pants out there?'

They stopped at reception, a black woman filing her nails behind the desk.

'Are you the boys summoned to see Mike?'

They said yes and she no longer made eye contact, turning her nose up at them in disapproval. 'In that case you better take a seat in the lounge.'

Bigz and Slim sat fiddling with their phones while Jay sat arms-folded. At present Jay was staying with his older and wiser cousin Trevor and last night they'd had a rum and a sit-down. Trevor had dropped the road life early on, re-done his studies and gone white collar. He had a decent flat and a respectable job with an insurance firm. He lived a life of low stress and relative comfort and was a much happier person for it. But it took effort and meant an overhaul of your mindset, adopting a new set of values and goals. Jay remembered his words. 'Ditch the negativity. It's just attitude and laziness. We can be legit and go places just like anyone else. If we have to try a bit harder, tough shit. The point is, it can be done. If you want to change your ways and thrive you can do it. I'm living testament to that.'

Trevor was lecturing him, saying he needed to go back to college as it's the only way he wouldn't end up in prison with all the other losers out there. Jay ended the conversation and went to bed before Trevor tried to persuade him to go to his church again, but he knew Trevor's heart was in the right place. He just

84

wanted to help a family member, even if it was Jay's mum who'd probably encouraged him. His mum talked about Trevor like he was a saint or something. But Trev hadn't grown up in Hackney. Wood Green had calibre and some mean faces these days, but Hackney had history, tradition, a criminal past that was prominent on the crime map before any of them were even born. The road life was everywhere in H-Town, drenched into the concrete like blood. Cockneys had the sound of Bow bells, Hackney mandem had the sound of police choppers hunting nightly for armed robbers and killers. You couldn't grow up in the middle of that without at least a fair bit rubbing off on you. But if Jay was honest, none of that bullshit even appealed to him. It was just a background noise that had been swirling around him from year dot. By nature Jay was a ladies man, a player, in it for the women. Everything else was just a complication.

Hot Iron Mike came down the hall.

'No worries my man,' he said into his phone, sporting a sharp Savile Row suit. 'I can get you as much council funding as you want. That's right,' he laughed, 'connections my friend.' Then seeing them he pointed: 'You dicks wait there,' and he was off.

'Shit,' Bigz said. 'He's definitely upset with us.'

'Don't even say that.'

Soon the receptionist appeared. 'This way.' She wore a tight two-piece suit that emphasised each curve. Following after her Bigz's eyes were locked on her ample behind. He nudged Slim. 'Nice big booty,' he whispered, trying to alleviate the tension, but Slim told him to shush, it was no time for jokes.

By the door she gave a kiss of her teeth. 'Knock before you enter,' and walked away.

They knocked and heard, 'Come the fuck in.'

Mike was behind his desk, staring the trio down with disdain as they stood before him. Two books were next to him: Machiavelli's *The Prince* and Sun-Tzu's *Art of War*. Nourishment for the mind. Navigation for survival in the world of hard knocks.

He pointed at Jay. 'Who are you?'

'Me?'

'Yeah you, motherfucker. What role do you play with these two?'

'He drives,' Bigz said. 'But he's one of us – we're all equal, we're a team.'

'He's the driver? Did I say to bring your driver?'

'Well, no but...'

He motioned a finger at Jay. 'Get the fuck out of here.'

Jay made a hasty exit and Bigz now wished he hadn't spoken.

Mike formed his hands into a triangle and glared at the remaining two with a menace you couldn't learn or buy.

'I hear you've been running around out of control for some time now. And not just misbehaving on my turf, but off my turf also. What have you got to say about that?'

Slim spoke first. 'Things have been a little crazy lately, but not all the rumours about us are true, I promise you.'

'I see.' Mike rose an eyebrow. 'So you're saying my people have been lying to me, taking me for some kind of pussy?'

'No way,' Bigz said. 'Slim didn't mean it that way. It's just that like most people we've got enemies and sometimes they spread stuff about us that isn't true.'

Mike widened his eyes. 'I think it's best, Mr Bigz, if you shut your mouth. In fact I recommend it for your own well-being.'

'I'm sorry.'

'You better be. Now I want to talk about some of your antics lately, because I've got a feeling you've been operating with no regard to the hierarchy in place out there, thinking you're several ranks above your station. Which right now is no higher than what's flowing in the sewers beneath the streets.'

Slim wanted to get their point across before things went any further south. 'Listen Mike, we admit we made a mistake with Tyson Brown's brother, but that stuff about it being us who barged into Lucifer's place, that just isn't true...'

'Hush,' Mike said, putting up a finger. 'I want to discuss one subject at a time. First you target one of my chicken shops for small change, when everybody knows I've got those shops protected. Then you target the younger brother of a promising striker in the football team I sponsor. And finally, most outrageous of all, you fuck around with a woman of one of the top Tottenham faces, in the home where the man himself is staying.'

Both were itching to speak now, biting their tongues.

'First we'll address that last one, because that's the motherfucker that intrigues me the most.'

'We didn't do it,' they both said.

Mike looked from one to the other, settling on Bigz. 'You - explain that to me.'

'It wasn't us. Men from South London did it. Lucifer has bare enemies down there after killing those two guys. All this talk about us storming his flat is bullshit, I swear on my mother's life.'

Mike stared hard at him for a long time. Then he broke into a grin and slapped his desk. 'I fucking knew it weren't you lot who did it.' Then he dropped the smile and righted himself.

'I mean, you two wouldn't have the balls to do a job like that. You'd need to be crazy to mess with a general like Lucifer. But of course I knew that from the beginning, and so did he. In fact when I had a chat with him to see if it was Hackney boys who did it, he laughed at that. So let's move on. Now, the Memphis Fried Chicken shop, what was all that about?'

'We didn't know it was one of yours, I swear down,' Bigz said. 'If we'd known, you think we would have hit it? No way.'

'Well let me tell you this. They're paying me more now because once word got around what happened to you, nobody's going to hassle them. Having acid behind the counter is a measure I've recommended - so maybe you've done me a favour there Bigz.'

They looked at each other and Mike laughed.

'I was angry at first though, I admit. I even sent out some of my boys to go find you. Thankfully your cousin Dreadman supplied your address and they broke in and pissed on your sofa.'

Bigz was puzzled. 'I thought it was the Tottenham lot who trashed my flat?'

'Uh-uh. But that's history now, so let's move on. Tyson Brown's bro. You licked him up. Normally I wouldn't give a shit, but Tyson's one of my most promising footballers and family woes affects his game. A West Ham scout is seeing him next week, which for your sake better work out, you feeling me?'

Mike sat back, exhaled and shook his head. 'By rights I should let nature take its course and let the Totty men deal with you. But two more dead roadmen on the Hackney streets, what do I gain from that? I earn diddly squat from these tit-for-tat killings. So I've got an alternative. You want to hear the proposal?'

They were all ears.

'You two are out there full time, dedicated soldiers without a cause. Maybe I can use that dedication, channel it in the right direction. Tell you what, I'll get the beef with Ty Brown and his crew squashed and in return you come work for me. Full time, no more freelancing, no more anarchy. I want your aggression harnessed and channelled. In other words, put to use when I say so. The leashes only get taken off for attack when I issue the command. Because I'll say in your favour, with all these stories flying about, you boys have built a nice little rep for yourselves, and I could use a few more pit-bulls on the payroll. What do you say?'

Both were more than grateful, expressing their thanks.

'Okay,' Mike said, nodding as he stared them down. His expression slowly darkened. Finally he pressed a button and said, 'Deanna, fetch my kit.' He stood up and came around the desk.

'Don't think for one minute you've got off this shit lightly, because working for me ain't easy street. I demand discipline, and as is well known, I enforce this discipline with the heat of my branding iron.'

The receptionist entered carrying a small steel bucket of red-hot coals, a branding iron set within them.

'Just what the doctor ordered,' Mike smiled as she placed it down.

'I'll be seeing you later, sweet,' he said.

By the door she smiled. 'Looking forward to that.'

Mike slipped on a protective glove. He picked up the red-hot iron rod. Both had heard stories of this initiation but never believed them.

'Lift up your sleeves and get your forearms ready. You first Slim. Lean your hand down on the desk and don't move a muscle.'

Reluctantly Slim stepped forward, baring his arm and closing his eyes. With a sizzle the iron connected on his skin. Pain shot through his body, a scream issuing shrill and harsh. Wincing, he grabbed his arm and stood back in place.

'Get the fuck back here. That was only the first line.'

Slim did as he was told and endured three further brandings until the letter M was scorched onto his skin. He dropped to the corner, huddled in agony.

'Now you Mr Bigz,' Mike said.

The room reeked of cooked flesh and Bigz felt nauseous. The door wasn't locked. He could make a getaway, run right out of the building, out of London and never return. He could move to a different town and start all over again. But Mike had contacts everywhere. He'd find him. It could be a week or six months, but the sure knowing would do his head in. Bigz couldn't live like that. Approaching the desk he braced himself for the pain.

Maybe he'd learn something from this. Perhaps his problem was he wasn't ruthless enough. He needed to become more like the people he feared, more like Mike, and maybe this would toughen him up, give him the kick he needed. He saw Mike's excited leer as the hot iron approached his skin. He decided he was going to take it like a man.

The pain hit him like an electric bolt to the heart, his scream involuntary. Several more shrieks and Bigz turned and dropped breathless to his knees.

Mike chuckled. He brought the smoking bucket out of the room and returned to see them groaning on the floor. 'Jeez, it smells like Dante's seventh circle of hell in here – sounds like it too.' He opened another window. 'What are you, little bitches? Get up on your feet, soldiers. Stand to attention.'

They rose and Mike sat on the side of his desk with the cool assurance of a CEO.

'You're my cattle now. You work for me. And furthermore, you'll conduct yourselves with the appropriate respect and etiquette when around me.'

Breaking his composure, he stepped to Bigz and grabbed him, anger refreshed.

'Another thing, I saw you from the window earlier playing the big man pushing my young artists around, and I don't like that kind of disrespect. Fuck with my artists and you fuck with me. One of those boys is flying out to New York next week to meet one of the world's top producers, and where are you going? Wherever I fucking tell you, that's where. Do you hear that?'

Bigz nodded and Mike released his grip. He made to turn, then spun back around and punched him hard. Bigz bounced off the wall and hit the floor.

'Now get out of my sight, the both of you,' Mike said, kissing his teeth.

Outside Jay was leaning by his car waiting for them to finish their meet. He'd been lucky up there and felt no envy for them right now. The youths were still by the entrance, laughing and joking, not a care in the world, and they reminded Jay of himself a few years back. No tensions, no worries, whereas now it seemed there was never anything but. He gazed at the lit window of Mike's office. What was happening up there didn't bear thinking about. He just hoped the guy wasn't going too harsh on them, not least because they'd only deflect their anguish onto him.

He paced up and down. It was a cool night yet he was sweating. A part of him wanted to jump in his car and drive, travel as far as possible and ideally never see either of them again. But he'd been part of the trio for so long now, his place cemented, that it seemed impossible. Slim he could handle, Bigz was another matter. Back in the day they'd been equals, but time had warped things and too often these days Bigz seemed more like an enemy lording his power over him. Take last week in that flat when Bigz pointed a gun in his face. It couldn't go on like this. He'd have to start making plans for an exit. Life in Hackney just wasn't cutting it any more.

Mulling on it, he concluded that he was probably just over-reacting when a scream pieced the air. His eyes zoomed to Mike's window. Again it came, a pained wail that reverberated off the nearby warehouses. The youths went silent; sensing danger they climbed on their bikes and dispersed. Further screams issued forth, harsher and ugly, and Jay recognised Bigz this time. Jay jumped in his car and started the engine. It was over. He wasn't sticking around. This was his getaway, his break; he'd had enough. From now on Bigz and Slim would have to ride out their woes alone.

Passing Lea Bridge roundabout, he considered the practicalities. If he really wanted to make a break he couldn't stay at Trevor's as they'd find him; he'd have to pack his shit and head further afield. A year ago he'd laid low for a few days with another cousin Syrus over in Harlesden, and they didn't know the address. The law had been hunting for them after Bigz robbed a guy's Rolex on the street. The man fought back, landing some decent punches until Bigz stabbed him up bad. He returned to the car fuming because the guy had busted his nose. The charges were eventually dropped due to lack of evidence. He'd have to give Syrus a ring.

He wondered what Trevor would think. Harlesden could be a gritty place, giving Hackney a run for its money, and he'd no doubt disapprove. Syrus was Trevor's polar opposite. There'd be no talk of happy-clappy churchgoing or nine-to-five wage slavery with Syrus, that's for sure. Syrus was a fellow ladies man and fresh territory to conquer was just what Jay needed.

He phoned Syrus and told him the score, amending his story for credibility. Running from his own crew could look snakey, so instead he said the local police were on his back and he needed a couch off-manor to rest his head for a bit. Sy was glad to hear from him, said he was welcome, come and stay for as long as you like blud. Jay thanked him, said he'd catch him later. So all was good. Jay was heading off the scene for a while. Maybe longer. He'd see how things played out. But the message to Bigz and Slim was clear: his chauffeuring days were done and they'd have to find a new mug. He imagined their faces. It was both nerve-wracking and exciting, but changes had to be made. He'd pick up his essentials from Trevor's then make the ride to NW10. But first he needed to grab some notes from a cashpoint.

He pulled over at Stamford Hill and crossed the busy road. By the machine he noticed a man loitering nearby, giving him furtive looks. Messy hair and dirty jeans like a junkie. Was the dickhead actually planning to move on him? Jay decided he was imagining it, until he suddenly approached, hand behind his back like he was concealing a knife.

'Got any change mate?'

Jay pocketed his cash then glanced left and right before

feeling in his back pocket. Reading the situation the guy took several steps back.

'Stand the fuck away from me or I'll cut you up,' Jay said, hand ready to pull his shank.

The guy hesitated, then muttered something and skulked off. What was happening to the hood? Even the tramps were getting ideas these days. He was glad to be seeing the back of it. He visited a shop for some rizla then headed across to his car. Climbing in he noticed a commotion by the cash machine. The junkie was pulling a woman around by the hair trying to grab her bag. Without a second thought Jay jumped out, dodging the passing cars as he ran over there. The man was wielding a machete.

Jay whipped out his blade. 'Leave her alone.'

The man stood shocked and the woman dropped to the ground. His tool was triple the size of Jay's and there could be a problem if the freak wanted a duel, but he gambled on a threatening step closer and it paid off as the guy suddenly turned and ran. Relieved he watched him turn a corner.

The woman sat on the ground crying and Jay got down and asked if she was okay. She nodded and thanked him for saving her. A man was phoning the police and a young couple ran forward asking what happened. 'A guy just tried to rob her. He ran off down the backstreet there.' Then Jay muttered an excuse and left. He didn't need the attention.

'You're moving in with Syrus? The man's a bona fide criminal.'

Jay shrugged as Trevor stood watching him pack his stuff. 'It's what's happening Trev, so you can take it or leave it.'

'What am I going to say to your mum about this?'

'She'll just have to get real, because I'm doing this to save my own skin. How are things ever going to improve for me if I don't get away from Slim and Bigz?'

Trevor paced up and down. 'What about Aunt Millie in

Northampton, you could stay up there for a bit?'

'Aunt Millie? She used to whip her own children to get the evil out of them. That worked well, didn't it. Last year Nigel topped himself and now her grandson Mark's a gangbanger.'

'Little Mark?'

'He ain't little no more. He's thirteen, six-foot-tall and running with the local crew.'

'No way.'

'Believe – Sharon told me. And besides, I'm not living in a house with three generations stuffed under the same roof. And I hate those little towns up country, they're depressing.'

'But going to Harlesden is madness. Syrus is still on tag for plugging a hundred rocks of crack.'

'He's not on tag no more.'

'So what, he's still living the same life. He spent a whole year inside and it taught him nothing.'

'It's a temporary measure. I'll stay round his yard until I find somewhere better.'

Trevor shook his head. 'And what if your two compadres come knocking at my door?'

'It's me they'd be looking for, not you. Anyway, they know the road but not the house number so there's not much chance of that.'

'There better not be.'

'I wouldn't be frightened of them two. I want them off my back but there's much worse out there.'

'Did I say I was frightened of them? I don't give a shit about the wasters you hang around with. Anyone who comes to my door is getting it slammed in their face.'

'So what's the problem then?'

Trevor stopped pacing. 'The problem is you. Your mum's worried about you. She thinks you're going to end up like your father.'

Jay turned around, riled now. Trevor had over-stepped the

mark. 'What are you mentioning my father for?' He threw his clothes down. 'Why don't you just shut your fucking mouth?'

When Jay was young his dad had walked out on the family for another woman, so it was a sore point, something he avoided thinking about. Jay had only vague memories of him, but photos showed a dapper dresser with a self-assured smile. The man was a ducker and diver, and did some stints in prison. Jay swore if he ever laid eyes on the wasteman he'd lick him up bad. His older sister reckoned she spotted him once with a bunch of street drinkers in Forest Gate, but Jay didn't want to know. The man was dead to him.

Pulsing with anger, Jay zipped up his holdall.

'I'm just saying Jay, you're heading for bad things.'

'My choice.' He shouldered his bag and made for the door.

Trevor stood arms-folded blocking his way.

'What is this? Are you going to move out of my way or what?'

'You're an ungrateful prick, do you know that?'

Jay dropped his bag and swung for him. Trevor deflected the punch and dealt him a hard left. Jay staggered backwards, then returned with a flurry of blows, most of which had little effect. They grappled for a bit until Trevor got him face-down, arm up behind his back.

'Are you done now?'

'Fuck you.'

'I said are you done?' He twisted his arm.

'Ahh… okay, I'm done.'

He eased off and they sat by the side of the bed. Trevor wiped some blood from his lips, turning to Jay who was doing the same. They looked at each other, then they looked again and both shook their heads and laughed.

'Jeez...'

Trevor put out his fist and Jay tapped it.

'Can't believe we just did that.'

'Madness.'

Trevor rubbed his jaw. 'You got me a good one there.'

'Same here. Several.'

On the floor the bag stared them in the face.

Trevor exhaled. 'Do what you have to do Jay. But look out, because people care for you. I mean that.'

Jay nodded. 'I appreciate that Trev.'

Outside he got into his car and hit the tarmac, driving the nine miles west to a new chapter in his life.

7

Nightmare Angel

Fly was pacing up and down in his flat, one pissed off motherfucker. A regular client had been bugging him about getting hold of a piece, so he gave him a number. But now he wished he hadn't been so accommodating. Helping people get strapped up wasn't part of Fly's customer service package. He offered pharmaceuticals only, not guns, not therapy, and certainly not a bailiff service to recover money lost through your own stupidity. He'd had Tarq mouthing down the phone saying he'd been ripped off, demanding names and numbers, and it wasn't on.

Fly tapped out his blunt. This new super-strong skunk on the scene was doing little to ease his vexation. The more he reflected on it, the more Tarq's violation infuriated him. He was running a business here and complications was the last thing he needed on his mind. Dreadman said he'd put the boy onto the right people, and if they chose to jack him it was out of his hands - the boy was probably just a lying little snake trying to cause friction.

Tarq was a good customer who put a lot of Ps his way, but a

client has to know their place and when to shut their mouth. Maybe he was blowing it up, overthinking it, but sometimes it just comes down to respect. By shouting down the phone at him Tarq had pushed his luck too far. A point had to be made. He dialled Hot Iron Mike. Fly paid Mike premium for selling on his patch, but unlike most in the protection trade he wasn't slow in smoothing out problems.

The bossman assured him the matter would be dealt with as soon as. Think of it good as done. Fly liked that. Iron Mike had a hard-nosed reputation but he was a man of his word. A businessman to the bone, he understood impediments to the flow of free trade can only be remedied with zero tolerance.

Tarquin sat on his floor, the detritus of his chaotic lifestyle all around him. It was daytime yet his ragged curtains hung almost fully closed, the flat barely lit. His glory days were over, it was indisputable, yet life had a cruel habit of gleefully rubbing the salt in.

The other night he saw his ex-girlfriend Tabitha walking with her new boyfriend. Tarq recognised him as a lead singer he used to know. They'd hung out occasionally. But Johnny's band was going nowhere while Tarq's was on the up. He remembered them in the Bricklayer's Arms in Shoreditch one night, Tarq laughing when Johnny said he planned for his band to be on the cover of the NME within a year. Now sure enough Johnny's group had pushed on and made it, their debut album fly-posted all over the streets of Hackney.

Tarq and Tabitha met eyes, shock turning to sorrow before she turned away. Johnny either failed to recognise him or wasn't remotely bothered, carrying on talking as he passed by.

At the time Tarq had been clucking for a fix, but now the bigger picture haunted him, the knowledge of what he'd thrown away cutting like a scalpel. Johnny had replaced him and he wished a world of bad luck on the guy, but the person he was most in hate with, was himself. He replayed the scene in Dagenham, opening the sports bag, except this time he pulled out a real loaded pistol. He wanted to hold it in his hands, put it to his temple and blow his brains out. Instead he reached for his wrap of heroin. It was his solution to dull the pain, help him become weightless, free and unburdened, no mistakes, no consequences. An escape from the sad reality around him.

A knock at his door jolted him from his stupor. For a second he thought it might be Fly. He'd spoken to him yesterday high on crack, trying to get the rip-off Rasta's number. Tarq had been angry and persistent and it wasn't the done thing. But he was a good customer and maybe Fly had now taken pity on him – Yo Tarq, I had a word with my friend and got some of your money back. Don't be stupid like that again okay. Though the knock was likely just one of his junkie mates looking for a fix.

He checked the spyhole and saw two black men standing there, one bulky, the other slim and light-skinned. He didn't know them. They knocked harder but Tarq didn't open it.

'What do you want?'

'Open up, we've got something for you.'

Perhaps Fly had sent them to deliver his refund after all. Could it be true?

He opened the door and they lunged for him. The largest held him by the neck, growling in his face. 'Mess with Fly and you're messing with some big people.' He threw him down onto the sofa and began beating him. The other guy tried to turn the light on but there was no bulb. He browsed the place for anything worth nicking, but must've been disappointed because soon he said, 'Let me have a go at him Bigz. He deserves a licking for bad hygiene habits alone. Has this place ever seen daylight? It's like a fucking rat's nest.'

Bigz stepped aside to let Slim take over. Tarq tried to reason with him but he said, 'Don't even look at me, wasteman. You're a tramp, you deserve all you get.'

The digs kept coming, both laying in now, until finally they stood back to evaluate their work. Tarq lay curled up on the floor aching.

'Job done. I think Mike will be happy with that. Now let's get out of here before we catch fleas.'

They made to leave, then Bigz stopped. 'One minute Slim, I forgot something.' He undid his flies and stood in front of the sofa.

'You evil fucker,' Slim laughed. 'A beatdown is one thing but pissing on someone's sofa is taking it to another level.'

Bigz finished up and tucked himself away. He was satisfied now. He'd wanted to pass on the favour for time.

*

Donning a white disposable boiler suit, Lil Killa carried a wrapped sawn-off shotgun as he followed an older guy called Tony the Pony towards an old Escort.

They stopped by the car, Tony cursing as he patted himself down for the key. Lil Killa eyed him under the streetlight, noting it was better to die young. The old G looked nervous, worn out, as if not only the job in hand but life itself was too much for him. That's what happens. Stick around too long and you lose your vitality, get stuck in the past, unfit for the challenges of the present. Lil would never let himself go like that. But more likely he'd never make it anywhere near to Tony's age. Fate had different plans for Lil. He had a limited time on these streets. It came with the lifestyle.

Tony the Pony noticed the boy looking at him, his dead-eyed stare creating unease.

'What you looking at, man? You're giving me the jitters. Stop eyeballing me.' He checked left and right. 'And remember – you don't know me, ain't never met me, agreed?'

Lil responded by unwrapping the shooter and aiming the business end at him. 'Likewise,' he said with a smirk.

Tony raised his arms in fright. 'Put that fucking thing down. Jeez.'

Lil lowered the gun, nodding in subtle amusement.

'You're crazy,' the Pony told him, checking for prying eyes. 'A dangerous little fucker pointing that thing at me like that. Now ain't the time for jesting. We get seen we're nicked, and I ain't being thrown in the slammer for nobody.'

They were behind some flats in Manor House. It was dark, nobody about, but you couldn't be too careful. He shook his head at the boy's stupidity, found the key and they climbed in. They drove along Seven Sisters Road, turning onto Amhurst Park, Tony less edgy now they were on the road. The destination was Homerton's Kingsmead Estate.

'Why do they call you the Pony?' Lil Killa asked.

'I used to collect money for bets - you know, on the horses, the ponies.'

'Used to?' Lil said, sensing something interesting here. 'But you don't anymore?'

Tony exhaled; he didn't want to discuss it. 'It's just a name like any other.'

He hadn't been a gambler's runner for over twenty years now, but still had the scar from when he was jumped one night carrying two grand. He remembered leaning by a wall on Sandringham Road, his intestines spilling out through his fingers, praying the ambulance would get a move on. But worse was losing the dough, which his bosses wanted back, stolen or not. He laid low for a while, then one night walking past the Hackney Empire they took some shots at him from a car, killing another guy who just happened to be strolling by. Things cooled off when the gang got into some problems with the law. Tony had done some grassing to get them off his back. The main face got a long stretch and the question of their dough got lost in the mix. He never ran for a gambling firm again, but the name stuck.

'Let's just get this shit done quick,' he said, not in the mood for idle conversation. 'Knock-knock, show the guy the shooter, say whatever Nelson told you to say and we'll hit the road. Because I don't know about you, but threatening people with guns ain't my idea of a fun evening.'

The boy was unresponsive. Tony turned to check if he was listening and saw him staring straight ahead, wearing the same morose expression since they'd first been introduced at Nelson's flat half an hour ago. Guy looked like a space cadet. He kissed his lips, said no more.

It was Hot Iron Mike who'd forced the Pony into all this shit. Sending him out on heavy work because of an unpaid debt. Three hundred poxy quid. But when a face like Mike issues an order you jump to attention or live to regret it - or maybe you don't get to live at all. He thought of a Jamaican he'd known called Righteous who'd left Spanish Town thinking London would be a breeze. He took orders from nobody, especially not the soft black English boys who thought they were big Yardie men. Righteous was caught selling in one of Mike's clubs and given a warning. He laughed and sent a message back for Mike to kiss his bare backside. The next day Righteous went missing. He was found floating in the River Lee. He had a bullet in his head and was minus a tongue.

Tony felt a chill pass through him. He was strictly a weed man, but since all this business of doing jobs for Mike he'd sought solace in the crack pipe, a habit he'd held at bay in recent years, and the relapse wasn't helping him financially or mentally. His head was alive with paranoia. Only this morning he'd dreamt he was locked in a burning car and couldn't get out. Red-eyed demons were squashed against the windows, leering as his skin began to melt. He woke up in a sweat.

With the sawn-off reassuringly heavy on his lap, Lil Killa eyed the passing scenery. Along Lower Clapton Road he gazed down a side-street to the flats where he'd grown up. Him, his mum and his older brother. His dad was around early on but Lil couldn't remember him. He heard he'd been sent to prison for raping some woman. Or maybe a number of them. He'd hide in the shadows then jump them on the road. That's what his brother told him anyway. His mum once said it wasn't true because their dad was a useless drunk who rarely satisfied her let alone strangers on the street. But when off her head she'd say all sorts of things. Lil once heard a different story, that his dad had killed some guy after being cheated at a card game, a renowned gunman who let nobody take liberties. Lil preferred that version. It was like something from an old film. He used to imagine he made his dough robbing banks, an outlaw with a fearsome reputation but a good heart, spreading his earnings around the community. But that was just make-believe.

His mother never told him the truth about his dad. She kept changing the story. But that's because she was an alky who used to bring strangers home, men who would stay for weeks and beat and abuse Lil and his brother saying they were driving their poor mother round the bend, when all the boys wanted was a bit of food and attention once in a while. As time went on they realised their mum wasn't like most mums, and when his brother Carl grew big enough he'd call her a lazy piece of shit to her face and they'd go out shoplifting for stuff to eat.

At night they'd dream that one day their old man might come back and whisk them away to start a new life somewhere. He'd return from prison or wherever the fuck he really was and surprise them. A sharp-looking dude with money in his pocket, hands full of presents for his two proud sons. He'd take control and from then on life would be fine, everyone talking about how Carl and Terrell had left the ends and gone on to greater things. Cruising along in an open-top Beemer. What do you want boys, you want to hit Nandos? Then how about we head up the West End and I'll buy you some trainers, get you kitted out? We can do this every day if you like.

But it never happened. And maybe his dad was just like a lot of other men in the hood, doing their own thing, not giving a shit. The guy probably never spared them a thought. Soon Lil's brother ran with a crew and was hardly ever home, going in and out of juvie until he topped someone and got life. Their mum was getting crazier, losing the ability to act sane, and even the social workers were beginning to notice. One day Lil was coming home from school. It was twilight and police lights and a crowd of people were by his flats. He saw his mum being stretchered into an ambulance, one arm slinging lifelessly over the side. There was a mess on the concrete, as if someone had thrown a bucket of red paint, and here was where his mum had thrown herself down from their fourth-floor window. The police were ordering people to stay back. But that's my mum, Lil said, and a policewoman took him aside and tried to soothe him. He pushed her away, told her to get her hands off him. He was on his own now, would have to look after himself from now on. He was eleven years old but looked younger.

He ended up in a council children's home. He'd blanked out much of what happened there, but memories still remained. They used to drug him. There was a pervert called Watson. He'd bring visitors in. Shadowy officials who worked for the council or the government. When Lil was zonked out, glued to the bed and the room swirling around like a nightmare, Watson and his friends would do things that afterwards he'd tell himself was all a dream. Denial for the sake of his sanity. A year ago after meeting an old friend he was told where Watson was living. It was a flat in Manor Park. One night Lil knocked on the door, a gun behind his back ready to shoot him, but an Indian family lived there now. The info was a few months out. One of these days, Watson, you better believe it.

The Pony pulled over on a street to the back of the estate.

'How about here, is this okay?'

Lil shrugged. It would mean a walk but he wasn't too fussy.

Tony watched the boy take out the shooter, check the ammo.

'That thing loaded?'

'It'd be pretty useless if it wasn't.'

'But you're only threatening the guy, right?'

'It ain't a guy.' Lil turned to see the man's reaction. 'It's a woman.'

'Rah.' Tony was taken aback. 'Is it a debt job? How much money does she owe?'

'Fuck knows. Could be twenty notes for all I care. It's work.'

Lil saw the old G whistle and shake his head. The man was a fool. He seemed to presume it wasn't a hit. Mike and Nelson must've been playing a little joke on the Pony here. If so, Lil wasn't going to spoil their fun.

'Man, you're cold. If that's loaded I'd be careful with that thing. I can't believe those rarse clarts are sending you out with a loaded gun. How old are you anyway? You look sixteen tops.'

Lil was twenty-four, but due to his height and build people presumed he was younger. He'd been on the scene for time now so didn't appreciate this kind of disrespectful tone. Like when girls called him Baby K, that pissed him off too. But luckily he wasn't too interested in girls. He shupsed his lips. The old G was going to pay for that comment, mark my words. But for now Lil put it to the back of his mind.

'Fuck this shit, I've got a job to do.' He pulled up the hood of his boiler suit, attached a Tony Blair mask and got out of the car.

'Be quick,' the Pony said.

Lil Killa walked into the estate gun in hand. The blocks stretched above him. This was the role he was born for. Gunman outlaw. Nightmare angel of the concrete ruins. He felt he was donning a coat of armour. Like if an army took aim the rounds would bounce right off him.

He remembered another job he'd done. He'd been sent to stab a guy called Drilz. Not kill him, just bore him in the leg or whatever. It was a favour for some Holly Street guys he knew, practically a freebie. He did it to impress, to show that he worked more for fun than anything else. To most people that was scary, made him unpredictable, the worst kind of dangerous.

Watching from the bushes of a small park, he waited for Drilz to leave his house. Daylight was fading when the door finally opened and he went strutting off with his girl. Lil Killa walked up behind them. He'd seen the guy around, a prick with a snarl who considered himself untouchable. Lil relished the fact he was about to shatter that belief. Drilz chatted to his girl, his voice sounding less menacing than usual. Lil called out and Drilz spun around. He looked surprised, but quickly reverted to type, screwing his face as he eyed Lil up and down.

'You talking to me, you little dickhead?'

'Come here and say that. I've got something for you.'

'Are you mad?' Drilz laughed, shook his head. He'd heard how this fool rated himself as a psycho, but to Drilz the PR campaign didn't fly. He passed his blunt to his girl. 'I'm gonna kick this midget's arse.'

Lil stood his ground as Drilz punched him square in the face. Confusion flitted across the guy's eyes. Lil hadn't even flinched which went against the natural order of things. Drilz pushed him in the chest and went to hit him again, unable to understand why he'd invited this on himself, a punchbag refusing to fight when suddenly Lil's hand dashed towards his face. Drilz saw a flash, then his vision was plunged into darkness and he staggered backwards. He realised he'd just been stabbed in the eye, then his mind went screwy. Blade still intact, he hit the ground. Lil leaned down to retrieve the knife as the girl screamed hysterically. Frozen to the spot, hands to her head, mouth open wide. A still from a film.

Approaching her, blade dripping, he was a screen actor issuing a killer line. 'Snitch to the feds and I'll slaughter your whole family.'

Lil had taken things to a whole new level and everyone was scared of him now. Even the boys who'd given him the job. Groups looked at him in awe, falling silent as he approached, nodding tentative greetings in fearsome respect. Thing is, behind all the loud talk, most of these so-called roadmen were just regular Joes, kicking footballs or chatting up girls, but Lil was a guy who pulled off mafia hits, slaying people on their doorsteps and stabbing guys in the brain for the sheer fun of it, putting all their petty antics in the shade.

He headed for the target's flat. Shadow extended before him, he felt vital and alive, proud to be part of a tradition, but happy to put his own spin on it, leave his own mark, a cold-blooded killing machine with a 12-bore shotgun and a war criminal's mask. Lil savoured every second. He spent the rest of his life half asleep, his whole existence geared towards these fleeting moments of invincibility. Two men sharing a spliff stood up when they saw him and backed away down a passage. This is what you call an entrance. He imagined a movie camera panning alongside him, recording the scene for posterity, showing the dreamers and wannabes how it's done. Life didn't come better than this, moving with power and purpose, the adrenaline soaring through him.

He reached the block in question and counted the numbers for the target's ground-floor flat. The door was painted blood red and Lil saw this as a good omen. He rang the bell, stood waiting. Inside he heard the wails of a baby, then footsteps, its mother call out that she was coming. The door opened, the woman in a white dressing gown, her tired expression turning to alarm. He blasted her in the chest and she jolted backwards. The baby cried louder and a young boy appeared down the hallway, silently staring as the woman convulsed on the floor, gown painted crimson. Lil stepped towards her. He aimed the barrel at her head and again fired, the walls at each side taking the gore.

He was back on the concrete now, walking fast beneath the blocks, faces peering down at him, his heart banging, film reel speeding up, on fast-forward until he reached the street and got into the back of the car.

'Everything cool?' Tony asked, pulling out and driving away. He caught sight of Lil in the rearview. 'Jesus man, you're covered in blood.'

'No shit,' Lil said, removing his mask and gloves

'What the hell happened back there?'

'Job's done. Target's been taken out.'

Tony doubletook. 'You killed her?'

'Uh-huh.'

'No way, you're kidding me...'

The old G was fretting away, a drone in Lil's ears, but he tuned out the transmission. He was coming down fast now, adrenaline dissipating, a joyless exhaustion creeping in. He'd taken a few pills earlier, some pick-me-ups. Maybe he needed a few more.

'I ain't going down for no fucking murder, you listening to me?' The Pony's voice returned to him through the static.

'Nobody's going down for anything, you can take my word for that,' Lil assured him. Then he noticed they were heading in the wrong direction. 'Where you going?'

'Bringing the car back to Nelson.'

'You kidding? Head over to Tottenham Marshes. We've got to burn this shit.'

'Nelson didn't mention that.'

'Not to you he didn't, but you're not the main player here. We were planning all this before you arrived. We've got to get rid of the evidence, so come on, move it.'

Tony turned the car around and they travelled in silence. Then he tutted and said, 'Nobody mentioned no murder hit to me, this is a pisstake.'

'Relax old G, you ain't killed nobody, I did. If anything goes down I'll just say you were a random cab driver I picked up. That way you've got nothing to do with it.'

'You'll say that?'

'Course I will.'

Reaching the Marshes they pulled off the road, the car bumping slowly through the bushy grass.

'Go further down, over by that tree there.' They passed a burnt-out car, a torched motorbike. 'It's the perfect location. Another car on fire down here, nobody will bat an eyelid.'

Coming to a halt, Lil removed his boiler suit.

Tony looked at him in the mirror. 'Just so you know, I won't snitch on you either. If they ask me if you had a gun or wore protection or whatever, I'll deny it all. You did nothing and nor did I. Is that agreed?'

Lil didn't answer him. Tony turned around. 'Are you listening to me?'

The Pony met the twin barrels of the shotgun. His eyes showed a mass of white before Lil Killa blasted him point blank in the face. Tony's features were no more, his body slumping back over the wheel in a mess of blood. Lil's ears rang from the blast, the cordite fumes in the enclosed space overwhelming. He chucked the gun in the front and got out of the car, retrieving a black bag he'd stored in a nearby bush. He washed the mess off his hands and face with a bottle of water, changed his clothes, then chucked all the evidence into the car. He doused it down with a can of petrol. Setting it ablaze he slipped away into the night as the hot flames burned.

The gear was cooked and ready, tourniquet tied and the needle about to go in his arm when the doorbell sounded. Tarquin froze. He grabbed a knife and jumped to his feet. If that was Fly's men back for second helpings they were in for a surprise this time. Once more the bell sounded, its shrillness cutting through him. He stood there, knife hand shaking, fearing the door being kicked in any second. Then there were knocks, more like taps, and he heard a voice.

'Tarq, it's Greg. Open the door. I know you're in there. I saw the light from the street.'

It was his sister's fiancé. He lived in Bournemouth and worked in Bristol, what the hell was he doing here?

'I'm working in London for a few days so thought I'd drop in for a chat. Just to see how you are. Charlotte's worried about you, so is your mum and dad. You're not answering the phone. Not responding to their letters...'

Tarq placed the knife back on the table. He lay down on the sofa and pulled a blanket over him. He curled up, covered his head.

'Just a chat, honest. Five minutes and I'll go...'

His family didn't understand him. They had no idea of what he was going through. They lived in another world, a parallel universe. Things were different now. He was a different person with a different set of needs. There was no going back. The person they knew and wanted to see happy again no longer existed.

'Come on Tarq...'

Couldn't the bastard go away. Leave him the fuck alone. He put his hands over his ears to drown out the voice, praying, willing it to cease. A minute later when he took his hands away there was silence. Finally alone, he sat up. The syringe was right there faithfully waiting for him, its sweet oblivion beckoning, then he noticed a note had been slid under the door. He thought for a moment, then went over and picked it up.

It said: COME HOME.

8

Killing of a Flashboy

Sunday afternoon and Bigz and Slim were heading for Jay's last known whereabouts, his cousin's place in Wood Green. Reduced to driving Slim's crappy Ford Fiesta, the sooner Jay and his GTi were back on the scene the better. Slim was willing to let any hard feelings go, he just wanted Jay back in the fold, but Bigz wasn't feeling so lenient.

'Fucking off and blocking us on his phone, his own bredrins? It's unforgiveable. I want to bang him out for that.' He swung the car off Lordship Lane and down into the backstreets.

'There's no need for that kind of talk,' Slim said. 'Jay ain't going to stay away forever. He probably just got stressed and needed a break, don't worry about it.'

'I'm not worrying, I'm just pissed off.'

They parked in on Trevor's street and got out of the car.

'You know the house?' Bigz asked.

Slim checked the nearby windows and spotted the religious poster he remembered from once before.

'That one,' he pointed.

At the door a man eyed them up and down. 'What do you want?'

'You Trevor?' Bigz asked.

'Who wants to know?'

Bigz heard the guy had been a gangbanger but went straight after finding God. Yeah, right. A guy he knew called Hot Step had got out on parole after playing the same trick. He wangled a council job as a youth worker which was good cover for the three crack houses he was running.

'We're friends of Jay's,' Slim said, taking over. 'We heard he was staying here recently.'

'Well he ain't no more, and it's not my concern anyway, so I'll let you gents go.'

He made to close the door but Bigz put his foot there. 'We're looking for him. Do you know where he's hiding out?'

Trevor looked at his foot but refused to rise to it. 'Wherever he's staying now is his business. He left one night and I haven't seen him for dust. Jay does his own thing, I do mine.'

'You saying he hasn't even phoned you?'

Trevor held his stare. 'What did I just tell you?'

Bigz wanted to slap him, but Slim stepped in before things escalated. 'Look, no probs, but if you hear from Jay tell him we're concerned. There's no beef with us if that's what he's worried about.'

'No beef, you sure?'

'Yeah, it's cool. We're bredrins. Just tell him to give us a bell.'

'Okay, I'll do that,' Trevor said, slowly closing the door, eyes locked on Bigz until he disappeared.

Walking back to the car Slim shook his head. 'Why the attitude Bigz? You want Jay to come back or not?'

Bigz threw him the keys and got into the passenger side. 'You can drive, I'm in no mood now.' He folded his arms as they pulled away.

'You were making things difficult back there, I swear.'

'Fuck off man. Did you see the way he spoke to us? I was this close to slapping him.'

'Then Jay would never come back. If he gives us a call we've got to be forgiving, that's the deal. He'll return eventually, I'm sure of it. He just got freaked by Hot Iron Mike and needed some time out.'

'Yeah well, Jay's got nothing to worry about on that score. Mike wasn't even interested in him.' The fact Jay got off without a scratch that night still bugged him something rotten.

But working for Mike had so far been fine. They'd been mainly doing collections and deliveries, the odd threat or beatdown. It was easy work. Things were going well.

Back on Lower Clapton Road they sat parked up eating take-out chicken.

'Look,' Slim said, pointing out a guy strutting along the street in their direction. 'That's whatshisname... Lil Killa.'

Bigz stopped chewing to look at him. 'The one they say stabbed Drilz in the brain?'

'Not only Drilz, I heard he done a hit job the other day on Kingsmead. Blasted some woman dead on her doorstep, then he shot his own driver and torched the car. The police think the driver might've done it then killed himself because they found the shotgun next to him, but most people reckon it was this little fucker.'

Bigz studied him as he walked along. He looked no more than fifteen, yet he had bare respect on the road. He wondered if the stories about him were true. It was hard to tell. Yet something about the guy unsettled him.

'He's a loner you know,' Slim continued. 'A lone wolf. Nobody wants to hang with him. Don't look like he's too bothered though.'

'Who sent him on the hit?'

'Who do you think? Hot Iron Mike.'

Coming level Lil Killa spotted them and came up to the car. Slim let the window down. 'What's up, Lil?'

'It's all good,' he said, leaning down to glance at Bigz, a

roguish glint in his eye. 'I heard you guys are Mike's boys now.'

'Makes three of us then,' said Slim.

'Uh-uh, I'm a freelancer. Nobody owns me, not even Mike. Has he branded you two with his ting yet?'

'What you chatting about?' Slim said, affronted.

'He brands all his full-time boys like cattle, don't he.'

'Not us. We're just doing him a few favours at the moment.'

'That's not what I heard,' Lil smiled, showing off a gold molar. 'I heard he took his iron out and you two were squealing and shit.'

Bigz had heard enough of this crap. He placed his lunch aside and reached under the seat for his Mac-10.

'Yo,' he said, leaning over. 'You heard wrong, little man. Nobody fucks with us. Or if they do, they get a taste of this.' He pointed the gun at him.

Lil Killa didn't even flinch. But at least Bigz had wiped the cocky smirk off him.

'If you say so, big man.' Eyes colder now.

'I fucking do actually,' Bigz said, trying to hide his humiliation at Lil's lack of reaction. He returned the submachine gun to under his seat. What a psycho.

Lil was giving a dead-eyed smile, staring at Bigz like he was a small animal he was going to mutilate for fun. He looked the type that would do that shit.

'Anyway, we gotta roll,' Bigz announced, closing his chicken box. He was freaked out and no longer hungry.

'Yeah, we got business.' Slim started the engine.

'I'll let you two go then. And don't forget, have fun,' he said, his eyes staring Bigz out.

Lil Killa stood watching them as they pulled away. Bigz's heart was hammering, the blood rushing to his face. He realised he was actually nervous and it angered him.

'Well there you go,' Slim laughed. 'Total nutcase. I liked the way you showed him the Mac – don't know if you should've pointed it at him though.'

'Fuck that prick,' Bigz snapped. 'I ain't scared of him or no-one. He's all hype, that's what I reckon. Who says he did the Kingsmead hit? That could've been anyone. The feds are probably right, it was the driver. He's just full of mouth.'

'I wouldn't bet on it B. The dude creeps me out.'

Bigz didn't like Slim giving him the credit. The guy had strutted up with bare disrespect, trying to belittle them. In Bigz's book that shit wasn't on, and not from someone younger, no matter how many hits he'd supposedly done. After being press-ganged by Mike, Bigz had planned to send out a compensatory message that he was a man not to be messed with. Instead, here he was in his own back yard getting spoken down to like some kind of bitch.

Mulling on it, the episode enraged him. 'Turn the car around.'

'You what?'

'Turn the fucking car around. I want another word with that cunt.'

'You're kidding me.'

'Did you hear the way he just spoke to us? I want a word with the guy. Right now.'

They drove down to Mare Street looking for him. There was no sign, but coming back around they spotted him walking in the distance near the church. He turned into St John's Gardens. They parked the car and hurried towards him.

'You sure about this Bigz?'

'You might want to let him diss you like that, but the outcome affects the both of us. Mike is one thing, a pill-popping adolescent loser is another.'

Slim was surprised Bigz was taking it so badly. Lil was just an oddball and he himself would've allowed it. But maybe Bigz had a point. They were on Hot Iron Mike's team now and should be respected for that. They carried on along the path, a pleasant patch of greenery lined with trees.

'There he is,' Bigz said, spotting him up ahead. 'You carrying anything?'

'Yeah, my Rambo.'

'Pass it over,' he said and took the blade.

They rushed ahead to where Lil was slowly walking along. A few yards behind him Bigz called out.

'Yo little man, I want a word with you.'

Lil turned and Bigz marched forward and grabbed him. He pushed him up against a tree. The boy didn't resist, staring back with unreadable eyes, a subtle weirdo smirk. Bigz found himself hesitating before speaking.

'You dissed us back there big time, so how about an apology for the both of us.' Bigz held the knife inches from his face, but Lil was unfazed. He gripped him by the neck. 'I'm talking to you pussy.' Again the boy said nothing, staring coolly into his eyes, right through to his soul.

Deep inside Bigz felt something collapse. Lil wasn't scared of him. Wasn't bothered at all. He wasn't feigning either, he simply had no fear. And somehow this knowledge was more distressing than even Mike's hot iron.

'Feds, quick, let's move,' Slim said, spotting two policemen trotting on horseback up ahead.

Bigz pocketed the knife, let Lil go, and their eyes never parted until Slim pulled Bigz along, urging him to move quick. Bigz walked back to the car in a daze. Slim drove and Bigz felt a headache coming on. Never in his life had he met someone with absolutely no fear like that. It was mind-blowing. When you held a blade to somebody you expected a reaction. Instead he'd got nothing, zilch. It wasn't human.

'That was close back there,' Slim said.

Bigz wasn't listening. His head ached. He'd had enough.

'Drive me home. I'm fucking done for the day.'

*

Slim was all suited and booted for Darren's funeral. After the burial, he'd gone back to his aunt's house for drinks and snacks, and now he was with a group of his English cousins taking the session to a local Dagenham pub. Approaching the place Slim inwardly smiled. A large St George's flag hung outside and bang on cue three shaven-headed, beer-bellied cockneys strutted out. Dagenham was beyond a cliché.

Inside, similar types lined the bar. The BNP had support round this way and Slim swore he was getting one or two dirty looks, though he'd had a blunt earlier and was probably just being para. Still, he was glad when his group stepped out from the dark smoky pub to the beer garden to catch some sun. He stood with the others drinking a pint of lager, going with the flow, though in truth he'd have preferred a Coke. His cousins were chatting about Darren, saying he'd been no angel, had his faults, big faults, but nobody deserved to die like that.

'Thing is though,' said Billy from Clacton-on-Sea. 'It was a case of live by the sword die by the sword, I suppose.'

'Exactly,' shrugged Gary from Basildon. 'I mean, you can't say the bloke didn't ask for it.'

'Did you hear the crap the vicar was banging on about? I was holding back my laugh. If there's a heaven Dal's had the gates slammed in his face, I know that much. You're not on the list mate, you ain't getting in.'

'With his track record, he's down below, dancing on hot coals with the man with the horns, guaranteed.'

The boys laughed and continued along the same lines, but Slim felt this kind of chat was inappropriate. A joke's a joke, but Darren's death was a tragedy. They should be showing more respect.

'Darren was a lot of things,' Billy quipped, 'but prize cunt was definitely one of them.'

Finally Slim spoke out. 'What do you mean by that?'

'Well Marvin mate, this for a start.' Billy lifted his shirt to reveal a nasty scar along his waistline. 'Me and Dal had a little row one day. A few inches lower and he would've taken my bollocks off.'

Slim didn't know about that. Then Ben spoke of the time Darren used a bayonet on a cab driver. 'I think he might've owed the bloke a fare.'

So he had his moments, was a bit nasty now and then. Fair enough. But it just didn't seem right bringing all this shit up now.

'Bit of a cunt on occasion was our Dal,' winked Mitch, a short but stocky ex-army man. 'Fancied himself a bit of a gangsta, *ya get me blood*?' and he pulled a street pose.

'Yeah, Ali fucking G,' Gary said.

'Anyway, I love funerals. I only come for the drink,' deadpanned Graham, a guy who'd once tried to join the police. 'More funerals, more opportunities to get pissed. Bring 'em on I say.'

People were cracking up, but Slim wasn't on the same page. He spent enough time wisecracking with Jay and Bigz, but the humour here was a different flavour. Like they didn't give a fuck. He had little in common with his cousins. Most were London-born but had moved out to Essex or Kent.

'Darren wouldn't want us sitting around crying, I know that much,' Billy said, trying to get Slim back onside. 'There's nothing wrong with a laugh. Dal was a wicked joker himself. I remember the time he superglued the door handle of these flats then called the police. We were waiting on the balcony for some dopey Plod to turn up and get his hand stuck. Instead some old codger comes along - Grr, for fuck's sake, hand stuck solid, shaking his stick at us. Bleedin' youngsters. Me and Dal were splitting our sides.'

Slim laughed. Maybe Billy was right, he was being too sensitive. He was handed another pint, but he'd already had some cans back at the house and he soon felt nauseous. After a while he realised he might need to vomit, get all the gassy beer out of his system. He went inside to use the toilet. He entered a cubicle, bent over the pan and let the liquid gush.

He felt a lot better now. At the sinks he rinsed his mouth. He liked the odd rum and coke, even the occasional Guinness, but how these men routinely shoved ten pints of lager down their necks he couldn't fathom. Washing his hands, the door opened and a man walked in. Slim caught his eye in the mirror and then the man stopped and stared. Here we go. He hadn't been imagining things at all. The pub was full of racists. He wished now he'd stayed back at the house, but he would've looked like a right girl not going down the pub.

The man was bulky, tattoos down his arms, t-shirt showing a gut. He wasn't young but wasn't exactly old either. His bright blue eyes stared at him.

Slim turned, shaking his hands dry. 'You got a problem mate?'

The man smirked. 'We've met before, haven't we?'

'I don't think so.' Slim made to leave but the man stood in his way.

'Well I'm pretty certain we have. Where you from?'

Slim looked him in the eye. 'Hackney,' he said proudly.

'That makes two of us. I'm a Hackney boy too.'

'Sure you are.' Slim shook his head. He'd had enough of this joker. He made to walk around him but again his way was barred.

'You know Homerton, that manor? That's my old stomping ground.'

Slim didn't like the sound of this; he couldn't work out the man's game.

'Can you step out of my way please?' he said impatiently.

'And guess what us Hackney boys did to thieves back in my day?' The bloke leaned in. 'We nailed their thieving hands to the floor. Because that way you can always identify the cunts by the big scars on their paws.'

The man laughed and Slim pushed past, back to the beer garden. What a nutjob.

Billy put another pint in his hand, but Slim said he was thinking of heading off. Billy put an arm around him, eyes glassy with drink. 'Nobody's going anywhere Marv, least of all you me old mucker. We're staying till closing, giving Dal a good send off. You want a chaser with that, I'm getting some whiskies in?'

The group was pissed and so it seemed was every other punter in the place. This drinking all day lark was a tradition Slim wasn't getting roped into again. Feigning a phone call he made for a quiet corner of the garden, puffing on a blunt to chill out.

'Look at Marv over there having a sneaky doobie,' one of them pointed.

'Someone call the Old Bill on the cunt.' More laughter.

When he returned the group were discussing how London had turned into a right shithole. 'The place has fallen now,' Mitch said. 'It's like it's not even part of England any more. We're a despised minority these days.'

'We're the wogs now, the new niggers,' said Graham. Then someone muttered in his ear and he turned to Slim. 'No offence Marv, it's just a figure of speech.'

'None taken.'

Slim was itching to leave now, get away from these dumb pissheads. By the back door his older cousin Ben stood chatting to the headcase he'd met in the toilets. Both laughed, slapping each other's backs like they were the best of friends. This place was mad.

When it got dark they all went inside. Slim used the opportunity to slip off, everyone so loud and rowdy now they likely wouldn't even notice his absence. He'd left his jacket round his aunt's place so he'd have to pop back there before heading home to Hackney. He paced street after street of near-identical houses, almost getting lost until he passed the alley where Darren was killed and knew his aunt's was the next road along.

He stopped in at the site for one last time. Flowers were laid and he looked at the messages. One on the wall said WESTBROOK WAS A BASTARD WHO DESERVED IT. He shook his head. That was out of order. Must be some sick idiot with a grudge. Bursting for a leak he went further up the alley, stood by the wall and unzipped.

'We meet again,' a voice said behind him.

Slim jumped and turned around. It was the same nutter from the pub.

Slim hadn't time to yell before the heavy blade crashed down into his skull. The world slipped to the side and he was floored, adrenaline flooding his body, consciousness flashing in and out like a malfunctioning screen. Wild sparks flew in his brain until again the axe came down, once, twice, three times, but by then the plug was pulled, the screen completely blank.

Bigz lay in bed, Leona resting on his chest. It was her day off work and she was spending it with her man in the best way possible.

'So when are we going to move out of London then?'

'We aren't,' Bigz said, confused.

'Well we've talked about it enough times. But half the time these days you're in another world. You know: moving out, getting married, having children. You don't want your kids growing up in the hood do you?'

'You're rushing way ahead,' he laughed. 'One thing at a time. Anyway, you don't have to move somewhere boring to have kids. I know plenty of men with kids – some of them with lots of kids.'

'Yeah, kids with baby mums they don't live with or even care about. That's why we're not progressing at the rate we should be. Making money, going places. Look at other ethnicities, rising right up the ladder.'

'Like who?'

'I don't know… Asians. Running lots of businesses. Making a decent wage.'

'Jeez, what is this? I'm not short of money. I make good money sometimes.'

'And how much tax do you pay on it?'

'What's that got to do with it?'

'If you're not paying tax it means the money's not legitimate, which means at any point you could be carted off to prison.'

'You think Asians don't break the law with their VAT fiddles and shit? They're the kings of that hustle. They're worse than the Nigerians.'

'Whatever,' Leona said, shaking her head. 'But don't you ever want to settle down?'

'Course I do. And I'd like to have kids and maybe move somewhere nice too. But in the future, not right now.'

'Inner-city living gets too much after a while. A 14-year-old was murdered just down the road the other week. It wasn't like this when I was growing up. We used to play on the street or down the playground. Now it's all needles down there.'

'Hackney's much worse than Islington and it never did me any harm.'

'Right.' Then she saw his wounded arm. 'You ever going to tell me how you got that scar? It looks like an M.'

He moved it away. 'I told you, I was at a barbeque. I tripped and fell on the grill. I'm lucky, it could've been worse.'

'Must've been a strange looking grill.'

'It was painful you know.'

They were silent for a bit, then Leona turned to him and smiled. 'I'm in the mood for another go round.' She climbed on top.

Bigz pulled her back down. 'We did it that way already. This time it's gonna be me in the driving seat.'

'Oh, is that right...'

Suddenly his phone went.

'Don't answer it,' she said. 'We're busy right now.'

Bigz checked the screen. It was Mike. 'Shit, I've got to take this.'

Leona crossed her arms as Bigz sat on the edge of the bed to answer it.

'What's this I hear about your sidekick?' Mike asked. 'Is he really dead?'

'I don't follow, what do you mean?'

'On the news online there's a picture of Slim – Marvin Green, yeah? - and it says an axeman attacked him in Dagenham. Says he's fucking brown bread.'

'Nah boss,' Bigz laughed. 'You're getting things mixed up. Slim went to Dagenham yesterday for his cousin's funeral – his cousin was killed with an axe, not him.'

'But it looks like Slim's been axed now too. I've got it right here on my screen. Go check it out. Evening Standard, Bizarre Axe Murder No.2.'

'I'll do that,' Bigz said, almost certain Mike was mistaken. He went to the dressing table to open the laptop and sat down.

'Are you getting back into bed or not?' Leona said, but he ignored her. Finally she jumped out of bed and put on her dressing gown. 'You can go pleasure yourself because you ain't getting no booty off me, not today, not ever.' She slammed the door behind her.

Bigz wasn't listening. He was reading of London's latest street murder, Slim's face staring back at him.

The front door bell made him jolt. He went to warn Leona not to answer it, but she was already there. Two detectives stepped forward, two uniforms behind them. Their words stopped him in his tracks. Bigz was under arrest in connection with the murder of Marvin 'Slim' Green.

*

Terry woke up in bed with a banging hangover. He'd spent most of yesterday in the pub and was now paying the price. Stacey was already up and about, and when she walked in he braced himself for an earful, but instead she put down a glass of water and some Aspirin.

'Don't think I've got any sympathy, I just want you up and running today because Aunt Linda asked if you'll go round and cut her other tree. Where's your axe, I was looking for it, is it still in the car from last time?'

He rose bolt upright. 'Yeah, it is. No problem, I'll do it.' Anything to get rid of her because now he remembered what happened after the pub last night.

'Oh,' she said, pleasantly surprised. 'I'll tell Linda you'll definitely be there then. She said you did a really good job last time. Thanks Terry.'

She left the room and Terry was alone now. Rewinding through the fog of last night's drink, disturbing images and scenes flashed back at him. No way, had he really done it again?

Yes he had.

He'd been at the bar when a group of men entered the pub and took their drinks outside. They'd been to Darren Westbrook's funeral and among them he met Ben, an old mate who'd moved to Margate. He learned he was related. Ben said Darren had had his problems, been a bit naughty, but who deserves an axe in the head? They were reminiscing, laughing about the old days. Then Terry spotted another familiar face, but this one brought no pleasant memories. It was Westbrook's thieving half-caste accomplice that night. Terry caught him in the gents and had a word. He couldn't recall what he said, but remembered the bloke didn't recognise him. Terry recalled only fragments after that. Watching him depart. Following him. Grabbing the axe from his boot as they passed down his road. A repeat performance in the same alleyway.

Terry looked at his hands. They were clean. He must've scrubbed them last night after coming in. Yesterday's clothes were tossed on a chair. Unfurling his jeans, he saw patches of dried claret. Thank fuck Stacey hadn't picked these up. He quickly bagged the lot and dressed in fresh clothes. He needed to check his jacket, but it was by the front door and Stacey was pottering about down there. He crept downstairs with the bag, grabbed his jacket and opened the door to leave.

'Where you going?' she called from the kitchen.

'Just got a call for a job. A regular customer, always tips well. Back in an hour.'

'You haven't even had a cup of tea.'

'I'm fine.'

'Well don't be long. And check the boot for your axe – you'll be needing it later.'

Opening the boot, there was his axe caked in blood. He slammed it back down. Jesus Christ. He'd have to bury it and buy another one. He got in the car and checked the state of his jacket. Sure enough there were blotches across the front. Thank God Stacey was in bed when he rolled in. He must've been fucking blotto last night. But it was even luckier she hadn't noticed it today. He set off for a quiet wooded park in Hornchurch and buried the lot. Returning to his car he was knackered and it wasn't yet noon.

'Hope you're feeling fit,' Stacey said when he walked in the door.

He was round Linda's all day. He felled the bastard, sawed the trunk into logs, then cut and bagged the branches. It took an age, and even with Linda's constant tea and cakes, he was shattered.

Driving home he stopped in at the pub for a well-deserved pint.

'Here he is, the axe killer himself,' Dan smiled.

Terry froze mid-stride. 'What are you on about?'

Dan looked at him. 'I'm having a laugh. What's up, you had a humour bypass?'

Terry relaxed. 'Just thinking of other things.' He sat in at the bar.

'How did you get on with the tree?'

'Butchered it mate. I should've asked to borrow your chainsaw. I would've had five or six pints in me now if I did.'

'Talking of butchering,' Dan said, tapping his paper. 'Me and Andy were talking about this new ripper. You heard about it? Have a shufti.' He passed it over.

FEARS OF A 'DAGENHAM RIPPER' AFTER TWO MEN SLAIN.

'*...a second victim, Marvin Green, 21, has been discovered dead in the same alleyway with similar injuries from either a machete or axe. A man charged with the first killing has been released unconditionally, and there have so far been no arrests for the second, leaving speculation of a random killer on the loose... Police are treating the murders as unrelated but are keeping an open mind. They urge the local community to stay calm but vigilant...*'

Terry's mind was galloping like an injected racehorse as he tried to make sense of it. The suspect had been released? They mustn't have had enough evidence to nail him. Not surprising considering he didn't even do it. But now the police would be out on the hunt tenfold.

'Sounds like the usual gang shit to me,' he shrugged, trying to sound casual. 'Dealers topping each other. It's happening all the time now. Look at this mug here pulling a gang sign. They're spreading out, bringing their turf wars with them. That's why the area's gone to pot.' He pushed the paper aside.

'Weird though,' Andy remarked. 'Same alleyway, similar injuries. It's got to be the same attacker.'

'Doesn't have to be,' Terry said. 'I bet that alley's a drug dealing spot. A rival smack dealer comes along selling his wares, then bosh.'

'My old girl said someone was mugged at knifepoint in that alley a few months back,' Dan said. 'She hasn't walked down there since. Now this. What's happening to the manor?'

'I'll tell you what's happening,' Terry said. 'There's scum moving in left and right. Every kind of cunt you can imagine.'

'Say it was a vigilante thing though?' Andy mused. 'Some bloke on a mission, whipping out his axe, cleaning the streets of scum. Like Charlie Bronson.'

'Which one?' Dan asked.

'Scraggy faced fucker with a shooter. Blows away spades and spics on the New York subway.'

'I was thinking of the jailbird,' Dan said. 'Nutty bloke. He took the name. In for life, spends his spare time attacking screws.'

'Oh him,' Andy laughed. 'Well that's what I reckon anyway. This Ripper's a vigilante.'

Barmaid Chloe came over to clear some glasses. On that note Andy finished his drink and zipped his jacket.

'That's me. I'm off home to beat the wife.'

'Not your missus,' Dan said. 'You walk in the door and she gives you the frying pan treatment every time.'

Chloe shook her head like they were a bunch of schoolboys and went off to serve someone.

Andy grabbed his paper. 'I'll leave you two chaps to do what you're best at. Chatting a load of old bollocks.'

'Be good,' Dan said. 'And watch out for the Ripper.'

They sat in silence for a bit, Terry's mind speeding with nightmare scenarios. Prison, isolation, his whole world turned upside down. But he needed to pull himself together. He had two options. Punish himself with stress, which would do him no good at all, or fall back on his usual method when faced with a problem he can do nothing about. Pretend it doesn't exist and carry on as normal.

Dan, meanwhile, was dwelling on the news he'd received

earlier from the Marriott brothers. It was hardly the end of the world, but was no cause for celebration either.

'Did I tell you about the job?'

'No, what about it?' Terry said, glad of the change of subject.

'It's not happening now. It's off.'

'The big one you've been banging on about?'

Dan nodded. 'It's down the shitter.'

Terry turned back to his drink. He wasn't sure he was happy or sad about it. He hadn't committed himself, but likely might've had Dan kept tempting him. But now the decision was made for him. It was for the best.

'I spoke too soon on that one Tel. But you know how it is, not everything reaches the final stage. Best to be safe than sorry though. Anyway, I'll be keeping my ears open, because I don't know about you, but I could do with a nice windfall right now. My ex and kids are crippling me. I've just had to buy Debbie a motor to drive Adam to school, and Kayleigh's asking for a loft extension so she can have a bigger room. They think I'm a bank.'

Dan stood up to go to the mens. He slapped Terry's shoulder. 'Could be worse though. As long as you're breathing it could always be worse.'

Terry wasn't bothered. The job being called off was a blessing. He'd been mad to even consider getting involved. Dan had a broken marriage, but in every other aspect he was a jammy git with a born streak of luck, certainly where graft was concerned. How many bits of work had he pulled off since Terry packed it in, and still he was walking fancy free, regular holidays, new car every year or two, not a genuine worry in the world. Dan was a bloke bad things rarely happened to, or who quickly found his feet when they did, while Terry nursed a head full of baggage, and when he tripped these days he tended to stay down. With Terry's luck going on a job would be a kamikaze mission.

9

Grey Day

Bigz walked out of Dagenham police station to a dull and drizzly morning. He'd been held for forty-eight hours, being questioned repeatedly. Talk about fucked up. Why would he murder his best friend? He'd never had any beef with Slim. They'd been like brothers. And anyway, he was with Leona that night. By the end they seemed to believe him.

He stood on Rainham Road, vans and lorries rumbling by, industrial units stretching as far as the eye could see. He hadn't enjoyed a moment's comfort in a whole two days and wanted out of this dump. He would've jumped in a cab but he'd left his wallet back in Archway. In a pocket he found some change. Chicken money. Great. He'd have to tube it home like a nine-to-five civilian.

Chugging back on the District Line took forever. He was still over-ground, passing West Ham, when Mike called.

'The feds give you any ideas about who wasted Slim?'

'They haven't a clue, which is probably why they pulled me in. The whole thing's crazy.'

'Well, I spoke to both Lucifer and the Tottenham boys and it was none of them. Like I said when I recruited you, that beef has been squashed.'

'I'm glad to hear that. That means the fuckers who did Slim were probably the same ones who did his cousin. Why I don't know. But Slim was hanging with him recently and Darren sounded like the kind of guy who had enemies.'

'Shit happens, I suppose. But something else, where's your driver these days?'

'Jay? He's gone fucking AWOL. Only thing I miss about him though is his car. And now I don't even have Slim's crappy whip to ride in – or Slim himself for that matter. Everyone's disappearing on me.'

'Listen B. Go home, freshen up, then report in for work. I'll be at my garage all afternoon. Some good news: I've got you a new partner.'

'Who?'

'You'll see.'

Bigz didn't like the sound of that and tried to push it to the back of his mind. To kill time he read a discarded *Hackney Gazette,* renowned for the most fucked-up headlines in London. A woman wanted to meet the 'hero' who saved her from a machete-wielding mugger in Stamford Hill. Then he read the cover story. An ex-Hackney Council official on trial for historical underage sex crimes was acquitted after a key witness was murdered. She was shot dead on her doorstep on the notorious Kingsmead Estate in Homerton.

Tarquin had begun stalking his ex-girlfriend. The other day he'd again spotted her with Johnny, this time strolling arm in arm through London Fields. He tailed them back to their place, standing by a tree across the road watching Tabby in her bra as she closed the blinds of their townhouse flat. The thought of them together up there made him want to throw himself in front of a train. He imagined his body being torn to ribbons under the wheels. Workers wandering the tracks with grabbers, bagging up his scattered pieces like litter. Because that's all he was now. A junkie piece of waste.

Once he'd been fizzing with dreams, excited by what the future held. Now he spent his nights like an animal out hunting the streets for prey, and the more junk and crack he used the more intense were his urges towards mayhem and destruction.

Today he was again by the tree. The house's street door opened for the third time in an hour. But this time it was them. Tarq watched as Tabitha and Johnny set off down the street, their backs to him. Perhaps he'd actually do it this time. Bury his knife into Johnny's back. He stepped out from behind the tree and slammed into somebody walking along. 'What the fuck?' A bulky black man stood before him, face screwed in fury. 'Some prick just bumped me on the street,' he said into his phone. 'I'll call you back.'

He pushed Tarq in the chest. 'What's your problem bruv, you blind?'

Tarq didn't need this right now; he was busy. He stepped around him to walk away, but the man grabbed him and threw him against the wall. 'You listening to me?' He was shouting in his face for an apology. Discreetly Tarq reached for his blade. He jabbed it into his stomach and ran.

Bigz froze in astonishment, arms out, looking down. The blade had gone no further than his stab vest. First time he wears one and some random civilian shanks him on the street. He turned left and right. Nobody had witnessed it and he wondered what he'd say if they did. Boiling with rage, he charged up the road to annihilate the fucker.

By the crossroads there was no sign. Only a couple ambling along. He was about to ask if they saw someone running, a young guy in a trilby hat, but didn't bother. He questioned if all the

131

skunk was getting to him, slowing him down. Then seeing the tear in his jacket he cussed loudly. Things were getting strange lately. Stranger than strange. He shook his head and walked around to Mike's lock-up.

Tarq ducked into an alley and stood breathing by the wall. The knife was still in his hand. Weirdly it was dry, without a mark. Considering he'd just stabbed the man it didn't make sense. But a more intriguing question was where he'd seen him before, because he definitely had, and at close quarters.

Then it came. He was one of the thugs Fly had sent round to beat him. The one who'd pissed on his sofa. He hadn't recognised Tarq - maybe because of his hat or his flat being semi-dark, or because beating people was something he did so often he'd never remember them all, who knows. But one thing was for certain, a stabbing was exactly what the brute deserved. Tarq would have to keep his wits about him, though, because the man was obviously local and another meet couldn't happen.

Two of Mike's security men, Moses and Rib Eye, stood guard outside the garage. Bigz nodded at them and entered.

'It's the man himself,' Mike smiled, leaning by a gleaming red Merc sports. 'Come in B, I've got you a new car and a new partner.'

Seeing the car Bigz stopped dead. He broke into a smile.

'No way, Mike. I don't know what to say – I love it.'

The incident on the street was a distant memory now. A fucking Merc. If working for Mike provided benefits like this, all was forgiven.

'This one?' Mike slapped his knee in laughter. 'This ain't your car. This is Red Betty, one of my favourites. She's just been serviced and waxed. A beauty ain't she? No blud, your car is over there.'

Bigz turned to see a used black Yaris hatchback. It was wet, a figure bent out of view washing it down. The car-washer stood up and Bigz started in shock.

'Meet your new ride and your new partner, right there.'

Lil Killa gave Bigz his best dead-eyed grin.

'So the feds let you go?' Lil Killa said when they were out driving, Bigz at the wheel. 'Some would say you're a lucky man.'

Sensing a wind-up, Bigz shook his head.

'Yeah, like I'm going to kill my own partner in crime. Get real.'

'Why'd he get killed then?'

'I told you, Slim's prick cousin was well reckless, attracting all kinds of attention. Hang with the wrong guy and their enemies become yours. The guy was a bad influence. Slim should've known better. He should've stayed in Hackney.' He struggled with the gearstick. 'All I know is this car is a piece of shit. Even worse than Slim's Fiesta.'

They were heading to meet the boss of a new chicken shop, to discuss terms and conditions, with a little persuasion if necessary. Lil was slumped low blowing gum bubbles. Bigz glanced at him, a question teetering on his tongue. Considering their last meet in the park they seemed to be getting on okay, bygones be bygones I suppose. But even so, it was best to tread carefully.

'Is it true you did the Kingsmead hit?' There, he'd said it.

Lil chuckled. 'Never confirm, never deny, that's my policy.'

'I see,' Bigz nodded, taking it more or less as an affirmative. 'Do you know why she was targeted?'

'That side of things don't concern me. All I heard is the Turks passed the contract onto Mike – which of course ain't the first time.'

'I read something about it in the paper,' Bigz said cautiously. 'About why the woman had a price on her head.'

'What paper?'

'This week's *Hackney Gazette*. I found a copy earlier on the train.'

'I don't read no papers.'

'They reckon she was whistleblowing on some guy who'd been high up in the council.'

Lil turned to him. 'Whistleblowing about what?'

Bigz looked at him, noting Lil's interest.

'The council's kids' homes. Apparently the woman grew up in one. And you know the score, nonces would come round to get their kicks. She was about to testify in court, get one of them locked up for stuff he did back in the day.'

'You read that?'

'Earlier today. And I thought, ain't that the job Lil K was supposed to have done? Then I thought, that's a shame because with the key witness taken out of the picture the old paedo has just walked free.'

For half a minute Lil Killa didn't say a word.

'You think if I didn't do it, some other fucker wouldn't have?' he said at last.

'Well, I wouldn't have done it.'

Bigz glanced over. He'd finally got to Lil in some way. Hit a chink in his armour and it felt good. Was Lil uncomfortable with what he'd done? Did the guy have a heart after all?

Lil turned to him. 'Who's to say I did it anyway?'

'Not me,' Bigz shrugged, pleased with himself regardless. 'I don't know if you did it, and quite truthfully I don't care.'

Reaching their destination, Bigz got out of the car. Lil followed.

10

The Joys of Negative Thinking

Terry's daughters were moping around with faces like thunder and Terry was walking on eggshells in his own house. Megan was suffering a bout of her usual teenage angst, while Leah had split from her boyfriend after he'd cheated on her. She was locked up in the bathroom crying buckets.

'I told you I saw him with another girl,' Terry said to his wife. 'He was two-timing her from the beginning, the little fucker.'

'Watch your language Terry, and don't tell Leah you knew that, whatever you do.'

'I won't, but if I see the bloke around he's in trouble.'

'No he isn't. He's out of the picture now, it's over and she's best rid of him.'

'But look at what he's done to her. I've never seen Leah like this. If I see him on the street he's getting a slap.'

'Do that and I'll be giving you a slap.'

'And what about Megan? Having a breakdown because some stranger online called her a name? She needs to pull herself together. What's going to happen when she steps out into the real world?'

'Keep your voice down.'

'I'm just saying it's about time she grew up.'

Stacey made some tea. She'd only just sat down when Leah came flying into the living room. Her eyes were red.

'Mum, can I have a word with you, privately?'

'Okay love.' She stood up and spilled some tea. 'Oh shoot, give me a sec...'

'Can you fucking come now please?' Leah stamped her foot.

'Oi,' Terry said. 'Don't speak to your mum like that.'

'You,' Leah pointed, 'can go fuck yourself.'

He was about to get up. 'Leave it Terry, we all get upset sometimes.' Stacey followed her into the next room.

Terry sat back. Then he went for a listen at the door. Leah was crying about what a fool she'd been. Her boyfriend hadn't only been cheating with some cow, he'd made a separate girl pregnant. Everyone was laughing at her behind her back and Ollie was boasting about it.

The door shot open and he pretended to be walking by.

'Terry, why don't you go out for a few hours, do your shift earlier tonight? We're having a heart-to-heart, we need the living room.'

'Okay,' he shrugged. 'Before I go I better nip to the toilet.'

Upstairs he heard Megan in her room punching her bed. 'I hate you, I hate you...'

Christ Almighty, it was like living in a nuthouse.

He set off in his car. He was only a few streets away when a white van came flying out from a side road. He slammed the brakes and the van halted just inches away. The driver jumped out and so did Terry, asking the lunatic what he thought he was playing at. The man was early thirties, swarthy, shouting at him in broken English. He pushed Terry in the chest and Terry smacked him in the jaw. The bloke followed with a solid right hander and suddenly Terry was on the ground, disorientated, the man's mate pulling the nutter back towards the van.

'You're lucky, my friend. Next time I kill you.' The van pulled away.

Terry stood up and dusted himself down. A red hatchback pulled up, a woman asking if he was okay. She said she'd witnessed the man attacking him, but Terry was embarrassed more than anything and laughed it off saying he was fine.

'Should I call the police?'

'Thanks love but definitely not, I've had enough hassle for one day.'

Back on the road Terry was fuming. His mouth was numb from the blow. A minute from his doorstep and some bastard jumps out and puts him on his arse. He couldn't believe it. He should have floored him, been stamping all over the cunt. Mind you, there were two of them.

Fuck this, he needed a drink. At a time like this the pub was the only place. Swinging a left he saw four youths by a bench on a green. One of them had a girl on his knee. Clocking the youngster's face, Terry slammed his foot down on the brakes. It was his daughter's ex. He got out of the car and headed over, the group falling silent as he approached.

Sensing trouble the girl got off Ollie's knee and his two mates stepped back, but Ollie remained sitting like butter wouldn't melt.

'Alright Mr Hart.'

'Don't try your charm on me you little cunt. Get up.'

Ollie shrugged and stood and Terry hit him with a right, bang in the face. A gasp rose from the others as Ollie landed back down on the bench like a sack of shit.

'That's for Leah,' Terry said. 'Nobody makes a mug out of my daughter, have you got that?'

Nobody moved a muscle and Terry walked back to the car, satisfied with a job well done.

He drove to the pub and parked in. At the bar he sat on his own. As he drank one pint, then another, the two incidents played in his head repeatedly. Now that he'd calmed down, the troubling aspects were shouting out loud and clear. He'd been attacked by a grown man, then he'd taken it out on a teenage boy, slim as a stick. He could feel a real downer coming on. But he pushed it away, refused to entertain it. What's done is done and he was sticking by it. He ordered another pint and a double scotch.

Dan walked in with a bloke called Ed the Red and they joined him. Straight off Dan noticed his cut lip.

'You been in the wars again, Tel?'

'Sit down and I'll tell you what happened.'

Ed got a round of drinks and they settled in as Terry recounted his tale.

'So you knocked the Romanian out flat, then a minute later you beat seven bells out of your daughter's ex?'

'The bloke could've been from Uzbekistan for all I know. But that's the gist of it, yeah. And Leah's ex deserved all he got. They wanted trouble, I gave them trouble, so everyone's happy now.'

'Well Terry mate,' Dan clapped a hand on his shoulder. 'That's the spirit. I'm impressed.'

Ed the Red got up. 'And I'm going for a slash.'

Now it was off his chest and made public Terry was left with only the raw truth, and it was far from satisfying. A total anti-climax if he was honest. But he tried to look on the bright side. The road rage episode had been an embarrassment, but the thought of Ollie getting a belt in front of his mates *and* another of his girlfriends more than compensated. Leah would hear about it and be proud of him. Spotting the prick had been a stroke of luck. He'd had it coming. If you don't want tears and regret don't mess with the Harts.

Dan peeled a twenty from a wedge and told young Chloe to put it in the charity mug behind the bar.

'Someone's in the money again,' Terry remarked. 'I thought you were skint.'

'I'm hardly rolling in it, but you know me,' Dan winked. 'I've always got something on the go.' He lowered his voice. 'I was down Tilbury yesterday. Me and Chris Tucker. We unloaded a lorry. Big fuck-off Sony TVs. Shifted the lot down Kent this morning. Payday mate.'

'Lucky for some,' Terry said, aware of the paltry few quid in his pocket and the stack of bills at home he'd have to work extra to pay off.

'Talking of Tilbury,' Dan continued. 'Do you remember that bird from there I went out with just before I met my ex. Blonde, big old knockers?'

'No.'

'Course you do. Looked like Sam Fox.'

'Definitely don't remember.'

'She was sharing a flat with a genuine brass. I couldn't believe it. A functioning smack addict. When she brought me back her mate's needles were right there in the kitchen. I said goodbye fast to that I tell you.'

'I ran a car front down there for a bit, early nineties,' Terry recalled. 'Didn't make much of a profit but it was handy for other financial purposes at the time.'

'The place me and Paul Nash torched for you in the end?'

'That's right. You did a good job there. I made a few bob on the insurance.'

'That's when you were driving the cherry-red Range Rover, wasn't it?'

'That was a beauty. I loved that car.'

'What happened to that motor, why'd you sell it?'

'I didn't. It got written off after I crashed it up Gallows Corner. Some bloke cut me up on the roundabout, nearly caused a fucking pile up. I was in hospital, remember? Smashed my head in.'

'That's right - me, Joe Bird and Pikey Pat turned up with a bottle of vodka.'

'We all got pissed,' Terry smiled.

'Then the nurses threw us out.'

It was funny looking back, but Terry had a close call that time. It was his second big head injury. The first was when he was ten years old and he lost his footing climbing up an old factory near the Eastway. He woke up a week later in hospital; spent a month there, missed school. They said he was lucky to be alive, but at that age you don't think about death, just shrug it off, can't wait to get back out and see your mates. They were always exploring, climbing things, breaking into derelict buildings. A lot of that area of the Lea Valley was gone now, getting done up for the Olympics, but he remembered sitting with his brother in a dumped banger, a pylon towering above them. Lee was at the wheel pretending he was at Brands Hatch, but they soon got bored and started smashing the car up. Under a seat they found a rusty old gun. It looked like something from a Western. They played with it all day, showing it off to other kids. When one boy tried to nick it, Lee threatened to shoot him. Heading home Lee threw it in the river, said it was for the best. Who would've thought he had only a few more years?

Terry looked at his watch. He'd been in the pub for hours now, but why rush home to a madhouse? Ed the Red was across the way talking with Jim Radley, a trade union man from Fords until they closed down production putting everyone out of a job. Recently Terry had seen him on the TV news warning of growing right-wing extremism among the local working class.

Ed was back, sitting in.

'So who are you voting in the local elections, Terry? It'll be time to put your X in the box soon you know.'

Terry shrugged; he wasn't interested. Then Dan said, 'Tel can't be arsed. He's never voted in his life, have you Tel?'

'Yes I have. Not since Blair got in though. That was the end of it.'

'Labour lost its way for a while I admit,' Ed said. 'But there's good things happening, changes on the cards. Labour's returning to its roots.'

Dan almost choked on his pint. 'You having a laugh?'

'I'm not actually.'

'And there's me thinking the Raving Revolutionary Party was more your thing, or whatever the commies call themselves these days.'

Ed ignored that. 'Labour has its faults, and Tony Blair is definitely one of them, but you've got to be realistic. They're the only left-wing party with any hope of ever getting in. It's best to unite and get behind them, especially at a local level.' He turned to Terry. 'So come on then Tel, who are you throwing your weight behind?'

Terry remembered when Ed would be outside the tube in all weathers flogging papers, even trying to punt them around the pub. He didn't have a clue. He was one of those mugs who still believed the left gave a shit about ordinary people.

Terry turned to him, holding his gaze. 'British National Party, that's who I'm voting for.'

Dan laughed while Ed looked disappointed.

'You're not serious, surely?'

'Why wouldn't I be?'

'I thought your wife was Jewish?'

'What's that got to do with it?'

'If the BNP have their way she could be getting shipped off to God knows where.'

'But they're not getting in are they. Your lot are getting in round here like they always do.'

'Not if everyone votes for the scum you're planning to vote for.'

'Everyone's going to follow my lead are they?'

'They just might. There's a good chance the BNP could win several local wards this time.'

'That's democracy for you,' Dan smiled. 'Terrible, ain't it?'

'It's nothing to do with democracy,' Ed turned to Dan. 'It's to do with being misguided. Believing propaganda and lies.'

'Like half the manor moving out because they don't recognise the place no more?' Dan said.

'That's just not true.'

'How about people not feeling safe?'

'Don't pull that old one. It's always been rough around here Dan, you know that.'

'I don't remember dealers chopping each other up in alleyways much in the past. It's nothing new in Hackney though.'

'Nobody knows who did those killings yet. And white violence happens all the time round this way, always has.'

'I got decked by a bloke straight off the boat earlier,' Terry cut in. 'Would that have happened a few years ago round here? No fucking chance.'

'I thought you were the one who decked him?' Dan said, winking at Ed.

'We decked each other. We were on the ground, weren't we.'

'Decked each other? That's a good one.'

'Whatever. I'm not having these cunts completely take over the plot, no way.'

'They're not all cunts Terry,' Ed told him. 'Do you know the problems some of these people suffered before they came here?'

'He suffers every time he goes home to the wife,' Dan thumbed.

'Couldn't give a shit,' Terry stared at Ed. 'We've all got problems. We need to pull up the drawbridge. There's no more room at the inn.'

'You tell him Tel. And something else,' Dan said, mischievously leaning over, 'it's not just Terry voting BNP either.'

'So the two of you are voting for the Nazi party?'

'I think you'll find the National Socialists called it a day six decades ago when we kicked their arses,' Dan replied.

'You know what I mean, it's the same thing. It's the racist National Front all over again.'

'Listen,' Terry said. 'This is England and I'm English. Labour wants to destroy the country and the Tories are useless too.'

'Labour is the only party who gives a shit about real people. That's the bottom line. The BNP are just out for themselves.'

'Not good enough,' Terry said. 'You've got God-knows-who flooding in. There could be rapists, war criminals in the mix, nobody knows.'

Ed looked at them both and shook his head. Then he stood up, put his jacket on. 'You know what, I'm going up the road. There's no talking to you two. You're a pair of fucking fascists.'

'Oi, watch it,' Terry said, tempted to smack him one.

Ed made for the door.

'Cheerio then,' Dan said as he left. 'Fucking plank.'

'What did you bring that miserable cunt in here for?' Terry asked.

'He lives up my road, I met him coming out of his house.'

'And you invited him for a pint?'

'Course I didn't, he was coming anyway.'

Terry ordered another whisky chaser. He ran his hands over his face.

'Watch with the shorts Tel. Shorts today, meths tomorrow. Did you hear about down the hospital, how the handwash keeps getting nicked because it's full of alcohol. The alkies are necking it.'

'I'm not surprised people want to get out of it. You should see my gaff at the moment. It's like a lunatic asylum.'

'Wife or daughters?'

'Daughters. Wait till your one gets a bit older, you'll see.'

'My Kayleigh's coming up thirteen now and good as gold, no problems at all,' Dan said. Then he stared into his pint. 'Only thing is I don't see her enough. Or Adam.'

They sat in silence for a bit. Then Dan turned to him. 'Here

Tel, you really voting BNP?'

Terry shook his head. 'Wouldn't trust the cunts.'

Dan laughed.

Terry rubbed his jaw. It was clicking from the punch. He finished his pint. It was best he headed home.

'You off?'

'I'm done mate.'

'Alright, be good.'

He stepped into the night and walked to his car. Approaching it he suddenly stopped. Two of his tyres had been slashed.

Fuck. Was it Ed the Red? Would he really do this over a bit of pub patter? No chance. It was the toerag he'd slapped earlier, Leah's ex. He scanned left and right, paying attention to the shadows. He wondered if the runt was watching him, savouring the moment. No, a bloke like that wouldn't have the balls. He was long gone.

But it didn't mean Terry wasn't going to find him.

He opened the boot and reached for his axe.

Tucking it under his jacket he felt himself come to life, fortified, a man on a mission. It was time to gain back some pride. He set off on foot to locate his quarry.

Ollie Albright was walking home from his girlfriend's house, chatting on the phone to his pregnant bit on the side. All was well until she started going on about him attending a pre-natal meeting, so he quickly ended the call, told her something was up. He'd call her tomorrow.

He pocketed his phone. Juggling two birds wasn't easy, but it was less complicated than three, which had been the state of affairs until only few days ago. But he wasn't sorry to see Leah go. The other day outside the cinema she'd marched up screaming, trying to batter him with a stiletto heel, his mates having to hold her back. She was mad. And her dad was a bit of a character too. Total headcase would be more accurate. Earlier he'd screeched up in his car and chinned him. Ollie could've done without the sore jaw, but to his mates he was a womanising legend, fathers having to lock up their daughters up and down the land. Three different girls? You da man Ollie.

Passing alongside the park he heard some rustling from the bushes. For a second he feared it was Leah's old man, ready to pounce for a second helping. But he was being paranoid. It was probably just a cat or a fox. He upped his pace. No cars passed along the road now, the houses dead, and some of the street lights were out. Earlier with his mates they'd joked about the local Ripper, winding each other up about a mad axeman on the loose, even though odds on it was just in-fighting amongst dealers, but it didn't seem so funny now. Ollie made a note to reduce the weed and restrict the powder for partying purposes only. He'd been burning the candle lately; maybe it was taking its toll.

Footsteps sounded from behind and he spun round. Twenty feet away a hooded figure stood holding an axe. He couldn't see his face but knew it was Leah's psycho dad. Ollie screamed and ran. A glance revealed Mr Hart hot on his tail. He raced towards the main road, the nearest sign of life. Finally there he ran out into the road, car lights screeching around him as he pleaded for help. Then it all went hazy. Next thing he was sitting at the kerbside, two women tending to him and a police car pulling in.

At the station he sat in an interview room as two coppers debriefed him. Their arms were crossed, neither in the mood.

'I'm telling you,' Ollie insisted. 'He was chasing after me with an axe.'

'So you were proceeding home from girlfriend number one's house, whilst talking on the phone to girlfriend number two, and then you looked around to see the father of girlfriend number three standing with an axe, is that correct?'

'That's right.'

'The same man who earlier slapped you in front of your mates.'

'Yes, he chased me and would've bloody killed me.'

'Were there any witnesses to this chase?'

'I don't know. What about the drivers of the cars that stopped?'

'They said you simply ran out into the road and had some kind of episode.'

'Somebody must've seen him.'

The coppers looked at each other, then the main questioner threw down his pen. 'Okay, this stops here. Do you have any illegal substances in your possession?'

'What? You're not listening to me. The bloke's mental. He probably axed those two in the alley as well. You need to arrest him for this.'

'Your pupils are dilated from what I'd guess is cocaine use and you smell of cannabis. What drugs have you consumed Mr Albright?'

'I don't believe this...'

They stood up. 'On your feet, Ollie, and stand with your arms out.'

He crossed his arms, remained seated. 'I'm the victim here. I've got my rights.'

'You don't know the law then. We can search anybody we suspect of carrying drugs or weapons. Refuse to comply and we can place you under arrest and conduct a full body search, forcefully if you prefer.'

Ollie stood up. They patted him down, put everything out on the table. One sniffed his bag of weed, pretending to be taken aback by its strength. The other held up his coke. 'Aha, it's Mr Charlie himself.'

'That's for personal.'

'And I'm a monkey's left bollock. Now we're busy men so I'll be brief. You're obviously in the middle of some kind of domestic drama and you're off your tits telling stories you've either hallucinated or are intentionally malicious. Either way it means a shitload of paperwork that we can do without. Either we charge you with possession or make this lot vanish and you'll not darken our door again. What do you say, Oliver?'

Watching him walk out of the station they shook their heads.

'If I hear one more tall story about the so-called Dagenham Ripper I'm going to do some ripping myself.'

Terry placed the axe back in his boot. Job done. He'd tracked the boy down, this time on his own. An hour watching from the bushes had proved fruitful. Terry smiled remembering the boy's face. He'd jumped almost a foot in the air, ran off screaming. Terry wondered what would've happened if the boy had stood his ground. Would he have attacked him? He liked to think he wouldn't, but yes or no, he'd scared the bejesus out of the boy, that's for sure. Which was enough. It was settled. Terry took out his phone to call the AA, get his tyres sorted.

'Excuse me mate, is that your car?'

An older bloke was walking towards him from a house; friendly face.

'Yeah, some scumbags let my tyres down.'

'I might've seen them earlier. There were some blokes messing around with your car. They looked dodgy. I wasn't sure what they were up to, thought the motor must've been theirs.'

'Kids, late teens?'

'No, these were grown men. Two of them. They had a white van parked further up. East Europeans.'

11

Home Improvements

Bigz sat in his pad smoking a blunt in front of the TV. Earlier he'd had a blazing row with Leona. She wanted him out of her flat, but when he started packing his bag she went even more ballistic. You just can't win. But he was best out of it. He'd miss the regular pussy but was glad to be having a break from her; she was doing his head in.

Other than that, things were running along quite nicely. Working with Lil Killa was turning out to be okay. He was definitely an unusual guy, but the fact people were so scared of him made Bigz's working day a lot smoother. Yesterday they'd been out debt collecting. A guy in the De Beauvoir flats tried escaping from his second-floor window. He bounced off the ground and legged it until Lil took aim with a little pocket pistol. Bang and he rolled to the floor, clutching his leg in agony. That was one supernatural shot. Downstairs they stepped on his wound and you should've heard the shrieks from the guy. It was echoing off the flats, full surround sound. A fold of cash appeared from his pocket, all six hundred and more. Mike was happy with that one, said they made quite a team.

Bigz got up and checked the fridge for some eats. The shelves were bare but for half a pack of stale pitta bread and a single slice of old pizza. He'd have to get a take-out. He grabbed his jacket, shoved on a beanie hat and went down to the street. What was it to be? Fried chicken, Chinese or McDonald's? His mouth watered at the thought. He decided on Micky D's. A couple of Big Macs, nuggets, fries, milkshake and apple pie would hit the spot quite nicely.

As he approached the junction a guy hurried past him and something made Bigz doubletake. He stopped to watch him turn up Dalston Lane. Scruffy clothes, strut wired and erratic. No way – was that the same white boy who'd tried to stab him last week? Bigz paused for a moment, McDonald's beckoning. But fuck it, it would have to wait. He turned up Dalston Lane and followed after him. He hadn't quite seen his face and wanted a better look.

The boy was up ahead walking a mile a minute. They passed the ruin of the old Five Aces club, then the line of boarded shops awaiting demolition. The more Bigz stared at his back the more he believed it was him. The boy crossed the road. Bigz went to cross too but almost got run over, a van beeping him, and he stepped back to wait for a break in the cars. By the time he got over his man was away in the distance. He saw him turn into a house. Bigz ran ahead and reached the spot. He wasn't certain of which door he'd entered, but guessed it was one that had a handwritten sign citing the squatting laws.

He rapped hard. Nobody answered. Then he shouted that they better fucking open up. He felt for the blade in his back pocket. If the prick was the same guy that moved on him he was getting it full-blown, guaranteed. He heard footsteps coming down the stairs and the door opened. A girl stood there, straggly fair hair and hippy vibes, a smell of incense and weed wafting through.

'Hiya, can I help you?'

'Did a guy just walk in here, tall, scruffy?'

'I'm not sure, there's a whole load of people here. Why, what's the problem?'

Bigz heard music; it seemed there was a party going on. A male voice shouted down the stairs. 'Steph, who's at the door? If it's Jehovah's Witnesses tell them we're Satanists.'

'Never mind my friend up there,' she laughed. 'He's just joking around.'

Bigz pushed past her and ran up the stairs. 'Oh,' she said. Then she shrugged and closed the door. Bigz entered a room where several people sat around, a stereo playing, some guy singing along strumming a guitar. They looked like they needed a wash.

'Yay, our man's here, that was quick,' a girl said, clapping her hands. 'That's good service, I only just phoned.'

'You got the gear bro?' a nerdy looking boy asked Bigz.

'Of course he's got the gear,' another tutted, 'or he wouldn't be standing there now, would he Henry?'

Bigz gazed around the room. 'Where is he – tall guy, messy dark hair?'

'I think you mean Rupert. He's your man with the funds,' said a girl lounging on a bean bag. 'He's just gone to the little boy's room.' Then she shouted, 'Come on Rupie baby, where are you?'

Bigz went down the hallway to find the toilet. If the man was doing his business in there, he was getting rudely interrupted.

The girl from the front door was in the kitchen making tea. 'Did you find who you were looking for?' she called. 'Sorry if my friends were rude, they're a little boisterous sometimes.'

Bigz marched past and stopped by the toilet. Sure enough it was locked. He rapped hard.

'Out you come man, I want a word with you.'

The girl stood sipping her tea. 'He'll only be a sec. Don't worry, he's got your money. Go inside and have a smoke if you like, he won't be long.'

Perplexed, Bigz turned to her. What drugs were this lot on?

'One second,' a voice announced from inside the bog and the flush went.

'Okay, whatever,' the girl shrugged and disappeared into the room, an old dance anthem now banging.

'Let's rave!' someone shouted. 'Acieeed!'

The lock sounded and Bigz crashed through grabbing the bastard by the lapels. He noticed he was wearing glasses and a lot shorter than who he was looking for.

'Oh,' said the boy, not displeased. 'What a surprise. So what's your name then?'

Bigz let him go. 'I was looking for someone… but it ain't you.'

'I see… what a shame.'

As Bigz walked down the stairs someone popped out from the room.

'Dude, don't go, where's the goods?'

'I don't think that's our guy,' another remarked.

'Well who is it then?'

'Just some random who strolled in I think.'

Back on the street Bigz shook his head. He must've been imagining things. The guy he'd followed obviously wasn't the one. The only blade those lot ever used was when they were chopping up vegan shit from the health store. He laughed to himself. He'd been smoking too much lately, just being paranoid.

He walked back to the main strip and entered McDonald's. He flirted with the fit lighty girl behind the counter as he ordered a feast fit for a king. Collecting his order he gave her a smile, planning on getting her digits next time, as a bit on the side might do him good right now, clear some of the strife from his head. Hands loaded, he made for the exit and some guy coming in held the door for him. 'Cheers bruv,' Bigz said, feeling good with himself.

'You got any change mate?' a voice outside said. He noticed a figure sitting on the ground. Fucking beggars man, always hanging in the shadows. Bigz walked on, ignored him.

'Please, just a pound for something to eat.'

Bigz turned round. He was about to tell him to earn his drug money elsewhere when both their eyes widened in recognition. Suddenly the boy sprang up and ran like a track star. Bigz dropped his load and raced after him. The boy darted across the main road, dodging a bus, then turned down a backstreet.

Rounding the next corner Bigz lost him. He stopped. A dim-lit back alley stretched ahead. His prey was hiding nearby, he could feel it. Bigz flicked out his blade, issued a cold laugh.

'You think you can run from me? Where are you blud? I'm gonna slice you up big time.'

He approached a pile of dumped rubbish, then a noise sounded behind him and the boy sprinted out of the alley. Bigz set off up the street after him, until he turned a corner and saw him throw himself onto a passing police car. It screeched to a halt. The boy was begging for help, pointing down the empty road towards him. Shit. Bigz turned and ran. Disappeared into the backstreets.

He stopped in a passage by some flats to gather his breath. The fucker was lucky this time, very lucky, but they'd meet again don't you worry and next time he'd be ready. Things too hot on the streets now, it was best to slip back home. He'd have to order something in.

*

Terry's home life had vastly improved. Leah had heard about her dad smacking Ollie and to say she was happy was an understatement. Stacey complained that he'd gone too far, but Leah stuck up for him and she relented. Maybe the boy did deserve a clip behind the ear. But claims of Terry later chasing him with an axe were too far-fetched for anyone in the Hart household to believe. His youngest Megan saw him in a new light, and locally the hearsay did his reputation no harm at all. Yesterday the gang down the road moved out of his way nodding, 'Alright, Mr Hart.' He was getting appreciation from his family and respect on the street and it felt good.

Saturday noon and Stacey was about to drive Leah up to Lakeside to meet her mates. They stood in the kitchen. 'I'm proud of you Dad,' Leah hugged him. 'You're a hero.'

'He shouldn't really be throwing his fists around like that,' her mum said, still sceptical but sporting a glint in her eye.

'He only pushed him, isn't that right Dad?' Leah winked.

'Yeah, I only gave him a tap. Make no mistake though, I told him what for. Mess with my family and you mess with me.'

'I love you Dad,' Leah kissed his cheek. Then she turned to her mum. 'What's that story you told me once, about when you two first dated and Dad warded off some bloke who tried chatting you up?'

Stacey smiled, her eyes misty with nostalgia. 'That was down the Ilford Palais.'

'You remember that Dad?' Leah asked.

'He remembers it well. They fought outside at the end of the night. Half the club was watching. In the end a police car came screeching in and your dad had to scarper.'

'It was no big deal, just a punch up,' Terry shrugged. 'Anyway, that was almost twenty years ago, I can't remember back that far.'

'Sure you can't,' Stacey smiled, slapping his arm.

'What happened exactly?' Leah asked her mum.

'This bloke came up to me when your dad had gone to the bar. Smartly dressed, a Jack the Lad type. He asked if I wanted a drink and put his arm around me and your dad went crackers. He knew him as well. It was one of his so-called mates.'

'Del Harper? He was never a mate of mine.'

'He had all sorts of mates back then. But he was always very protective of me.'

'I still am.'

'Of course you are,' she said and put her arms around him. 'But no more getting into scrapes with teenagers, okay?'

'Wouldn't dream of it.'

'Okay lovebirds,' Leah said, skipping off. 'I'm going upstairs to get my bag. I'll be ready to go in a minute Mum.'

Stacey spoke in his ear.

'Maybe I'll slip into something nice when I get back. That basque and stockings you bought me at Christmas. Megan's gone to Becky's up Wanstead. We'll have the place to ourselves.'

'I see.'

'It's about time we had some intimate time together, no screaming kids about the place. What do you say?'

'The man from Dagenham, he say yes.'

When Stacey and Leah had gone Terry sat in front of the telly. He remembered back to 1987, that scrap with Del Harper outside the Ilford Palais. But what happened when they crossed paths a few weeks later would've left Stacey appalled.

Terry and Dan were on a night out back in the old manor. A pub disco in Lower Clapton. Harper was across the bar in a shoulder-padded suit jacket, gold chain, eyeballing him. Terry heard he was into burglary, hitting big gaffs out in the suburbs. Lurking around in people's homes sounded about right for the bloke. The men with Harper looked a bit tasty, but if Harper wanted a straightener Terry was game. It was early, the place filling up with good-looking birds out for a dance and more. Dan was out to pull but Terry was a taken man.

'Are you saying you wouldn't give that a workout?' Dan said, nodding at a cracking brunette in a white mini, dancing around her handbag.

'No mate. Straight up, I wouldn't.'

'How about that one?' Dan pointed to a tidy blonde bird.

'I told you, I'm with Stacey now.'

'You're insane. What about that sort then?' The bird had a black perm, black skirt and boots.

'Must say you're tempting me now, but still. I've met the woman I'm going to marry. That's it, I've sown my wild oats.'

'The night's young so we'll see about that.' Dan got some drinks in then said, 'Have you seen who's across the bar, keeps looking over?'

'Clocked him already.'

'You reckon he'll start?'

'Only if he wants to be eating tomorrow's breakfast through a straw.'

'I know one of the blokes he's with. Geoff, the big unit. I might have a word, see what's up.'

Dan chatted to Big Geoff and returned. 'Geoff said in my ear that Harper's a mug. If he has a go he'll be on his own. Doubt he'll start though, you gave him a right pasting the other week.'

Cameo's 'Word Up' filled the dancefloor, Dan joining in, but Terry was happy by the bar. He watched Dan pulling shapes with a decent ginger bird. Dan was a soul boy, but Terry had always been into a bit of everything; Oi, Two Tone, Rockabilly. Anything lively. But these days his tastes were mellowing. At home he liked a bit of Level 42, Dire Straits, Phil Collins if he was in the mood. He wondered what his brother Lee would think of that. He'd probably laugh, call him a wanker.

Lee's favourite band was The Stranglers and now whenever Terry heard their new stuff he wondered how Lee would rate it. Golden Brown had gone to number one a few years back; it was mad he'd never heard it. Then again, maybe he had. Terry saw the band do a Kinks cover on Top of the Pops recently and they still looked the dogs. Lee would agree.

'You alright Tel, you look a bit down?' Dan had the ginger bird on his arm.

'I'm fine mate, no probs,' Terry put on a smile.

'Meet Susan - this is Tel,' he said, leaving the girl with him as he ordered more drinks.

'How come you're not dancing?' she said, bright lively eyes. She had a fair bit of cleavage on show and he tried to keep his eyes away. Dan was doing well.

'I'm fine, honestly. I'll have a boogie in a bit.'

Another girl appeared next to her. Dark hair, dark eyes, just Terry's type.

'This is my friend Joanne,' Susan said. 'This is Terry.'

'Nice to meet you Terry,' Joanne smiled. They got chatting and soon were dancing and the next few hours passed in a blur. Terry's vow of staying faithful to Stacey seemed lost in the hot sweaty night. At one point he was in the bogs on his own. He was by the urinal finishing up when Harper flew in with a Stanley knife. 'You fucking shit cunt.'

Terry kicked out and grabbed his arm just in time. They grappled by the sinks, limbs twisted as Terry yelled at him to drop the blade. Harper tried to bite his ear, instead burying his teeth into his neck. An electric bolt of pain made Terry throw him to the floor, blade clattering aside. Terry kicked and stomped him.

Out of breath he retrieved the Stanley and squatted down for a word.

'I'm sorry Tel, I didn't mean it,' Del begged, 'I'm speeding off me head.'

There was no excuse. He grabbed his face. 'Come for me again you cunt and I'll put you in the ground.'

Terry striped him and Harper screamed like a caterwaul.

*

For Jay, life in Harlesden was swinging along nicely. Hearing about Slim's death had been a shock - and he still felt a little guilty for not attending his funeral - but it only emphasised how moving on from Hackney had been a wise decision. He was chilling on the corner with Syrus and three others, passing spliffs, joking around. Then Syrus groaned as a police van turned slowly up the close.

'Here we go. It's the bacon brothers coming for a meet and greet.' PCs McKevitt and Jobson were the only coppers with the bottle to roll into the Stonebridge Estate without backup. 'They must be bored tonight so think they'll try and harass the local youth.'

Syrus was a couple years Jay's junior, and two of the crew tonight were younger still. One was a mad ginger guy called Shots, renowned for carrying a sawn-off under his coat. The other was a light-skinned black guy called Blue. The duo were a laugh but well reckless. Jay had been told of the time some Acton guys came up for a football match. Shots and Blue chased them down into the station, Shots letting off his 12-bore, blasting one in the arse. They knew not to grass though. Syrus said they were handy boys to have around, especially in battles. Not all was peaceful in NW10 between the crews, the tension between Stonebridge and Church Road constant.

As the police van edged closer, Syrus said how last week they'd drenched a couple of pigs with a bottle of piss. Seen them walking along then splashed it down from a window.

'That's nothing,' laughed a fat guy called Goonz. 'In Aylesbury I saw this brother throw shit in a screw's face. No lie. He had a big lump of it in his hand, the screw opened his pad then splat, he gave it to him straight in the face.'

The van pulled up alongside them.

'Evening chaps.' McKevitt's meaty arm hung from the window. They'd heard other feds call him Robo, as in Robocop, but the boys refused to give him the credit. 'How's everything swinging in the hood this evening, Sy?'

Syrus stared straight ahead, not deigning to play the copper's game. Then someone mouthed, 'Go fuck yourself officer,' to a group guffaw. Syrus cracked a smile.

'Who's the comedian?' McKevitt looked over to Shots and Blue. 'Considering you two girls have school in the morning, shouldn't you be in bed?'

'School? Joking aren't you? That's done.' Shots blew a raspberry and Blue said, 'How come I suddenly smell pig meat? Fucking stinks man.'

McKevitt shook his head. 'Only thing that stinks round here is what you lot have been smoking.'

'Quiet night out there is it?' Syrus remarked. 'If crime never sleeps, how come you're not busy catching criminals?'

'I'd say that's what I'm doing right now, because last I heard possession of cannabis was still a punishable offence. That makes you lot law breakers – on top of all your other list of offences.'

'You saying you never like a smoke, officer?' Goonz asked.

'Weed is a black man's drug. And I ain't a black man.'

'I know, you're a fucking pig – oink, oink,' Blue said, dodging behind the others.

'Watch your mouth you cocky little cunt.' Then the copper turned back to Syrus. 'How much of that shit do you smoke a day? It lowers your brain power you know, fucks your IQ. That's why every time you lot do anything you get caught red-handed. You need to wisen up mate.'

'You don't know the half of what I get up to and never will,' Syrus crossed his arms. 'I'll be driving a Porsche, living the Cris life when you're still earning peanuts.'

'You tell him Sy.'

'Oink, oink.'

'Go suck your mother, pig.'

McKevitt turned at that one. 'Oi, half-breed,' he addressed Blue. 'Come here and say that.'

'Rah,' Syrus said, mock-shocked. 'The copper's a racist. I'm stunned. Call the cops man.'

'I didn't say jack shit,' Blue said. 'You did though, you just called me a fucking half-breed.'

'That's because you are. You're half black, half white, am I wrong on that? But you're better looking than this ginger cunt,' he said, turning to Shots. 'You still carrying the long shooter, big man?'

'What shooter?' Shots said, turning to lob a spit down the street. 'I was acquitted of that shit.'

'You were questioned, then they dropped the enquiry due to lack of witnesses. Doesn't mean you didn't do it though.'

'Yes it does,' he tutted. 'I'm an innocent man innit.'

'Man? You wish. But in your case I actually believe you are innocent, because a low-level mug like you wouldn't have the balls for such a thing.'

'Go back to the nick and suck your superintendent's tits. He's a fat fucker like you so he's got big ones.'

Everyone cracked up, whooping and snapping their fingers.

McKevitt stepped out of the van; his sidekick followed.

'Up against the wall you little cunt,' he told Shots, moving with a weightlifter's strut.

Jobson, another lumbering steroid abuser, came for Blue. He had him by the wall, spreading his legs. 'The rest of you, get back, or we'll call the cavalry and you'll be kipping in a cell tonight.'

'You're taking the piss,' said Syrus. 'Those boys ain't done nothing and you know it.'

'Couldn't give a fuck. If we find drugs or weapons they're getting nicked. And so will you be, so button it.'

Blue wasn't spreading his legs wide enough so Jobson hit his stick against the side of his knee. Blue yelped. 'Ah, that fucking hurt man, what you doing?'

'That's police brutality,' Syrus said.

'They ain't done fuck all,' Goonz said.

The boys were getting vexed, and when the copper again threatened Blue with his stick Syrus stepped forward, hand instinctively reaching for his back pocket. Jay had a quick word in his ear. 'It ain't worth it Sy. You can't win this one. Ride it out.'

Sy looked up and down the close for backup, but nobody was around tonight. 'I want these harassing fuckers off my ends. A man can't chill outside his own fucking house these days.'

'There's nothing we can do right now, allow it,' Jay said, hoping things wouldn't escalate.

Blue was clean so they let him go, but Shots was found carrying a steel comb with a sharpened handle.

They put the cuffs on him. 'Keiran O'Shea, you're under arrest.'

'What you nicking me for? It's a fucking comb blud, it's harmless.'

'It's an offensive weapon. Put that to someone's neck and you could sever an artery. Which is why you're carrying it. Now don't argue fella, just get in the van.'

'You should be doing what you're paid for,' Syrus told them. 'Instead you just want to bring in a body so you can get back to your canteen.'

'Go home Syrus. And tell your boys to disperse or we'll send in the heavy brigade to kick down some doors – yours first. Biggest gang in London you're dealing with here mate, don't you forget that.'

Everyone was standing around complaining. As the van pulled off down the close Goonz chucked a stone. Then Blue ran and lobbed a chunk of brick. It connected, denting the mesh where Shots was locked in the cage. The van screeched to a halt and everyone ran.

Robo put his foot down on the brakes. They were taking the piss. Behind them the gang had scarpered, the road seemingly deserted now. Both cops could remember not too long ago when Stonebridge was a brutalist hellhole of colossal blocks replete with warren-like walkways, as if solely designed to assist the criminal community in their getaway from either police or whatever old lady they'd just mugged. The old estate was mostly levelled and replaced now, but the scrote quotient seemed pretty much the same.

'What do you reckon, Jobs? Radio for back up, flush the fuckers out?'

'I don't fancy the runaround. They're gone. We'd be lucky to bag a single one of them.'

The prisoner in the back kicked the cage. 'Let me out of here pigs, I didn't do nothing.'

'Ah, our delightful guest. Almost forgot about him.'

They got moving, turned out onto the main road.

'So where we going?' Jobson asked wryly. 'Not the nick, I presume?'

'Course not. The lovely Church End Estate. See how our brave soldier likes being dumped in enemy territory.'

Within minutes they were there, cruising slowly past the shadowy housing. Up by the playground lurked a gang twelve-strong.

Robo stopped the van, got out and opened the cage. He undid the prisoner's cuffs. 'Out you come Keiran mate.'

'You're fucking joking, aren't you?' He looked terrified. 'I ain't stepping foot out here. Are you trying to get me killed?'

The gang had left the playground and were edging closer, hooded zombies smelling meat.

'That's funny, I thought you liked hanging out with big black boys. I thought that was your thing.'

Shots sat back and crossed his arms. 'Just bring me to the nick, do whatever you like, but I'm not getting out of this van.'

'Yes you are you mouthy little cunt.' Robo pulled him out of the cage.

'Please, let me back in...'

'Not a fan of the Church Road crew then?' he said, laughing as he slammed the back doors and returned to the driving seat, leaving the boy stranded.

The gang was at close range now, spread out wide, a pack eyeing its prey. Pulling away, Robo and Jobson watched Shots take to his heels, the group setting off after him. They disappeared into the darkness of the estate.

'And there they go, enjoying their favourite sport,' Robo remarked.

'And ours.'

Back on the road a call came in about a rapist on the loose in Kilburn. IC2 male spotted running along Carlton Vale. All available units.

'Right then,' Robo said, whacking on the disco lights. 'Time for some real policing.'

12

Body Work

Lil Killa was in an internet cafe doing some research. The fact he'd undertaken a hit to assist the kind of people he'd spent years wanting to wipe from the face of the earth wasn't sitting well with him. It was like a sick joke. But one thing was for sure, somebody somewhere was going to pay for this shit.

He necked down some benzos and continued reading blogs from people who'd endured similar care home experiences and wanted justice. Most abusers were never charged because they were units of a larger swarm. Rings protecting its members. Connections that stretched from the slums to the establishment. In Islington the problem had been at epidemic levels yet denied for years. In Lambeth whistle blowers had been violently targeted. A council worker who tried to tell on senior abusers was mysteriously burned to death in his house. Another was knifed on the street. A woman was attacked with acid. The perpetrators were never found. Police investigators who pried too closely were warned to rein it in, and that was by their own bosses. Government ministers and council staff aware of what was happening were complicit in their silence. MPs had supported a paedophile lobby group. Perverts were intentionally installed in children's care homes. Some returned to their jobs after serving sentences for abuse. The pattern was countrywide. Investigations ending with predictable rounds of denials, lost evidence, dropped cases, acquittals.

Lil scrolled through photographs of wrongdoers, trying to match the faces to his memories. He wanted to track them down. Take action in the only way he knew. But it was no use. He was getting nowhere. Simply filling his head with misery upon misery, reading how the bad guys always won, which was something he'd always known anyway.

He stepped out onto Lower Clapton Road. Grey sky, spits of rain. Times like this he hated everyone and everything. Hated the whole rotten world. As he walked he stared at passing faces just to see what might happen. All turned away. He felt an urge to do something radical. He imagined walking into McDonald's, a gun in each hand. Screams. Mayhem. Here's a taste of what it feels like in my shoes.

Fuck it. Maybe he'd just go home. Go back to bed.

A car pulled up next to him. 'Lil man, I've been looking for you everywhere,' Bigz said, leaning out. 'You turn your phone off? Get in. Mike's got some work for us.'

They headed for an address near Springfield Park. Watching the streets go by Lil was glad to be in company. Back in the real world again. Away from the confines of his head. Maybe he'd leave the online research alone. Leave the past where it was. Why incite a legion of demons?

'A guy called Shine is expecting us,' Bigz said. 'That's all I know.'

'Shine? Never heard of him.'

'We're probably just collecting some shit, shifting it from A to B.'

They pulled in by a block and headed up. A small Jamaican guy opened the door. He scanned left and right. 'Come.'

Passing the living room, a junkie lay out cold on the floor.

Shine led them to the bathroom. 'I would've done this job myself but it ain't my ting.' A fully-clothed black guy, late fifties, trilby, suit, was face-up sleeping in the bath. 'Here's your man.'

'What a place to rest your head,' Bigz laughed. 'Who is he?'

'Didn't Mike fill you in?'

'He told us fuck all.'

'Rarse,' Shine tutted. 'This is the man with the cargo and you've got to get it.'

Bigz turned to Lil, who in turn shrugged his shoulders. 'You're going to have to start from the beginning here,' Bigz said, 'because all I can see is an old guy sleeping in the bath.'

'He ain't sleeping brother, the man's dead.'

Lil held a mirror to the man's nostrils. 'He's right, he's gone.'

'Shit,' Bigz said. 'What about the man in the room, is he dead too?'

'Nah, he's fine. He's my friend. We were having a little social time earlier. He likes his brown so he won't be with us today. But this guy, he flew in from Kingston earlier and passed out before he unloaded his stash.'

Lil kissed his teeth, but Bigz didn't get it. 'What can we do about that?'

'He wants us to cut him open,' Lil said.

'No way.'

'That's the drill,' Shine nodded. 'He's carrying a bellyful of goods but some of it must've leaked into his system. You should've seen him earlier. He was shaking and sweating then, bang, he hit the floor out cold. Fucking bumbaclart.'

'What tools you got available?' Lil asked, knowing they had a fair bit of work so might as well begin

'Hang on a sec,' Bigz put up his hands. 'I ain't dissecting no-one. Human butchery ain't my line of business.'

Shine was in no mood now. 'Mike told me you were the men for the job.'

Bigz stepped forward with a glare. The Yardie was beginning

to piss him off.

'Leave it B,' Lil said, putting an arm between them. 'We'll do it.'

'That's right,' the Jamaican said. 'Or I'll have to phone Mike to tell him he sent the wrong men.'

Bigz backed down, and Shine laughed as he walked away. 'You want tools, go check the kitchen.'

'I'm gonna kill that cocksucker,' Bigz hissed.

'One dead body's enough for one day,' Lil said. 'It's gonna be messy, but when Mike gives us a task it probably ain't wise to argue, you know what I'm saying?'

In the kitchen they searched for tools. The walls were mouldy, crusted dishes piled high. The drawers were bare but for a long rusty carving knife.

Lil held it up. 'Looks like we found the tools.'

'We should head to a shop, get some proper equipment,' Bigz said. 'Protective wear and that.'

Shine appeared. 'You might want these.' He passed them some overalls and gloves.

'Yo, what about knives?' Bigz asked.

'What's your man holding there, a fork?' Shine said and strutted away.

Changing into their scrubs they could hear Shine cackling away at the TV, his sinsemilla filling the air.

'Guy won't be laughing for long, believe. He'll be crying tears for the way he spoke to me.'

'Forget about him,' Lil said, his mind on the job. He stared at the bath. 'I suppose we'll have to strip him down.'

Lil did so and the man's bare belly was distended like a balloon.

'You telling me that gut's full of cocaine?' Bigz said.

Lil slapped its girth. 'Packed solid. He swallowed too many packets and his stomach acid must've burned through the latex. It's a risky game. There's got to be easier ways of making money,

I swear it.'

Bigz had an idea. He smiled, closed the door.

'Let's skim some of the gear for ourselves. That fool won't know the difference. I say we earn ourselves a bonus for doing this shit.'

'I suppose we could siphon some off, yeah.'

'Come on then.' Bigz nodded at Lil's knife, eager now. 'Get carving. Let's see what we're looking at here.'

Lil got down on his knees to begin, while Bigz sat on the toilet trying to face the other way. Apart from the odd expletive Lil seemed to be handling the task admirably. But as time passed, the constant sound of squelching flesh was making Bigz curious. He turned to take a peek. Lil's arms were covered in blood as he tugged at the man's bloated intestines.

'Jesus.' Bigz felt his vomit rising. He jumped up, aimed for the pan.

'I know how you feel,' Lil laughed.

'I don't know how you can do that stuff.' Bigz wiped his mouth.

'What do you think surgeons do in hospitals?'

'But a surgeon's a surgeon.'

'That's right, he's working to put bread on the table just like we're doing here.'

'But look at that… what is it?' Bigz creased his face.

'Innards. We've all got them you know.'

Shine stuck his head in the door, making sure to avert his eyes from the mess. 'How you getting on, star?'

'So far, so good,' Lil said, pulling out a golf-ball sized packet.

'Nice, man. Here.' Shine put down a black bag. 'Wash each one and place them on this.' He turned to Bigz. 'You alright there, big man?'

'I'm fine, how are you?' Bigz said, eyes blazing.

'Glad to not be in here watching this shit,' Shine chuckled, closing the door behind him.

The packets kept coming, Lil handing them to Bigz to wash the gore from each one, a pile building, until at last Lil wiped a forearm across his forehead, smudging it with blood. 'That's it B, that's all she wrote.'

'Thank fuck for that.'

Lil stood up, his overalls covered.

'Jeez man,' Bigz laughed. 'You look like a serial killer - but hang about, the amount of jobs you've done you actually are a serial killer.'

'Professional hitman actually. Serial killers are usually sad white psychos.'

'True,' Bigz conceded.

They got cleaned up and then Shine appeared. 'You finished extracting?' He took a glance at the mutilated mule. 'Bloodfire,' he turned away.

'Job done,' Lil announced.

'You guys were quick on that. The last lot spent half the day getting to this stage. All they did was complain as well.'

'Okay, we better be off,' Bigz said and they made for the front door.

'Hang on, where you going?' Shine said.

'Home,' said Lil.

'But what about him?' Shine pointed back to the bathroom.

'That guy ain't going anywhere,' Bigz laughed.

The Yardie blocked their path. 'Nor are you until you get rid of him. I was told you'd be providing retrieval of the goods and disposal of the carrier, guaranteed. I'm paying top dollar for this.'

Bigz and Lil looked at each other, then Bigz said, 'Are you taking the piss?'

Shine stepped forward. 'You leave all the hard work to your boy there and now you want to leave when the job's only half complete.' He pushed Bigz in the chest. 'Get in there, rudeboy, and finish what you came here to do.'

Bigz grabbed and slammed him back against the wall. 'For a little guy you've got a big fucking mouth.'

'You better get your hands off me or you'll be one sorry fucker.'

Lil urged Bigz to leave it but he leaned in closer. 'I want an apology or you'll be joining your man in the bath there.'

Shine grinned, eyes wide. 'We'll see what Mike has to say about this.'

Bigz punched him twice in the face. Shine looked stunned, then he whipped out a knife.

Bigz grabbed his arm and they grappled down the hallway, stumbling into the living room. Tripping over the comatose junkie, Bigz toppled backwards to the floor. Shine smiled as he approached him wielding his blade. Then the Jamaican froze, mouth open and eyes wide, knife hand suspended in the air. Blood appeared at his chest where the end of a carving knife protruded.

With a suction sound Lil pulled the knife out from his back and Shine collapsed out cold.

'Jeez man, close call,' Bigz said. 'I thought I was a goner there. Thanks.'

'No probs.' He gave him a hand up and they both flopped down on the sofa exhausted.

Shine lay face upwards, shirt drenched in blood.

'You must've got him directly in the heart there,' Bigz observed.

'You could be right.'

'So what do we do now?'

Lil ruminated on it. 'The drug mule goes in the car to be dumped. We bleach the bathroom. Then we get my prints off the knife and give it to him,' pointing to the junkie. 'Make it look like they had a disagreement. What do you say?'

Bigz was impressed. 'Let's go with that.' Then he thought of something less comforting. 'But what about Mike, what do we tell him?'

'Just tell him we did the job, said goodbye to Shine and split.'

Bigz nodded in relief. They had a plan.

'So I suppose Shine was right about one thing,' Lil said, standing up. 'We're only half finished.'

*

Night-time and Jay and Syrus were out cruising the North-west streets. They had a shopping list and were doing a bit of car spotting. Clock the right make and model parked in someone's driveway then call the youngers to come and do their magic. It was an earner they had going for a firm based in Rickmansworth. Good pocket money.

Last night they'd been down the Funky Buddha in Mayfair, full VIP, clubbing in style. It was heaving with the finest females London had to offer and they bagged themselves two wannabe Page 3 types, bringing them back to a hotel for some late-night entertainment that lasted till dawn.

'Last night was class,' Jay said, leaning back free and easy with Syrus at the wheel for a change. 'Those girls were something else. How did you get on the guest list?'

'Contacts, my man. You've been over the east side too long bruv. In north-west we do things executive style. No half measures.'

'Well I know one thing, I want more of that. Do you think Donna and Cindy will want to meet for a sequel?'

'No, they were just temporary arm candy. But it works both ways. We get what we want and they get a night of quality attention. Everyone goes home happy.'

'But Donna said she definitely wanted to meet again.'

'That's what they all say,' Syrus laughed. 'Didn't you notice how come morning things had thawed? Like when you said you'd call her, she said I'll call you first. What they really mean is: I had a fun time but nice knowing you. But hey, I ain't complaining. It's give and take.'

Syrus was ruining Jay's high.

He'd been thinking about Donna all day and was planning on asking if she wanted to meet tomorrow night. He'd felt a bond there, something more than you'd get from a standard one-nighter. But Syrus's negativity was casting a new light on things. Maybe she had been a bit frosty in the morning. Rubbing coke on her gums then doing her lipstick. Giving him a peck on the cheek and no eye contact when he said goodbye.

'What, you in love with the woman or something?' Syrus grinned.

'Not exactly. I just thought we might've had something going.'

Fuck it, Jay took out his mobile.

'You gonna phone her?'

'Yeah, maybe I will.' He selected then pressed her number.

'I want to hear this man. Put it on loudspeaker, go on.'

The ring tone ended. 'Hello?' Music and voices were in the background like she was in a bar or a club.

'Hi Donna - it's me, Jay.'

'Who?'

'It's Jay. Great time we had last night. I really enjoyed your company.'

'Oh right - yeah, it was mega. Er, listen Jay, I'm a little tied up at the moment…'

'I just wanted to ask if you fancy meeting tomorrow night - go for a little drink or something?'

'I'm busy tomorrow I'm afraid babes.'

'What about the night after? We can go to a club if you like, or maybe just take things easy.'

'No can do I'm afraid. It was a nice night with you Jay but I'm pretty busy at the moment. Tell you what, I'll give you a buzz sometime and we'll see what happens.'

'Oh, okay. You sure you don't want to set a date?'

'No, I'll call you.'

'I see. Okay, fine...'

The line went dead.

Syrus laughed, slapping the wheel.

'What's fucking funny?'

'You ain't been clubbing up central before, have you Jay?'

'Yes I have. I've been bare clubs all over town.'

'But no exclusive joints like last night. We were partying with the rich and famous in there. You've got to be realistic. These types are gold diggers. It's written all over them, loud and clear. If you're not a banker or footballer then it's just short-term fun.'

'Nothing wrong with trying.'

Jay sat there sullen for a bit. But not for long. Fuck it, it was history.

Passing through Harrow he spotted a Mitsubishi four-wheeler in a driveway. 'Look, is that the model on the list?'

'Could be.' Syrus reversed to check it out. 'Yeah, bingo.'

*

Tarquin sat on the pavement next to a *Hackney Gazette* placard: *DEAD MAN FOUND IN GRAVEYARD GUTTED LIKE FISH.*

He was begging for his next fix. A few more quid and away he'd go. He caught the eyes of a well-dressed girl. Long hair, stripy tights, the type he'd have once socialised with, asked out, bedded. He asked her if she could spare some change and she gave him a fiver, telling him to get something to eat. He thanked her saying he would, then counted up his funds and went to score.

He sat in an alley smoking crack. By his feet a rat picked at a take-away box.

A Turkish guy in a bloody apron appeared from a rear shop door holding a meat cleaver. He told him to get his junkie arse away from here.

Tarq paced the streets. It was dark now, the air full of police sirens, squad cars flying after some unknown prey.

A youth tore past him on the pavement, stopping by a bush to quickly deposit something. He carried on sprinting. A police car screamed after him, turning at the next corner.

Tarq went to the bush to investigate. He pulled out a carrier bag, something weighty inside. It was a handgun. Quickly he pocketed it and kept walking.

Turning a corner three police vehicles were parked in the road, lights swirling, the same youth handcuffed on the ground. The boy was shouting and a group had gathered, some on bikes, complaining about police harassment.

One was shouting into a policeman's face threatening action. Suddenly the copper dropped him, his colleagues helping to pin and cuff the man.

The crowd was jumping now, growing in number, and another van pulled in. A bottle came from a window above, smashing on the roof of the police van. Up went a cheer.

It looked like the beginning of a riot. Tarq turned at the next corner and left the scene behind. He finally had a gun.

'I spoke to my dad today,' Stacey said, dipping a biscuit in her tea.

'Old man Katz?' Terry said, sitting back, arms folded in front of the telly. 'Was he slagging me off as usual?'

'No, as a matter of fact he wasn't,' Stacey tutted. 'I told him about that bloke you met.'

'What bloke?'

'The old bloke.'

Terry looked confused. 'Who?'

'Stanley Dawson.'

He turned to her, sitting up.

'Oh, the old boy I drove to Stansted,' he said. 'That was weeks back and you remembered his name?'

'Why wouldn't I? You told me they'd been good friends.'

'Well, yeah. He was a decent bloke. Not like some of the scumbags I pick up. He's going to call me next time he needs a lift. He goes to the airport several times a year he reckons. Gave a decent tip as well.'

'The Gravedigger,' she said.

'You what?'

'That's what my dad called him. The Gravedigger. He said that was his nickname, because back in the day he dug people's graves.'

Terry laughed. 'He's a character your old man, I'll give him that. Spins a good yarn.'

'I wish they were only yarns. He was harping on but I told him I didn't want to know about the good old days thank you very much. I mean, some of the things he says about the Krays for instance I wouldn't want to repeat. I remember back at school we had to stand up and say what our fathers did. Everyone said builder or milkman or whatever, but I didn't know what my dad did so I said businessman. What business? the teacher said. I didn't know what to say.'

'I know what I would've said.'

'What?'

'Mind your own effing business.'

She smiled. 'I reckon you would've as well.'

The local news came on, something about a double murder in Leytonstone, two men shot in their car. Then some expert was talking about rising knife crime amongst teenagers.

'That's another thing, Dad was saying it's getting dangerous round here and we should move to Southend.'

'Dangerous? He can talk. I reckon East London's crime rate took a nosedive when your old man moved out. The Old Bill must've been celebrating.'

'Terry, do you mind?'

'Sorry, I'm joking. He just wants you nearby, at his beck and call. He'd never be off your back.'

'Don't worry, I told him we're going nowhere. It's just all this talk about Rippers and stuff.'

'It's toerags targeting toerags, who cares.'

'Terry,' she chided. 'Don't talk like that, we're all human beings you know.'

'I'm just saying.'

They watched a film, some romantic Hugh Grant crap that Stacey liked, but Terry's mind was elsewhere. He remembered Stanley at the airport, pointing out the blood on his neck. Asking if everything was okay, Terry saying he must've cut himself shaving.

But what was he supposed to have said? Oh that's because I just butchered a bloke in an alley. Went fucking postal on him with an axe. Eye for an eye, times a thousand. Though judging from his nickname Stanley was a bloke who understood those type of things.

That night Terry couldn't sleep. He kept slipping in and out of dreams, waking up with a start, tossing and turning. His head was alive, it wouldn't shut down. He was tripping back through the past, back to scenarios real or imagined, it was hard to tell.

He remembered changing into his football boots by some public bogs on Hackney Marshes. What was he, fourteen, fifteen? It was already dusk but the lads would often play into the night. He was late and wanted to get over there and join in, but first he needed a leak.

Inside a man stood by the urinal trying to make conversation. The more he talked the more Terry boiled up inside.

The man was trying to proposition him.

Terry zipped up, then by the door he told him to go fuck himself.

The man laughed and said something about next time. Next time son, you'll see. You won't be so cocky then.

Terry walked away. His face was burning hot. He'd give him fucking next time.

Instead of running over to join the lads he found himself searching the bushes for a stone or a rock, something heavy. He found a knife handle stuck in the earth. He pulled it out, silver blade gleaming.

Terry returned to the bogs. The man was still playing with himself by the urinal. He glanced around just as Terry plunged the knife into his back. He staggered then collapsed to the floor, rasping in shock.

Terry watched as the man's body trembled, stunned as a dark pool of blood emerged on the tiles around him. Then all was still, his eyes lifeless, mouth wide open. He was dead.

Panicking, Terry dragged his body into a cubicle, stuffed it in and closed the door. A shocking trail of blood remained. He grabbed a mop and pail from the corner, dragging the blood round and round on the wet floor. It was no use; the place was like an abattoir. He threw it down and ran through the night.

He spent the following week in a daze.

Had he really killed somebody?

When football night came around he returned to the toilets. He half expected to see the man still there, stuffed into that cubicle. But there was no body, no blood.

Terry stepped back. He turned to the wall. Writ large in blood were the words:

THOU SHALT NOT KILL.

Part Two
County Kilburn

13

Back from the Dead

Bernie Riordan was in his Watford repair garage, working under an Audi A8 when his phone went. He wheeled out and answered it. Phil O'Malley, his mate from back in Kilburn, was talking a mile a minute, sounding panicked.

'The fucker's out Bern, he's actually out. I was pulling a pint, I look up and there he is staring straight at me. I thought he had a dozen more years at least, I don't understand it.'

'Slow down, who are you talking about?'

'Sean Quinn.'

Bernie's chest went cold. 'No way, you've got to be mistaken.'

'I've just spoken to him. I gave him a pint on the house. He was right in front of me.'

'Is he still there?'

'He's just gone now.'

'Where to? Listen Phil, you better not have told him where I am.'

'I fucking had to. If I said I didn't know he wouldn't have believed me.'

'For fuck's sake. Is he on his way over here now?'

'He said he might pop in on you later.'

Bernie kicked out sending his toolbox clattering across the floor.

'What was that noise?'

'Nothing,' Bernie said. He started pacing. 'Was he friendly?'

'He seemed fine. But you know what the bloke's like, it's hard to know what he's up to.'

'Christ Almighty. I don't need this now Phil.'

'Tell me about it. When I saw him I almost had a heart attack. I think he knows Bern, I'm telling you.'

'He knows fuck all. You hear me? So keep it shut. No matter what happens you tell him nothing. Have you got that?'

'You think I'm fucking stupid?'

Bernie's eyes shifted to the entranceway. Nobody was there. He'd only just sent the two lads who worked for him down the cafe, but still, he entered his office for some privacy.

Sean Quinn had been the planner, the main man. As an armed team they had a good run over several years, but it ended after Quinn shot a copper in a getaway. The copper survived, but for a while it looked like he might not. Quinn had the book thrown at him, while Phil and Bernie were acquitted; the judge reprimanding the police for a shoddily put-together case. The police had discovered all but one of their stash locations, so fresh out of remand Bernie and Phil had their hands on a large sum of cash. They planned on keeping Quinn's third of it back for him, but in the end got greedy and split it two ways. As past associates they couldn't visit Quinn in the nick, but sent word to him that the Flying Squad had found everything, but hadn't officially logged that last one. Considering how bent the bastards were, Quinn bought it, so all was good. Bernie put his share into a garage business, moved his family from Kilburn to the leafy outskirts of Watford. Phil relocated to Spain, squandered it and returned a year later to take over his uncle's pub on Kilburn High Road. Occasionally there were rumours that Quinn knew more than he'd let on, but they refused to believe them. What did it matter? He had a minimum of twenty-four years to serve before he'd be considered for parole.

'If he turns up don't upset him,' Phil said. 'Even if he lashes out... Jesus, I'm going out of my mind here.'

'Just calm down and tell me what he said. Everything.'

'Not much. Just small talk really. He was in a pretty good mood as it goes, but it didn't seem genuine. He kept giving me this knowing smile.'

'Fuck...' Bernie wiped his forehead. 'Look, I'm hanging up now, I've heard enough. The bloke could walk in any minute.'

'Listen Bern, I might just grab the missus and kids and have a break. I was thinking of Spain for a bit. I could leave the pub in good hands, get a flight, tonight maybe.'

'Are you trying to get me topped? Step one foot off the manor and you'll have more than Sean Quinn to worry about, I'm telling you.'

'Okay, I'm just not thinking straight right now...' Phil's voice cracked. 'I'm fucking worried mate.'

Bernie pictured Phil ten years ago on that final job. Pointing a loaded sawn-off at a guard who was flat on the ground, threatening to blow his bollocks away. They got the cash, all six hundred grand of it, Bernie at the wheel speeding off. Then next thing the police were behind them and Quinn was firing shots, one of which hit a copper in the chest. They were arrested within days.

'Just pull yourself together Phil, what's happened to you?'

'It's not me, I'm worried about my wife and daughters.'

'Quinn wouldn't hurt women and kids. You're blowing this all up. Are you still knocking back the Martell for breakfast? How many shots have you had today?'

'A few. Not too many.'

'Heard that one before. Now come on, we'll be alright. If Quinn wants a chunk of money we can sort it.'

'I'm skint Bern. The pub's making a pittance. I'm hardly getting by.'

'I'm not exactly rolling in it either, but as I say, we can sort it - if we have to.'

'What, do a job?'

'I never said that.'

'Well what then?'

'I don't know, I haven't had time to think about it. I'm going now. Just hang in there, and if you hear any more news call me straight away.'

Bernie left the office. He was deep in thought when young Baz and Wayne returned.

'You all right boss, you look lost?' Baz asked.

'I'm fine mate.' He stared at the Audi he should've been working on. Then he turned to the doorway and imagined Quinn walking through it. Demanding answers. Shoving a shooter in his face wanting to know where the fuck his money was, because all that old bollocks about the filth nicking it was a fucking fairy story, wasn't it Bernie mate?

He needed time to think. He slipped out of his overalls, told the lads he'd be back in an hour. He walked down to O'Reilly's and took his Guinness to a corner seat where he could keep an eye on the door. Bernie would have to be convincing. But could he hack it? Perhaps Quinn had mellowed, lost his fire and he could pull it off no problem. But he sounded like he hadn't changed. A dark horse you didn't want to get on the wrong side of. But fretting about it would get him nowhere. They'd committed the ultimate betrayal on a friend. But what's done was done. Who knows, perhaps there was nothing to even worry about. Either way, he'd play it by ear.

Back at the garage, nobody had called so he continued working under the Audi. An hour later he sensed something, saw a shadow maybe. A voice called his name. Bernie wheeled out. A figure stood silhouetted in the entranceway, right arm raised as if armed. Bernie froze. 'Bullseye,' the man said, hand shaped into a gun. Then Quinn stepped forward and smiled, spread his arms. 'Well, don't I even get a hello?'

Bernie stood up and threw his spanner to the floor. 'You silly fucker. You gave me a fright there.'

'Your face. Who did you think it was, the grim reaper?'

'Come here.' They gripped hands, leaned in for a hug. Bernie offered him congrats on his release, eyed him up and down. 'Let's have a look at you - you're looking fucking well mate.'

Quinn still had his dark hair, heavy brows, intense blue eyes. He still wore their uniform of the nineties: leather jacket, jeans, boots. He'd bulked up a good bit. 'You been working out?'

'In-house gym. When the services are free you might as well use them.'

'Phil phoned earlier, told me the news. I couldn't believe it. We'll have to throw a welcome home party. Do it round Phil's maybe.'

'Maybe. I've already had a drink-up with the family. I've been out a few weeks now. Still settling in. I've got digs in Edgware. My brother Noel lives not too far. He still drinks back on the manor, says he hasn't seen you around for years.'

'I'm out of the loop mate. Only spoke to Phil for the first time since before Christmas. I'm just working away, behaving myself these days.'

'You still with Jen? How is she, still a nurse?'

'Yeah. We've got two kids now - you remember Conor though, don't you?'

'Course. You used to dress him in the Arsenal strip. He was just this high then.'

'You should see him now. Sixteen. Right nightmare.'

'Can't be any worse than we were.'

'Hope not. He's a good lad really. Just needs to do better at school; he's suspended at the moment. But he'll sort himself out.'

They went and sat in the office. Bernie took out two cans of

Fosters from the fridge, passed one over.

'Not bad little place you got here,' Quinn said, looking about. 'How's business?'

'Could be better at times. Can't complain though.'

'Is that your big Land Cruiser outside? You must be coining it in.'

'Joking aren't you, I'm still paying that thing off.'

'Still doing bits on the side?' Quinn winked.

'Nah, those days are gone mate. After what happened, Jen gave me the ultimatum. I hope you've dropped the naughty ideas too, it just ain't worth it.'

He saw Quinn study him for a second, shrug it off.

'Suppose every villain's got to hang up the old six gun someday.' He picked up one of Bernie's business cards. 'Just wondered how you could afford a nice cushy business like this – you know, on the straight?'

'Went cap in hand to borrow from a greedy bank manager, just like all the other mugs out there.'

'Don't talk to me about bank withdrawals,' Quinn smiled. 'I've just done a big stretch for that shit.'

'I was meaning to ask, how did you get early-release?'

'You know Carson who nicked us? He got done for corruption. Then they reviewed his old cases and found untold discrepancies. I put in an appeal and it paid off. They basically walked into my pad one day and said I was free to go. I think the government are worried about bad publicity. There's been some other releases but it's all a bit hush-hush.'

'That's one stroke of luck.' Then Bernie turned serious. 'You did a fair old stretch there Sean. We only did a year on remand. I've never felt good about that, you know. Nor has Phil.'

Quinn put his hand up. 'No need.' Then he changed the subject and they joked about Phil running his uncle's old pub now. He's getting the same red hooter. Is he still knocking back the brandy? Probably pours it over his cornflakes.

Bernie got down and took five hundred quid from the safe. Told him to have a drink. I know you need it.

'Cheers Bern.'

'Least I can do.'

They headed out and stood in the cobbled passageway.

'We should meet in a few days,' Quinn suggested. 'Have a few quiet pints, catch up.'

'Yeah, anytime,' and they shook hands.

Bernie watched him walk down the passage, disappear at the corner.

Back at his desk he took out his phone. 'Phil. He came over. I've just seen him off. It went well. Things are fine. The last thing he's out for is trouble.'

'You sure about that? Did he mention the stash?'

'No. It's history, forget about it. Seems he's taken his time inside on the chin. He said he wants to meet for a drink in a few days. It might just be talk, but I'm not bothered. If he wants a pint we'll go for a pint.'

'It sounds too good Bern. Say he's just buttering you up? Creating a false sense of security. Have you forgotten what he can be like?'

'That's not the impression I got. Look, back in the day we were close. I know him.'

'In the pub he had an edge. You know the last thing he said to me? I'll be back. It might sound like a joke, but somehow it wasn't funny.'

'Yeah right. Any second Big Arnie's going to come crashing in with the hardware. Listen you drama queen, we're off the hook. Things are sweet. Now go and pour yourself a triple on the house. I'll bell you in a few days.'

Bernie left the office with a spring in his step. So the bad news hadn't been so bad after all. He jumped when he saw Quinn in the entranceway staring at him.

'You're back.' Despite flinching Bernie tried to sound casual.

He wondered if he'd been heard on the phone, but with the radio on it wasn't possible.

'So I am.' Quinn held up his mobile. 'You forgot to give me your number.'

After swapping numbers, Quinn looked at him. 'We'll have that drink. Tomorrow night maybe. Me and you. A little talk.'

'Yeah, we'll do that,' Bernie nodded a little too eagerly. 'Looking forward.'

Quinn disappeared and Bernie was left standing there. He went to the toilet. In the mirror his face looked drained. That second appearance had left him unnerved. Quinn hadn't smiled this time, seemed colder. Bernie felt clammy and splashed his face with water.

It had been a strange day and maybe he was over-reacting. He didn't know. He recalled his optimism on the phone to Phil and hoped he hadn't spoken too soon.

*

Tarquin stood by the dark water of the canal debating whether to throw his gun in and be done with it. Things weren't working out the way he'd imagined and he wondered if the weapon was jinxed. First there'd been the off-licence in Essex Road. The guy behind the counter stood there arms-folded, completely unfazed. Get that gun out of my face. Do you even know how to use the thing? Is it even loaded? The man continued his taunt, saying where he came from they used rifles and AK47s and you, my friend, wouldn't last a fucking minute. He tried to grab it from his hand and they struggled across the counter. Then three men with sticks came flying out from the back and Tarq couldn't get away quick enough. They chased him through the estates and he was lucky to make a clean break.

Then there was the betting shop in Homerton. The girl ducked behind the counter and Tarq was left standing in a balaclava talking to the air. On the way out some guy tried to trip him up and he nearly went flying. This wasn't how it was supposed to be. He was supposed to be making big money.

He took the unloaded pistol out of his pocket, looked at its worn finish. It had obviously been around, had some history. Maybe it had a list of victims to its name and one of them had cursed the thing. The other day he'd tried to sell it to a guy called Reggie. He was interested until Tarq took it out to show him.

He held it in his hand then quickly passed it back, said he wasn't feeling it. Reggie would spend hours talking about government conspiracies and liked to tell people he was psychic. Tarq remembered him one night reading a man's palm in a crackhouse by Hackney Downs. Reggie shook his head, said unfortunately some bad luck was coming his way and advised him to keep a watchful eye. Brian was happy go lucky and laughed it off, said he didn't believe all that mystic stuff. A week later he was knocked over and killed in a hit and run. It could've been a coincidence, but then again who knows.

Two men were approaching along the towpath so Tarq put the gun away and went home. That night he got a call from a Venezuelan guy on the scene called Billy the Fence. Tarq regularly sold him stereos, phones, whatever, the man's flat an Aladdin's Cave, but Billy was into more than fencing - he had connections. He said he'd heard what Tarq was getting up to, and knew he wasn't having much luck. But that's because he needed direction. Guidance from someone in the know. In this game inside-knowledge was everything. Billy offered him some work. Cash in the pocket. He knew of businesses where the security was slack or the owners were willing to get robbed for insurance purposes. For a fit young man like yourself it would be a walk in the park. What do you reckon T?

* * *

187

Entering the pub Dan saw Terry sitting at the bar smiling into his pint.

'You're in a good mood Tel. Thought I was seeing things.'

'What are you on about, I'm always in a good mood these days.'

'Why's that then?'

Terry leaned in. 'Won three hundred quid in the bookies earlier.'

'Must have been a lot earlier because you look like you've been on the sauce for hours.'

'Had a few chasers, so what?'

Dan scrolled through his messages. 'From the news I've heard today I'm a happy man too, I can tell you.' He spoke quietly: 'You know Concrete Kelly, my Paddy brother-in-law from Kilburn? He's got a job coming up. Filthy fucking lucre mate. I'm going to be loaded. Come summer you won't see me, I'll be lying on the beaches looking at the peaches.' He rubbed his hands together. 'Roll on summer, eh?'

Terry turned back to his pint. He hadn't brought his family on a decent holiday in three years now. The last was a cheap deal in a Spanish hotel overlooking a noisy building site. Stacey and the girls hadn't been best pleased.

'That's the thing with my brother-in-law,' Dan continued. 'When he puts out work you know it's going to be major. Big money.' Then he said the magic words. 'Kelly's looking for a driver. I'm thinking of asking Mickey Swan – you know Swanny, runs that lorry park down Rainham. He needs the cash. And after this bit of graft he'll have so much he won't know what to do with it.'

Terry turned to him. 'Hang about...'

'What?' Dan said, looking at his phone.

'Kelly's looking for a driver, you say?'

'Yeah, I'm giving it to Mickey Swan. Good old Mickey. In fact, I might give him a bell now as it goes.'

'Don't bother,' Terry said.

'What? Why is that Tel?'

'Because I want in.'

Dan feigned shock. 'You sure on that?'

'I'm sure.'

'Sure it's not the beer talking?'

'It's me talking. Loud and clear.'

'No changing your mind in the morning? Because if I confirm it there's no fucking about.'

'I said I want in.'

14

Fathers and Sons

It was a week since Quinn's appearance, and despite talk of them meeting up Bernie hadn't heard a peep. He sat tucking into a steak after a hard day, but could already feel the indigestion coming on. He was thinking of maybe picking up the phone. He didn't want Quinn thinking he was blanking him. He imagined Quinn one day knocking on his door and butting him in the face. 'You were doing well with me off the scene, weren't you Bern?' Maybe he'd make that call. Go for a dreaded drink. But perhaps it was a better idea to sit on it, see what happened.

Jen was collecting their daughter from a kids' party and his son Conor was upstairs playing music far too loud. Bernie brought his plate to the sink. As he did the washing up his mind shifted back to the nineties. Pulling off jobs and throwing money around. Part of an extended firm that nobody fucked with. After big jobs they'd tell the women they were heading out of town to lie low; instead they'd book into a hotel for the weekend, five, six, seven of them living it large. How many times this happened he couldn't calculate. Bernie remembered waking up one time, the suite a devastated party zone of wasted bodies, Quinn singing along with Axl, a bottle of Jacks and his trousers round his ankles as he rode the tart in front of him. Welcome to the Jungle. The two hired birds must have been serviced a dozen times that weekend. But Sean Quinn was the king. Load him up with powder and away he'd go.

Photos began circulating. It was Gary Fitzgibbon, snapping off shots thinking it was funny. It's one thing being off your nut for days banging anything that moves, but sober it's the last thing you want to see slapped down on the bar in front of you. 'Here you go Bernie you dirty fucker.' Fitzy pulled that stunt more than once. Bernie remembered a snap of himself in his boxers, a Thai bird on his knee, naked but for a pair of boots. In another he sat grinning for the camera, kecks round his ankles and a blonde's head between his legs. He was smoking a fat cigar, tapping the ash down onto her hair. Who was that wanker sitting there, because it certainly wasn't him. He couldn't recall the shots being taken, was obviously out of it, but the images stayed with him. He couldn't remember half of what they got up to on those nights. His missus was his fiancée then, but they'd already had Conor. What if she'd got hold of those shots? He decked Fitzy on the pub floor, tried forcing the picture down his throat. Then he went round to his place with a gun one night and got him to burn the lot. But what if some were still out there? A little evil intent and he'd be fucked, his marriage over. It didn't bear thinking about.

But it was all in the past now. And God knows what happened to Fitz, he hadn't seen him in years. Most of the lads had moved away. Some were back inside for other stuff. Bernie was lucky. He sat in front of the TV. The noise of his son's music finally sent him upstairs for a word. He banged on his door, asked him to turn that racket down. The volume lowered slightly. 'Not good enough. Right down. In fact put your headphones on. Do we all have to hear your rubbish taste in music?'

Conor opened the door; he wore a backward baseball cap. 'This ain't rubbish, it's NWA. Classic rap.'

Bernie felt like laughing. 'I was listening to all that before you were born. Beastie Boys, Public Enemy, Niggas with Attitude. It was silly then and it's even more silly now. You'll get over it.'

Conor shook his head, closed the door. The volume reduced, but not enough. Since Conor's teen rebellion phase they hardly talked. But in fairness, things with Bernie and his old man had been the same when he was that age; they only really connected years later. Maybe with fathers and sons it's just the way things go. A few years back it seemed the friendship thing was on the cards. He'd bring Conor down to Arsenal. Then they started going fishing together. Bernie bought up all the best gear and everything. Conor lost interest. The forced bonding thing felt artificial so Bernie decided to let things happen naturally. Now the boy was in trouble at school after years of doing okay. It wasn't good. Bernie had been in non-stop trouble too at school and look at the road he'd taken.

Jen insisted Conor was just going through a phase and if anything he'd learn from it. Hopefully she was right. Bernie went downstairs and sat back in front of the telly. Frustration gnawed at him. Eating away. It was Quinn. He needed to know where he stood with him. The bloke was up to something, but he didn't know what.

He heard Jen and Caitlin return home and went out to the hallway. His six-year-old daughter ran to him, told him all about the party. Jen said she had a boyfriend now and Caitlin denied it saying she didn't like boys. Jen said she was telling a white lie and they all laughed. Caitlin went to catch something on TV and Bernie followed Jen into the kitchen. He held her as she rinsed a cup, nestling into her shoulder.

'What's all this? You're in a good mood.'

'I'm giving my wife a cuddle. Anything wrong with that?'

'Of course not. I was just wondering where my husband went.'

Bernie laughed, kissed her neck. 'Let's go upstairs.'

'What, right now?'

'I'm in the mood. Conor's up there blaring out his music. Nobody will hear a thing.'

'You randy so and so.'

Jen laughed as he kissed her ear.

'Go on then, big boy, get up there and wait for me. I'll be a few minutes.'

Bernie went upstairs and waited faithfully under the sheets for his wife to join him.

NWA's 'Fuck tha Police' was Conor's personal anthem, because the people he hated most in the world right now were his teachers and Five-O. Both authorities fucked with his rights to party and do what he wanted, whenever he wanted. He pulled a pose, mouthed those words in the mirror and ended up laughing. It was a bit of a joke, but there was some truth in there somewhere.

After beating the crap out of Danny Payne, a guy who'd pushed him around for too long, he was hanging with a new set of friends. People respected him now and he enjoyed the feeling. It was a new lease of life. Like he'd broken out of a shell. It was a shame he was suspended though because at school he'd been appreciating the recent female attention.

The track finished and Conor heard a steady knocking against his bedroom wall. No way. His parents were next door banging. Couldn't they do that shit privately, or quietly at least? Or even better, how about not at all. He turned up the next track, opened his window and lit a spliff.

He scanned the cul-de-sac below. The houses were all the same red brick, the development built a decade ago when they'd moved up from Kilburn. His old mate Matt Feeney and his sister Gemma walked by. Matt was dribbling a ball, Gemma thumbing her phone. All the guy ever did was chat football. He was even into Gaelic football, hurling, the whole GAA thing. Sport was well and good but it wasn't the be all and end all. Matt needed to extend his sights, get out more.

The last time they spoke Matt said, 'So Con, you're running with the brothers now?' They pushed each other for a bit before Conor called him a fool and walked away. It's not as if all his new mates were even black, it was a multicultural crew. But Conor was moving in different circles now, Matt being left behind. Conor still liked his sister though. Gemma was a year younger and always gave him a smile whenever they passed. He'd never taken much notice of her before, but she was growing up nicely, had a bit of shape going on. He imagined the two of them in her house with her parents out, Matt walking in to witness the scene. Give me a sec mate, I'm just boning your sister.

But Conor's lack of experience in that area needed addressing fast. Last week he'd premiered his talents with Amy Thorn, a girl from the park the world and his dog had been with, but it was over too soon and he needed to improve his skill set. Sharpen his technique. But for the time being he'd wing it. 'Straight Outta Compton' came on and he rapped along with passion. In an hour he was meeting the boys. Marcus said there might be a party later, he'd let him know. Half the time these parties never materialised, but something would happen, it always did. He decided on a quick shower, his second of the day, wanted to stay fresh, just in case.

Jen got dressed and went downstairs while Bernie stayed in bed for a nap. A roll in the sack had done him good. He'd been fretting too much lately, letting it all get to him. But the return of Quinn was a shock. A ghost from the past, bringing with him that former state of mind, when they'd lived for the easy cash, the craic, the camaraderie. He remembered those nights in the Green Dragon, their informal HQ. Laughing at their success, at a system that couldn't stop them. Towards the end the Old Bill knew they were at it, but couldn't catch them in the act and nobody would talk. Life was good and it seemed their run would never end. But end it did. They got careless. He remembered the night Quinn gave Happy Jack Gavin such a battering he was lucky to survive. He was in intensive care for weeks and it brought undue attention. Jack had nicked a key of sulph from a Greenford mob Quinn was friendly with. At the trial the attack was brought up to show the jury what a nutter he was. They said it was unprovoked, only happened because Quinn was in a bad mood. But there are reasons for everything. The police knew only a fraction of what they were getting up to.

Bernie remembered Johnny Mac, a mate and active member of the team. He was reliable, one of the best, until the partying side of things took their toll. He'd be out on jobs half-cut, a liability. On one job he bashed a guard over the head because the old boy wasn't opening a gate quick enough. The man had a seizure on the ground. They called an ambulance, aborted the job. Quinn was livid, but Johnny was his closest friend, so he was lenient. He took him off the team for a bit, so he could sort himself out. But Johnny got heavier into the Class A's, became a local nuisance. In the pub he'd be shouting his mouth off, starting fights; he even got cocky with Quinn. It was strange to see; growing up they were like brothers. But enough was enough. Quinn had him dragged down an alley off Kilburn High Road. He held a knife to his throat, said he was sorry things had to end this way but he had no choice. Johnny cried and begged, saying he was sorry, he'd clean up, he'd change. Quinn barred him from the Green Dragon, said he'd better fucking change or else.

Johnny Mac was on a downward spiral. He was off his nut half the time on crack and his own parents could hardly recognise him. They appealed to Quinn for help and he promised he'd try. He arranged a meet, but Mac wasn't so contrite now. Get fucked, he said, their friendship was over. Violent burglaries were happening locally and word was it was Mac and the group of junkies he hung with. Some of the victims were elderly and Quinn was fuming. If Mac did one more job he was getting a Belfast six pack: elbows, knees, feet. Johnny was unrepentant, sending Quinn a message that it was him who better watch his back. That was it. He'd crossed the final line.

The boys were guests at a black club one night. Quinn's was the only white firm the blacks would have dealings with. They all knew club owner Sammy T from school and now he was one of the manor's top dealers, sporting a full-blown Jamaican accent. He'd just sent a bottle of bubbly to their table when word came through that Mac and two mates were putting themselves about in a pub in Willesden. This was their new thing, heading to quiet pubs on the manor and bullying the drinkers. Quinn, Bernie and a bear of a man called Tommy Gun had to postpone Sammy's kind hospitality.

They jumped in Tommy's motor. Quinn was packing a .44 Magnum, Tommy never went anywhere without his Browning 9 mill, while Bernie had a hunting knife. Quinn put plastic sheeting down in the boot of the car and got everyone to wear gloves. Johnny Mac was being taken off the street.

They walked into the pub, Irish and Jamaican old timers looking away as they entered. The landlord was silently wiping a glass with a face like thunder. Two of Mac's waster mates were over by the pool table chucking balls at each other, taking the piss. Both had long greasy hair, jeans, track-suit tops. Seeing the three men enter they ceased fucking about.

'Where's Mac?'

Both shook their heads, nervous now. Tommy checked the gents, said they were empty. Quinn stepped closer, asked again. They looked at each other, shrugged their shoulders. Quinn pulled his Magnum and whipped the nearest one to the floor. Then he grabbed a handful of his hair and put the gun to his head. Mac had run up to St Raph's to get more gear. Quinn stomped the bloke until he pled for no more. Patrons stared silently into their pints. Landlord wiping that same glass. 'You better not be lying.' They threw him out of the pub, kicking him up the arse. The other man came with them into the car. Quinn stuck his head back in the pub door. 'Everything all right now, Eamon?' the place now alive with chatter. 'Grand,' the landlord winked. 'And none of us saw a thing.'

Tommy was behind the wheel, Bernie and Quinn in the back, smackhead between them at gunpoint. They drove to St Raphael's Estate, touring its rundown streets looking for Mac. No sign of him.

'What's your name you little prick?' Quinn asked.

'Fergie.'

'Well Fergie, I think you and your mate are taking me for a cunt, that's what I think. Where's Johnny living now?'

'I don't know, I swear. I only see him on the street.'

They turned onto the North Circular. By the warehouses of Staples Corner they pulled off into a stretch of wasteland. The headlights lit up tall weeds as the car crept along. 'Where are we going?' he whimpered. 'Please don't kill me...'

Fergie was pulled out, dumped on the ground. 'Go on lads,' Quinn said, lighting a fag. 'Go to town on him.' He stood watching as Bernie held the junkie from behind, Tommy thumping his fists into him. They let him collapse.

'Good work boys.' Quinn picked up a broken bottle. He got down on one knee, grabbed the man by the throat. Bernie turned to face the distant cars as his screams sliced through the toxic air.

The feud with Mac dragged on. One night Tommy Gun was driving along Cricklewood Broadway when he spotted him on the street. He took some shots from his car but lost him down the backstreets. Tommy was kicking himself that he'd let him slip but Quinn was amused by the episode, his arm around Tommy's shoulder in the pub, saying how Mac must be shitting himself now.

They were having a session one night in the Dragon. Quinn was at the bar; Bernie at a table with Tommy Gun and some others. It was almost time for a lock-in when Johnny Mac walked in with a revolver. A song on the dukebox faded out, the pub silent now. Mac stood eyes unblinking, gun levelled at Quinn.

Nobody moved but Tommy. He stood, his bulk covering Sean. 'You'll have to shoot me first.'

'Out of the way you fat cunt or I'll fucking do that.'

Tommy reached for his own piece and Mac blasted him twice in the chest. Tommy dropped to the floor, lying motionless, his pistol next to him.

'There goes your minder Sean,' Mac laughed. 'Now get down on your knees.'

Quinn stared back, refused to move.

'Fuck you then.' Mac pulled the trigger. Click. He tried again; nothing happened. Tommy sprung to life, retrieved his gun and fired two rounds. Mac staggered to the deck, blood at his fingers, gurning in confusion. The lads rushed to Tommy's aid, but he waved them off, staggering to the bar demanding refreshment. He gulped a brandy then ripped open his shirt to pull out a Kevlar vest, two bullet marks visible. The lads cheered. From that day on he was a hero.

The landlord locked the doors, everyone helping to clean up. Mac was carried down to the cellar and placed on the stone floor. It was just Quinn and Bernie now, staring down at him. He was still alive, on his side coughing blood.

Quinn took a shovel from against the wall and passed it to Bernie. 'Finish the cunt.'

Bernie was unsure. Quinn kicked Mac in the face, cursing him. Then he pushed Bernie forward.

'Don't piss me off Bern. Just do it.'

Bernie hesitated and Quinn kept goading him. Telling him it was about time he showed his worth. Stood on his own two feet instead of leaving everything to him. What sort of man are you? I plan the jobs, put money in your pocket, and look at you now. The cunt just tried to fucking murder me.

Bernie brought the shovel down hard on Mac's head. He paused, heard a groan, then with a roar he brought it down repeatedly until his body was still. He stepped back, staggering.

Quinn laughed heartily, slapping his back. 'Jesus Bern. Didn't know you had it in you.'

He leaned down, smiling over his dead ex-mate. 'Who's winning now Johnny boy?'

Bernie still held the shovel. It was covered in blood. Then the beer came up his neck and he vomited in the corner.

They wrapped Mac in a roll of carpet and carried him up through the barrel hatch to the car. Quinn phoned his building contractor brother and they headed for a site in Wembley.

'I've got a new respect for you Bern,' Quinn said at the wheel. 'You did well back there. And did you see Tom Gun tonight? Jesus, the man's a legend.'

They drove in silence. Then Quinn turned to him. 'How's it feel to kill someone Bernie?'

Bernie stared at the road ahead. 'I didn't kill him – he was dying.'

'You killed him all right Bernie boy. You gave him that shovel right in the bonce. I'm jealous, I wanted to take the fucker out myself. I just didn't want his toxic junkie's blood all over me,' he laughed.

Now Bernie wondered if Quinn had really uttered those words. Probably not. His dream was distorting, going off-kilter.

Mac was buried in the foundations of an office extension. Bernie spent half the night doing the work on his own, Quinn leaving him to it, saying he'd better attend to the forensic clean-up back at the pub. Now Quinn was back by his side, standing by the freshly dug pit. They dragged Johnny's body across the muck, dropped him down into the hole. A bloody moon shone bright as they stared down at his twisted form. 'Good riddance to bad rubbish, that's what I say.' Quinn turned to him. With one mighty push Bernie was off his feet, laughter echoing from above as he crashed through the endless darkness.

Bernie shot bolt upright. He was awake, sweating in his bed. What time was it? It was dark outside. Then he remembered going upstairs with Jen. The door opened and he jumped. Jen stood there, then her face changed.

'Bernard, are you okay?'

15

Riffraff in Chiswick

'I'd love to fire a bit of kit like that,' Bigz said, driving along the Great Cambridge Road, shades on, sun shining down. 'Metalwork of that calibre is being wasted on those Enfield mugs.'

They'd just made a drop. Mike had warned them not to look in the holdall, which of course only piqued their interest. They weren't disappointed. It was an AK-47 machine gun.

'You like your guns big, yeah?' Lil said.

'Who doesn't? I've always wanted to fire an AK, let rip like Rambo in the jungle. This country has a serious lack of artillery. America pisses all over us in that respect. So does Africa, Russia, everywhere. Yeah man, I'd love some of that.'

'You want to go waste somebody then?'

Bigz paused. He turned to Lil who was slumped low chewing gum. 'What did you just say?'

'I said, do you want to go take a life today, end some fucker?'

Bigz studied his face. Lil was cool as you like, unreadable as ever.

'You mean right now?'

'Why not,' he shrugged. 'We can get the ball rolling right now if you want.'

Bewildered, Bigz shook his head. 'You're serious, aren't you?'

'I don't fuck about.'

'I know you don't. Jeez. Tell me, just for the record, who's the lucky man?'

'It's a guy on my list. My own personal list.'

'You've got a personal hit list?'

'Don't we all?'

'No. Though come to think of it, there are a few men out there I wouldn't mind seeing the back of. Everyone's got their enemies, but it's risky though.'

'Doesn't have to be. Look at me. I've sent bare men to the next world.'

Bigz frowned, unnerved at Lil's casual confidence. Was the guy for real? He was freaking him out again.

'I don't doubt that, but if you went round putting bullets into everyone who's ever pissed you off you'd never see daylight again.'

'Ask me, the risk is part of the fun.'

'Who is this guy on your list anyway?'

Lil produced a picture of a fat old white guy. He said his name, said he was a highly regarded member of the establishment.

'Never heard of him,' Bigz said.

'Well, he don't exactly roll in our circles. But you've already read about him. He used to visit the children's home I lived in.'

Bigz remembered the *Hackney Gazette* article. 'Oh right... I see.' He was getting the gist of it now.

'The woman shot on Kingsmead was the main witness trying to get him locked up for his crimes. The job ended up on Mike's desk, and he gave it to me - which considering my past link to the matter hasn't exactly left me too happy.'

'Shit Lil, I can understand that. With the witness dead the guy walked.'

'But there's a happy ending, because I've got a nice gat prepared, all ready to collect. Dum-dum bullets, the works.'

'Hollow point, type that explode?'

'Burst your head open like a ripe tomato.' Then Lil turned to him. 'Just wondered if you wanted to come along for the ride. I mean, if you've got the balls?'

Evening. They collected a fake-plated ringer and drove to Chiswick, West London. Bigz had never been out this way before, Lil saying it was a posh area where all the media fucks lived. They found a space a few doors down from the man's address and parked the car. The houses were terraced but well-to-do, neat streets oozing comfort and wealth. A sleek blonde walked by talking on her phone. She disappeared around a corner.

'So this is where you find all the pricks on TV?' Bigz grimaced.

'Here and places like Hampstead. Or maybe Richmond and Barnes.'

'Richmond and where?'

'All the pussy areas basically,' Lil said, checking his weapon. 'Anyway, you gonna wait in the car?'

'It's probably best.'

'Well one thing's for sure, I won't be long.'

Lil put up his hood and stepped out into the night. Reaching the house he walked up the short path. The lights were on, the target seemingly in. Lil rang the bell.

A figure approached through the mottled glass. The door opened. The man stood there. It had been years but he looked the same: plump, red faced, impatient.

'What did I tell you before about coming early,' he said, looking at his watch. 'You'll just have to sit in the car and wait.'

'What the fuck are you talking about?'

Lil Killa raised the gun and blasted him in the forehead.

Blood hit the wall and he jerked backwards, eyes shocked. Lil fired again, the man's white shirt turning crimson. He fell to the floor. Lil stood over him. He aimed for the genitals.

Helmsley sat at home enjoying a fine malt to the strains of Mahler. He had a spare hour to savour before meeting with his esteemed associates for their monthly gathering. A banquet in a top London hotel, then on to a patron's Richmond home for a private soirée. Youthful entertainment would be amply provided, inhibitions left at the door.

It was only weeks since the outcome of his trial, an unfortunate affair that despite his acquittal still left a bad taste. But it was soothing to recall the judge's final words. Helmsley had been a victim of a malicious campaign of lies and could leave this court with head held high, his name unblemished. He'd been granted a lucky escape, but it was sad to recall his many acquaintances through the years who'd been less fortunate. Thrown to the lions, their reputations destroyed because of their natural needs and desires. Yet with so many men of power and influence working hard to bring change, Helmsley was confident of the day their good names would be restored and celebrated.

Years before, he had occupied a senior position at Hackney Council. He recalled that militant era with fondness. It truly was an age of anything-goes, when those in respected positions could expect discretion. Accusations of wrongdoing in the council's care homes were frankly absurd. What Helmsley and others had partaken in did not constitute a crime. Pleasure was taken and pleasure received, and to claim otherwise was most certainly financially driven.

In court his defence had fought with impressive verve, his QC a secret affiliate whose skill was second to none. Ensuring the no-show of a key witness hadn't exactly done any harm either. It had cost money but was worth every penny. Helmsley chuckled into his drink. He'd soon have to change into his evening suit. He was just finishing his malt when the doorbell chimed. If that was his driver the damn fool was early.

Bigz heard the shots and saw Lil Killa pacing briskly back to the car. He jumped in.

'The man's dead, let's roll.'

They journeyed back along the North Circular, Lil sitting back coming down from the high, Bigz praying they hadn't made a big mistake.

Roadworks at Finchley delayed them, so the appearance of Edmonton's tall incinerator chimney was for once a welcoming sight.

At Tottenham Marshes they doused the car and set it on fire. Excitement over, they made for the River Lea towpath to walk the two or three miles back to Hackney.

'When you get home, make sure to shower yourself down with bleach,' Lil said. 'Just in case.'

'I know the score.'

'Get rid of your clothes too.'

Bigz rose an eyebrow. 'Good job I've got an extensive wardrobe.'

Down by the canal it was quiet, not a soul around. The moon shone down on the still murky water, and a heron appeared, its enormous wingspan moving slowly across the night sky.

'Look,' Lil said.

'Weird. I hope it's not a bad omen.'

They were edging Springfield Park when Bigz's phone sounded. It was Mike.

'Get over here now,' he said. 'I want a word with you two cocksuckers.'

The line went dead. They looked at each other.

'What have we done to upset him?' Bigz wondered.

'Could be he's just in a bad mood,' Lil said. 'But one thing's for sure, he's definitely getting crazier these days. You hear what he did to Jugs, white guy from Frampton? He was sent on a punishment shooting but the victim saw the gun and ran for it. Jugs went back to tell Mike the news. Bad move. Mike ordered him to put his hand down on the desk and close his eyes. Jugs was expecting a branding, but Mike pulled a Samurai and chopped his fucking hand off.'

'What the...?'

'Then he picked it up off the floor and said, Here Jugs, you want a hand?'

'No way.'

'Mike's ramping the crazy shit to eleven these days. Everyone's saying it. We better watch it.'

Bigz thought about it. Then he clicked his fingers. 'I know why he's got the hump with us. It's the Jamaican mule job we did.'

'Shit, I forgot all about that.'

They went up onto Lea Bridge Road and headed for Mike's studio. Inside the receptionist led the way. 'You better knock gently. The bossman ain't in good spirits right now.'

Lil did the honours.

'Come the fuck in,' they heard.

Mike was behind his desk swivelling restlessly. The air smelled suspiciously of crack fumes. Was he hitting the pipe now?

'I'll ask you,' Mike pointed at Lil, 'because you're the one with the brains and he ain't got jack shit. Now what happened with the Yardies?'

Lil feigned confusion. 'Nothing. We did that job no problem, boss.'

'Well how come Shine is fucking dead?'

'He the guy that was there?'

'No, he's your mum's fuck buddy, course he's the guy who was there. What happened?'

'We extracted the cargo and dumped the body. No problem.'

'And where was Shine?'

'He was there in the flat. He said well done and we said goodbye. One thing though, he had a junkie friend there. I remember we didn't like the look of him.'

'Mmm.' Mike studied him sceptically, eyes going up and down. 'That's the official line, that his friend killed him. But I don't always believe official lines.'

Bigz spoke now. 'But it was obviously that guy who did it because…'

'Shut the fuck up!' Mike snapped at him. Then he opened a drawer and took out a Taser. He got up and walked around the desk. 'I don't like it when people interrupt me. In fact I fucking hate that shit.'

'I'm sorry Mike, I was only saying that…'

'There he goes again.' He shot him with the stun gun. Bigz froze from the voltage then collapsed sideways to the floor.

'Now that's better. That's what a prick like you needs to learn some manners and respect round here.'

Mike pressed his foot down on Bigz's head as he spoke to Lil Killa.

'I've got eyes and ears all over and you two have been running round wild-style, up to all sorts of unsanctioned shit out there. You cross me I'll nail you to the wall and roast you up with my iron, is that clear?'

Eyes crazed he removed his foot and kicked Bigz in the face. 'Now take yourself and this piece of shit out of here before I get angry.'

It was official now. Hot Iron Mike was getting more difficult.

16

Guns and Roses

The shutters came down as Bernie locked the garage. It was dark; he'd done a late one. He still hadn't heard from Quinn, but he'd received some silent calls lately, numbers withheld, which could be the bloke playing games but was probably just a coincidence. He didn't want to worry about it, yet it niggled him. To put it to rest he took out his mobile to ask Phil if he'd noticed anything unusual. If the answer was no, Bernie would go home a happier man.

He'd hardly said hello when Phil fired the same question, saying he'd been getting silent calls, six times today.

'Shit.' Bernie paced up and down on the cobbles.

'It's him isn't it,' Phil said. 'It's Quinn.'

'We don't know that.'

'Who else could it be? He knows we took his money and he's playing games with us. I could sense it from the start.'

'You're a worrier, Phil. Stop shitting your pants until we know for sure.'

'He's planning something, I know it. He's probably been watching us. All that time on his hands and we haven't seen hide nor hair of him.'

Phil was banging on but to Bernie it was just noise. He told him to calm down, he'd speak to him later and hung up.

Christ Almighty. He walked up the dim-lit passage towards his car. He'd go home, have a bite to eat then go straight to bed. Maybe in the morning he'd be able to think. He pressed his key and Quinn stepped out from the shadows. 'Busy day, Bern?'

Bernie drew back in shock. 'Jesus, I didn't see you there.'

'Thought I was some scumbag come to rob you?'

'Something like that,' he laughed, trying to make light of it. Quinn stood with his hands in his leather coat.

'Going home to the wife and kids?'

'Yeah, just finished up now.'

Silence followed and Bernie didn't know what to say.

'You never did phone me did you Bern? For our little drink.'

'No, I've been busy mate, big workload at the moment.'

Half his face in shadow, Quinn looked him up and down. 'Always were a grafter, I'll say that. Even if it was a different line of business.'

Bernie wondered how long he'd been out here, lurking in the dark waiting for him. But the reason why bothered him more.

'So how about now?' Quinn asked.

Bernie looked puzzled.

'That drink.'

'Oh right. Okay,' Bernie shrugged.

'You don't seem very committed?'

'To what?'

Quinn stepped forward, eyes set on him.

'To me, Bernie,' he said quietly. 'To me.'

Bernie didn't like the way this was going. 'Look, I don't know what you're talking about.'

'I think you do Bernie boy.'

Bernie looked at his key, then his car. He should've been driving home to his family, putting his feet up after a hard day. Instead he was standing in the gloom facing a malevolent ghost from the past.

Quinn stepped closer. Bernie could smell the drink on him now. He imagined him in the pub all day brooding, stewing away.

'You know what I reckon?' Quinn poked his chest. 'You'd prefer it if I was still in the nick. Because with me away all these years you've been doing just fine for yourself. What do you reckon?'

'That's bullshit.'

'You're a better actor than Phil, I'll give you that.'

Bernie shook his head. It was late and Jen would be wondering where he was. He'd had enough of this. He looked his old friend in the face.

'If you've got something to say Sean, just say it. Because these riddles are pissing me off.'

'What did you do with my money, Bern?'

'What fucking money?'

The blow took Bernie by surprise, the force sending him staggering. Quinn grabbed him and slammed him against the shutters, breathing close.

'I've been watching you, keeping a close eye. And you know why? Because you two pricks have been taking me for a fucking mug.'

Bernie tasted blood. 'That's not true.'

'You and O'Malley cleaned out my lock-up and blamed it on the coppers, ain't that right Bern?'

'No fucking way.'

'Don't insult me you lying cunt, I'm warning you.'

'We didn't do it.'

Quinn slammed him hard in the gut, let him slide to the ground. Bernie was winded, struggling for breath. Quinn got down.

'Look at me,' he held his face. 'You and that cunt know what you did, so let's not even go there. Let's move onto the next stage, because I'm in charge now and I'm telling you what's going to happen. You got that?'

Bernie nodded.

'You're going to do a job for me, a big job, and you're paying me back every pound note and more. You listening?'

Bernie nodded, said yes, and Quinn stood up.

He offered him a hand, cheerful now. 'Come on mate, what are you doing down there? Up you get Bern.'

Upright he was still wincing. He didn't know where to look.

'With you out earning you're going to be a busy man, aren't you. You and Phil, two busy bunnies. Unless you have other ideas of course. But then you'd be putting some close loved ones in real jeopardy, and we don't want that, do we?'

Bernie glared at him and Quinn smiled, glad the message had hit home.

'So if you're not feeling too put out, I'd say it's time for that drink,' he slapped his shoulder. 'We've got some catching up to do. You want to hit somewhere local or head down the old manor? Choice is yours.'

Phil was busy serving a Friday night crowd when his phone went. He ducked in from the bar, put it to his ear.

'Quinn knows.'

Phil steadied himself. 'No.'

'He knows everything. I've just spent the last two hours drinking with the bastard. But he's offered us a way out. To pay him off. We're going back to work. Something he's lining up with Concrete Kelly. I can't talk about it on the phone, we'll have to meet.'

'Jesus Christ.' Phil was sweating now.

'He's been watching us, knows our ins and outs. He knows where our kids go to school, what car your wife drives and about her relatives in Spain. So don't even think about it Phil.'

'Fuck… but what if we do the job and it's still not enough for him?'

'He reckons once he's paid he's fucking off out of the country and not coming back. That sounds good enough to me.'

'You really believe he's going to let us off?'

'I wouldn't say he is letting us off, we're going to be risking our arses for the cunt.'

'A job with Concrete Kelly?'

'I know, I don't like the sound of it either. With Kelly it definitely won't be no small-fry thing. But I will say Kelly's a professional - you know, police in his pocket, the works, so at least we've got that.'

Phil had to sit down. All of a sudden he felt fucked.

Concrete Kelly climbed back into bed after taking a leak. It was 5.30am, the sheets warm and inviting. His wife lay sleeping next to him as pretty as a picture. He was a lucky man, lived a charmed life, that's for sure. And since being invited to join a major race-fixing syndicate things couldn't be better. Perhaps it was time to scale back a few other interests, or put them in the right hands at least. He'd definitely have to cut down on those grass-roots jobs he got involved in, graft he had no real need for apart from enjoying the thrill of being back near the coalface. He was pushing on now and perhaps it was time to wise up. Then again, he'd see. The sense of risk kept him feeling youthful.

His family had moved from Connemara to London when he was eight. Then as a 14-year-old tearaway he was recruited as an unlicensed bookies runner. Larry 'The Knife' Murphy was a local face who took him under his wing, sending him out to collect wagers from the pubs and digs around Kilburn and Cricklewood. The Knife taught him the tricks of the trade, how to make a pound note, and Kelly graduated onto greater things, eventually running a crew of gun-toting heavies that had that Irish corner of North-West London sewn up.

Considering his numerous dark deeds through the years, he was lucky to still be in the game. He thought of the others who hadn't got this far, ending up lifed-off or erased from the scene completely. If you fucked up in this line of work you paid for it with your hide. He recalled the time one of their own men, Doonan, ran off with a pile of their money. They'd just done a cash delivery lorry so we're talking a fair old chunk. They found Doonan drunk in his brother's pub up in Bedford, having spent the evening boasting about his new-found wealth and how he was off to San Francisco in the morning. Perhaps he should've kept his mouth shut. Kelly had him concreted into an oil drum and dumped in the arse-end of the Thames.

Then there was Tony Boyle. He'd been an IRA man in Belfast, but sang to the Brits like a blackbird when pulled into Castlereagh. He ran off to London rather than face the 'Ra's nutting squad. Boyle got in with a team pulling off bank jobs, but Kilburn probably wasn't the wisest choice for his drinking. The IRA spoke to Kelly asking for a favour. One night Kelly and a bloke called Gaughan were drinking with Boyley in the Black Lion, listening to him regale them with his heroic exploits over the water while they plied him with Mickey Finns. At closing they lured him to a flat with the promise of women. When he entered he saw the plastic sheeting and tried to make for the door. Gaughan stuck a knife in him. They waited for a 'Ra man to come and identify the body. He took one look, said *Tiocfaidh ar la,* our time will come, and left. Then Boyley went under the M25.

Looking back there were quite a few of them. Kelly remembered the black fella who'd been visiting a pub in Willesden threatening to have the place firebombed if the governor didn't pay monthly security. He mentioned some heavy names but must've been slow in the head because everyone knew the boozers were already paying out to the Kelly Gang. The governor told him to knock round early next morning before opening and they'd come to an arrangement. Next day when he walked in he was met by a welcoming committee. His eyes widened in surprise and he pulled out a machete. Out came the baseball bats, and for a full minute tables and chairs were flying before he was finally unarmed and pinned down on the wooden floor. Even then he was effing and blinding.

'Hold the fucker there,' said Wild Bill O'Reilly, before returning from his van with a hammer and nails. 'Hold his hand out.' He did one hand, then two, but still the fella kept cursing. 'Off with his shoes,' he said and then he did both his feet. Nothing would stop his shouting and ranting. Finally Wild Bill slammed the claw side of the hammer into his head and only then was there silence.

'I think that calls for a pint,' somebody said, and for an hour they sat laughing and drinking with the man nailed to the floor and a hammer sticking out of his head. Then it was opening time so they had to drag him out back to the van while the landlord got a mop and pail. He was ten minutes late opening the boozer and a line of old timers were banging on the door gasping for their morning jar. It turned out the fella was a drug-taking nuisance from Stonebridge who liked to follow old women back from the post office on pension day. He wasn't missed.

Kelly wondered how many more there'd been through the years. He remembered Big Patsy Breen. He was a regular around the pubs, a fierce brawler and womaniser. Occasionally they'd bring him on debt jobs but mainly he worked on the buildings. He had a brief romance with the sister of one of the gang, a man called Gallagher. Maggie was a fiery type, and a few weeks after they split she claimed he broke into her flat and brutally raped her. She'd been out dancing at the Galtymore that night and when she got home, there he was naked in her room after breaking in through the window. Maggie was known as a bit of a trollop and Kelly was sceptical, but after she met them in person, bawling her eyes out with a black eye and swearing she was telling the truth, she had them convinced.

They found Breen drinking in The Crown on Cricklewood Broadway. They wanted to bring him in for questioning but he refused to go quietly. Breen battered his way to the door, ran and wasn't seen for weeks. Then one night word came through that he was in a backstreet pub in Kentish Town. They walked in wielding a sawn-off as Breen sat at the bar. Fair play to the man, he hardly flinched. He asked if he could have one last swig of his pint then grabbed the gun's barrel and a hole was blasted through the ceiling narrowly missing a lodger who was upstairs watching TV. Breen was kicking and punching, nobody able to get a hold of him. Finally he flew out the door and they headed after him. They found him in a nearby park hiding up a tree. 'I didn't do it, the woman's lying to you, you stupid cunts,' he said. Gallagher was itching to get at him, but Kelly assured Breen that if he came quietly he'd get his chance to air his side of things. Breen climbed down, but hitting the floor again he was off. Kelly took aim with a Colt .45, shot him and he fell.

Breen was bleeding from his shoulder as they dragged him into the back of the van. Gallagher was beating him all the way to the lock-up and by the time they got there he was in bad shape. They sat him on a chair but he fell unconscious and died in front of them. What a balls up. They'd planned on interrogating not killing him, but it was a bit late now for regret. They'd have to get rid of his body. Someone suggested Epping Forest, but they'd done one out there a year before and were almost noticed by a couple frolicking in the bushes. One of the lads knew a pig farmer in Essex that a certain East End firm used. Kelly remembered the farmer had a squint and two fingers missing from one hand. As they handed over the body he seemed giddy with delight. It's funny the things you remember.

When Maggie heard Breen had taken a permanent holiday, it was suddenly a different story. She'd only wanted him beaten, not fucking killed. It turned out she'd been jealous after he'd left her for a prettier girl and she'd made the story up, even bashing up her own face. None of the lads were happy with that, some giving her brother a severe thrashing for it. Big Pat had his faults but he was no rapist and hadn't deserved such a send-off. But it was just one of those things. A few years later Maggie got into drugs and whoring and ended up strangled to death in a hotel room in Paddington.

Looking back, Concrete Kelly had made his share of mistakes, but he had no major regrets. He'd only done a few short bits of bird early on and had kept quite nicely under the radar considering. He supposed he was born lucky. Crafty old goat that he was.

*

Lil pushed his empty plate aside and reached over to the next table for a *Hackney Gazette*.

'You hear about the Palace Pavilion?' he said, reading an article on the troubled nightspot.

Bigz was head-down tucking into a Full English. 'No, what's the score?'

'It's closing down.'

Bigz looked up. 'No way.'

'And it looks like for good this time.'

'Nah, never.'

'It says here. That last shooting was the final straw.'

'I don't believe that. It's a local institution, been there for years. My late brother used to go to reggae nights there when I was this high. It'll stay open, you'll see.'

'Doesn't look like it,' Lil said and read aloud, '*Local MP Diane Abbott has released a statement saying, 'The Pavilion has a history of attracting trouble. Now another young man has lost his life. It is time this club is permanently shut down. A history of gangland-style executions in the area surrounding Lower and Upper Clapton Roads have earned it the terrifying tag 'Murder Mile'. Once again it has lived up to its horrific reputation. I support the police in their campaign to revoke the club's licence, blah blah blah...'*

'She supports the police? Of course she does. She ain't got a fucking clue. Beef kicks off now and then, but shit can go down anywhere. She just wants to gentrify the hood. Bring in the yuppies with all the money and get rid of the real people born around here.'

'I remember your bred Jay used to go there a lot,' Lil said, eyeing a photo of the building from 1921. 'He was down there all the time, pulling and that.'

Bigz fell silent. He put down his knife and fork and pushed his unfinished plate away as if Jay's mere mention had put him off his food. He sat back, staring off into the distance.

'Fuck Jay,' he muttered.

Lil continued reading. 'Did you know the Pavilion used to be a cinema? Like way back in the day. An old picture house? Then in the 80s the club was called Dougies. Then of course in the 90s Chimes. Then they had to change the name again because of all the beef going down...'

Bigz wasn't listening. He stood up, said it was time to go.

*

Terry and Dan got a black cab all the way from Dagenham to Kilburn. Sitting back watching East London's grey sprawl give way to cosmopolitan Hackney, Islington and Camden, both were in good spirits, excited to be getting the ball rolling. The journey was bringing back memories. They passed pubs that as younger men they'd drank, danced and fought in. Sites of music venues long gone. Highbury and Islington station where they'd brawled with a job lot of Arsenal one night in '82, Terry chasing one of their main men with a chain. Dan remembered everything.

'Well then,' Terry said. 'I'm finally going to meet your brother-in-law.'

'Yep, Concrete Kelly himself. You'll like him I reckon. He's good company, a bit full of himself but he's a real laugh.'

'How long's your little sister been married to him?'

'Three years now. You should see their house. Big place in Stanmore. She always wanted to marry a rich man. She was working in a hotel in Kempton when she met him. He was there for the nags and it was his birthday. Liz is thirty-five, he's sixty-two,' he laughed.

'Has Kelly been married before?'

'Three times. He's got seven kids.'

'I don't envy him there. How did he make his fortune?'

'Shipments of you-know-what in the eighties, early nineties. He was living out in the Dam for a while. Then he moved into VAT swindles and property and made an even bigger packet. He's into the nags now, always hanging around the racetracks. He keeps a legit front but can't resist these little one-offs though. The more you earn the greedier you get I suppose. But he stays behind the scene, keeps his hands clean. Mind you, he wasn't so careful when he was younger. You should hear some of the stories. There was this mob he used to run with. Some bloke ripped them off by twenty grand, saying a rival firm had nicked it. Kelly's lot knew he was lying. They were in the back room of a pub listening to his sob story. When he finished they looked at each other and laughed. Kelly gave the nod then one pulled out a hatchet and buried it straight in his head. They carried him out to the boot, all of them pissed, and drove down to Camden Town to lob him in the canal. They filled his pockets with rocks but he kept bobbing back up, so in the end they flung the fucker from a towerblock roof. Splat. Then they rolled back to the pub to continue the session.'

'Nice,' Terry smiled.

'Yeah, they're a bit wild over that way. Or certainly were back in the day anyway. Kelly's full of tales like that. I take them with a pinch of salt myself. He's a great craic though.'

Alighting at Kilburn High Road they paid off the cabbie. Across the road a group of black men were shouting and pushing each other. They sounded African. One pulled a long blade and the chaos escalated. A squad car sounded in the traffic and they fled down a backstreet.

'What happened to County Kilburn?' Terry said. 'I thought it was supposed to be Irish up this way?'

'It's turned into County Congo mate.'

They entered the boozer. The barman brought them upstairs to a private bar where Concrete Kelly held court. Sinatra crooned, two minders murmuring at the counter. Kelly occupied a table further up. Black suit, open-necked white shirt. Two men leaned forward as he recounted a story.

Kelly paused his flow when he saw the Dagenham boys.

'Here they come,' he smiled, flashing expensive dentistry. 'The terrible twosome.'

Dan introduced Terry, and Kelly offered him a firm handshake. 'Good to see you Terry son.' Then Kelly introduced the blokes at the table. Phil was a wiry man with alert eyes, one to watch, while Bernie was stockier, standard armed blagger written all over him.

Terry helped Dan bring the drinks over. As the barman prepared the Guinness Terry earwigged the conversation back at the table. He'd imagined Kelly to be a full-blown Paddy but he had a London accent, only the slightest Irish discernible.

'So the copper said it was impossible, he couldn't do it. So I says to him, anything on this earth is possible mate if you put your mind to it. Just get cracking and bring me that info or one of these days your wife will be receiving a nice set of photos in the post, and they won't be snaps of your last family holiday in

Greece either. No kids building sandcastles on the beach in this batch I'm afraid. I pulled one out to show him, gave him a little taster. Next morning he had everything we wanted. He never let me down again. He was always paid though, I'm not a complete cunt,' he laughed.

'What was on these photos anyway?' Bernie asked him.

'Let's just say they exhibited his enthusiasm for young teenage boys. We got the negatives from a safety deposit job. It's not all jewels hidden from the taxman you know; there's guns, powder, all sorts of shit. I heard an Islington firm found a stash of celebrity pictures of a similar nature and were so disgusted they handed them over to the law. Guess what happened? Fuck all. The snaps disappeared. The superintendent I had dealings with should've been in the slammer, no doubt about it, but what would he have got? Two, three years? Rob a bank and it's a different story. He was on our books for years. Paying for his sins. It was good while it lasted.'

'What happened to him?' asked Phil.

Kelly took a sip of whiskey. 'He shot himself in the head in the end. His wife walked in and there he was, his brains up the wall. Shame really. He wasn't half handy.'

Terry and Dan brought the drinks over and sat in.

'How's it swinging then Danny boy?' Kelly asked.

'To the left last time I looked.'

'Silly fucker. And finally I get to meet Terry. How are you mate?'

'I'm good. Glad to be here.'

'Dan tells me you're an experienced man.'

Terry laughed modestly. 'I've done this and that.'

'He knows what he's doing,' Dan said. 'He's done it plenty of times before.'

'So you're fit and willing?'

'I'm ready to make some money, yeah.'

'That's the best incentive.'

'It's the only incentive,' Dan grinned.

'Well on this bit of work you'll be pulling in six hundred large apiece,' Kelly said, quieter now. 'How does that sound?'

Terry pulled his chair in and smiled. 'Sounds like music to my ears.'

They all chatted for a bit, got acquainted, then Kelly took Terry aside for a talk about the work. It involved four mill that was stored in a lock-up in an unknown location near Luton. A money depot hit three years ago netted twenty-eight big ones. Most of the main players were tugged and a fair few mill returned. One of the gang however was only charged with handling, but unknown to the police had played a much larger part. He was due to be freed in a few weeks to enjoy his slice of the bounty. Their job was to kidnap him on the day of his release and relieve him of the cash. 'After all,' Kelly said, 'it's not his money is it, the thieving cunt.'

They laughed, clinked glasses. 'You've come well recommended Tel. So here's to success and financial comfort.'

Terry liked the sound of that, and as the night drew on he found Kelly to be an entertaining presence. Bernie and Phil seemed like decent blokes too. They were five or six years younger than him and Dan. Phil was a bit quiet at first, but he soon opened up. Bernie was sound from the off. Just like Terry, both had been out of the game for a while, but they'd done some hefty graft in the past and what's more, got away with it. These were the kind of people to work with. Men with normal jobs or businesses. Under the present radar. It turned out Phil was the governor of the pub and Bernie ran a garage up Watford.

Terry felt a renewed sense of motivation. The return of his old fire. He hadn't been himself in recent times. He'd been getting up to all sorts, venting his frustration in some careless ways. Moneywise he'd been scraping around at rock bottom, but the future looked different. It would be a whole new start.

Dan leaned in with a gleam in his eye. 'So what do you

reckon?'

Terry nodded. 'I think I made the right decision.'

'Stick with me and you'll have the big villa in the Marbella hills before you know it. Living the dream. Lying next to the pool tanning your bollocks.'

Terry knew this was it. The big one. There wasn't a problem on this earth a fat wedge of cash couldn't solve. He was sick of scratching around skint. A lack of money just caused aggravation. Grief at home and grief in your head. He looked around the table at the other men. All were happy, looking forward, as excited as him.

'So what do you say boys,' the London Irishman smiled. 'You reckon we can pull this one off?'

'Piece of piss,' Dan said, and all agreed.

'In that case,' Concrete Kelly rose his glass. 'Here's to success.'

*

Bigz sat watching *Eastenders*. The soap pissed him off no end, but it reminded him of Leona and he missed her. He called her number. Again there was no answer. She'd been ignoring him for weeks now and he wondered if they'd ever get back together. Then he had an idea. He grabbed his jacket and headed down to Sainsburys. He bought a box of chocolates and the largest bunch of red roses on offer. Then he jumped in his car and drove over to Archway. Twenty-five minutes later he was approaching the Elthorne Estate. One side of the estate was cordoned off with tape, police everywhere, probably a stabbing or some shit, so he parked on a street nearby and walked around to the next entry.

By Leona's block a group of youths were hanging by the concrete stairs. One of the guys was sitting in his way. Bigz screwed his face at him to move, which he did slowly and reluctantly.

'What ends you from?' one of them asked. 'You Finsbury

Park?'

Bigz turned to him, a thin African looking guy, guessed he was the joker of the pack.

'H-Town, E5,' Bigz said proudly, jutting his chin. 'You got a problem with that?'

'Just asking,' the boy said, a little rattled now. 'It's just that some of Six Acres came up earlier.' Then he added, 'They're in hospital now,' to a round of sniggers.

Bigz scanned the group. Six bodies, late-teens; three black, three white. If he didn't have a poncey bunch of flowers and Milk Tray in his hand he might've set the cat among the pigeons. But fuck it, he was on a romantic mission right now. He gave a laugh and headed up. The day you start fearing crews like Archway it's time to get out of London.

He stood outside Leona's flat. The lights were on and he could hear the TV. He readied himself. They hadn't spoken in a while so at least she'd be calm, even if she did tell him to piss off. He rang the bell and waited. He heard her approach, undo the bolt. 'Jeez, I'm coming.'

Opening the door she blinked. 'Oh, it's you.'

'I know you weren't expecting me, but I thought I'd just give you these.'

'Er, thanks.' She took the flowers and chocolates but seemed distracted. An awkward pause followed.

'Aren't you going to invite me in?'

'It's a bad time right now.' She glanced behind her.

'Who's at the door, Lee?' a male voice called from inside.

Bigz and Leona locked eyes. He was shocked at her betrayal, while Leona looked almost sorrowful. She dropped her gaze, 'I told you it wasn't a good time B.'

A Turkish-looking guy appeared up the hall dressed in a white towel.

Bigz stormed through and pushed him in the chest. 'Who the fuck are you? What you doing with my girl?'

The man was all muscle no fat, and he pushed Bigz back with force, telling him to get the hell out of here. Then Bigz pulled out a little .32 and pointed it at him.

The guy flinched at something over Bigz's shoulder; Bigz gave a quick glance to check and the piece was snatched from his grasp.

'Down on the floor now!' the man ordered, gun trained in two hands.

Bigz was stunned. How did he fall for that trick? Hands-up, he slowly lowered himself. Impatient, the Turk pushed him face-down.

He told Leona to frisk him. She found a knife tied to his left shin. He ordered Bigz to crawl to the corner and sit. As Bigz moved he eyed the man with hatred. His reward was a gun-smack across the head.

'What the fuck?' he said, fingers coming away bloody.

'You're lucky I don't blow your head away.'

Leona passed Bigz a towel for his wound, then stood next to her man. 'Don't try anything B. Mehmet spent two years in the Turkish army and four in the police force over there. You're lucky you're still alive after bursting in here with a gun.'

'I was shocked after seeing you weren't alone, is that okay with you?'

'No, it's not actually. You've just proved I made the right decision in terminating our relationship.'

'First I heard. We've had breaks before and you haven't run off with other men.' He looked at the man then dropped his eyes, all the fight gone from him. 'What are you still pointing that thing at me for?'

Leona nodded and Mehmet lowered the gun. He removed the ammo clip and tossed the weapon back to Bigz. 'It's yours. Have fun with it.'

Bigz put it away, towel piled up on his head.

'You need to sort yourself out,' Leona told him. 'Stop running around thinking you're this big gangster, because you're looking pretty pathetic right now.'

Bigz removed the towel. The blood seemed to have clotted.

'I think you better go.' She stood back to let him stand up.

Bigz turned to Mehmet. 'You gonna give us a moment of privacy to say goodbye or what?'

'I don't want a moment of privacy with you Bigz,' Leona said. 'Those days are over. I'm moving to Hertfordshire with Mehmet, so don't come over again, I won't be here.'

Bigz looked at her. Then he shook his head and left. By the front door Leona said good luck and it closed behind him.

Downstairs the youths were still there. 'Where's your flowers bro?' one quipped and the group burst out laughing.

Bigz lunged forward and punched him to the ground.

The pack set on him.

For a while Bigz held his own, kicking and striking out, deflecting the worst of it, until he was coshed over the head from behind and his vision burst with stars. He hit the deck, their shouts distorted now, fading in volume, kicks mere vibrations as he slipped into the black.

Further up, a witness stood watching from the shadows. Six figures laying in to a prone body. 'Enough,' one said and finally they stepped back. He got down to check the man's pockets. He pulled out something shiny, held it in his hand. A phone, knife, gun, it was impossible to tell. The boys gathered to look at it. Then they ran.

17

Tall Dark Handsome

Quinn walked into Phil's pub and pulled a stool. A girl served him a pint and he spied Phil at the end of the counter reading a paper, knowing any second he'd look up and jump when he clocked him. Quinn counted the seconds, one, two, and Phil didn't disappoint him. He glanced up and almost leapt out of his skin. Talk about subtle. Quinn raised his drink and smiled. Fucking plank. He watched Phil right himself and walk over as if all was fine and dandy. He'd noticed how Phil put on the charm for customers, always a quip and a smile. But not far below the surface was an uneasy man indeed.

'Thought you were going to have a coronary there, Phil.'

'I was just surprised. How are you?'

'Good, you?'

'Doing my best - just getting on, you know.'

'You'll be doing your best soon,' Quinn winked discreetly. 'I know that much.'

Phil went to serve a punter and he let him stew on those words. He took a look around the pub. It was still a bit early, the place scattered with mostly old timers.

As the barmaid came to wipe the counter in front of him, he

noticed a resemblance and realised she must be Phil's daughter. She had the same dark hair and eyebrows. She smiled politely and he said, 'So what's a nice girl like you working in a tip like this for?'

She stopped smiling, narrowed her eyes. 'My dad runs this place. And last time I looked it wasn't a tip.'

She marched away and Quinn laughed, eyeing her up and down as she went. He liked her already. She had more spunk than her old man, that's for sure.

Phil had heard their exchange and looked embarrassed.

'Go and take your break,' he hissed.

'I just did half an hour ago.'

His face was red. 'I said go and take a fucking break.'

The girl disappeared and Quinn looked away, pretended not to hear. Let the man have some pride at least.

Phil came over. He threw the towel over his shoulder, leaned over the bar.

'So tell me,' Quinn asked him, 'how did it go last night?'

'We met the rest of the team. It went well.'

Quinn took a lug of his pint. 'You're all set to earn me a packet then. Better late than never, don't you reckon?'

Phil looked down. 'We meant to pay you. We thought we'd have made the cash back by the time you were released. We just didn't think...'

'Shut up Phil.' He couldn't believe the gall of the cunt. Lying to him yet again. 'Just do the work and get me my money, you fucking cockroach.'

Phil nodded, then went to serve somebody.

The job's date was only a few weeks away. And it was all thanks to Del Daly. Sharing a cell with the Luton crim had been a stroke of luck. Daly was no pushover, and part of a serious firm, but found doing time a mental strain, which can be a weakness up for exploitation. He liked his pills and hooch, crutches that can expose you to vulnerability. Del was a talker and Quinn a good listener. Del was loose with a secret one night and it was pure gold. The one thing preventing him from topping himself was the windfall stored away for him when he got out – which was now coming up. Quinn used this intel to the best of his ability, but naturally he needed to keep his own hands clean right now. That's why he'd called in Concrete Kelly. There was no better man to oversee such a job to completion. Where there was cash to be found, Kelly never went home empty handed. Quinn didn't want to jinx it by getting too excited, but a few weeks from now life would be a whole lot better.

He went to the gents, got chopping and hoovered up a fat one. It's funny how in the nick the most he'd done was a bit of hooch, he hardly even touched weed, then out he comes and he's back on the drink and powder like there's no tomorrow. He washed his hands, looked at his face in the mirror. He might've been away for a while, but he still had his looks, that's one thing. He smoothed his hair, had a bit of a quiff going these days. Pride in your appearance was an important thing. He considered how many blokes let themselves go to pot. Let it all hang out. Gave up caring. Either that or they got bogged down with responsibilities and lost their spirit, their sense of adventure. Turned into old men before their time. Take Phil for example. All nervous energy, craving the next belt of brandy to see him through the day. What sort of life was that? He drove a tatty-looking Mondeo with a key mark up the side. Must have pissed all that money up against the wall. Bernie was the smart one. Shrewd as fuck when he thought about it. But old Phil was like an open book. A real snake of a man. If you're going to practice the dark art of deception, be good at it at least. He'd never fully trusted the bloke, even in the old days. He was good on the team, had a lot of drive, or plain old greed more like, which in the blagging game is no bad thing, but shake the cunt's hand and you'd do well to count your fingers afterwards.

Back at the bar he took a few more inches off his Guinness.

'You doing alright there Sean?' Phil called over.

Quinn nodded. He recalled his chat with Bernie the other night. Emerging from the shadows to freak him out. It was comical now thinking about it. He'd given it the psycho touch, hinting how he'd been watching his family. Phil's too. How things could turn nasty on that score. He wasn't sure about that now and wondered if he'd gone too far. They were mad if they thought he'd harm women or children. But what choice did he have with the conniving cunts.

Phil's daughter was back behind the bar. She was acting sulky, something Quinn, with nothing much else to do with his day, found greatly entertaining. She was an average-enough looker in the face but had a decent bit of shape to her, he had to admit. He wondered what Phil would think if he got to grips with his beloved daughter. The more he considered the idea, the more it grew in appeal. Watching her, he liked what he saw. Before the night was out he planned to make the feeling mutual.

'You like working here don't you?' he said as she poured him another drink.

'Not when I'm serving you I don't.'

'Don't worry, you'll get used to it,' he laughed, watching Phil turn his head, concerned at that prospect.

'I don't think so.'

'You will,' he smiled. 'You'll come round eventually. They always do.'

She met his gaze. 'Do they now?'

'Yes they do.'

'Well maybe I'm different.'

He noticed her big blue-green eyes, could almost see the rolling Irish hills reflected in them. Freckles sprinkled her nose. He'd been wrong about her face. The girl was pretty.

'You're right on that score,' he agreed. 'You are different. I noticed that as soon as I walked in.'

'Is that a compliment then?'

'What do you think?'

She shook her head. 'Men.'

'That's right, real men. There's a shortage of them nowadays.' He glanced at Phil, up the way pulling the bitter pump, pretending not to hear.

'You're not wrong there,' she said, not getting it.

'So naturally it's nice to see a real woman around,' he continued. 'Like you.'

'You really need some better lines,' she said. But he'd got a smile out of her at last.

'What's your name?' he asked.

'Tara.'

'Quinn,' he put out his hand. 'Sean Quinn.'

'Suave, aren't you?' She shook it, squeezing hard.

'Jesus,' he said. 'You're quite the tiger, aren't you?'

'I take no shit.'

'I can well see that.'

The pub was locked for the night and Phil was upstairs having a row with his 19-year-old daughter. Tara was bold and wilful, the type that would do the opposite just to spite you. The more he warned her never to speak to that customer again - the man she'd spent half the night flirting with - the more she insisted she'd talk to whoever she liked and he wasn't going to stop her.

He slammed his fist on the table. 'In that case you'll get out of my fucking house.'

'That's enough.' His wife Maureen, Tara's stepmum, got between them. 'Now stop over-reacting,' she told him. 'Calm yourself down.'

Tara stormed off but he kept talking.

'I'm telling you now, young lady. You'll do what I say in my house or you can pack your bags and piss off.'

'Go fuck yourself.' She slammed her bedroom door behind her. Then she grabbed a cushion and flung it across the room.

Her dad was a nutcase - worse, an alcoholic nutcase. She'd been talking with a customer? Big deal. The bloke was probably twice her age. It was only a bit of a laugh. Why was her dad going crazy over a harmless bit of fun? Because he didn't want her to be happy, that's why. He wanted her to be miserable like him. She took out her phone and looked at the man's name: Sean. She felt like phoning him right now just to piss her dad off. She put in so many hours behind that bar and never got a word of praise from him, even though all the customers liked her. And now a man came in saying she was attractive and full of life and was wasting herself working there, and her dad didn't like that.

Sean seemed to be an old acquaintance of his, but her dad hadn't been very friendly with him, that's for sure. Maybe they didn't know each other that well. Tara hadn't liked the bloke at first either, but he won her round and in between serving they'd spent the next few hours bantering. Her dad disappeared upstairs at one point and when he came down to lock up he was half-cut. He must've been up in the office, knocking back the brandy as he watched them on the CCTV monitor. He'd been acting so strange lately, nothing would surprise her. But if she wanted to talk to a male customer and accept a few drinks it was her business.

As he left, Sean said he'd phone her, and she'd carried on the game: 'You know I won't answer it.' Then he'd winked and said, 'We'll see about that.' And here she was thinking of calling him right now. He lived in Edgware and never went to bed until the early hours. 'Oh well, another night alone.' He'd practically been saying come-home-with-me all night. She pictured herself in his strong arms. Somebody who liked her, appreciated her. She imagined them in bed, Sean on top of her. He had a fire in his eyes, a way about him that promised excitement, a world away from the run of the mill, and she needed some of that right now. Her finger teetered over the ring button. Then she put her phone down. No, it was a silly thought. She stood up and looked at herself in the mirror. She hated her body and wished she was slimmer. She turned to the side, held in her belly and pushed her chest out. But maybe Sean didn't care about things like that. Maybe he liked a fuller figure. Why else did he show her attention if he didn't like what he saw? Again she picked up her phone. She was unsure what to do. But anything would be better than sleeping in this madhouse tonight.

Maureen knocked and Tara told her to come in.

'Your father's had a bit too much to drink tonight, take no notice of him.'

'That's what you always say. I'm sick of him, I hate him.'

'Come on Tara, don't talk like that. He said you were giving a man too much attention down there.'

'What's wrong with that? Does he think I'm still a child or something?'

'Some of the customers are rough. You don't want to be getting involved. Remember last time.'

A few weeks ago she'd gone out with a Dubliner called Joey. The eejit had been begging to take her out for weeks. He wasn't much of a looker, had teeth not far off Shane MacGowan, but she couldn't deny he was a laugh. They went to a late music pub down the road and got seriously pissed. Walking back to his tenth-floor flat in the South Kilburn Estate, Joey spent half the journey wearing a road cone over his head and got into two fights, the first with an idiot who was singing Oasis songs in the road, the second with two East Europeans that earned him a black eye and some kicks on the ground, but still she slept with him. At dawn they were woken to his front door being kicked in as armed police stormed the place. They tore Joey out of the bed yelling about firearms, while Tara clutched the sheets. Finally a copper came in with a bagged handgun saying, 'Found it lads.' Joey was arrested; they let Tara go. The replica belonged to one of Joey's flatmates who was out.

'You don't want to go through all that again, do you?'

'Of course not, but we were only chatting. Dad's just blowing this up.'

'Maybe he knows something about the man you don't.'

'If that was the case he'd say.'

'He's worried about you, that's all.'

Maureen left the room and again Tara looked at herself in the mirror. She lit a cigarette, pulled a sultry face. I suppose she wasn't too bad-looking when she thought about it. She opened the window and smoked, looking down at the cars and night-buses passing along the High Road. An angry drunk staggered along the pavement, tipping over a bin behind him. A couple gave him a swerve.

Just then she got a text. It was Sean.

*

Lil Killa's internet sessions were paying off. He'd tracked down another of his abusers. Popping some pills he set off in a stolen car to a new build-estate in Epping. He was dressed in a boiler suit and gloves, and for good measure he'd brought a meat cleaver. Meat was how the man had treated him, so as chopped-up meat would the bastard meet his end. His name was Chapman. Back at the kids' home he was one of Lil's guardians, paid to keep those in his care safe and well. He lived alone. Lil took the A104 and in thirty minutes approached the Essex commuter town.

He parked in and sat watching the house. Memories flooded his senses. Chapman had been particularly brutal, a man who had revelled in other people's pain. Lil remembered one night being driven to the forest, Chapman and two others in the car, men in suits with loud demanding voices. Men of high standing who commanded respect, Chapman told him. They were drunk, passing a bottle of red wine, Lil between them in the back hallucinating from the drugs they'd administered. He was pulled out of the car and led through the woods. Demons flashed in and out of the trees, jeering, shrieking. They stopped at a clearing. The men wore animal masks now, one holding his neck so tight he couldn't breathe. He remembered the taste of soil, an evil symphony screaming in his ears, the forest on fire around him. Ritual over, they dragged him back to the car. They travelled in silence now. Chapman warned him not to tell tales or his life wouldn't be worth living. He was a lowly nobody and they were powerful men, units of a larger swarm, a network that ran to the very top of society. There was no escape, nowhere to run. Laughing as he said we're everywhere, in every crevice, even inside your own head.

Lil grabbed his cleaver and kit of tools, got out and walked over to the house. He knocked, the man answered and Lil Killa led him inside at gunpoint. Chapman looked shrunken, different from the ogre of his memories, but he smelled the same, wore the same glasses over rat-like eyes. A laptop was playing porn, the television low in the background. On the sofa his former care-leader began to cry. Lil Killa explained who he was, asked if he remembered him. Chapman said no, yes, maybe. He said he was sorry, admitted he'd done things he wasn't proud of and regretted everything. The man was a liar. Lil Killa threw him a roll of tape, told him to put it over his mouth.

'Don't kill me, please.'

'Just do it.'

'I can't.'

'Do it and you might live. Don't and I'll shoot you in the fucking balls right now.'

Chapman did it.

Lil ordered him to stand, hold his arms behind his back. Taping them, he kicked him to the floor and taped his legs. He set down his tool kit and began working on the bastard for a full thirty minutes. By the time he was finished Chapman was nailed and sawn and cut to ribbons.

Lil Killa stood to survey his work, the room now dripping red, swirling around him; in his ears the whooshing and whispering of ghosts. In a trance he left the house carrying Chapman's severed head by the hair. The road was quiet, people tucked safely in their homes staring at their screens, lost in distraction. Lil slung it in the back and drove.

Bigz woke up in hospital with a body full of aches and pains. Two feds were sitting at his bedside.

'So Joe, you're finally with us? I'm Detective Reilly and this is Detective McKay.'

'Hi there, Joseph,' McKay said. 'Or should I say Bigz?'

Reilly was your typical cockney copper, while McKay was an older no-nonsense Glaswegian.

'We're from Trident,' McKay continued, 'and your mug has been on our wall for quite some time now. You're a wee bit of a celebrity in our office. So tell me, why the long face?'

Bigz crossed his arms, refused to speak.

'Got yourself in a spot of bother, didn't you mate,' the cockney said.

'That's right. Had seven shades of shite kicked out of you by those pesky Archway boys,' the Scot added. 'And there was me thinking you Hackney men were the top dogs? All this running round working for Hot Iron Mike is making you careless I daresay.'

Bigz was stumped at that but tried to hide his shock. How did they know all this?

'If I'm not under arrest then you're wasting your time.'

'In case you've forgotten, you were carrying a gun the other night, so shortly you will be under arrest and facing serious charges. Let me see now,' McKay scratched his chin. 'How many years inside for possession of an illegal firearm?'

'A mandatory five,' Reilly said. 'But with all your previous, you'd be looking at double that.'

'You can't prove it's mine though can you?' Bigz said. 'You could've planted that shit on me.'

'With your fingerprints all over it? Don't think so mate. You're taking a long holiday.'

'Don't forget to send us a postcard,' the cockney added. Both laughed.

'Anyway,' Reilly checked his watch. 'We're off duty now, so I've got a date with a pint of lager.'

'Count me in and add a wee dram.' They stood, put on their raincoats.

'All I can say fella, is get yourself a good lawyer.'

This wasn't the first time Bigz had been through this pantomime, but they'd got his gun, his prints all over it, so without a doubt he was looking at time.

'Wait.'

'No can do,' the Scot said putting up his coat collar. 'We're off to the boozer – and you, my son, are going to jail.'

They left the room. 'I said wait,' Bigz called.

McKay popped his head around the door. 'You know the score, Bigz. If you're no gonnae talk we're wasting our time.'

'I'll talk, if you drop the charges.'

For an hour they filled their notebooks, pending a lengthier kiss 'n' tell.

'Okay, you've just earned yourself a get-out-of-jail card. Behave yourself and we look forward to continuing the conversation.'

Walking along the corridor McKay put his hand out to his partner. 'I told you he'd talk. Now you owe me twenty quid.'

Reilly handed over the cash. 'I can't believe it worked.'

'My methods always work, son. You'll learn.'

'We had hardly anything on him and he was singing away.'

'All you need is a few key facts - you make up the rest. The witness thought he saw a gun.'

'He also said he wasn't sure, it could've been anything.'

'I took a gamble and it paid off. For me anyway,' the Scot added, patting his pocket.

'Drinks are on you then, I presume Mac?'

'I wouldn't get carried away there, young fella.'

*

Quinn rolled off her and they lay back on the bed.

'You're a lively one, I'll tell you that.'

'You're not too bad yourself,' Tara smiled.

'Wonder what your old man would say about all this.'

'No doubt he'd have a fit. You should've heard him earlier, ranting at me to get out of his house, all because I talked to you.'

'He's a character your dad, I'll tell you that much.'

'He's an alcoholic more like. He drinks real Martell himself but fills his optics with cheapo shit from the cash 'n' carry. He's a crook.'

'All pubs do that, don't they?'

'Don't care. It's dishonest. I don't know what my stepmum ever saw in him. Or my real mum.'

He didn't reply to that. He knew that Phil's first wife had died young from cancer.

'He's got his bad points, but he's alright your dad really. Deep down I mean.'

She leaned up on her elbow and looked at him.

'You knew him back in the day. What crimes did he commit?'

'Same stuff as any of us. Just making money. But that can get you into a lot of trouble.'

'If you steal it, yeah.'

'The banks steal it. They're the biggest crooks out there.'

She rolled her eyes. 'So he didn't hurt anyone?'

'Of course not. He just did a bit of borderline stuff here and there. Still does with his optics.'

'Is it true he did armed robberies?'

'Ask him yourself. I'd be interested to know what he'd say.'

'I asked my stepmum once, because he was away for a while when I was younger. Almost a year. They told me he was working on a building site in Germany.'

'They told you that?'

'Don't worry, I know where he really was because my cousin told me. He was inside.'

'And does your stepmum know you know that?'

'Of course, and my dad. We had a row a few years back and I told them never to lie to me again.'

'You can understand why they lied though. They were trying to protect you. You were a kid.'

'Yeah, suppose.'

She leaned up and turned to him. 'Were you close mates back then?'

'I knew everyone on the manor. But then I moved to Ireland, been there for the past decade or so. It's kept me out of trouble.'

'So you weren't in the slammer with him back then?'

'No chance,' he laughed. 'They'd never get me alive. I'd go out guns blazing.'

She lay back down. 'Don't talk to me about guns. I went home with a bloke a few weeks back. In the morning armed police steamed in and pulled him out of bed. One of them was pointing a machine-gun at me.'

'Really?'

'Yeah.'

'Were you naked?'

'I was actually,' she smiled.

'I'd like to have been there.'

They leaned in to kiss.

When Tara got home her dad was at the table, an uneaten plate of toast in front of him, eyes bloodshot like he'd had a hard night.

'Maureen, she's here,' he called, then to Tara: 'Where have you been all night?'

'That's my business.' She went to the fridge for some orange juice.

He scraped his chair back, came towards her.

'You tell me right now where you've been, you little madam, or your days are numbered here.'

Maureen entered the kitchen. 'Now that's enough, will you two stop rowing?'

'I want to know where she was last night.'

'And I'm telling you it's none of your business,' Tara said.

'You were with him, weren't you?' he shouted.

His wife urged him to keep it down.

'Answer me, girl.'

Tara turned to him, unable to hide a smirk. 'So what if I was?' She held his stare. Her dad was the first to back down. He turned away and seemed to crumble, reaching behind him for a seat. Suddenly he seemed old.

'Look at what you've done to your dad now,' Maureen said.

'I didn't do anything.'

He sat there, leaning on his temples, all the fight gone from him.

Maureen comforted him. 'Are you all right Phil?' He gave a slight nod, but looked defeated.

Maureen shot her a wicked look. 'You've fucking well upset your father now, that's what you've done.' She didn't often swear.

'Dad,' Tara said, guilty now as she'd never seen him like this. 'I was around my friend Fiona's house. I spent the night there.'

Phil turned to her and they looked at each other. Her birth mum Angie had died when she was two years old and first Phil's parents, then Angie's parents, looked after her until he married Maureen six years later. He wondered if the trauma had affected Tara; losing her mother then moving from one set of people to another, not to mention being fatherless when he'd spent that year on remand. Phil hadn't been a good father. He knew that. He had a criminal past, had led an irresponsible life without a care for those closest, those who worried about him while he had run around living it up with selfish greedy men who were just as rotten as him.

He even blamed himself for the cancer that killed Tara's mother. Angie was a needy type and he hadn't often been there for her, always out drinking, earning, or going with other women, leaving her to bring up Tara alone. Then he'd carried on the same way when Angie was gone. He wasn't a good man. And now look at the state of him. His sins were coming back to haunt him.

Tara looked the spit of Angie but had inherited all his own worst traits. His stubbornness and short fuse - and the way she threw back shorts behind the bar she could soon be sharing his drink problem. She was making mistakes, involving herself in people best avoided, just like he had. Craving risk and excitement. In his case it had been the mates he hung around with; with her it was men.

And here she was, denying that she'd spent the night with that bastard Quinn. He looked into his daughter's eyes, both of them knowing she was lying.

18

Head on a Plate

Bigz was back in his pad after several days in hospital. He sat watching daytime TV. A panel of four women discussing men and depression. Men tended to suffer their woes in silence, refusing to tell anybody or seek help, which was a factor in why their suicide rate was three times higher. Damn right, Bigz muttered, as he glumly puffed on a blunt. He'd never felt this low. His girl had betrayed him, some lowdown pussies had kicked him into hospital, and to his eternal shame he was now a fucking police grass.

He'd given Reilly and McKay the kind of shit they wanted to hear, but soon they'd want some real-life info to chew on or he'd be doing jail time. They'd even phoned this morning about some murder in Epping, a guy nailed to the floorboards and mutilated. As if Lil would do shit like that. He exhaled. Then he thought of Leona and groaned. He felt like going back to bed.

His phone rang and he picked it up. It was Lil. He asked if he was home.

'Nah fam, I'm sunning myself on Montego beach.'

'You're home then. Let me up, I'm outside.'

Bigz buzzed him up then let him into the flat. They sat down.

'I got 'em,' Lil smiled. 'I got two of them.'

'Who?'

'The Archway crew. I pulled up last night, fired into a bunch of them and two are in hospital now all fucked up with bullet wounds. I made sure to shout Hackney too.'

Bigz sat up, grinning for the first time in days. 'You did that?'

Lil nodded. 'The police think it's some feud they've got with Finsbury Park. Clueless or what? But Archway know so who gives a fuck.'

'Rah man,' Bigz said, the news warming him like a happy pill. He slapped the armrest. 'That's the best thing I've heard for fucking time.'

'They won't mess with H-Town again, that's for sure.'

'I appreciate this Lil, I really do.'

'No worries. How you feeling considering?'

'Still a bit rough, but I'll pull through. One thing though Lil, watch out for the feds. They were all over me at that hospital.'

'Fuck the feds, they're clueless.'

'Not as much as you think,' Bigz said.

His comment was met with silence. Lil had sensed something, his eyes scrutinizing him. Suddenly Bigz wished he hadn't spoken.

'What do you mean by that?' Lil asked.

'Nothing. I'm just saying be careful.'

Lil leaned forward. 'I'm always careful, but I get the feeling you meant something specific there. Like they told you something.'

'No way. They were just firing a lot of questions. But you know me, I don't speak to the fuckers. I just sat there waiting for them to piss off.'

Lil Killa left those words hanging as he observed him like a shark. Bigz didn't know where to look.

'You were carrying your piece that night, weren't you B?'

Lil's intuition stunned him. Was the guy a freaking mind reader?

'You're lying to me,' Lil said and stood up. 'I can see right through you.'

'You been smoking crack or something?' Bigz laughed. 'I told you, just be careful in case they know more than we think.'

'They caught you carrying and turned you, didn't they?'

Bigz got up. 'You calling me some kind of grass?'

They both stared, Bigz in vexation, Lil with a knowing glint. 'You tell me.'

'I just did. I have a policy, I don't talk to no cops, ever.'

'I bet you did in hospital though.'

Bigz tutted, tried another tack. 'Are you trying to piss me off?'

Lil Killa looked him up and down. Then finally he relaxed and swiped the air. 'Forget about it. Calm yourself.'

Bigz shook his head and they sat back down.

'I've been through untold shit lately Lil. A little bit of sympathy wouldn't go amiss you know.'

'Forget I said anything.' Lil put his fist out and Bigz spudded it. 'You've been through the mill, I know that. It must've been hard - what happened with your girl and stuff.'

'Yeah well, you just have to move on. Keep your head up. No point moping around about it.'

They watched the box for a bit, laughing at how lame daytime TV was, then Lil got up. 'Wait here, I want to show you something.' He headed for the door.

'Where you going?'

'Just down to the car. I'll be back in a minute.'

He left and once more Bigz felt uneasy. Was Lil playing with him? What if he was going down to get a gun or knife? Just in case, Bigz checked for the blade he kept down the side of his chair, made sure it was easy to access.

Lil returned holding a plastic bag with something wet and weighty inside. Bigz caught a scent and wondered if it was some kind of food. It smelled like off meat. Lil told him to put a plate on the table. Then he pulled out the contents and placed it down. Staring back at them was a severed human head.

'Jesus fuck!' Bigz said, jolting back.

Lil Killa calmly sat down, lacing his fingers. 'That's one I did the other night.'

Suddenly the smell was rancid. Bigz turned to Lil, knowing for certain what he'd probably always known, except now it was flashing loud and clear in neon lights. His partner was a full-blown psychopath.

'What did you bring that in here for?' Bigz gasped.

'To show you, B.'

Lil stood up and made for the door. 'You know what, I'm going to leave him here so you can have some company tonight. By the way, his name's Chapman.'

'Why are you doing this?'

'Because I want to see if you blab to your new friends about it. Think of it as a test of allegiance.'

'I want this fucking thing out of my flat!'

'He ain't going nowhere. So sit down and have a long think. You're either on the road or with the feds. You can't do both. But if you think you can, take a good look at that guy there.'

Bigz knew he was defeated. He turned to Lil with imploring eyes and his confession seemed to silently pass between them.

'Aha...'

Lil stepped away from the door and Bigz wondered if the guy possessed some kind of juju powers, because next thing he was spilling all, the confession gushing out of his mouth. Gently, Lil led him to his seat. 'Take it easy,' he said with the calm assurance of a priest. 'One thing at a time now.'

'They found my gun and said I'd go down for years, so I talked. But I only told them a pile of shit, I promise you. I said nothing incriminating, I swear down.'

Lil told him he'd made a mistake but honesty was the best

policy now. Yes, he should've taken his chances, but it didn't have to be a disaster. If they played it clever they could even work this mess in their favour. You run your handlers while they think they're running you. So he'd have to start at the beginning, remember everything he'd told them.

Bigz felt the lifting of a great burden, but one he might have hell to pay for.

19

Daytime Drinking

Bernie's phone sounded just as he'd begun spraying a motor. This had better be important.

'I'm going to kill him,' Phil said. 'I'm putting one in the back of his head.'

'You what?' Bernie went to his office and closed the door.

'You heard me. He's gone too far now. I want the fucker taken out.'

'Okay, you've been drinking. What time is it? Eleven a.m and you're already lagging?'

'You don't know what the bastard's gone and done.'

'I know well what he's done, but it's not the end of the world. Actually I was thinking, I reckon we can do a deal with him about maybe getting a cut of money from the job ourselves. Obviously give him the lion's share but...'

'He slept with my daughter.'.

'What?'

'He fucked my daughter, Bern.'

For a moment Bernie was silent. 'Tara? No way.'

'He was in the pub last night, chatting her up right in front of me. Upstairs I had a row with her about it, then she disappeared and spent the whole night with the cunt.'

'I don't know what to say Phil... I mean, are you sure about this?'

'I'm sure about one thing, I'm putting a bullet in him. I've still got a gun you know.'

'Hold on. We need to meet and talk. I know you're raging and so would I be, but nothing done in anger or haste ever works out, you and I both know that.'

'I hear you, but I've had it with him. He's laughing at us, the both of us. For all we know he could be setting us up with this job, wanting us inside doing time just like he's done. That's the sort of thing the bastard would do.'

Bernie hadn't considered this possibility.

'Don't tell me you trust the fucker,' Phil went on. 'He just wants to send us down and have a good old laugh about it. Did you see that smarmy old prick Kelly last week? Full of shit. The bloke has probably never got his hands dirty in his life. He gets other mugs to do it for him. And those two cockneys, who the fuck are they? We're dealing with strangers here. The whole thing's a game of revenge. We're being set up.'

'I don't know Phil - one of those blokes is Kelly's brother-in-law.'

'Yeah, right. We don't know them from Adam. Quinn is gunning for us. Look at what he's just done to headfuck me. He's playing a game here. Even if we do the job and he gets his pay-off, you think he's going to leave it at that? What he's done with my daughter is probably only the beginning. I wouldn't be surprised if we end up riddled in bullets. We've got to take control of this.'

Finishing their call, Bernie was worried.

It wasn't yet noon and Quinn was on the bus travelling down Cricklewood Broadway. He'd just done a gym session on the weights and planned on some lunch, then maybe he'd pop into the pub, see how Tara's auld fella was doing. He passed The Crown, a big old Irish boozer that since he'd been away had turned into a posh hotel-restaurant complex. Its grand terracotta frontage remained, and apparently you could still get a pint at the bar, but after a multi-million internal makeover it was far from the grass-roots haunt of old. It was hard to believe the site of so many sessions spanning generations had gone so upmarket. Along the Broadway with its tatty little shops, such opulence seemed out of place. He imagined the fights through the decades on the forecourt, friendships made and maintained in the smoky bars inside. For as long as he remembered, men lined the road here each morning awaiting the subby vans that picked them up for a day's labour on the buildings. He heard it still happened, except now it was East Europeans waiting for the start.

Quinn thought of his old man, long deceased now. He'd been in the building game all his life and all he had to show for it at the end was a knackered body full of aches and pains. Playing the straight game didn't pay. If you wanted money and weren't born with a silver spoon up your arse, you had to get out there and take it. He remembered his first big job. He was nineteen and carrying bricks for thirty quid a day when the Donnelly brothers took him on a jeweller's raid. Balaclavas, sledgehammers, shotguns. The buzz was unbelievable. Smashing fuck out of the place, he knew he was made for this kind of work. It certainly beat shovelling shit for a living. He was paid eight hundred quid. God knows how much the D brothers made, but to Quinn it was like winning the pools. He wasn't complaining. They spent the weekend drinking and clubbing, having the craic, enjoying the best of life, and from then on frequent graft kept his pockets lined, until the Donnelly's did an impromptu bank job on their own one time and it all went tits up. During a high-speed chase they smashed into a lorry on a slip-road off the A1. Ray was killed instantly; Kevin lived but was in bad health and later topped himself in prison.

But life goes on. Quinn had apprenticed with the best and he put a team together to take things to the next level. Success became their second name. His firm were the boys now. Out doing jobs, scams, fingers in all sorts of pies. Nothing happened on the manor without their say so. It was good while it lasted.

He considered his time away. He was lucky to get released, but after a decade inside it's a different world out there. Everything's changed, your network is defunct and you're back to ground zero, working from scratch. But fuck it, things were on the cards. With Concrete Kelly taking care of the Del Daly job he'd soon be laughing.

Kelly was his dad's cousin. The two never got on. His dad saw the bloke as full of himself, in the pub showing off his gold cufflinks, a man who'd started on a concrete lorry. For years Quinn wondered why they rarely talked. Then he heard that back in the day they'd had a big fight one night outside the Gresham on Holloway Road. His dad left Kelly minus some teeth. It was the only time anyone remembered a man walking away from such a slight. But they were family after all. Kelly would always joke, How's your auld fella, has he still got the big old fists on him? But one thing was for sure, he was a man that got things done.

Quinn was looking down at the passers-by as the bus crawled along Shoot Up Hill towards Kilburn tube. His phone went. It was his brother Noel. He said he had some bad news. Kelly had been raided and charged with being part of a race-fixing syndicate. They also found a loaded gun and a bag of precious rocks from some big jewellery job last year. He was being held on remand and it was unlikely he'd be able to buy his way out of this one. Basically, Kelly was fucked.

Hanging up Quinn had to compose himself. The job was up in the air now, but an even bigger worry was if Kelly started singing to the police. Trapped in a corner people do all sorts of things and he wouldn't put it past him. If he grassed about the upcoming job, pushed it all onto Quinn, the police would start watching him which he definitely didn't need. It was all too risky now.

But he refused to worry. He'd already been flirting with some other ideas, keeping a few things on the backburner. Last week he'd spent some days out on a bike spying on a money depot near St Albans, watching the vans come and go, noting times, patterns, gathering intel. Something for the future just in case. Now it looked like he might have to put in the hours, think more seriously about that one. But there were others. Smaller bits and pieces Bernie and Phil could pull off for him no problem. Pocket money for the time being. It was a fucking shock about Kelly though, the bastard getting banged up just when he needed him. The whole thing unsettled him. He'd left the house in a good mood today as well.

A youngster at the back of the bus was conversing loudly on his phone. He was spitting the street lingo, some wannabe gangsta, the type who in a Cat A nick would be swiftly brought down to size. Quinn recalled the time in Long Lartin when a similarly noisy upstart who'd just hit twenty-one came on the wing upsetting the equilibrium. He thought he was still roleplaying on the street. When confronted he listed off some supposedly-feared names. Nobody had heard of them. People weren't happy and something had to be done. When he made the mistake of swiping some tobacco from a lifer's pad, it sealed his fate. Inside, burglary doesn't get you a slap on the wrist. He was woken from a nap with boiling water. Then Quinn prised his jaws open while a murderer from Leeds tried to cut his tongue out. They never saw him again. He imagined the boy got the message. On the outside however, unless pushed, Quinn would live and let live. He thought of the Kelly job and stopped smiling. It was all down the can, but getting pissed off wouldn't put money in his pocket so he'd try to stay positive, see how things went.

Again his phone rang. It was Bernie.

'Alright Bernie boy, how's the craic?' he said, trying to sound upbeat.

'Not good. We need to talk.'

'Go on then, shoot.'

'Phil's not a happy man.'

'No, and why is that?'

'His daughter Sean. I mean, it's not right, is it?'

'She's a fully-grown adult, old enough to make her own decisions.'

'Phil doesn't see it like that and nor do I. You're just trying to piss him off and I don't think it's a good time for that.'

'Talkative today, aren't you Bern?' Then more quietly: 'If I were you I'd watch what you fucking say.'

'It's gone beyond all that now. You want us to pull off some major work and at the same time you're trying to fuck with our heads. I don't think that's wise.'

Quinn hadn't expected this kind of defiance and felt his blood rise. He held himself in check.

'Get yourself down to the old manor. I want a talk to you.'

'Not in Phil's pub we won't.'

'The Black Lion then. Three o'clock.'

Quinn hung up.

'Cunt.'

Bernie walked in to the pub. Drinkers were sparsely scattered, Quinn sitting at the bar with his arm around a woman. She had long curly auburn hair, wore a tight green dress. Quinn threw back a whiskey before leaning in to nuzzle her neck. The woman laughed, the two of them looking half cut, woman especially. The barman on duty was a skinny young bloke with glasses, Adam's apple going up and down as he tried to ignore their antics.

'Riordan, you ol' cunt,' Quinn said loudly. 'How are you, my old mate?'

Bernie recognised that arrogance of old and knew he was on the charlie.

Quinn muttered something in the woman's ear and she sniggered as she looked Bernie up and down. He ignored it.

'Anyone want a drink?' Bernie asked, taking out a twenty. He received no answer.

'This is Siobhan,' Quinn told him as he tickled her side. 'She's from Limerick. Stab City. Friendliest town in Ireland. She wants a drink, don't you Shiv?'

'Will you get off me, you big eejit?' she laughed. Their glasses were empty so he ordered three pints of Guinness .

She turned to Bernie, inspecting him. 'Will you look at your man here, he's so feckin' serious.'

'That's because he's a dark horse,' Quinn said. 'Don't trust him with your money whatever you do. Because when you come looking for it it'll be down the fucking swanny. Ain't that right Bernie boy?'

He'd just arrived and was already sick of the pair of them. When the round of drinks came he asked Quinn if they should find a seat.

'You find one,' he said. 'I'll be over when I'm good and ready.'

Bernie stared at him. 'I came here to talk to you.'

'I came here for the drink, the women and the craic,' he said, pulling Siobhan close. He slapped her on the hip, grabbed a handful.

'Ow, that hurt, you bastard.' Then she shot Bernie a dark look. The newcomer had arrived to ruin her afternoon. 'You heard him, my fella's not going anywhere.'

'Tell you what Shiv, give me five minutes while I talk to this miserable cunt.' Quinn stepped off his stool. 'We've got a little business to discuss. Then me and you will continue where we left off.'

Siobhan held his face and kissed his lips. 'Don't be long, I miss you already.'

Quinn and Bernie headed to a table and sat in. 'You certainly know how to ruin a good afternoon, I'll give you that much.'

'This is no joking matter,' Bernie leaned in. 'We need to talk, big time.'

'About what? You and that cunt up the road are earning my money back, so what's to discuss?'

'The job's a set up, just admit it.'

Quinn stared back, trying to read his intent. He laughed. 'A set up by who, me?'

'At the minute you're doing everything you can to act the cunt, so it wouldn't surprise me.' Bernie glanced over to see the trollop swaggering off to the toilet.

'I just want my money off you thieving fuckers.'

Bernie dropped his gaze. 'I understand that, but there's other ways we can get it without going through Kelly.'

Bernie was unaware of Kelly's misfortune and the job's current status. Quinn held that card back.

'Why, you don't trust him?'

'I know he's related so no offence, but he's slippery, always has been. We'd kidnap the bloke, get the cash then probably get robbed by another crew on the way back. It wouldn't be the first time he's pulled a stunt like that. And those two Dagenham blokes, who are they, they could be anyone.'

Quinn exhaled, sat back for a few moments.

'It's not a set up. I'm the one who brought the job to Kelly. I'd do the work myself if I could.'

'Well maybe you shouldn't have trusted Kelly with organising it.'

'He's family, he wouldn't rip me off.'

'You don't know that.'

Quinn shrugged. 'I still want my money Bern.'

'I'll get your fucking money. My way. I'll plan something with

Phil.'

'Don't talk to me about Phil. Half an hour ago he left a message on my phone. You want to hear it?'

Bernie shook his head. 'Probably best I don't.'

'He reckons he's going to rip my head off and shove it up my arse. Funny how people change. Though I must say he sounded off his tits so I'll forgive him this time.'

'Hi, you,' his bird called from the bar, sulkily over her shoulder. 'You coming back over here or what?'

'One minute,' Quinn said.

'So are you going to tell Kelly we're off the job?'

'You know what this means don't you? It means I'm losing cash here, and all because you and Phil haven't got the arsehole to do the graft.'

'I told you, I'll plan a different job.'

'You've been out of the game for years.'

'So what?'

Quinn looked him up and down, then shrugged. 'Go on then. Impress me.' He leaned close. 'Plan it, organise it, do it. But if I don't get the kind of cash I was expecting from the Kelly job, you and that weasel Phil are finished. Because you know what Bern, I've fucking had it with you two. And my lenience can only stretch so far before I end up grabbing a shovel and doing what you did to Johnny Mac.'

Shocked, Bernie checked left and right. 'What are you bringing that up for?'

Quinn smiled, delighting in his transgression. 'Why am I bringing up the time you bludgeoned a friend to death in front of me? It's hardly one of those things you'd forget now, is it?'

'We promised we'd never talk about that.'

'We promised a lot of things back then. Things you happily disregarded. Like if any of us got sent down we'd be well compensated when we got out, because we were all mates. You certainly stayed faithful to that one,' and he added, 'killer.'

'It wasn't even me who killed him.'

'No, who was it then?'

'Tommy Gun shot him and he would've fucking died anyway.'

'Maybe. But you made sure of that by caving his head in with a fucking shovel. It was down the basement of the Dragon. I remember it like yesterday.'

'Mac tried to kill you.'

'Tell that to a judge up in court, see what he says. And tell him you buried him under an office block in Wembley where he remains to this day. Tell him that. I'm sure he'll understand.'

Quinn was enjoying himself, while Bernie was trembling. For a moment he pictured himself grabbing Quinn's neck, both hands in a vice-like grip, staggering through the tables and chairs, refusing to loosen his hold until the bloke was stone dead on the floor. But Bernie was frozen where he sat, he couldn't move.

'You're a murderer, Bernie. You could've phoned for an ambulance that night but you didn't. Maybe it should've been you doing all that bird, not me at all. Because believe you me, I met enough killers in there. All I wanted on the out was a few quid in my pocket but I ended up inside doing all your time. That's certainly one way of looking at it.'

Again his bird called over. 'Will you get over here, or do you prefer your stupid ol' mate to me?'

'You buried Mac down in a hole, his parents living out their days not knowing if he was alive or dead. Then I was in the nick while you enjoyed your freedom, suburban life with the missus, watching your kids grow, your garage set up with my fucking money. And today you phone me telling me who I should and shouldn't be screwing. You're a joke mate.'

Bernie stared at the table. 'If it came out about Mac you'd be implicated too. We'd both do time.'

'Who said it's going to come out? Not me. But if it did, I've got nothing to lose, have I? I'm not the one with the business, the wife and the kids. I'm here scratching my arse still waiting for my cut of the money you pinched.'

'You forgotten about me or what?' His bird sounded weary now, placing her head down on the bar. 'Men, I swear to God...'

'Calm down woman,' Quinn smiled, taking his glass and rising from his seat. 'I was having a nice little chinwag with an old friend.'

He looked down at Bernie, satisfied he'd hit the right buttons. 'Go home Bern,' he said quietly. 'You look ill.' Then he joined Siobhan at the bar, the two laughing and tossing back drinks like he'd never arrived.

Bernie walked up the High Road to stop in on Phil. Tara let him through, warning that her dad was under the weather at the moment. Aren't we all, Bernie thought, going upstairs. Reaching the landing Phil's Dobermann McQ came bolting down the hallway, barking in front of him. Bernie knew not to react. The dog cautiously smelled him, remembered his scent and slunk off. Bernie wasn't a regular visitor these days.

Phil was brooding in front of the telly, curtains drawn, a bottle in front of him. Bernie sat down in the next chair and Phil turned to him. 'I'll fucking murder the bastard,' he said, as if Bernie having strolled in uninvited was an everyday occurrence.

Bernie poured himself a brandy. 'I'm with you on that one Phil.'

'So you should be,' he replied half a minute later.

On the TV a panel of women were talking about alcoholism, sex, men.

'Will you listen to these bitches rabbiting on,' Phil said.

They sat in silence for a bit, Bernie letting the cognac soothe him.

The topic on TV was cancer now and Phil turned it over to a tanned man in a bow tie pricing a set of Iberian antiques.

'We never should've left Spain,' Phil said bitterly. 'It's been nothing but shit since I came back to London.'

Bernie didn't reply. Perhaps Phil should've stuck around and been wiser with his share of the dough. Then again they shouldn't have nicked it all in the first place.

'I was happy back then,' Phil went on. 'Well, happier anyway. Now look at me, I'm completely fucked.' Then he turned to him. 'Who let you upstairs, my slut of a daughter?'

'Come on Phil. We were all that age once. She's just rebelling. My son at home's doing the same thing. They're a pain at that age. Anyway, she doesn't even know who Sean Quinn is. You haven't told her, have you? To her he's just some bloke putting on the charm.'

Phil stood up on shaky legs. 'Come here, I want to show you something.'

Bernie followed him into his office. He unlocked a cupboard and took out a sawn-off shotgun.

'Put that thing away. You're mad.'

'I've got ammo too. And you know what, it's got the bastard's name on it.'

'Get that thing out of the house Phil. If the coppers come sniffing around you're fucked.'

Phil put it away and they sat back in the room.

'I was in the Black Lion just now chatting to the fucker,' Bernie said.

'Watch your wife and daughter and anyone else female around him, that's all I can say.'

'I told him the Kelly job's too risky and we want out.'

Phil shook his head. 'Quinn's not going to accept that. He wants us in prison or set up to be shot dead.'

'Well listen to this, he did accept it. He said okay.'

Phil was puzzled.

'I've told him we'd plan a job ourselves. Do it and pay him off.'

'And he agreed to that?'

'Yes, he did – which is the only way we'll get the bastard off our back.'

Phil eyed him. 'There's always another way,' he said. 'Don't you forget that.'

Bernie turned back to the TV. He didn't respond to that suggestion.

Quinn came out of Siobhan's flat on Carlton Vale and walked back around to Kilburn High Road. The flat was her aunt's, the biddy out for the count on the sofa, a pile of sherry bottles in the corner. Siobhan had the box room where they'd spent two hours getting closely acquainted. Meeting a woman in need today was just what the doctor ordered. As she slept, Quinn crept off to catch last orders. Back on the main drag he bumped into Tara.

'Look who it is.'

'Oh no, it's trouble,' she said, only half joking.

'How's your auld fella?'

'Drunk,' she said, blowing fag smoke aside. 'He knew I was with you last night and wasn't best pleased.'

'So I heard.'

'From who?'

'Word travels.'

She took a drag, blew it out. 'Anyway, I better go.'

'You're not escaping me that easily. Come for a drink.'

'I only popped out for some milk.'

'Come on, just the one. Live dangerously.'

Tara considered it, looking up the street towards the pub, its upstairs living space a den of misery. They set off. 'I can't believe I'm doing this.'

They entered a place that was doing a late one.

'You got a boyfriend then?' he asked once they'd brought their drinks to a seat at the side.

'Don't talk to me about men. Everyone I meet turns out to be some kind of criminal, including you.'

'Me?'

She shook her head. 'That's how my stepmum acts about my dad. It's like a joke in the family: never mention his shady past. He's got a gun you know, I've seen it.'

'Your old man with a shooter? Never.'

'A shotgun. He took it off a drunk in the bar once and kept it for himself. Then one night these robbers came in at closing. The barman hadn't locked the doors yet and two of them burst in. My dad saw it on the monitor. Next thing he's down wielding a sawn-off and you should've seen them run. We've never had a problem since.'

'I see the old dog hasn't changed his spots,' Sean laughed.

Tara looked at him; his stubble, undone white shirt. He smelled of drink and musky sweat, a masculine scent she couldn't deny she was fond of.

'Tell you what, I'm heading to the gents for a pick me up. And before you ask, yes you can have some. I'll be back in a minute.'

He disappeared and a man came over and sat opposite. It was her one night ex, Dublin Joey. He was smiling like a fool.

'How are ye, Tara? Who's the big ol' gangster with you tonight? I'm jealous.'

'Well don't be. He's Sean, one of my dad's old friends. He's probably twice my age.'

'That didn't stop him having his arm around you.'

She changed the subject. 'Had any early wake-up calls by the fuzz lately?'

'Don't ask. Sorry about all that by the way. That was my mate Liam's fault. He's over there. If you're into shooters, don't go round the place shouting about it, that's what I say. Ears everywhere.'

'Did he get in trouble for it?'

'No, they couldn't prove it was his. There was a shower of troublemakers living in the flat before us, so the police believed it must've been theirs.'

'Hey, Sean's coming back, you better go.'

Joey said quickly, 'My mate saw yer man on the pull in the Lion earlier. He went home with a drunk redhead.' He left the table, passing Sean as he went.

'Who was that?'

'Just a friend.'

'I'd watch him. He looks tricky.'

'You two would get on well then.'

'Look, he's looking over,' Sean laughed. 'I should go and slap him one.'

'Stop it. You men are like little boys sometimes. I'm nobody's property, you know.'

'A strong woman. Nothing wrong with that.' He leaned in: 'You want a toot?'

'No, not tonight.' She moved away from him, crossed her arms.

'You in a sulk with me or what?'

'I am as it goes.'

'What have I done now?'

'Who was the redhead you slept with earlier? It was me last night, another woman today. You certainly get through them.'

'Your mate came over to gossip, did he?'

'So it happened then?'

'No. Unless you mean my cousin Mary who I had a drink with earlier.'

'Your cousin?'

'I do have relatives you know.'

She studied him. 'Are you sure?'

'Course I'm sure.'

'Okay, I believe you. But I'm not the wisest of people or I wouldn't be sitting here, would I?'

He put his arm round her. 'Don't be so hard on yourself. I think you're beautiful, a really attractive woman, do you know that?'

She blushed. 'Do you really?'

'Course. You're the nicest girl in this pub.'

She looked around, seeing virtually all men. 'Oh, thanks.'

'No seriously,' he leaned close. 'I knew you were special from the moment I saw you.'

'Shut up,' she said, but wanted more.

'And I really enjoyed last night too,' he said.

They were face to face now. 'So did I.'

'Then stop fretting all the time and go with the flow.'

Joey and Liam were by the pool table, watching the couple as they left the pub.

'Looks like your girlfriend didn't listen to you about the redhead then,' Liam smiled, leaning down to fire a shot.

Joey's eyes were still on the door. 'I don't like the look of that bloke at all.'

'Why, because he's bringing your missus home for a riding?'

Joey ignored that. 'Liam, have you bought a replacement piece yet?'

'What, you want to go and shoot the fucker? Word of advice. Never let a woman push you over the edge. There's plenty more carp in the old fish pond, believe me.'

'You're right,' Joey said at last, trying to shrug the whole thing off. 'There's other birds I've got my eye on anyway. Have you seen that new one behind the bar in McGovern's?'

'Anne Marie? She's got a boyfriend. Bloke from West Belfast. I wouldn't mess.'

'Oh. Well there's Magda from the Sunshine Café. I think she's got a thing for me, you know.'

'You reckon you might be lucky on that one?'

'I think I might be very lucky.'

'Guess what? She's just got engaged to an eighteen-stone rugby player. Works on the door of some club down Camden. He'd have you for breakfast.' He potted the black then slapped Joey's back and went to the bar for more beers.

Joey handed the cue to some blokes who were next up and sat down. He'd liked Tara ever since he'd first walked into her pub three months ago. When she'd agreed to go out with him he felt he'd struck gold. The gun raid messed up everything.

'Cheer up Joey,' Liam said, returning with two pints of the black stuff. 'The boys are on their way. Larry, Jimmy and Keef the Teef. What's women when you've got a jar in your hand, your mates and the craic?'

Fair point, but Joey was still jealous of Sean. The man was a snake. He knew he was bad news from the moment he'd walked in. With some people you can just sense it. He planned to ask around, dig something up on the bloke. Prove to Tara she was making a mistake. Tonight he'd drink and be merry, but tomorrow he'd make it his mission.

20

Urban Foxes

Terry and Dan were in the pub talking of second homes in the sun. Who knows, at some point they could even up sticks and make it permanent. Money made things possible, opened up the options. Look at Charlie White from up the road. After some graft he fucked off to Northern Cyprus, now ran a bar out there. He loved it, said he never wanted to see a rainy day in Blighty ever again. Terry knew Stacey would never go for the full decamp, not with all her relatives here, but the thought of even a taste of sunny climes was making Terry's mouth water. Soon he'd be flush and without a worry in the world. He felt like grabbing Dan around the shoulder and planting a smacker on his cheek. This job would provide the fortune he'd always dreamt of. Or a hefty lump of it at least.

He considered the last few months, years even, and couldn't believe how miserable he'd allowed himself to become. Moping about like it was the end of the world. Negativity was in the head. It was a choice. It was like after he'd been robbed in his car. He'd let it get to him, gnaw away and erode his pride. But not for long thankfully because he'd got off his arse to remedy that. He'd been hasty and put himself on the line, but lady luck had been there smiling all the way. Sometimes you just have to take a chance, do what's right. It's the same with this upcoming graft. If you want changes there's no use sitting around thinking about it, you just have to kick down some doors.

Dan's phone chimed out The Final Countdown and Terry watched him answer it. It was his sister. Dan didn't sound too chirpy at what he was hearing and Terry wondered if somebody had died. If so, he hoped it wasn't anyone close. Family woes or a death would only spoil the mood.

Dan hung up and exhaled. 'That was Liz. Bad news I'm afraid Tel. Old Kelly's been raided. Six different charges. Serious shit too. He's being remanded.'

'What?' Terry saw an avalanche of bricks and mortar crashing down over his plans and dreams. 'No way.'

Dan supped his pint. 'The job's off,' he shrugged.

Terry stared at him. 'What do you mean?'

'It ain't happening now. Kelly's been nicked, he's in the slammer.'

'What the fuck happened?'

'Well, Kelly joined some bent racing syndicate the Old Bill must've had their eye on. What can I say? I don't envy him right now, I know that much.'

'What's going to happen then?'

'He's facing a stretch. They also found a shooter and some jewellery on the premises linking him to a job. I'm surprised at that, it's pretty careless of him leaving all that tom sitting around at home. He's up shit creek mate.'

'So what's happening with the job?'

'It ain't happening now,' Dan said, once more shrugging his shoulders.

His phone sounded, that riff again. Terry hoped it was Liz, this time saying the whole thing was a wind-up.

'Yes mate,' Dan said. Then he broke into a grin. 'Wha-hey....

brilliant... top man.... Yes, definitely, will do... fantastic… Okay, cheers for that, catch you later.'

'What's the news?' Terry asked eagerly.

Dan rubbed his hands together. 'Just earned four grand sitting on my arse. I put down two large on an investment a while back. The old wacky baccy. Completely forgot about it to be honest. Doubled my money.'

'The call wasn't about Kelly?'

'No, that was my mate Griff, he works up Felixstowe docks. Loves a good earner I tell you. I could sit here telling you stories all day about the cunt.'

Terry slammed his fist down on the bar. 'I'm talking about Kelly and the fucking work.' Several drinkers across the way woke up and looked over.

'Whoa, steady on,' Dan said, lowering his tone. 'If you're upset about the graft, there's always more where that came from. Something else will come up, it always does, mark my words.'

'That's all very well for you to say. I was relying on this.'

Dan shook his head. 'Not a good thing to do Tel. It's easy come easy go in this game, you know that yourself. Kelly getting nicked at this point has probably done us a favour. Imagine if we'd gone ahead with the job while the coppers were still scoping him. We'd all be done. In fact, even now we better keep an eye as we recently met with the fucker. They've nicked him so it's likely their operation's over, but you never know.'

Terry thought about it. 'The coppers were on him?'

'They must've been. For his racing caper. Watching him night and day. Thank your lucky stars the job didn't go ahead sooner. We'd be sitting in the nick with him.'

Dan's way with words took away the sting, but still Terry was devastated. He'd gone from cloud nine to ground zero with one poxy phone call. He looked at his pint. It looked like somebody had pissed in it.

Dan had a paper out, pointing to some soap-star slapper in a bikini pushing her tits out.

'Here Tel, how much would you give for a test-run on that, eh?'

'Fuck all, that's how much I'd give.' He stood up and put on his jacket.

'Come on Terry, cheer up.'

'No, I won't. In fact, you know what, you can get fucked.'

'Me?'

'Yeah you, you silly cunt.'

Dan laughed, watching him go. The bloke was acting like a three-year-old.

Just then Andy walked in, Terry shouldering past him at the door.

'What's up with him today?'

'He didn't get a shag from the missus last night.'

'You sure? He wouldn't be that upset.'

'A little enterprise we had planned got called off.'

Andy sat in at the bar, then he lowered his voice. 'Talking of earners, Paul Croxton phoned. He tried to bell you earlier but your phone was off.'

'Yeah? What's the score?'

Andy glanced left and right. 'He's offered us a little job.'

Terry walked out into the drizzle, got in his car and drove. He was heading in the direction of home until he realised he wasn't in the mood for home. He was too fired up, too fucked off. He wondered if he should sign in for work, pick up some custom to get his mind off things. But with several pints in him it probably wasn't a good idea. Maybe he'd just drive around, try to get his head together. God, he was a fucking idiot. There he'd been walking around with a spring in his step thinking he was already in the money, which just goes to show how rusty he was these days. How fucking straight he'd become. You dream no dreams until you see the fucking pound notes in your hand. Even a cunt knows that. Dan knew, he'd give him that much. He never let anything touch him. Just shrugged his shoulders and carried on, happy go lucky. But Terry wasn't Dan.

He turned a corner, a white van passing on the other side. He caught sight of the lone driver at the wheel. Where did he see that face before? Then he flashed to the road rage confrontation, getting a smack in the road. It was the same bloke. Without debate Terry turned the car around and followed after him.

They were heading south towards the old Ford plant, the roads quiet at this time of night. Terry kept his distance, road stretching ahead, industrial units on one side, dark open space on the other. Finally the van indicated left and pulled off the road. Terry drove by and saw him parking in between two boarded-up factories. Terry pulled in further along. He got out on foot, tooled, edging his way to the scene.

Low in the shadows he watched the man on his phone, pacing by his van. 'Where the fuck are you boss, we said ten o'clock?' Terry crept closer, tight to the factory wall, a light rain blowing. The man turned his back, shouting into his phone. A lorry thundered by on the road and this was it. Terry made his approach. He swung his axe. The blade plunged deep into the man's back. He screamed and hit the ground. Terry once more raised his tool. More blows followed.

Terry hit the road. He felt better now, laughing and bouncing in his seat. He was back on form and all was well with the world. The Kelly job didn't matter now. It was a triviality. Dan was right. There's always other jobs, always will be. He could even look around for something himself. Or maybe even push the boat out, plan some graft of his own. It wouldn't be the first time, would it?

Then again, why bother? Life has its ups and downs, financial and otherwise, but you ride out the hurdles. Maybe he'd just keep rolling along as he was, accept things the way they were. After all, he had the respect of his family now. They loved and appreciated him and the feeling was mutual. What more do you need? Whatever he planned to do, including nothing, was up to him. He'd play it by ear, see how things panned out. As Dan said, easy come easy fucking go.

His phone rang.

'Danny boy,' he said cheerily.

'That's how it is now, is it? You were calling me a cunt earlier.'

'That's because I'm a stroppy sod at times, which ain't now.'

'At least you admit it.'

'Anyway mate, business or pleasure?'

'You confuse me Tel, you really do,' Dan laughed. 'It's business as it goes. There's an earner on the cards if you're up for it. I just spoke to Mr C.'

Paul Croxton was a local boy they'd knocked around with growing up. He'd been a good fighter down West Ham, but long-term was too ambitious to waste his Saturdays kicking arse for no financial gain. He took up with his uncle in the powder trade and went on to make a killing. These days he moved in different circles, a respectable businessman with an eight-bed pile in Brentwood. But he still threw crumbs to his old mates occasionally. Terry had refused to take part in the last few jobs offered, while Dan and Andy had ended up flush for months.

'There's a lock-up down the old manor full of top-end sports cars he wants us to collect and deliver. Should be a piece of piss as whatever dopey fucker's storing them has nothing more than a couple of padlocks on the door.'

'In Hackney? Sure there's not a pack of pit-bulls inside waiting to pounce? Could be a trap. Nobody's that silly.'

'You're on the ball Tel, but it's kosher, believe me. You know Hackney these days, the estates are shit but a fair few of the houses are tarted up and full of yuppies. You know how clueless that lot can be. There's a nice few quid in it too. Bit of pocket money, tide you over for a bit.'

'Count me in Dan, cheers.'

'Will do mate. One thing though you mad cunt, how come you're so happy now?' In the background Terry heard Andy shout, 'Because his missus just opened her legs.'

'Tell Andy to go suck a big fat member,' Terry smiled.

'Seriously Tel, you on the schizo pills these days?'

'Not last time I checked, no. And tell Andy I get my oats on a nightly basis. Several times.'

Clicking off Terry wondered how he'd gone from sad to elated so quickly tonight. Then he tasted blood on his lips. Of course. Our little friend back there. He checked his face in the rearview, a full smear up one side. Talk about war paint. He'd have to clean himself up. But what happened was unimportant now. It was done and forgotten. Looking back got you nowhere. Life was all about moving forward. Marching on.

*

'There you go,' Lil said, handing over the cue after potting half the balls. 'Beat that, big man.'

Bigz clicked one clean in, then messed up on the next, almost sinking the black.

'Jeez, I need another drink.' He shook his head as he made for the bar. 'Back in two.'

'Don't play the master if you ain't got the moves,' Lil smiled, leaning down to wipe him off the table.

Bigz returned with two bottles of Bud and they sat down for a bit. The pool hall was above Stoke Newington Road, a one-stop-shop where you could buy or sell anything for a price.

They surveyed the dim-lit room. Mus and his mate were at a table across the way, doing a good trade, junkies arriving every few minutes for his bargain three-for-two's. Three white guys were at a table to the far side, all leather jackets and jeans, probably coke dealers. Also in the house was Billy the Fence, a pony-tailed Venezuelan accompanied by the Scottish goon he used as muscle. Billy accepted whatever the shoplifters brought him, but was known to pay peanuts. Bigz heard a rumour Billy had a new sideline on the go robbing jewellery shops. If so, he was moving up in the world.

'This place is like a den of thieves,' Bigz observed. Then bang on cue Dreadman swung through the door. The guy looked riled, like he'd had a difficult day. He joined another dreadlocked local who greeted him with sympathy.

'Did you hear what happened?' Lil said, nodding over. 'This morning Dreads got raided. The police pulled him out of bed, turned his yard over. He's probably just been released now.'

Bigz checked the time: 6 pm. That meant he'd spent most of the day in a cell. He smiled. 'They find anything?'

'Just a bit of weed I heard. Dreads ain't stupid, he's not going to stash anything at home. But it just goes to show, the feds are taking heed of what you're telling them. You said you heard he was dealing guns and in they went.'

'Jeez Lil, you knew this today and didn't tell me.'

'I'm telling you now.'

Bigz watched as Dreadman shared his woes, waving his arms about as he recounted his day. His companion shook his head, no doubt cursing the bloodclart evils of Babylon.

Bigz sniggered. 'Serves him right for snitching my address to Mike's men that time. He's lucky he didn't get stitches for that.'

'This one was just a test. Now we know five-o are taking your claims seriously we can start working things in our favour.'

Bigz nodded. Then he turned to him. 'But how exactly?'

Lil leaned in. 'Say we wanted to get some people off the street. Now we know we can do that.'

'Like who?'

'I'm thinking ahead here, but let's just say we raided a stash of gear off some crew. They'd be out armed and loaded hunting for whoever did it. But with your new arrangement we could clear the fuckers off the road, out of harm's way, you understand what I'm saying?'

'You want to start taxing dealers? That's big-league shit.'

'What are we, small league? We've been playing things straight with Mike for time now and I don't know about you, but I'm not exactly feeling it in the pocket.'

'You can say that again,' Bigz agreed. 'I'm seeing young guys, seventeen, eighteen, cruising the hood in brand new Beemers now.'

'That's the thing. There's money out there but too many hands grabbing for the same pot. Sometimes you've got to use your initiative, go that extra mile to ensure you're earning your fair share. Otherwise, what are we risking our arses on the road everyday for, fun?'

'Uh-uh,' Bigz shook his head. 'I get my fun when I'm banging pussy. Not when I'm gofing around all day for the likes of Hot Iron Mike. That's just work.'

'Exactly. But work has to have its perks or it ain't worth getting out of bed for. With all our jobs and deliveries, I've been taking note, collecting intel. If you're willing to take the plunge, we could be pulling off some decent earners.'

Bigz pondered it. Messing with Mike was risky shit, but maybe it was worth the punt. Only the other night he'd been scratching around for pizza money. He deserved more.

'It's something to think about,' Lil said. 'What do you say?'

Bigz pouted in thought. Then he nodded, 'I'm up for it.'

'Well there you go. Happy days,' and they smiled, spudded fists.

Bigz set the table for another game. It was good to have something to look forward to. Future prosperity. Or a few extra quid in the pocket at least. He was chalking his cue when across the way a familiar face walked in the door.

'What's up B?' Lil asked, seeing Bigz transfixed.

'It's that boy I told you about. He tried to stab me once. Then next time I chased him and he ran up to the fucking cops.'

They watched Tarquin approach Billy the Fence.

Bigz checked for his blade. 'I've lost this fucker one too many times.'

'Wait up,' Lil said. 'The boy ain't going nowhere. Let's watch this.'

Tarq pulled out a pile of gold chains and placed them down on the green baize. Billy inspected the carat with an eyeglass, his minder looking left and right. Finally Billy counted off the agreed cash. Tarq tapped his fist and made for the toilets.

'You see that wad he pocketed?' Lil said

'It's ours,' Bigz smiled. 'Let's go.'

'Wait.' Lil nodded to the right. 'I don't like the look of those three white guys over there. They could be undercovers. Let's head to the exit, approach him on the stairs as he leaves. Shuffle him out back, get him in the car. Then we can fuck him up wherever you like.'

'I'll do more than fuck him up, trust me. You carrying?' he asked and Lil nodded.

They loitered out by the top of the stairs pretending to chat. Bigz reached up to swivel the CCTV camera aside. When Tarq came through the door, Bigz turned and showed him the gun.

The boy looked shocked.

'That's right pussy, we meet again. Now get down the stairs before I take your fucking head off.'

They headed down towards the rear fire door. Bigz prodded him on, then out in the twilit yard he held the gun in his pocket for fear of prying eyes. 'You're gonna pay, fucker, big time.'

Shaking his car keys Lil walked slightly ahead towards the road. 'Where we heading B?' he asked over his shoulder.

'Abney Park Cemetery. I want to cut him up before I bury him.'

Lil laughed, then suddenly the boy spun around holding a gun and - BANG – he shot Bigz in the face.

Bigz fell backwards and Tarq raced off towards the road.

'What the fuck?' Lil rushed back to where Bigz was floored, clutching his face.

'He just shot me! I can't fucking see!'

'Take your hands away, show me.'

There was no wound, no blood; Bigz blinking his eyes trying to regain his sight. Then Lil saw a burn mark where the bullet had grazed his scalp.

'You're lucky B. That round flew just shy of your head. You must've ducked just in time.'

'But my eyesight?'

'That's probably just the muzzle flash, it's temporary.'

Lil helped him up, Bigz's vision slowly returning.

'Hey boss, you okay?' A Turkish guy called down from a window.

'Fine,' Lil said curtly. 'No problem.'

'I saw him running. He had an automatic. Powerful weapon.' He smiled, pointing his cigarette hand at Bigz. 'You're lucky, my friend. You must've been saying your prayers.'

Tarq ran like billy-o. Rounding a bend he crashed into a woman with a push-chair and three kids, bags of fruit and veg flying everywhere. Ignoring the tirade, he carried on running. He turned up a passage to the rear of some shops and crept through a gap in a fence into an overgrown back garden. Entering a barely-standing shed, he settled on a low seat. He'd been here before, shooting up. And another time hiding from the police after he'd grabbed a man's wallet. That time they'd come close - he'd seen their torches - but not close enough.

They wouldn't find him here, he was sure of it. But if they did, he'd have to shoot his way out. He looked down at the gun that Billy had provided and wondered what he'd have done back there without it. Getting into the car with those psychos would've meant death. He'd been lucky three times with Bigz now, but the idea of a fourth meet didn't fill him with confidence. It felt like the bullet hadn't connected; Bigz had ducked and seemed to fall away too quickly. That meant the chance of seeing him again, even angrier next time, was almost certain.

Maybe it was time to get out of Hackney. Move onto fresh territory. But how? His flat was here, his parents paying the rent. In his pocket he felt the reassuring wad of cash he'd got from Billy the Fence. He'd done a jeweller for him and been paid five hundred. It was small fry for what the haul was actually worth, but it wasn't bad cash for a few minutes' work.

It was dark now. Low by the shed's half-open door he saw a pair of eyes looking in on him. He flinched until he realised it was a fox. He'd seen it before in this garden, recognised its scrawny frame and missing ear. Some bastard had probably shot at it for fun. The fox took a step forward to inspect the uninvited human on his turf. Tarq put out his hand and the creature eyed him for a few seconds, before it cautiously reversed and disappeared. Tarq understood. Animals were right to deem humans untrustworthy. Trust nobody in this life and you have a chance of surviving.

'So who the fuck is this guy?' Lil asked as he drove Bigz home.

'I told you, I was walking along the street once and he bumped me, no apology or nothing. Then next thing he's trying to fucking shank me.'

'Some random? Did you provoke him?'

'Course I didn't – well, I might've pushed him maybe. What would you do? Then another time I saw him outside Dalston McD's and he ran like it was fucking dinnertime. I just can't catch the fucker.'

'I'm going to ask around about this guy. He's a junkie, yeah?'

'I guess so.'

'But a junkie hawking piles of gold jewellery and running round with an automatic? That ain't normal.'

Bigz scowled as he probed his scalp.

'Tell me about it.'

*

Bernie was at work tucking into a kebab when Phil called. They hadn't spoken for two days, since Phil had flashed his sawn-off.

'You sobered up yet?'

'I haven't changed my mind Bern. I want him done.'

Bernie reached over to close his office door. 'Things have changed since the old days Phil. You can't get away with all that now.'

'You can if you keep your hands clean. We'll hire somebody.'

'A hitman?'

'A professional.'

'I don't know about this.'

'Keep yourself several steps away and you can't go wrong.'

'For starters there's the money - you're skint.'

'I'll borrow it. I'd sell my right arm to get him off the street.'

'This is mad talk, but just theoretically speaking, who would you have in mind?'

'I know a bloke who can sort the whole thing. He's a Turk, connected to the Green Lanes crowd.'

'And you trust him?'

'One hundred per cent. I've done bits and pieces with him before, known him for years. We shared a cell back in the 'Ville. He's half Turk, half Irish, he's sound.'

Bernie paused. 'I'll have to think about this.'

'Don't bother, let's just do it. I want Quinn out of the picture.'

'We'll see.' Bernie rubbed his face and exhaled. 'Any more news?'

'Yes, Tara didn't come home again last night. Guess who she was with?'

'Come on Phil, you don't know that for sure. Youngsters stay out all the time.'

'They were spotted together in Doyle's place. They were drinking there till past midnight.'

Bernie exhaled.

'Agree to it Bern or I'll fucking do it myself. The cunt's taking the piss.'

'Steady on, I need to think about it.'

'You've got one hour before my Turkish mate comes around. We're having a talk.'

'You mean you've already told him?'

'I'm just waiting to okay it with you.'

'Jesus – look, I'll phone you back within the hour. I can't even think right now.'

Bernie binned his food and paced up and down outside in the passage. The days were getting warmer, the sun beaming down. The postman came along and handed him the mail. Most was junk, but an A4 envelope he had to sign for. He opened it and pulled out some photographs. His younger self beamed back at him. There he was sitting jeans round his ankles, eyes coked to the hilt, a peroxide head between his legs. Another showed him on a bed, a naked Thai bird straddling him. Gary Fitz's shots from the hotel parties. A message read: *What would the missus say? Plenty more where these came from you thieving cunt.*

Bernie was sweating. That snake Quinn. He'd got his hands on them and wanted to destroy his life. He imagined Jen at home opening the post, seeing what he'd just seen. It couldn't happen, no fucking way. Back inside one of the lads popped out from behind a car, asked him something, but he put his hand up, locked himself in the office, pulled the blinds. His hands were shaking. He had some brandy miniatures somewhere, found them and knocked one back. Again he confronted the photos. His son must've been three or four at the time, he and Jen either still engaged or actually married. Jen wasn't the forgiving type. Not with sex. If she got her hands on these she'd fucking divorce him.

He picked up his phone, called Phil.

'Do it,' he said.

'The hit?'

'Go ahead with it.'

'Now that's what I like to hear Bern. It's the best option, trust me. Dev will be here any minute. I'll tell him it's on. It's great you're on board.'

'How long will it take?'

'I'll tell him we want the ball rolling as soon as possible.'

'The fucker's just sent me some pictures. Shots from the old parties, threatening to send them to Jen.'

'Pictures?'

'From that cunt Gary Fitz. He was always snapping them off, the bastard.'

'I haven't seen Fitzy in an age, didn't know he was still around.'

'I nicked a load off him years back, thought I'd got the lot but I obviously hadn't. Maybe Quinn had some all along. I can't believe we ever allowed photos to be taken, it's madness.'

'You know what it was like in those days. When we celebrated it was like there was no tomorrow. I can't remember half the shenanigans.'

'I don't even want to think about it. I just want Quinn dead. Worse, I want him to suffer for this.'

'God, I can't believe the mad fucker did that. What does he want from us?'

'He wants us to be his slaves, that's what. Out doing jobs for him, just like you said, till he decides to get us sent down or taken out. The bloke's evil.'

'Well he's not going to be on the scene for much longer so you can rest easy.'

The job was twenty grand, a big discount for a friend. Phil was borrowing seven grand from his brother; he'd told him it was for a car. Bernie would have to provide the rest. I'll raise it, Bernie told him. Phil said he'd pay him back.

'Now go and talk to the bloke. Let me know all the ins and outs.'

Hanging up, Bernie saw the photos sitting there on his desk. He ripped them into tiny pieces. Christ, the sooner Sean Quinn was gone from this world the better.

'Result.' Phil slammed his desk in triumph.

He knew those snaps would come in handy someday. Always have that extra card for when need be. He'd played a conniving hand on Bernie, but it was a move that would benefit the both of them.

Phil recalled the night three years ago when Fitzy walked into the pub. He hadn't seen him in years and he'd really let himself go. He said his liver was fucked, but that one was obvious. At closing Fitz wanted to carry on drinking, but Phil said his wife was strict so they grabbed a bottle and cabbed it to Fitzy's place in Northolt. The flat was a sad mess, smelled of prison. Sure enough, Fitzy took out his box of snaps. He put on an old Pogues tape and the reminiscing was merry. Some showed the lads in pubs, glasses raised, or on holidays in the sun. A few revealed guns, stacks of money. Talk about careless. Finally they came to the parties, the ones Phil was after. Fitz laughed how Bernie had once showed up with a shooter demanding the lot, but he had a lot of the negatives so he had them reprinted. Two hours later Fitz had passed out on his seat and Phil took the entire box with him, negatives included.

Fitz returned to the pub the next night distraught, asking where his precious collection of memories had gone. Phil brought him out to the back and showed him a bin full of ashes, said it was something Fitz should've done long ago. There were incriminating things in there. What if the police got hold of them? In reality Phil had only burned the ones incriminating to himself alone. Fitz wasn't pleased but nor was there much he could do. Six months later he was gone from cirrhosis.

Phil poured himself a large one. On the monitor he saw his daughter enter the pub, returning from her latest tryst with Quinn. He smiled knowing the romance would soon be over.

21

Fight for Your Right to Party

Bernie's wife was concerned about his behaviour lately. Longer hours at the garage, brooding silences, always tired. They stood in the kitchen talking about it.

'If I find out you're seeing another woman...'

'I'm working my arse off more like,' he laughed, pressing the kettle on. 'Business is good at the moment. We're making money. You should be celebrating.'

She studied him for a few moments. Then at last she relaxed and shook her head. 'Come here you.'

Fresh from the shower, Conor stood listening from the top of the stairs as they hugged and made up. He laughed. Another woman? Get real. In his bedroom he whipped off his towel, exuding a heady dose of Lynx. Watch out ladies, here I come. It was Saturday night and the boys were heading to a party in Kingsbury. He pictured his crew rolling in, all the girls lined up in admiration of those slick Watford boys. The house apparently had plenty of bedrooms and Conor was feeling lucky.

Dressed, he smoked a blunt out of his window. Gemma

Feeney exited her house with a friend, walking along the close, pony tail swinging. He'd friended her online and she'd sent him back a message saying she didn't chat to her brother's enemies. Matt and Conor had fallen out, but was she taking it personally or playing hard to get? The other day on the street she'd blanked him until he said, 'I'll get a smile out of you one of these days,' and sure enough he got a smile. But right now he was thinking of the older girls at the party tonight. It was an eighteenth birthday, no little kids' affair, and if he wanted results he'd have to max up the charm. But with his crew confidence wasn't a problem. Quite the opposite in fact. He just hoped they'd behave.

Zipping a pack of rubbers into his jacket he thought of Amy Thorn. He'd gone back home with her again last week for second helpings. He'd lasted a bit longer this time, but the thought of the whole thing depressed him. She'd been a bit more vocal, but it didn't feel genuine somehow, more like she was going through the motions. He remembered their conversation afterwards as they smoked a zoot. Amy lying there staring at the ceiling saying she'd been doing it since the age of twelve, men using her for one thing only. It wasn't something he wanted to hear. Her voice sounded dull and toneless and at one point she started crying. He hugged her, told her to chill. Then she put it down to weed, said it just made her emotional sometimes, talk rubbish. No probs, he said, we all talk rubbish. I talk rubbish all day. But the girl was weird. By the time he left she was turned in towards the wall, slumped there motionless, and by the stairs he passed her dad who was heading up to the toilet. Conor said hello and the man just looked at him and grunted. Talk about awkward. No way was he going back there again, that's for sure. But end of the day, experience is experience.

He collected his phone and wallet. All set, he checked himself in the mirror. It was time to roll. Down by the front door his mum said she'd be worrying about him; make sure to be back by midnight.

'Midnight? What am I, twelve years old? The party's round Marcus's house so there's no problem. I'll probably stay over.'

'Just phone to let us know you're okay,' his dad said, coming down the hall.

'Course I'll phone. I always phone.'

His mum touched his hair, said he looked really handsome. 'Don't be misbehaving tonight. You know, be safe,' she winked and he groaned in embarrassment. His dad told him to look after himself and handed him twenty quid. This was a little uncomfortable as he'd already lifted a twenty from his wallet earlier, but the more the merrier.

Conor met his eye and said thanks. Sometimes he wished the stories about his dad were true. About him being an armed robber. But they said he'd got off that charge because he was innocent. He'd hung with some dodgy mates but he'd never been a criminal. Not much of one anyway. And that's why he was released after time on remand. The subject was rarely brought up, a family taboo. But it made Conor wonder if his dad was a pussy. His mates were out robbing, but he himself hadn't done a thing? Had he been landed with a coward for a father? He'd asked him outright once when they were fishing – did you do it Dad, what they accused you of? His dad looked taken by surprise, but Conor thought he'd be honest with him. But he said no, he was innocent

If he'd been a crim, couldn't he just admit that fact to his son? Or did he view him as not old enough yet, a little kid to be kept in the dark about such things. If he'd hung out with active badmen but hadn't been one himself, the man must've been one sad fucking pussy. Conor never went fishing with him again, or to the football, and he lost a lot of respect for him.

He thought of Marcus who had only vague memories of his dad. He'd asked him once where he thought his old man might be now. Marcus toked on a blunt considering it. 'In prison or dead I reckon,' he shrugged, like he didn't give a shit either way. Right then Marcus was the coolest motherfucker on this earth.

On the train to Kingsbury the five boys were living it up, loud and rowdy, but it was Saturday night after all. A bottle of Martell was doing the rounds, and Conor had just thrown back a swig when a cute girl turned and smiled, getting off at one of the stops.

'You see that, guys?' Marcus said. 'Conor's getting all the attention from the ladies. He's gonna pull tonight guaranteed. Which is more than can be said for you,' and he kicked out towards Rio who was swinging from the bars.

'Fuck you man, I'll be having a twosome while you're sitting on your ones scratching your balls bruv.'

Marcus kicked out but missed.

Blue, a mixed-race guy, said, 'I'm all set for party animal mode tonight, fucking trash the place, blatant.' He was Marcus's Harlesden cousin who was staying the weekend in Watford with him. He ran with the Stonebridge Crew and got bare respect from the boys.

Marcus carried on winding up Rio who was necking from the brandy full tilt, showing off.

'He'll be puking his guts up tonight if he hits the liquor like that, believe.'

Rio was laughing with his tongue out like he was already pissed. 'All I care about tonight is pussy.' He passed the bottle, again swinging from the bars, narrowly missing a man in a suit sitting trying to mind his own business. Rio was the new boy in the gang, an honour Conor was more than happy to hand over. Until recently he'd done all his homework, accompanying his strict Ghanaian parents to church every Sunday, but like Conor he'd woken up, realised life was for living. 'If I don't get to bang at least two decent girls at this place I'll be viewing the night as a failure.'

'You're dreaming blud,' Louis laughed. 'At that party last week you couldn't even pull one. You spent most of the night chucking up in the garden. You were blotto.'

Rio lunged for him and they started play-fighting.

People up the carriage were looking at the group like they were crazy, but it was only a bit of fun. Conor took out a bottle of Stella. He removed the cap with his teeth, getting some admiration until the beer fizzed up drenching him. 'Shit.' He jumped up.

'You're a dick, man,' Blue laughed, setting everyone else off. 'That's like this Hackney bredrin I know called Jay. He was in brand new threads chirpsing up these girls on the street and this bigarse bird flies by, dumps a load of shit over him. We were cracking up.'

At Kingsbury they headed up onto the street. Conor felt a sense of pride coming down to this manor as it was near to the badlands of his roots: Kilburn, Willesden, Cricklewood.

'Anyone know the address?' he asked.

'I've got it on my phone you numpty,' Blue replied, and Conor saw some of the boys laughing at that, including Marcus.

Blue had status, but Marcus's cousin or not, the guy was beginning to bug him. The boys hardly knew Blue, yet already he had them all crawling up his arse. Maybe Blue had a problem with Conor because he wasn't doing that.

They stopped in a shop, Louis and Rio throwing sweets at each other, and then the old Asian guy came out from behind the counter demanding Blue turn out his pockets, saying he'd nicked a bottle.

'Are you mad? I ain't even selected what I want yet, you mug.'

The man tried patting down his jacket and Blue pushed him in the chest. 'Put your hands on me again Paki and I'll knock you out.' The man stared at him, then shook his head and returned muttering to the counter. Blue strutted out.

Paying up Rio said, 'You're out of order, old man, accusing

people like that.'

'I won't have anyone stealing from my shop.'

'No-one's stealing nothing. You just see a bunch of youths and paint them all with the same brush. You're prejudiced innit.'

'What was all the drama about?' Marcus asked Blue when they were back on the street.

'Must be this,' Blue said, pulling out a beer bottle. 'I got these too,' and he showed two packs of Haribo. 'I don't give those shops nuttin. You should see us down my ends, we just waltz in and take whatever we want. They know not to make a scene. One guy tried it once and he found his VW firebombed.'

Blue led them down the residential streets towards the house. The gaffs were pretty decent down this way, classic semi-detached.

Hitting the last of the brandy, Rio ran up onto a car roof shouting, 'Who's ready to party, motherfucker?' He launched the bottle through the air and it landed in a front garden.

'Look at that,' laughed Blue. 'The guy's already drunk.'

They turned a corner. A teenage boy and girl were approaching. Nerd types. Passing, both kept their heads down. Blue splashed some beer into the boy's face, pushed him.

'What you got for me, pussy?'

'Leave him,' the girl said. 'We don't want any trouble.'

'Am I talking to you, you ugly mutt?' Blue pushed her.

'Leave her alone,' the boy stammered and Blue backhanded him round the face. 'What did you just say?' He pushed him against a garage wall. Voices laughed as Blue demanded his money, while Rio and Louis cornered the girl, asking if she did blow-jobs. She called them bullies and Conor saw Marcus joining in, pulling her hair and laughing. Blue was wielding a blade, getting the boy to hand over his phone.

'Jeez guys, check out this cheapo shit,' he announced, holding up the budget Nokia. 'You know what blud, you can keep that,' he laughed, handing it back. 'I don't roll with no fifteen-pound phone, you get me?'

The boy was sucking from an inhaler and Blue turned to the girl, who was struggling to get away from Rio, Louis and Marcus. Blue grabbed her arse and Rio copped a feel of her tits, then she started screaming and they scattered, laughing as they went, turning up another street, carrying on towards the party.

Conor hadn't taken part, but he hadn't done anything to stop it either, standing with his hood up tight in case any neighbours were watching. It was out of order. The boys never picked on harmless geeks, but Blue was bringing a different flavour, setting a new precedent.

'Nothing but little pussyoles round these ends,' Blue said. Then Louis pointed over to Rio who was standing in someone's garden pissing onto the tulips.

'You're well rowdy,' Blue said, arm around him when he returned. 'I've gotta bring you down Stonebridge bro, meet the crew.'

Conor wasn't happy. The boys were making dicks of themselves.

'You okay, Con?' Marcus said. 'What's up?'

'Your cousin's got quite a mouth on him, hasn't he?' He nodded ahead to Blue who was now telling Louis and Rio how he'd once got off with a mother-daughter combo, describing the details. 'He's a bit of a muppet.'

'You fucking pissed? Chill out blud, it's party time,' Marcus said, choosing not to take his claim seriously.

They approached the party house. A black guy in a bomber jacket stood arms-folded at the door. He was the birthday girl's dad. 'Not tonight Blue,' he shook his head.

'Come on Leon, I've brought all my bredrins. We come in peace, man.'

After a minute of negotiation, he let them through. The place was heaving, 50 Cent's 'In da House' pumping out as Conor and Marcus hit the front room. It was packed with dancing girls, black, white, Asian, you name it.

Conor got smooching with a hot girl called Sonia. Marcus chirpsed up her mate. Conor thought he was well in there until her friends pulled her away. Marcus was solo now too, so they went to the next room where Blue introduced them to a shaven-headed ginger guy called Shots who was slouched back on a chair, a cute black girl on his knee. Despite being pale, freckly and not exactly built, the guy oozed a couldn't-give-a-fuck confidence. It turned out he was a well-respected Stonebridge man.

Conor tried it on with a few more girls, getting into a near-ruck when some fit Filipino bird let him chat her up knowing her boyfriend was due back from the bog. 'You fucking want something, bruv?' The guy was older, built, shouldering him out of the way. Conor didn't fancy it. Guy would've battered him.

'What was all that about?' Marcus asked.

'Bitch was a prick teaser.'

'Aren't they all.'

At the punch bowl Rio dipped his head in, got slurping like a dog. 'You dirty fucker,' they laughed. Then Blue bounced over and said all the action was upstairs. 'There's a line-up in one of the bedrooms.' Blue banged on the door, voices inside telling him to go away. Finally it opened a crack, a topless guy in a gold chain telling him to piss off, it's a private party. The door closed and Blue started kicking it. Then bouncer Leon appeared and told him to leave. Rio jumped in telling the man to go fuck himself and a scuffled ensued. Bodies flocked to the scene taking Leon's side. Punches swung and Rio ended up toppling down the stairs. Blue was escorted out the front door. The music had halted, the hallway full of girls loud-mouthing, and Conor saw two guys set on Marcus. He jumped in. One hit him in the mouth and he fell back onto some girls, one pushing him back hard with both-hands. Conor swore at her, then a punch flew from nowhere and Conor wrestled with some guy, until Leon pulled him out the front door, having just ejected Marcus. It slammed shut and the music resumed.

The rest of the boys sat on the garden wall nursing bruises. Conor joined them. Rio was holding a bloody tissue to his nose, and Blue and Marcus started beefing about some shit. They stood up, pushing each other. Then Blue caught Conor's eye. 'Where the fuck were you tonight, dickhead?' Marcus told him to leave Con out of this, he's safe. 'Nah bro, everyone gets a licking and I didn't see this fucker helping out once.'

'I was dashing out licks like everyone else.'

'That's the truth,' Marcus backed him. 'He jumped in to help me out then I saw some guy set on him.'

Blue spat by Conor's feet. 'You're a fucking pussy.'

Conor got in his face. 'Go fuck yourself.' Blue looked stunned, like he wasn't used to men fronting him up. He reached into his back pocket. 'Knife,' Marcus yelled and grabbed his arm. Blue and Marcus fell, tussling on the ground. Conor twisted his wrist until he let go of the blade, then he dashed it down the drain. The fight was over.

'Your man's out of control,' Conor told Marcus, the cousins breathing on the ground, a defeated Blue screwing his face at him.

'You owe me a shank.'

'Shouldn't have pulled it on me then.'

Rio was drunkenly taking Blue's side, saying they were out of order. Shut your mouth, they told him, and Marcus helped Blue to his feet.

Back on the wall everyone looked pissed, stoned, worn out.

'Anyone get any pussy then?' Marcus joked, but got no more than murmurs.

Music suddenly poured from the front door. 'You lot still here?' Leon said. 'You better fuck off home before I call for reinforcements.'

'We're going in a minute,' Conor said.

Leon came down the path. 'Don't ever come back unless you want your arses kicked again.'

Everyone started moving on, apart from Conor who made a point of finishing his cigarette.

'You – you got a problem, you little cunt?'

Conor got up and kissed his teeth.

'You shupsing your lips at me? I'll smack you in the mouth, knock your fucking teeth out.'

Conor walked away. 'Try it,' he smiled, knowing he could outrun the big lump any day. 'Your party's a pile of crap.'

'All mouth when you're strutting away from me, yeah? I know your face now, little boy. I see it again I'll fucking break it.'

Conor caught up with the others. Blue was eyeing him with a hint of admiration now, pointing his spliff hand. 'You're safe you know that, fam? You don't let nothing faze you. I like that.'

'Course Con's safe,' Marcus said. 'I told you he was safe.'

Rio was staggering and Louis draped an arm around him helping him along.

'What a fucked-up night,' Blue said, passing his spliff to Conor.

They walked along some main roads, reaching a stop for the nightbus. During the hour's bus journey nobody talked much, some snoozed. Reaching Watford people split off for home, until Conor was alone turning up his street. Blackbirds sung, the sky glowing pink at the horizon.

Passing Matt's house he saw Gemma in her doorway having a cigarette.

'Alright Gem. Bit past bedtime, ain't it?'

'Hi Con.' She came over. 'I was round my friend's place tonight. Thought I'd have a sneaky fag before going in. You know what my parents are like.'

'Same as mine, they hate smoke. They're both ex-smokers so they're hypocrites really.'

She offered him a Marlboro Light, lit it for him.

'You been fighting tonight? Your eye looks bruised and there's blood on your lip.'

Conor hadn't noticed. He mentioned the party but spared her the details. She asked if he was still hanging with that bad crowd and he laughed. They're not bad, just a bit wild, that's all. She nodded cynically: Right. Asked if he was still suspended from school. He was going back next week, he'd have to behave for once.

'How's Matt? I've been meaning to give him a call.'

She looked at him. 'You should.'

'I will. He's still a mate as far as I'm concerned. I've just been, well, not myself lately.'

She smiled. 'I knew you weren't a scumbag.'

Finishing their smokes they said goodnight. By her door she smiled at him.

He went to bed feeling strangely peaceful. Then his phone was buzzing next to him; it was twelve noon. Marcus was chatting about what a great laugh the party was last night, and Conor wondered if they'd attended the same one. Marcus said him and Blue took some speed and were up all night watching action films, rushing off their tits. Blue had just gone down the shop now getting some munchies. Conor said he'd call him back later, he was knackered right now.

'Nah, let me tell you the news. Blue wants to bring us down Stonebridge later, introduce us to his boys. They're having a get-together and there'll be a load of girls down there.' Conor was silent. 'You still there Con?'

'I've just woken up, I need more kip...'

'Knock round mine about five, yeah? We'll head down NW10.'

'Hang on Marc. No can do I'm afraid, not today.'

'You what? Blue's getting us aligned with Stonebridge and you want to pass on that?'

Conor exhaled. 'I don't know, I'm just not feeling it.'

'What do you mean?'

'I just don't want to do it.'

Conor was surprised at his own honesty. But after last night things were different. The feel-good factor was gone.

'You gone fucking mad? You sound like a dick.' There was an edge to Marcus's voice that reminded him of Blue. He remembered the shop last night, Blue pushing that old man. Then targeting that couple. The guy's behaviour was grubby.

'Maybe you should go Stonebridge and stay down there with him Marc.'

Marcus paused. 'Rah,' he said in shock.

'Look, I know he's your cousin but I didn't gel with him. That's just the way it is. He was acting like a prick last night, and so was everyone else, including me if I'm honest.'

Another stunned pause. 'So you ain't coming?'

'No.'

'You're out of order Con. Blue respects you, reckons you're the only decent guy in the crew.'

'He pulled a knife on me.'

'I know, and you dashed it down the drain like it was no biggie. He respected that.'

'It doesn't change things Marc. We didn't hit it off so I'm not going down his manor.'

'What the fuck? You've changed Con, I swear. You've lost it big time.'

'Look Marc...'

'Go suck your mum,' he said and hung up.

Conor lay back down. Had he done the right thing? Maybe. Maybe not. Time would tell. But at least he was honest, did what he thought was right. But another thing, throughout the call he'd been thinking of Gemma; she was on his mind. And maybe that's why he felt calm, like everything would work out. He hadn't been lying to her either, he really was going to talk to Matt. He wanted some of his old life back.

'Where's Con, ain't he coming down?' Blue asked Marcus as they hung by the corner in Stonebridge with his boys, sitting aside for a one-to-one.

'No, he's chilling at home. He's still fucked from yesterday.'

'I reckon your other boy's feeling even worse – guy who was puking from the brandy? He's a clown that one.'

A police car cruised up the close. 'Shit,' Blue said, putting his hood up.

PC McKevitt opened his window and motioned Syrus over for a word. 'Sy, my old friend. Surprised you're still out and about after your Osman warning.'

Syrus had received a police threat-to-life letter but wasn't bothered. Tensions between Stonebridge and Church Road were in the red all year round.

'I'll hardly get done on my doorstep, will I?' Really he should've just been honest, told them he was wearing a vest.

'Be careful, that's all we're saying.'

'Thanks for your concern officer, but I can look after myself.'

'It's just that, another body, we could do without the paperwork right now,' the copper smiled.

'Yeah course, should've known.'

The car moved on and Syrus returned.

'What was that about?' Jay asked, sitting with a girl called Mel on his knee. Everyone awaited his answer.

'Church Road want me dead, what's new? The police are just covering their arses in case I get wasted.'

'Man,' Mel said, sucking on a lollipop. 'You boys are heavy rollers.' She was new to the scene.

Things were hot right now because of a feud between Vince, a Stonebridge man, and Andre, allied to Church Road. Vince recently rolled up on a motorbike and shot at Andre as he stood chilling with friends. It was the result of a long-running beef between the two about a girl. The bullet missed, then one of

Andre's friends fired back and Vince shot that guy dead. It was no longer a personal dispute now, but gang war. Vince fled to Ibiza, and in his absence Church Road vowed that in revenge two Stonebridge men were getting taken out. According to police intel Syrus was in line as a victim. But what did the feds know?

'I know nuff brothers that have been murked,' Blue boasted to Marcus. 'Back at school my mate got done on his fifteenth birthday. He was down near Mozart Estate with his cousin when he got shanked up by about twenty men.' Then he smiled. 'After the funeral I met this well nice bitch. She was from Ladbroke Grove. I banged her in some alleyway down there.'

'Hey yo,' Syrus called, and they saw the boys heading off. 'Come, we're going up Frosty's.'

'Party time,' Blue said and they followed along.

'So there'll be girls there tonight?' Marcus said.

'Last time round Frosty's I swear there was more girls than men. His flat's massive, a big lounge and three bedrooms. You'll see for yourself. Large-screen TV on the wall, plush leather sofas. This girl Keisha's coming down tonight so that's me sorted. But fear not, I told her to bring her friend Loretta.'

'She nice?'

'You like big boobies? Like supersize?' he said, tongue darting in and out.

'What do you think?'

They turned onto the main road, cars flying by. It was a fifteen-minute walk over the North Circular and they'd have to watch it: enemy territory. They laughed about last night's shenanigans, embellishing some heroics into the mix, saying they could've had any girls they wanted but it was good to shake things up sometimes, leave your footprint. Leon wouldn't have been so cocky with a knuckleduster rammed down his throat, but that'd have to wait till next time. Suddenly a shot rang out from somewhere, echoing off the buildings.

'Gun!' someone yelled and everyone ran. Marcus froze in shock, losing a second or two, then set off towards the others. They were already way ahead, Blue included.

Another shot echoed out and he saw Blue vanish around a corner. Then a third blast sounded and he tumbled to the pavement. He tried to get up but couldn't feel his legs. The small of his back ached and he realised he'd been shot. Time slowed. Where was Blue? Why had he left him here all alone? Any second he expected his cousin to reappear and pull him up, help him to safety, but the pavement ahead was empty. Streetlights blurred, cars speeding by. He'd never felt so alone. Through a break in the flow of traffic, a figure approached him from across the road. Figures behind goaded him on. 'Do it, fucking blaze him.' Through a balaclava the youth's eyes glared with hatred as he levelled his gun. It was the last image Marcus ever saw.

Down the backstreets Blue met up with Syrus, Jay and his girl who were hiding in the doorway of some flats. 'Jeez man, there you are,' Blue said in relief. 'I was wondering where you lot got to.' Then Shots' ginger head emerged from a nearby bush. 'Get over here,' they said, laughing from all the shock and adrenaline. He bolted over. Everyone was pretty cool, apart from Mel who looked spooked. Jay had his arm around her, Mel leaning into his chest sucking her thumb. Blue spudded him. 'All in one piece, Jay?'

'Thankfully yeah. I swear a bullet whizzed past my head back there. Mel reckons the same thing.'

'It sounded like they were emptying a whole clip.'

'Must've been four or five rounds I reckon.'

'Felt more like ten,' Shots said.

'I heard six for definite.'

'Hey, where's Marcus?' Blue said, looking up and down the street.

'Who the fuck's Marcus?' Syrus asked.

'My cousin – the guy I brought down tonight.'

'Oh. Don't know, everyone ran.'

'I'll phone him.'

Blue kept getting no answer. 'Marcus ain't picking up. I don't get it.'

Shots said, 'You don't think he was hit, do you?'

'Don't even go there.'

'Where was he when it all went off?' Syrus asked.

'He was right next to me.'

Multiple sirens began wailing from the main road.

'Fuck this, I'm going back there, I've got to find him.'

'I'll go with you,' Syrus said. 'Anyone else coming?' Nobody volunteered. 'How about you Shots?'

'Nah, I'll leave it.'

Syrus kissed his teeth as he went, but Shots wasn't risking his arse for no stranger, cousin of Blue or not. Marcus had been part of that batty-boy Watford crew who'd had their arses whipped at the party last night. Blue was lowering his standards with wannabes like that.

Syrus and Blue reached the main road. Police and an ambulance were there now, the road cordoned off, flashing blue lights illuminating the scene. Up ahead paramedics were huddled over a body on the pavement. No way. Rushing closer Blue's worst fears were confirmed. Marcus lay stripped down in a pool of blood as they worked on him. Blue ran under the tape and a policeman tried to stop him.

'That's my cousin,' he pushed past.

Syrus watched. Even from a distance he knew Marcus was gone. They were pumping his heart, trying to revive him. Six months ago Syrus had watched them perform the same procedure on his friend Cornetto to no avail. Cornetto was now in Kensal Green Cemetery next to his uncle who'd gone the same way. Pools of blood and cut-up bits of clothing were scattered around, swirling blue lights painting the whole scene otherworldly. The paramedics stood up, Marcus's body motionless on the ground.

Blue was causing a scene now, three feds restraining him. Syrus turned away. Those bullets had been for him.

22

Dog Eat Dog

Bernie drove down to Kilburn with five grand on him. The rest would be settled when the job was complete, hopefully very soon. He parked in and entered the pub. Quinn turned from the bar and Bernie hesitated. What the fuck was he doing here?

'Talk of the devil,' Quinn said, sounding like he'd had a few. 'Look who it is.'

Phil stood red-faced behind the bar polishing a glass. Quinn stepped off his stool. 'I want a word with you two.' He nodded to a corner table expecting them to run.

Bernie stood his ground. 'I want a word with you as well.'

'Feeling's mutual then,' Quinn laughed. 'Get yourself a drink lads and come over.' He settled in the corner.

At the bar Bernie discreetly handed over the cash bag as Phil pulled him a pint. 'Easy now Bern,' Phil said, eyeing the scant patrons. 'Don't wind him up and cause a scene. In light of what's happening let's show no tension.'

'I still want a word with him. Let's bring it upstairs.'

Phil called to Quinn, pointing to the ceiling. 'We're going up.' Quinn shrugged, took his drink and stood. They headed upstairs, entered the empty function room. Quinn pointed to the little stage.

'Hey Phil, you should have go-go dancers. Strippers on a Sunday afternoon. Jazz this place up a bit.'

Behind him, Bernie saw red. He pushed him with both hands in the back. Quinn jutted forward spilling his drink.

'What are you sending me photos for, you cunt?'

Incensed, he turned round. He threw a right hander that sent him staggering back. Bernie wasn't sure if he'd been glassed. Quinn grabbed him, pushed him up against the wall. 'Photos? What the fuck are you talking about?'

'I'm sick of your games Sean, now get the hell off me.'

Quinn thumped him in the stomach, followed with an uppercut and Bernie was decked and winded. He turned to Phil who stood there frozen. 'Do you know what this cunt's on about?'

Phil shook his head, but could see the bloke already putting two and two together. Head cocked Quinn walked towards him. 'You been up to your dirty tricks again Phil mate?' In his hand now was a Stanley knife. Phil backed away. He said he didn't know what he was talking about.

'Yes you do, I can see it in your face. Trying to blacken my name, is that it?' Quinn grabbed a glass and threw it at him. It smashed against Phil's raised arms.

'Please, stop...'

Quinn kicked out at him and Phil toppled back over some chairs. On the floor he held the knife to his face. 'I want to know the story about these photographs.'

'Bernie thinks you sent him some pictures from the old days, a kind of blackmail thing.'

Quinn glanced back at Bernie who was trying to stand, get his breath.

'I see. One of Fitzy's collection. That you must have got hold of, right?' The blade was close to Phil's eye now.

'No, I promise you...'

'Of course you do. Because as per usual you're a grovelling little liar.'

Quinn pressed the knife to his cheekbone and Phil shrieked. The blade pierced his skin and Quinn was tempted to carve the bastard cheek-to-mouth when the door opened.

'Dad!' Tara screamed. 'Get off him!'

Quinn stood up and Phil was clutching his face, fingers bloody.

'What have you done to him?'

'Nothing, it's just a nick. Your old man's lucky though, he's been asking for it.'

'I'm calling the police. You're an animal. You're going to jail for this.'

Quinn lunged and grabbed her by the throat, showing her the knife.

'Do that, you little slapper, and your life won't be worth living.' Tara was stunned. He shook her. 'Do you hear me? I'll slaughter the fucking pair of you.'

He threw her down onto Phil and she held onto her dad.

'You'll say fuck all to nobody,' Quinn pointed. 'Do you hear me?'

'You're an evil bastard,' she cried.

'Just do as he says,' Phil told her.

'That's right, listen to your father.'

He went over to Bernie who was standing looking pained. He clapped his shoulder. 'Come on Bern, you and me are getting out of here.'

Rain fell as they walked the evening streets in silence. Quinn offered him a fag, Bernie accepting even though he hadn't smoked in years. As Quinn lit it for him, Bernie noticed a hint of regret, as if Quinn knew he'd gone too far back there. He wondered if it was Phil who'd sent him the photos after all. An incentive so he'd agree to the hit. If so, it was a fucking slippery move.

Quinn nodded him into a small pub. Bernie sat at a table and Quinn brought over two pints and whiskey chasers. After washing down the short with a lug of Guinness Quinn looked less troubled.

'You can talk to me now,' he said.

'There's nothing to say. You left Phil and Tara in a state back there. Do they really deserve that?'

'You started it Bern, getting physical and shouting the odds, so you can blame yourself.'

He had a point. Phil had only just warned him to be careful.

'I received some photos.'

'So I heard. Of you shagging a tart back in the day?'

'More or less.'

Quinn shook his head. 'It was Phil. You don't have to believe me of course, it's up to you.'

Bernie looked down. 'I don't know who to believe,' he said, despite it being obvious now.

Quinn gazed around the pub in disgust. Once a snug little Irish boozer, it had gone yuppie and was now bland and spiritless, quiet as the grave. He remembered the wild lock-ins held here in the nineties. The jukebox was full of rebel songs and the governor looked like Ronnie Drew. The boys would come down for a session, staggering out at eight in the morning when everyone else was heading to work. He eyed the sparse middle-class clientele with malice.

Quinn took a final lug, scraped back his chair. 'Believe who you fucking like. I'm sick of the pair of you.' He walked out of the pub.

Bernie remained. He waited twenty minutes or so, finished his pint and left.

The rain was heavier, slapping down drenching him as he went. He heard a shuffle, then he was yanked sideways into an alley. Back to the wall he faced Quinn's fierce eyes.

'All I want from you two cunts is my money, you got that?'

Bernie nodded and again the breath was blown from him as Quinn pounded his gut. Bernie dropped, splashing beery vomit across the cobbles as Quinn vanished into the wet night.

Tara drove her dad to the A&E to get his face stitched. The wound was small but deep and wouldn't stop bleeding. If anyone asked – nurses, Maureen - he'd been jumped on the street, they agreed, but it was dark and he saw little.

Bernie, meanwhile, drove back home to Watford. He had a fat lip and his gut ached. He'd tell Jen he had a problem customer at the garage, but he'd sorted it.

Quinn didn't feel like going home at all. He walked down to the blocks lining Carlton Vale and threw a stone up at Siobhan's window. Two floors up he saw her red tresses. She let him in, said she'd been sleeping. 'You're a right one you are,' she smiled as they crept past the living room where her aunt slept on the sofa. In the bedroom they didn't mess about, Quinn releasing his stress in the most efficient way he knew. Ten years without a woman was something he still marvelled at. He got a rhythm going, headboard thumping the wall. It was like a workout, like banging out reps in the prison gym. The thought of how he'd lost his cool with Phil enraged him now. It meant no more Tara and he'd been enjoying their regular thing together, a young bird on his arm, even if she was a bit of a soppy cow. But maybe he was wasting his time with youngsters like her. After all, if he'd wanted to piss Phil off he'd certainly achieved that now.

He needed to get back to the drawing board, get some real work done. He thought of the money depot near St Albans. That would be a masterstroke. He'd have to get on that, put the time in. You had to think big these days. But for now there were some jewellers he had his eye on. A few cash transit runs worth considering too. He planned to get Phil and Bernie out working as soon as possible. Get them out there earning even if it meant shoving them into a bank on Kilburn High Road with tights over their heads and a pair of bananas. Silly fucking mugs. But he needed pocket money. If only to cover the amount of charlie he was shoving up his nose. He concentrated on the job in hand, the tension building. No matter what happened, the future looked fruitful.

*

The next day Tara sat in the Corrib Rest with Joey. His arm was around her, her head resting on his shoulder after she'd told him what happened last night. She'd got through an eleven-to-seven shift behind the bar today, trying to pretend everything was normal, but with a shoulder to cry on it had all poured out. Joey said he knew Sean was a bastard from the moment he saw him. And another thing, that ginger bird wasn't his cousin either.

'How do you know that?'

'My mate says she's a right alco, always flirting and cadging drinks off men. She's been around for a few weeks now.'

'She still might be his cousin.'

'Would you eat your own cousin's face off right there at the bar?'

Despite everything Tara felt an involuntary streak of jealousy. What was wrong with her? She hated the man now, so why was she jealous? Maybe it was because she still liked the old Sean. The new version was a stranger.

'I've found out all about him,' Joey went on. 'From my Uncle Frank. He's out in Ruislip now but he lived in Kilburn for years, knew everyone. Sean and your dad were part of an armed firm. There was a whole crowd of them. Sean would plan big robberies, pick the right men for the jobs.'

'I've heard bits and pieces,' she said. 'Even looked it up on the internet but there's little there. All the older people in the pub won't talk about it.'

'That's not surprising. In the late eighties and nineties they were running round up to all sorts. They were a tight crew and the police couldn't get them because they were clever and nobody would talk. In the end they put a case together and charged a few of them, but the case was so full of holes and the police so corrupt a lot of it was thrown out of court. Only Sean got sent down because he'd shot a copper, and even on that they fixed some of the evidence. Your dad was one of the ones who got off. Don't tell anyone I told you this though. Sean was dangerous in his time.'

'He still fucking is.'

'There's other stuff too, darker stuff,' Joey spoke quietly. 'Some believe he played a hand in the death of his own best friend. Johnny Mac. He was shot and his body was disappeared. They'd been best mates but had a long running dispute. Johnny Mac was no angel apparently, but still. He went in an unmarked grave, just like the IRA used to do with grasses.'

'Your uncle told you all this?'

'His friend ran a pub that the firm drank in, The Green Dragon, a real criminal's den. It's gone, there's flats there now. Mind you, my uncle was a bit worse for wear when he told me all this. We were having a little drink of poteen together. Next day he denied it all, telling me to take his late-night fireside tales with a pinch of salt. He must've regretted spilling the beans.'

It was all too much. Tara broke into tears and Joey held her. Her dad had warned her about Sean and she'd not only refused to listen but rubbed it in. The guilt was eating her up.

'I wish I'd never met him. I never want to see him again.'

*

'I was over in Harlesden yesterday,' Lil said.

Bigz took a hand off the wheel to turn down the car radio. 'What were you doing out that way?'

'I buy my ammo from a guy out there. You know me, I like to keep my hardware loaded.'

'Sensible thing,' Bigz nodded.

'We were driving in his whip to pick up the goods. This player's Church Road and he pointed out a bunch of Stonebridge by a chicken shop. And listen to this, you'll never guess who I saw hanging with them.'

'Who?'

'Take a guess.'

'Fuck guesses, just tell me.'

'Your man Jay.'

Bigz turned, eyes stunned. 'You're kidding me.'

'I'm telling you. And I thought, I know that face. That's Bigz's boy. But what the fuck is he doing hanging with the Thugs of Stonebridge?'

Bigz was staring ahead, breathing hard through his nose now. 'You certain on this?'

'I swear down.'

After a minute digesting the news he said, 'Makes sense come to think of it. I remember Jay's got some family out that way.'

Suddenly Bigz swung a left off Tottenham High Road onto Bruce Grove.

'Where we going?'

'Taking a detour. I want to stop by his cousin's place in Wood Green.'

Reaching their destination, they parked in.

'You carrying?'

Lil nodded, passed over his piece.

When the door opened, Trevor seemed distracted, holding out a twenty quid like he'd expected a takeaway. Then his eyes widened and Bigz snatched the note off him and marched him inside at gunpoint.

'Where's Jay?'

'How the fuck would I know,' Trevor said, hands in the air. 'I ain't seen the man for time.'

Bigz bashed him with the gun and he landed back on the sofa

clutching his head. 'Rah, that fucking hurt.'

'You can blame your snake of a cousin. Now you're giving him a message. Tell him I know where he is and who he's hanging with. And if he don't contact me I'll be straight back here and I won't just be butting you with this ting next time, you hear me?'

Lil Killa came from the kitchen drinking a can of strawberry-flavoured Nurishment he'd taken from the fridge.

'Mind if I help myself?'

'Silly question,' Trevor answered.

'It's up to you now Trev,' Bigz said. 'Get Jay to call me or I'll be coming back trigger-happy.'

They made to leave. By the door Lil turned for a smirk. 'Apologies for the inconvenience.'

'Fuck you, you weird little prick,' Trevor almost said, but stopped himself.

Outside a delivery driver was coming up the path. Bigz handed him Trevor's twenty and took the pizza with him. 'Cheers boss, hot and on time,' he said, tucking into a slice.

Jay was with Syrus and the boys when Trevor phoned. He sounded livid. Jay went to take the call out of earshot and listened to the news. Bigz had burst in with a gun and attacked him in his own home.

'I swear down,' Trevor said, 'if Bigz and his little freak sideman darken my door again they'll be leaving in body bags.'

'So it's true he's teamed with Lil Killa now?'

'A small fucker was with him, yeah. Laurel and fricking Hardy. Guy was helping himself to my fridge. You think I need this hassle? I've had to contact some old friends over this shit and I'm packing a piece now. Risking my arse over your fucked-up shit. I left this gangbanging crap behind years ago and you're dumping it all back on me.'

'I'll sort it Trev, I promise you.'

'You better. Now phone the motherfucker pronto or he'll be paying me another visit.'

Syrus came over and sat on the wall.

'Was that our law-abiding cousin Trevor? What did he want?'

'Nothing much, he was just seeing how I was doing,' Jay lied. 'You know what Trevor's like.'

Syrus smiled knowingly. 'Was he phoning about your Hackney man? Come on Jay, I've heard things. You weren't really running from the Hackney cops when you came here, you were fleeing some beef with your crew.'

Jay didn't want to burden Syrus with complications. They had a good thing going at present, were making good Ps now. Bigz was trying to throw a spanner in the works.

He came clean. Told him the whole story.

Done, Syrus lit a blunt, took a long toke then passed it over.

'Seems to me there's only one solution.'

'Which is?'

'Take a little trip down east and take him out of the picture.'

The idea of Bigz not being around was an appealing one. But offing somebody was a major leap. It wasn't Jay's style. But he wondered if he had a choice now. Bigz would fill Trevor with holes just to get at him. And he wouldn't leave it there either.

'We'd have to get him on his own, away from his new partner,' Jay said, almost to himself, running the idea through his mind.

'Not a problem. Has Bigz got enemies?'

'Gee, where do I start? I'd be here all day. He's not an easy guy to get on with.'

'That's good, means the feds won't have a clue, and nor will anyone else.'

Jay took a deep drag, still unsure. 'It's a big step.'

'Not really. Happens every day.'

Jay nodded as he pondered that. People get thrown into prison every day too, he thought.

'We're family,' Syrus said. 'If he wants a piece of you and he's onto Trevor now, that's the final straw. A straight-goer like Trev don't need this shit.'

'He told me to phone Bigz immediately.'

'Go on then, do it now. Put it on loudspeaker. Considering we're popping the prick I want to hear him while he's still alive and kicking.'

He called him.

'Hey Bigz, it's me, Jay.'

'Rah… you finally want to speak to me after doing a runner? About fucking time. You're a cunt Jay. I've had your back for years and the minute things get hot you don't want to know.'

'Look B, I needed a break. Things were getting too lively out there.'

'So you run off to fucking Harlesden, hanging with the Stonebridge boys?'

'I was but I'm up in Coventry now.'

'Coventry? What the fuck?'

'I'm staying with my aunt at the moment.'

'You better get yourself back down to London quicktime, you hear me? There's bare shit I need help with. You can't just abandon your bredrins Jay, that's Judas-style. Me, you and Slim were rolling for life and this is how you treat his memory, by fucking off without a trace? You hear what happened, the guy got hacked to fucking pieces.'

'Course I heard. It's terrible.'

Bigz left a pause. 'You owe me for this big time.'

'I'm coming back, but not for a few weeks. My aunt is sick and I'm looking after her, helping out.'

'You're dealing merchandise up there more like, fresh territory, probably making a roll. You better be bringing some of those riches back with you, you hear me?'

'Nah, Coventry's well grimy, it's over-saturated on that score. There's no dough to be made up here. I told you, I'll be back in two weeks.'

Bigz kissed his teeth. 'You fucking better be.' He hung up.

Jay looked at his phone and exhaled.

'What a total dickhead,' Syrus laughed. 'He thinks he's in his own movie. I can't believe you ran with a clown like that.'

'Well, you can't pick the people you grew up with.'

'Suppose not, but you can get rid of them though.'

They headed back to their little bunch.

Shots was doing circles on a tiny BMX. 'Were you two chatting top secret shit?' he smiled. 'Is someone getting iced?'

'Something like that,' Syrus replied. 'Nothing out of the ordinary.'

23

Turkish Song of the Damned

Devrim Patrick Halim climbed into his Audi and drove the six miles over to Harringay, the area where he grew up. He had some business to sort for a friend. He'd first met Phil O'Malley a decade back when they were on remand for separate crimes; luckily both were acquitted. They were Kilburn locals and shared several things in common. Both had mothers from Cork, loved an easy pound note and neither discussed business with their wives.

Dev parked in off Green Lanes, a bustling stretch of 24-hour groceries, restaurants and Turkish social clubs. He entered a café and went through to the office where his brother Ossie stood giving a teenage delinquent a bollocking. His hand was raised to slap the youth, but seeing Dev he exhaled and returned to his desk. Dev took a seat at the side, popped a gum. Ossie skipped a greeting. 'Tell me Dev, what can I do with this prick?'

Dev gave a neutral shrug. Ossie had inherited their old man's temper; he didn't want to incite him.

'I give him a legit full-time delivery job to get him off the street and he gets nicked for fighting in the road with a complete stranger. Where's the logic in that? You want to end up in fucking jail?'

'Guy cut me up and did a wanker sign,' the youth tutted.

'You tutting at me, you little cunt?' Ossie jumped up and grabbed a meat cleaver, held it close. 'If I have to call you in here again I'll cut both your fucking hands off. You listening to me? Now get out of my sight.'

The boy slunk off and Ossie sat down, placing the cleaver on his desk.

'Anyway, what were we saying?' Dev said.

Ossie smiled. He put the chopper away, shook his head. 'I'm just wound up mate, serious. The boy's risking jail for shit that don't even bring in money. How dumb is that?'

Dev shook his head. Neither him nor Ossie had been wise at that age either, but it was easy to forget. Dev remembered the time they'd tried to burgle a Finsbury Park clothing warehouse of its Calvin Klein knock offs. They ended up crashing through the roof. It turned out the owner was a top Greek face, and one thing the kingpins on either divide didn't like was ethnic disharmony. It brought attention and was bad for business. They were in deep shit. The Turkish don of the area called them in to explain themselves. Known as the General, his paramilitary credentials back in the old country were well-renowned. People spoke about him in hushed tones, apart from their father who behind closed doors called him a tyrant and a thief. Their old man had no respect for men who earned their living dishonestly, a belief that was to cause much friction with his two sons through the years.

Dev still remembered that first time in the General's office, both standing there in bandages like it was yesterday. Flags and political figures adorned the walls, a revolver propped ominously on the desk. It was in the back room of a bakery only doors from where they now sat.

'So you're the two hooligans bringing problems to my door?' He slapped each around the face. 'You think you're big men, hah?'

He lectured them on behaviour and honour, implying their wayward ways were the result of a man marrying outside of tradition, but the bollocking would have been worse had their father and the General not hailed from neighbouring villages. In the end he said their father was an honest working man who deserved better sons. Little did he know what their dad thought of him. But now Dev and Ossie had dues to pay, remittances to make. Henceforth they worked for the General for many years, became trusted soldiers. Did time for him. Even killed for him.

Dev recalled his first hit. The hot summer night they sat parked off Newington Green. They were waiting for the target to exit the Turkish club and return to his car. A singer was audible from the club's open back doors. Folk songs of old. Love, loss, patriotism, death by war. The man appeared on the street. Dev got out, Ossie keeping the engine running. The man sung to himself as he went, suit jacket over his arm. He stopped at his car. He turned and saw the gun.

Dev's hand shook.

'Go on then you little bastard, do it,' he said, standing with both arms out. Defiantly he continued to sing, louder now. A song about a son not returning from a war. Dev considered running back to the car. Admitting he wasn't cut out for this. But the moment passed and he fired the gun; one, two, three. He was blooded now.

Ossie lit a B&H, downed a glass of raki. He pointed to the bottle. 'You want one? Join me.'

Dev shook his head, moved his chair in opposite. 'It's business not pleasure today I'm afraid.'

'Shame.' Ossie turned on the radio and they leant close on the desk.

'I've got a job. It's from my manor, an Irish mob up there.'

'A hit?'

He nodded.

'And the target?'

'Some lag, just got out after doing a ten.'

'Old friends?'

'Spot on. They owe him and he's causing problems.'

'You trust them?'

'I've known Phil O'Malley for years, he's safe. We were in the nick together and he runs a pub near me. Wives know each other, the works.'

'Is he the blagger you did the weed job with a few years back?'

'That's right. You've met him.'

Ossie mulled over it. 'Maybe I'll sub it to Ali's lot. He carried that last one off pretty well. Then again, there's always Hot Iron Mike - though I'd have to put a note in to keep it strictly clean.'

'Up to you. As long as they're professional.'

'I'll have a word with Ali's crew first. Last couple got coroner's suicide verdicts. Can you believe that? They might be charging top dollar now though, I'll see.'

'Phil wants the job done quick. I'm talking maybe this week.'

'You know the details?'

'Everything. I've been out with Fat Chris, keeping an eye. The target drinks around the same pubs every night.'

'What if he's under observation?'

'Old Bill? I would've spotted something by now. It's safe.'

'Okay. Send the details. Encrypted. And the money to the usual.'

'One last thing.'

'What?'

'I told him we'd do it for twenty grand.'

'You having a laugh?'

'Friendly discount.'

'You can say that again. More like a freebie if you ask me.'

Dev shrugged.

'Alright, go on then. It'll have to be Mike though.'

'Nice one. Over and out?'

Ossie nodded and turned off the radio.

Dev stood up. 'Okay, I better run.'

'Hey, come and visit soon, see the kids.'

'Will do. Come over to ours maybe. Marie will cook some of her spaghetti again.'

'No wonder you're getting a belly.'

Dev held in his gut. 'What belly?'

Ossie patted his own. 'I shouldn't be talking.'

'On that note I better hit the road.'

'Be good,' Ossie said and his phone rang.

As Dev left, he was on the phone alternating English and Turkish. Their father used to do that. It would be English until he got angry and the mother tongue took over. He walked back to his car. It saddened him thinking of his father. He hadn't approved of their lifestyle, but he mellowed in his last years and they were closer – well, talking at least.

Dev remembered the night he was alone with him in the hospital when he was dying of cancer. It was visiting time but nobody else had arrived yet. The doctor had said he had only several weeks left in him. Tonight he looked particularly frail. Dev leaned close as his father tried to tell him something. He caught the words. 'You and your brother have been nothing but a disappointment to me.'

He wondered if he'd misheard him. Then his father started trembling. Dev shouted for the nurse. Within minutes he was dead. His mum, sister and Ossie arrived. Tears flowed. His mum asked what his last words had been. He said he loved us all, Dev replied. The memory still burned. He drove back to Kilburn.

*

Tarquin stood by a line of derelict shops on Dalston Lane, staring at the flyposters of a trendy magazine that covered two

313

entire shopfronts. *London's coolest couple Johnny Long and Tabitha James talk sex, bullets and rock 'n' roll in Hackney.* The pair lounged in boho garb, Tabby oozing a languid insouciance that he recognised intimately. He stood entranced as her face gazed back at him twentyfold. He hadn't seen the couple around for a while, not since he'd fired a gun up at their window one evening, but they'd clearly been busy scaling new heights.

He stole a copy from a newsagent and sat on a bench to torture himself. A six-page photoshoot saw the couple posing in familiar sites across the East End. He recognised a Bethnal Green tower block, The George Tavern on Commercial Road, a graffiti-covered alley in Whitechapel he'd once jacked up in. Gritty urban chic. Johnny's band were all set for a sell-out UK tour, while Tabitha had signed up as the face of a cool high street clothing chain. Aside from modelling Tabitha enjoys moonlighting as a club DJ for London's in-crowd and says demand for her funky MC skills is booming. 'If only,' she laughs. 'I'm pretty awful at it actually, but it's all good fun.'

Both love London, even after being at home in Hackney when a stray bullet from a gun-blazing gang fight in the street below shattered their living room window. But is it really true that the bullet lodged into a copy of William Burroughs' *Naked Lunch*? 'Absolutely,' says Johnny. 'It was a hardback original on our bookshelf and the police took it away as evidence. It seems oddly fitting as Burroughs was of course something of a gunslinger himself,' he says, referring to when the novelist allegedly shot his wife in a game of William Tell. 'But in truth it could've blown my bloody head off,' he adds. At this Tabitha smiles, admitting it would've been impossible as they were somewhat busy in the back bedroom at the time. 'Johnny's so randy,' she laughs, slapping his knee, to which he replies in his best mockney: 'Not 'arf, darlin'.'

After their arguable dice with death, the amorous literature-loving couple have moved their lovenest to the less crime-ridden but no less fashionable Shoreditch. London native Johnny insists The Smoke will always be his home, guns and all, while Devon-raised Tabitha admits the experience was unsettling but she's an urban girl at heart.

Tarquin put the mag down and stared off into the distance. It was good to hear Tabby hadn't moved too far away, but surely she was lying about the gang shootout. Surely she knew it was him?

But he needed to get real. He didn't register in Tabitha's consciousness these days. She was on magazine covers now, hanging with the crème a la crème. Why would she waste her thoughts on a fuck-up like him? He got up and walked. It was too painful to dwell on. He needed escape. Needed a hit.

By a corner shop a man stood begging. Greasy hair, khaki jacket, another waster raising funds for a fix. Passing by Tarq felt a hint of recognition. But no, it couldn't be. Then their eyes met and sure enough it was Alex, the singer of the Sevilles. Alex hesitated, but Tarq hid his surprise to put him at ease. Everyone knew Tarq had fallen on his luck, but now he wasn't the only one.

'Al, how are you, man?'

'Haven't seen you in an age Tarq, what's up?'

Alex had hollow cheeks and a pleading look that certainly hadn't been there two years ago when he'd been strutting his stuff on stage. He had mouth sores, a front tooth missing. He admitted things had gone a little downhill. He'd been living in Brixton with his girlfriend but she kicked him out.

Tarq remembered their last meeting. It was at a penthouse party in Notting Hill thrown by a Sony bigwig. Alex's band were the stars of the night after signing a deal. Introducing their acoustic set the Sony guy said they were alumni of Highgate School, joking about nepotism, the old boy network. Later Alex took Tarq into a large dim-lit bedroom. The Seville's bass player Charlie was writhing on a water bed with both an upcoming TV actress and a girl from a B-rate pop group. They snorted some

MDMA, Alex saying he was off to New York tomorrow to play an industry gig with the Yeah Yeah Yeahs. Crack America and it's happy days. He'd try to put in a word to get Tarq's group out to the States too. Do some gigs together. The best British invasion yet.

It was party talk, but it was good to hope. The actress pulled Alex down onto the bed, began to tear at his clothes. She ordered Tarq to get his kit off too, wanted both of them, but Tarq declined and returned to the main room where Tabitha asked him where he'd been. The Sevilles never did crack America, nor did they get very far in Britain. Their first Sony single skimmed the charts and their big expensive album flopped. Bass player Charlie, high on a cocktail of drugs, later threw himself from a window in Brighton.

Tarq marvelled at how somebody who'd had everything going for them, connections, looks, talent, could have landed in the same position he himself was in. Then again, it was so easy. Alex said he'd met one of Primal Scream recently who might get him on the crew helping on their next tour. Tarq nodded along but Alex was kidding himself, even if the claim was true. Nobody would take on a liability. You fall and you're on your own. They spoke some more, then Tarq wished him luck.

Alex stopped him. 'I heard you've got your own place round here, your own flat.'

'I did at one point, but I'm kipping with a mate now,' Tarq lied. More late-night knocks at his door for gear, he didn't need.

Something caught Alex's eye and he said he'd better get going. He hurried away and a dealer stepped from a car, pumped arms, gold chain.

'Come back here you little shit,' he called and Alex ran.

The man strode up to Tarq, backed him against the wall.

'You tell your mate he owes me fifty quid and if I don't see it by tomorrow he's getting capped.'

'He's not my mate.'

'I don't give a fuck, just tell him.'

The man stared him out as he returned to his car. 'You pricks are all the same. Fucking vermin.' He revved away.

Tarq walked. He needed to raise some dough. Since doing regular jobs for Billy the Fence the pressure had eased somewhat, but even fat wads have a habit of running out. He stopped by a bush for his screwdriver. There was a car-park nearby that usually yielded fruit so he headed there.

*

Bigz and Lil Killa cruised along discussing last night's arson job.

'So you're telling me the council hires Mike to burn their own buildings down?'

'When need be, yeah,' Lil said from the wheel. 'Who can complain when there's nothing left to save? They flog the land to a developer for flats and it's back handers and profits all round. More, they get praise for reducing council expenditure.'

Bigz tutted. 'But that's corruption.'

'They call it business.'

'And there's us doing all the risky work.'

'Mike threw us four hundred each so I ain't complaining - you?'

'Course not. It's about time he gave us a bonus.'

Lil swung a right and they drove along Graham Road. He laughed recalling last night's capers, the pair of them creeping about in the dark with petrol cans. 'When you threw that match I thought you were going to go up in flames.'

'Tell me about it,' Bigz laughed. 'The fire went whoosh and almost blew me off my feet. I'm lucky I wasn't dancing in those flames boy. The fire brigade could've been pulling out a charred corpse last night - me.'

'I was cracking up all the way to the car. Oh yeah, Mike texted earlier to say job well done. He reckons the whole place burnt down to a crisp.' Then Lil's phone rang. 'Shit, that's him now.' He answered it.

'You heard the news?' Mike said cheerily.

'No chief, what happened?'

'Nothing much, but you know that bit of work you did last night? I heard they pulled out a body. Someone had been sleeping in there.'

'No way.'

'Some homeless guy apparently. It's funny because they're thinking it's him who must've started the fire by accident. Like smoking or some shit,' he chuckled. 'Convenient or what?'

'I see what you mean.'

'Anyway, you boys are busy so I won't keep you. Make sure to deliver that food.'

'Will do boss,' Lil said and hung up.

'Did he just say what I thought he said?' Bigz asked.

Lil nodded.

'Jeez, that's like a fucking omen.'

As they turned up Queensbridge Road something caught Lil's eye.

'What's up?' Bigz asked.

'You see that guy there,' Lil pointed. 'Is that...?'

Bigz zoomed in on a white guy walking along. He jumped in his seat.

'That's the fucker who tried to shoot me in the face!'

Tarq heard a screech of brakes and turned to see Bigz climbing out of a hatchback. He took to his heels, dashing into the Holly Street Estate.

Bigz set off after him. But as he watched his quarry vault a wall far ahead he knew he had no chance. He stood there out of breath, yelling into the distance.

'I'll find you man, and when I do your life is over, you hear me whiteboy?'

Lil came up behind him.

'That guy's got some legs,' he said, 'I'll give him that.'

'Not when I get hold of him he won't. I'll take a chainsaw to those legs, see how fast he can run then.'

Lil patted his arm. 'Come on, there's always another day. We've got some drop offs to do.'

Nearby a bunch of loitering kids, eleven, twelve, were enjoying the entertainment.

Bigz turned to them. 'You find something funny?'

A light-skinned black boy asked, 'That guy you were after, what did he do?'

Bigz ignored him and turned to walk away, then on second thoughts he replied, 'He boned your mum up the batty. That's how you came about.'

The group fell silent. As Bigz and Lil walked on, a bottle smashed a few feet behind them.

Enraged Bigz spun around ready to charge the fuckers, but Lil took his arm.

'Take it easy B, they're just a bunch of tinys. Allow it. We're at work now, it ain't playtime.'

'Did you see what those pricks just did?'

'It don't matter - now come on, we've got stuff to do for Mike, more important shit.'

Bigz cursed and they headed back to the car.

Peeking over a wall, Tarq watched them walking away. Lady Luck had saved him yet again. He felt like a cat with nine lives. The question was how many he had left.

24

Rippers

Dan turned from his stool at the bar as two strangers entered the pub. Cheap suits, slimy-looking. One was short and stocky, his pal tall and thin with the countenance of an undertaker. They were Old Bill.

'Tel,' Dan said from the side of his mouth, as Terry ordered another round.

The coppers came straight over. 'Terence Hart?' The short bloke flashed his ID. 'Police. I'm DC Llewellyn and this is DC Hawkes. We need to question you on a serious matter.'

Terry looked from one to the other. 'What matter?'

'Murder.'

Terry was mute, but Dan stepped off his chair. 'Is this a fucking wind-up?'

'Stay out of this mate, we're talking to Mr Hart. You need to come with us to the station for questioning.'

'I'm not going anywhere.'

'We can do this the easy way or the hard way.'

'How about we do it the piss-off-and-leave-me-alone way. Yesterday some kids were stabbed just over the road, how come you're not out searching for the culprits?'

'We're aware of that attack and enquiries are underway. But unfortunately this case is even more serious. It involves three people murdered on the street with an axe. Do you own an axe Mr Hart?'

'I don't have time for this bollocks. If you want to bring me to the nick you'll have to arrest me. Now I'm having a pint, so you can fuck off and take Laughing Boy with you.'

Hawkes stepped forward. 'That's it, you're under arrest.' He read him his rights and tried to cuff him. Terry pushed him backwards, saying he could shove those cuffs up his arse, while Dan squared up to Llewellyn.

Four men from across the way rushed over carrying pool cues, asking what the fuck was going on. Outnumbered, the coppers decided to retreat, talking into their radios.

'That's right, fuck off out of it you cunts,' Terry said in triumph.

'Enjoy your pint Terry,' Llewellyn said from the door. 'Then pack your bag because you're coming in. The heavy mob are on their way.'

A few minutes later, fuss over and Terry coming to his senses, he thought it best to wait outside. Dan took his drink and said he was coming out with him.

On the street they stood in silence for a bit. Then Dan turned to him. 'What have you done Tel?'

Terry met his eyes. At that moment he felt like telling him everything. Getting it all off his chest. He knew Dan would understand and do what he could to help him - and it wasn't as if the victims weren't pond life whose absence only made the world a safer place. But then again, why make an issue of it? Perhaps he could ride this out. If the police had any real evidence they'd hardly be requesting a chat, they'd be kicking his door down mob-handed and pulling him out of bed. Maybe this was all hot air. Just an enquiry. How many suspects did they pull in for these kind of things? He'd be questioned and ticked off their list and that would be the end of it.

'Are you seriously asking me that Dan?' he said.

'Come on, we all know you can be a bit of a nutter on occasion. What happened?'

'I've done fuck all. They're getting nowhere solving those killings so they're scraping the barrel. You know what the Old Bill are like. They'll probably be pulling you in next and anyone else around here with form. We all know who did it. The manor's gone to shit, it's crawling with scumbags these days.'

'You're right,' Dan said. 'And the filth are a bunch of lazy mugs. Remember they couldn't solve that sledgehammer murder down Rainham so they tried fitting up John Bradley?'

'Exactly. They couldn't get him for his other jobs so they planted evidence, the works. But they were sorry in the end because he opened a can of worms and two of the filth ended up inside. Bent cunts.'

Dan nodded. He looked at his watch. 'They'll be here soon Tel. It's best you get it over with. Phone your brief. It's bullshit so they'll probably only keep you for a few hours.'

Minutes later a police van pulled in and a troop of plod poured out. Terry put up his hands to show he was coming quietly, but still they floored him and knelt hard on his back as they tightened the cuffs.

Hawkes leaned down. 'Hurt does it, you cocky cunt.'

Llewellyn pointed at Dan. 'Pull that stunt again, scrote, and you're nicked. Count yourself a lucky man Daniel Cooper. That's right, I know you're name and I'll be keeping a close eye from now on.'

'I'm quaking in my boots,' Dan retorted, standing arms folded.

'Don't push it fella, I'm warning you.'

At the station Terry conferred with his solicitor. The police had no evidence, were merely eliminating the drivers recorded in the vicinity on the nights of the killings. The lack of functioning CCTV in several sites had hampered their investigation from the start. All three victims were known drug dealers, most likely killed in a turf war. Without witnesses or a murder weapon the police were clearly getting desperate. All of which was music to Terry's ears.

'In short, all they've got is footage of your vehicle passing the shops on The Heathway on the night of the first murder. As far as credible evidence goes it's very lean.'

In the interview room Terry's brief emphasized his client's innocence. Mr Hart is a family man and law-abiding member of his local community who works hard to provide for his wife and daughters...

Starting the interview the coppers looked bored, aware it was a formulaic waste of breath. Terry Hart had some form in the past but nothing too serious, and it seemed he'd gone straight in recent years. The man was a timewaster. If he'd agreed to come in with no drama he'd have been eliminated a lot quicker, but instead he'd dug in and pushed their buttons. In the last hour, as it happens, the murder team had received some viable intel that pointed in another direction completely. Llewellyn and Hawkes looked forward to joining their colleagues in the investigation, but for now had some timewasting to do.

Afterwards a young uniform escorted Terry back to the cells. The copper pushed him in the back then quickly slammed the metal door closed. Terry saw him peering through the slot grinning. 'Come on cunt,' Terry said, spreading his arms. 'Open the door, me and you, let's have it.' The copper sniggered, then closed the slot and trotted off. Cheeky fucker. Terry lay on the hard rubber mattress for an uncomfortable night. Some bloke nearby was kicking his cell door, ranting away like a loon. Another bloke yelled that if he didn't shut up he'd break in there and rip his fucking throat out. I'm trying to sleep you noisy cunt. The din intensified and it took Terry right back to prison where the sound of men kicking off was constant. But a single night of this madness was tolerable. It was just a temporary inconvenience.

His brief was right. Terry was a family man. No matter what he'd done in the past, or even recently, he wasn't a bad person. Not intrinsically. There were some proper wrong 'uns out there who deserved all they got, but he wasn't anywhere near that category. Like the shitstains who'd picked on a group of 14-year-olds the other day not far from the pub, robbing their phones and stabbing two of the boys for fuck all. Terry was no role model, but the violence on his record was old as the crows, mostly youthful punch ups or pub brawls.

But he'd be lying to say there wasn't naughty stuff in his past too. And to this day it didn't sit well with him. He recalled the time he'd used a hammer on a shop owner. It earned him his first bit of bird. But he'd been twenty years old for fuck's sake, practically a kid in today's terms. Didn't every young man make mistakes here and there? He'd got involved with the Burnett brothers who were pretty heavy at the time. In a Plaistow pub they'd watched him batter a woman-beating burglar unconscious and were impressed. He was signing-on at the time and when Len Burnett offered him some work he didn't say no. Dan thought he was mad to work for those psychos, but Terry was young, still finding his feet. They paired him with a Hoxton bruiser, Barry Rafferty, and sent them to collect payments from businesses across the East End.

Terry hated the work. It was bullying, no better than robbing a working man on the street. The pubs pulled in good cash back then, paid up no problem, but a lot of the small shops made a pittance. He remembered a tailor crying saying he couldn't make the payment, he had a family to feed and his business was on its last legs as it was. Big Raff dragged him out back and threatened him with a clothes iron. Terry gave the man another fortnight.

One day Terry was out doing the rounds on his own. A Stratford tool shop owner was usually friendly, but this time he refused to pay. A lump stepped out from the back wielding a hammer. Terry fought with him, beat him bad and the bloke staggered up and ran away. Then the owner came forward with a wheel brace. Terry saw red. He was holding the other bloke's hammer and he lashed out. Next thing the man was on the deck, bloody and groaning. Terry knew he'd over-reacted. He phoned for an ambulance, went on the run for a day then handed himself in. Terry was done for ABH; luckily the man wasn't too badly injured. He got two years, served one and never worked for the Burnetts again.

But he was never happy with that one. It was unnecessary. He thought back to when he lived in Hackney, just before he left school. He had a Saturday job on a fruit and veg stall in Well Street market. A girl would stop by with her gran and they'd always have a chat and he'd give them a discount. Carol was a stunner, too good for him, but he mustered the courage to ask her out. She said he could call round straight after work if he liked, she was having some friends round. She lived on a big estate nearby that had a reputation. It was dark when he was walking through it and, sure enough, he noticed a bloke up the way following behind him. Tall, white, shifty-looking. Several turns later he was still there. The bloke must've seen him on the stall and knew it was payday. Terry was carrying a knife at this point because of all the muggings that were going on. The bod was closer now; but one thing was for sure, Terry was handing his hard-earned wages to no fucker.

He slipped into a derelict garage, standing in the gloom with the smell of rats and dogshit waiting for the prick to turn the corner. Here he was, hurrying past. Terry jumped out and threw him to the ground. He was a lanky streak of piss and Terry got to work kicking away. The bloke was curled up, grunting with each blow, and not for the first time Terry wondered why people assumed he was easy pickings. Was it the way he looked, walked, some kind of aura he gave off? But things were going to change. He was going to get into weights, build himself up so nobody would mess with him ever.

The bloke cowered, said he hadn't done anything, and Terry got down to search him. Shut your mouth you fucking wanker. He was pocketing the bloke's flick knife when he suddenly sprang to life. They tussled and Terry stabbed him repeatedly. The would-be mugger dropped away and Terry stood there breathing. Nobody was around, the dim-lit scene lined with burnt-out cars, a bleak concrete nightmare. He walked back home, threw his jacket and both knives in a skip; he'd get rid of the rest of his clothes later. Back indoors he had a bath. Then his mum said someone was on the phone, a girl called Carol. He told her he was sorry for not coming round, he'd finished work late and had a hard day. Then he realised she was crying. Her brother had been murdered tonight, she said, just a minute from her door.

He never saw Carol again. He got a new Saturday job in Broadway Market. The death made the local paper, someone saying the victim was a decent boy but started to mix with a bad crowd and got into drugs. It was a blip, lost among all the other stories of the time, and soon Terry moved out to Dagenham and it was a whole new start, even better when six months later Dan's family did the same thing.

The next day Terry walked into the pub.

'Old Bill keep you all night?' Dan asked.

'Till ten in the morning mate.'

'What did the missus say?'

'What do you think? She was worried out of her mind. And the girls.'

'Guess what,' Andy said. 'My neighbour got a tug for it too.

Indian bloke. They just wanted to know his whereabouts and he was on his way within the hour.'

'Your neighbour?'

'A cabbie like you. The police are clueless. Looks like they're stopping anyone who drove a car in Dagenham that night. Real Sherlock Holmes effort then. We must be talking thousands. It's harassment if you ask me.'

'Tell me about it.'

'Anyway,' Dan said. 'Whoever did those attacks did the world a favour. I hate all these druggy cunts you see about. They're everywhere nowadays. The axeman should be knighted.'

'Yeah, but the culprit's probably a druggy himself,' Andy pointed out. 'Look at this.' He read from his newspaper. 'Man killed wife because his dinner was cold. Can you imagine it? His fish fingers aren't the right temperature so he grabs a kitchen knife and goes fucking loopy. That's drugs, it's got to be.'

'I'll be going loopy if you don't get another round in,' Dan said.

'I'll get this one,' Terry said.

Andy turned a page. 'Christ, look at these two.' A bleary-eyed Kate Moss and Pete Doherty staggering out of a club. 'State of them.'

Dan said, 'That's what Terry looks like when he hits the whisky.'

Terry shook his head; he paid for three lagers, handed them over.

'Cheers big ears.'

'That reminds me,' Andy said. 'Did you hear about Gary Steele?'

'What about him?' Dan said.

'He's another one.'

'Another what?'

'Crack merchant. He got into the old crack pipe, didn't he. Lost his job, his car, his girlfriend. Next thing he's out on the street doing all sorts to fill his pipe. Some pikeys down Dartford give him a shotgun and two hundred quid and sent him down to Canvey to top someone. Gary knocks on the door, bloke grabs the shooter and Gal gets his fucking foot blown off. He's in the slammer now. Minus a foot.'

Dan shook his head. 'I remember he used to be a snazzy dresser. Drove a nice VW sports at one point.'

'Then the gear took over.'

'Silly cunt.'

'Here, didn't you knob his sister once? Jane or Janice or something?'

'What, back in the day?'

'No, last night with your ex watching.'

'Fuck off.'

'You did though, didn't you?'

'Big girl?'

'Yeah. Big old baps. I saw her down Lakeside once not too long ago. She's got about five kids now.'

'Any of them look like me?'

They laughed.

Dan noticed Terry had gone all quiet. 'You still with us Tel?'

He picked up his pint. 'Just thinking.'

'Thinking never made any man happy ever,' Andy chipped in.

'True in your case,' Dan said.

'Shut up you donut.'

Terry had been dwelling on the murders. It had been nibbling on his mind all day. What if the police never found anyone to charge, would they pull him in again? Without evidence there wasn't much they could do, but say they discovered some evidence? Or even invented some? It wasn't a comforting thought.

Across the way, the TV volume suddenly went right up, a group staring at the screen.

It was the London news.

'A man has today been charged with three murders in East London. In a case dubbed 'the Dagenham Ripper killings' the police say they have finally caught the man they believe is responsible...'

'Wha-hey. Looks like you're off the hook, Tel,' Dan smiled.

'It's an Albanian,' said a local who'd just walked in. 'They arrested him earlier in Barking, right near my old girl's house.'

Viktor 'the Butcher' Bujanoc sat in a police cell considering his predicament. He'd been charged with four murders, only one of which he'd actually committed. It didn't make sense. The other week he'd killed a fellow Albanian in Ilford. He followed him one night and got him in an alley with a meat cleaver, a job he'd been well compensated for. Sadly the police had evidence on that one which would be difficult to dispute in court, but the three Dagenham murders were nothing to do with him. As he told them, he was seeing a woman in the area so was a regular visitor. They said the similarities in injuries were striking, proving it was the same attacker - but what did that prove?

The bastards had him for one kill so were simply trying to nail him for others to help clear their unsolved backlog. He'd killed other men, fair enough, but even so. He recalled a few highlights. Last year he did a Kosovan in a flat in Wood Green. The man hadn't been paying his debts. He was pleading his case, but Viktor swiftly silenced him with a shot to the head. Then he cut up and bagged his body and put it in the boot of a car. He parked it by a derelict industrial estate off the A13 where it remained for six weeks until somebody complained about the smell. He'd heard the boot was opened by a lady police officer. He smiled imagining her reaction.

Another job was in Leytonstone. The man was on his knees swearing he hadn't skimmed from those kilos of heroin, swearing on his mother's life. Viktor let him beg, feigning consideration, as if he might be lenient this time, just this once.

But it didn't work like that. Since coming to London three years ago Viktor had offered his services to the highest bidder and his countrymen paid generously.

He lowered his gun. 'You're lucky my friend.'

The man broke into tears of relief, saying how grateful he was.

Then Viktor slowly rose his weapon, just to see the man's face, and blew his head open. Tasting blood on his lips, he let it linger on his tongue. The fresh blood of a dead man always tasted good.

He thought back to life in the old country. He was the village butcher, scraping a meagre living from selling meat just like his father and grandfather before him, but after the civil war of '97 the nation was penniless and business was bad. He closed up shop and joined his wayward brother Edi in the cigarette smuggling trade.

With officials paid off and their warehouse stacked with tonnes of tobacco, life was better than ever. They decided to branch out, broaden their interests. They began gun running. That was profitable too. Then they got into the heroin trade and here was where the real riches lay. They ploughed money back into their home town, providing jobs and putting food on tables, and became local heroes. All was good until a rival gang began muscling in on business.

Viktor and Edi sent their men to execute this gang. One by one they were slain – apart from leader Arjan Tamare who went into hiding. Edi tracked him down to a distant village cafe and approached him with a gun. He pulled the trigger but it misfired. Tamare shot him and walked over to spit on his dying body.

Viktor made it his life's mission to hunt down the son of a whore who'd murdered his brother. For the next six months the mission consumed his every moment. His gang were busy men. Rumours placed Tamare in Bosnia, Amsterdam, Berlin, and there were kidnaps, tortures and lives lost along the way.

Ultimately he was tracked down to an apartment only forty miles from where the feud began.

Tamare was held down as Viktor produced his customary cleaver. He raised it high and, in front of his wife and children, took the head from his shoulders. Arjan Tamare's body was returned to the town, his severed head paraded for all to see. Then it was let loose and kicked about like a football by the men in the square. Finally, explosives were rigged to his corpse and it was blown to pieces to a victorious applause and gunfire in the air. Two days and nights of lavish celebration followed.

Life continued until one morning the Albanian police pulled Viktor from his bed. He was jailed to await trial for murder. After a daring escape that involved the killing of two policemen, he laid low in Germany, before settling with a new identity in Barking, East London. He lived quietly with his new English wife and kids, only emerging to socialise at his local Albanian café, undertake the occasional hit job, or bed a mistress on the side. The warm familiar embrace of women from his proud homeland was something he missed.

His cell door opened. A uniform stood there flanked by several armed police in balaclavas and black combat gear.

'Okay mate, you're being moved to Paddington Green. It's Britain's top security police station.'

'Why?'

'We've just heard all about you. You're wanted by Interpol for several murders in Albania. That makes you too hot to handle in this nick.'

'This is bullshit,' Viktor yelled, pushing him away. 'I fuck your mother.'

The armed boys got him on the floor.

✳

Mike called just when they were tucking into their Nando's lunch. Lil took the call, nodding along not saying much.

'What did he want?' Bigz asked when Lil hung up.

Lil wiped his mouth with a napkin and leaned forward, 'He's giving us a hit.'

Bigz stopped chewing. 'He say that?'

'No, but when he sends you to see Magnum I can't think of any other reason.'

Bigz was puzzled. 'Who the fuck is Magnum?'

Back in the car Lil filled him in. 'He's a gun nut. From East Ham originally. Provides the tools and info for jobs. The story goes he once tried to join the army but they laughed him out of the recruiting office. He returned armed and loaded and shot the place up.'

'Man sounds like a clown,' Bigz laughed.

'Don't let him hear you say that. His best friend once told him he had a BO problem and he pulled out a .44 Magnum, shoved the barrel down his throat and choked the guy to death. That's how he got his name.'

They turned off Urswick Road and pulled in by Marian Court. The blocks were well grimy. Inside a grizzly-haired junkie sat on the stairs smoking crack from a Coke bottle. Bigz kissed his teeth as he brushed past. 'Fucking tramp. Council needs to do a clampdown. Get rid of these zombies.'

They reached Magnum's door, screamy rock music coming from inside.

Bigz frowned. 'Sure this is the right flat?'

'I can hear it's the right flat,' Lil nodded.

Magnum opened up, standing there in army fatigues, khaki headband over his Afro, eyeing them bluntly up and down.

'I know who you are,' he said to Lil, 'but who's this guy?'

'This is Bigz. He's safe.'

The man could benefit from a lesson in manners, but Bigz let it go. Trouble with Mike he didn't need.

They stepped in. The place was bare and grotty and smelled of stale sweat. Magnum nodded to a sofa, told them to take a seat. He pulled a chair opposite, sitting backrest forward and legs akimbo and produced a folder. 'I'm a busy man so I'll be brief.'

Lil nodded while Bigz grimaced at the boom box on the floor, the source of the repellent racket. If the guy wanted to punish his ears in his own time that was his problem, but why now?

Magnum looked at him. 'What's up?'

'This music, what is it?'

'Slayer. *God Hates Us All*. Why, you a fan?'

'Not exactly no. How about you turn down the volume, I can't hear myself think here.'

Magnum shook his head then reduced the noise. 'You happy now?'

'Not quite.' The flat was clammy and airless and Magnum's battered trainers were emitting a stink. Bigz got up to open a window.

'What you doing?'

'Letting some air in. Some of us need oxygen.'

'The windows are screwed in, security measures, so sit the fuck down.'

Kissing his teeth Bigz returned to his seat.

Magnum handed over a photo and papers. 'Right, here's the info. You've got to memorize this shit because in a minute it'll all be going up in smoke.'

Bigz looked at the target's photo. Dark hair, built, self-assured. He reminded him of some of the white guys he'd seen during a weekend stopover at HMP Chelmsford, their old-school cockney accents and loud Essex banter grating on him. He noticed the job was in North-West London, Jay's adopted territory.

Lil wasn't too thrilled either. On personal missions he'd travel anywhere, but on hired hits he preferred to keep things local, on terrain he knew like the back of his hand. But fuck it, it was money so why complain. He memorised the details and handed back the papers.

Magnum held them over a small metal bin, took a lighter to them.

'Okay, usual precautions Lil. Arrange an alibi just to be safe. Though of course that's up to you. But if you're tugged by Five-O you keep quiet or... well, you know the score.'

'I know the drill. Been there, wore the underpants.'

'You might because you're the meanest little fucker on the block, but your friend here I'm not too sure.'

Insulted, Bigz leaned forward. 'Now you listen to me...'

Magnum leapt to his feet. 'You got something to say, big man? Because if so I want to hear it right now.' He stood revealing the gun in his waistband.

Bigz dropped his gaze. 'Forget it,' he muttered.

Magnum sat back down but continued to stare at him.

'Look at me,' he said.

Bigz met his eye.

'Next time you leave your attitude at the door, you hear me?'

Bigz wanted to tear the man's face off now, but instead found himself nodding in compliance. So often these days he was having to submit to men whose throats he'd rather be slicing. Maybe Lil had the right idea about that kind of shit. Heads on plates and whatnot. He swore if he ever got the chance this man would be one sorry fucker.

'Another thing Lil, the job's to be undertaken pronto. Like this week, no later.'

'Not a problem.'

Briefing over they got up and headed back down the hallway, Magnum behind them. He tapped Bigz on the shoulder. 'Hey, you forgot something.'

Bigz turned to face the close-up barrel of a gun. He winced as Magnum clicked off some empty shots. 'Bam-bam-bam, motherfucker,' he smiled.

Bigz fought an urge to lunge at the bastard.

'Here, take it,' Magnum said and handed it over. 'It's the tool for the job. And here's the ammo clip. Good luck guys, happy shooting.'

Heading down the communal stairs Bigz was silently fuming. That last stunt had been a trick too far.

'Didn't exactly hit it off with him back there, did you B?' Lil smiled.

Bigz didn't reply. The smell of acrid crack smoke was nauseating. Reaching the final set of stairs the junkie was still sitting there. Bigz lunged, booting him in the back. He toppled to the floor. A flurry of kicks followed. 'Fucking junkie piece of shit, I'll kill you.'

Finally Lil pulled him away towards the car.

'Jeez B, you need to chill, serious. We don't need the eyeball right now.'

Breathing heavily Bigz climbed into the driving seat.

'Make no mistake, sometime, someplace, that joker's gonna pay for his performance back there.'

25

Sexy Motors

Dan sat behind the wheel of the Transit, Terry beside him, Andy and his workmate Rob in the back as they barrelled along into London. They were heading for the old manor to collect three top-notch sports cars from a lock-up, deliver them to a Romford warehouse. The van would be handy for any other bits and bobs worth pinching.

Reaching Hackney they drove along a lonely and neglected Homerton High Street. By some boarded-up shops two druggies were pushing each other, a mouthy-looking woman trying to prise them apart. One bloke punched the other and they both staggered back, landing on a pile of bin bags.

'You see that?' Dan laughed.

'Dear oh dear,' Terry shaking his head.

Curving into Clapton they passed Sutton House, now a museum.

'Remember that old place,' Dan pointed. 'It used to be derelict. Everyone said it was haunted. Tommy Croft's lot broke in there once and he said he got chased out by a ghost. An old woman or something, coming down some creaky old stairs with a candelabra screaming at him. Even recently he swore it was true.'

'Chased out by a drunken tramp more like,' Terry said. 'They used to doss in there. Oldest building in Hackney that is.'

On Lower Clapton Road they noticed The Lord Cecil pub was boarded up.

'Another boozer bites the dust,' Dan said. 'I remember you had it off with some girl in the bogs in there once. We must have been what, eighteen, nineteen? We used to drink back on the manor quite a lot then. I was trying to get off with her mate and she spewed all over me. You got your end away in the jacks, I ended up going home covered in snakebite and black.'

Terry laughed, said he couldn't remember that.

'That's probably because we were dipping into the old sulphate. We used to be bang on it right through the weekend back then. We got up to so many capers in those days I can't remember half of it myself.'

'Well that's saying something, because you remember fucking everything.'

'Not really.' Then Dan paused in thought. 'But looking back there's always the rose-tinted glasses thing. You only remember the good. Most times anyway. I mean, in our day Hackney was as rough as it got. There was violence everywhere, more than now I reckon, but I don't remember that side of things as much. I just remember the laughs, the good things that happened.'

Terry didn't quite agree, but said nothing. Hackney was bittersweet for him, with an emphasis on the bitter if he was honest. His brother's death coloured things. From that day on his parents became shadows of themselves. They were no longer fixtures that would be there for him forever. It was a case of counting down the years, months, days; Terry learning for the first time about death, finality. Things most youngsters don't dwell on.

A memory came to him. It was a few weeks after Lee died. Terry was in a small park close to where they were now, idling on a swing. Along walked two kids that like him were bunking off school. He sensed trouble. They chatted, sizing him up, then the largest one stepped forward and changed his tone, told him to hand over his money or he was getting battered. Terry didn't delay; he sprang at him and they grappled across the cracked tarmac. The boy was shocked at Terry's vigour, the smaller kid frozen, not knowing what to do. Neither had properly read the situation, hadn't expected Terry to fight, but since Lee died he had a burning knot in his chest, a rage longing for release. Why was Lee not here anymore? What had he done to deserve an end beneath the wheels of a train? Life was cruel. It was sick. It pulled these mad strokes and laughed in your face.

Terry headbutted the boy and he fell away. The fight was over, the smaller kid backing up saying he was sorry. Terry told him to fuck off and he ran, disappearing out of view. His mate was staggering to his feet when Terry grabbed a lump of brick and brought it down on his head. The boy dropped. He was motionless, bloody, and Terry wondered if he'd killed him. The brick was still in his hand and for a second he felt like finishing him off for definite. Getting down and pounding out the frustration. Instead he threw it and ran.

'Looks like we're here,' Dan said. They turned down by some railway arches and parked in at the end. Dan passed Terry a bike helmet and put one on himself. 'Better mask up unless you want to be on Crimewatch.'

They got out and Andy and Rob stepped out from the back. Andy was in a helmet, Rob wearing a joke shop face mask.

'Who's that supposed to be then?' Dan asked.

'Schwarzenegger – I'm the Terminator.'

'You plank.'

'Fuck you asshole.'

'You got your tools?'

'Course,' he said, carrying out a little kit.

'Get to work on the locks then. I'm itching to see the wares.'

Job done, they turned on the light and took in the scene. A Porsche Carrera, Lamborghini Gallardo and Mitsubishi Eclipse were sitting there as described.

'Fuck me,' Dan whistled. 'By the way, I'm driving the Gallardo.'

The walls were piled high with boxes, car accessories, electrical goods.

Terry counted roughly fifty boxes of Kenwood car radios. 'You know how much one of these goes for?'

'Money in pocket Tel. Let's whack the lot in the van. Remember, Croxy only mentioned the motors so anything else is ours.'

They began loading up. After a bit, Dan had a root about in the office. There didn't seem much worth nicking. Then in a cupboard he found a large holdall. He zipped it open. It was stuffed with bags of white powder, fat rolls of cash.

Jesus Christ.

With the boys still busy he gave Terry a discreet nod over. He showed him the contents. Terry's eyes widened in shock.

'This is ours, just me and you,' Dan whispered. 'Say nothing.'

Dan slipped the bag into the front boot space of the Gallardo. 'I'll stash it somewhere safe on the way back. You drive the van. We're fucking rich Tel.'

Terry was stunned, adrenaline fizzing through him.

'Looks like this is definitely no yuppie's garage then,' Dan nudged him. 'A dangerous firm more like. The quicker we're out of here the better.'

Van loaded, it was time to get these beauties on the road. Andy and Rob couldn't wait to climb into their wheels, laughing like two kids. They watched them go.

'Thank fuck those two didn't find this little lot,' Dan said, peering into the goody bag. 'Wouldn't be fair having to split it four ways, would it?'

The cash was all twenties and fifties, perhaps a hundred large in paper alone. They counted twenty-five blocks of white, a kilo each. 'Look at the texture, it's near pure,' Dan said. 'We're going to make a mint on this.'

Terry was worrying now. 'What if Croxy hears about it? He's in the trade so there's a chance he might. He'll know it was us and want a cut.'

'If he knew there was a monster stash of gear hanging about he would've told us. Don't worry about it.'

'I just wouldn't want him thinking we're fucking him over. Look at what happened to Rolex Roy.'

Dan knew the fate of Roy McLeish well. He ripped Croxton off in a property deal then had the gall to say, 'Sue me.' A month later he was found dumped near Beckton sewage works, covered in burns from a blow torch. Two men were jailed for his murder. The police couldn't prove Croxton's involvement, but it only upped his stature as a man not to cross.

'Tell you what,' Dan said. 'If Mr C finds out we'll cut him in. But only if necessary. Who knows, if all goes well we could even sell the stash to Croxy himself. Say we got hold of it elsewhere. He's a businessman, only cares about the bottom line.'

Dan zipped up the bag and let down the boot.

'Whatever happens,' he said, slapping Terry's back. 'Me and you are in the fucking money mate.'

He tossed Terry a roll of fifties. 'Take that. It's just the beginning.'

*

Hot Iron Mike sat in his office chair gazing with pleasure at the big-haired mixed-race girl in silver hotpants who was head-down working at his crotch. A knock sounded at his door.

'Who is it?'

'It's Clyde, boss. Some urgent news.'

'Come in,' he told his head minder.

As Clyde entered he saw Mike leaning back, a girl's head

340

going up and down. He drew back.

'Sorry chief, I didn't realise you were busy.' He ducked out, quickly closed the door. His boss was becoming more decadent by the day. It wasn't a good sign. When standards slip at the top the whole edifice can crack and things get dangerous.

'Come back in,' Mike laughed, and Clyde re-entered. 'Tell me, what is this urgent news?'

Clyde saw the lines of coke on the desk and the girl still working away and wished he'd left it for later, especially as Mike wouldn't be pleased with the news he was bringing him.

'It's your garage, boss.'

Hand buried in her hair, Mike halted the girl's movement and tilted his head. 'What about my garage?'

Clyde gulped. 'It's your cars. They're gone.'

Mike abruptly threw the girl aside. 'What did you just say?' She landed on the floor and one of her heels snapped. It was a Jimmy Choo copy as well. Fucking bastard. But she knew not to make a fuss.

'What do you mean my cars are gone?' Mike was on his feet now, doing up his flies.

'There was a break-in.' Clyde stepped back and put his hands up. 'Look, I got the call just now, I'm only relaying a message.'

'How could there be a break-in when Nasty Man's looking after the place? He's sleeping in there, ain't he?'

'Nasty's gone to Jamaica,' Clyde said of Mike's full-time mechanic. 'I mentioned his holiday to you last week and you said you'd sort it yourself, get someone else in'

'You're my head of security and you're blaming it on me?'

The girl said that she better be going. She grabbed her fur coat and handbag and made for the door.

'You do that bitch, fuck off,' Mike said, approaching the short but very wide Clyde. He stood over him, breathing angrily.

'I ain't blaming no-one boss,' Clyde reasoned, a pain growing in his chest. 'I'm just saying you took it out of my hands, said you'd arrange for someone to guard the place yourself.'

The last thing Clyde needed was a physical confrontation. Secretly he wasn't a well man. Recently he'd collapsed at home and was diagnosed with diabetes, plaqued arteries and other complications, the doctor explaining how his immense level of body fat was killing him. Despite his fearsome bulk he was on medication and feeling vulnerable right now.

'I've heard enough of your bullshit.' With crazed eyes Mike removed his belt and looped it around Clyde's neck. He began choking him. They lurched across the floor, Clyde trying to free his air passage.

'You telling me my beloved car collection is gone? Every fucking one?' Clyde's eyes bulged. 'I had other shit in there too, a bag of cash and supplies, has that disappeared too?'

Mike threw him to the floor and Clyde's crash land shook the room. Clyde gasped, clutching his neck.

'Who did this?' Mike shouted. 'Everyone knew about my lock-up. No crim would ever go near that place. Who hit it Clyde? Was it you, putting the word out thinking you could pull this shit on me?'

'No, I swear,' Clyde rasped. 'I'd never do that.'

Mike punched the wall, his fist going right through the plaster. He'd been caning the pharmaceuticals all through the weekend and hadn't slept in two nights. He'd been loosening his grip on the reins, letting things slide. Now this.

He kicked his security man in the belly, ordered him up. Clyde was convulsing on the floor, frothing at the mouth now. But Mike wasn't in the mood for his play-acting. The guy had fucked up major. Again he kicked him in the gut, then again, and finally stamped on his head.

'Get up you slimy fucker.' He hated it when his men pulled cheap stunts on him, especially ones who were supposedly loyal. You couldn't trust anyone nowadays. There were snakes crawling everywhere you looked. Then he recalled that Clyde had in fact notified him about Nasty-Man's holiday and he'd planned to get Lil Killa to kip in the place. But he'd forgotten all about it. He imagined a team of pussies out there right now with his precious whips, taking him for a fool, laughing at him. He looked at the fat lump by his feet, eyes closed and body trembling now. What did the guy want from him, sympathy?

'Get up Clyde, I ain't joking.'

His minder was unresponsive. Incensed, Mike rummaged through his desk drawers for his stun gun. If the guy wanted to play the unconscious game he'd soon wake him up, that's for sure. He Tasered Clyde's chest, shooting a hundred thousand volts through the fucker. Clyde's chest lifted then crashed back down. He repeated the process to no avail, finally tossing the gizmo across the room.

'I said wake up cocksucker!'

Mike knew he'd surpassed all reason now, but he was on a roll, venting off in hot blood. The idea of a bunch of lowdown street rats driving his prized cars was twisting his sanity. He grabbed his samurai off the wall, roaring as with two hands he brought it down into Clyde's chest, staking his trusted employee to the floorboards.

Clyde's eyes shot open as he exhaled his last breath, then they clouded over and their lights went out. Mike remained leaning over the sword as the tension drained. His head was clearer now. At last he stepped back to admire the scene. His cars were his babies, carefully customised to his every specification. He was in love with those whips. They were a part of him, an extension of his essence. But all wasn't fatal. The beauty of high earning was that anything lost can be replaced. He was thinking logically now. Cars, apartments, soldiers, women. All were disposable and available for re-purchase. Even the guy on the floor could be bought again. That was the beauty of capitalism, of free trade, free choice. And maybe it was time for some upgrades. Perhaps he could do even better this time. The possibilities excited him.

He recalled as a kid growing up in a council flat, always paging through the Argos catalogue, longing for the consumer items his skint mum could never afford. But things were different now. He could purchase whatever he wanted. Anything at all. Even if something wasn't for sale, his men could seize it. Anything in this world was his at the click of a finger.

Then he remembered the bag of product and cash. That meant a sizeable loss. Money he didn't have. He'd been wildly overspending of late and his finances would now be in serious shit. But even money can be replaced. He'd simply have to crack the whip. Get his men to work harder. Get out there every day, scheming, robbing, dealing, hauling in the cash by the shedload. The men who raided his garage were going to die. He'd have them torn apart limb by limb. There would be a full investigation and he'd use every tool in his arsenal to find them. Of that he was certain.

The ringing of his phone pulled him from his reverie. He returned to his seat to answer it.

'I heard some noise,' Deanna said. 'Is everything okay, boss?'

'Yes... well, no. Get Moses and Rib-Eye up here. Tell them to bring deep cleaning gear and a body bag.'

'A body bag?'

'You heard me,' he snapped. 'Big Clyde's had an accident. He's no longer with us. I want it all cleaned up nice and discreet, do you hear me?'

'Er, yes, no problem,' she said. 'Oh, something else boss. I paid the girl but had to give her extra for a broken stiletto? A couple of hundred. She said she okayed it with you, is that right?'

'You did what? You tell that Jezebel ho next time she'll be practising her oral skills on a burning hot iron, you got that?'

He kissed his teeth and hung up. He snorted some white lines then sat back in his chair. Frustration snaked through him like a curse. He searched in his desk drawers for his crack pipe, but couldn't find it. He tapped his fingers. The sight of Clyde slumped there messing up his top-dollar Persian carpet was making his blood boil. Here he was breaking his balls trying to run a tight ship and all he got in return was insubordination. What next, fucking mutiny? Clyde had got his just desserts coming at him with news like that. He thought of his interrupted play with Miss Hotpants. Can't a hard-working exec window in a little leisure time or was slavery back on? He shook his head, then stopped as a memory hit him.

He was twelve years old on the long-demolished Clapton Park Estate of his youth. He was being ambushed by a gang of boys. 'Stab him, stab him,' they chanted as a half-caste guy with freckles and slitty eyes came forward with a sharpened-up screwdriver. He said he was going to stick it in his head. Two of them pinned Mike down, the rest laughing and goading, before Big Clyde flew in fists flying and scattered the lot. The older youth helped him up. If those dickheads hassle you again, speak to me. He'd seen Clyde around but they'd never spoken. Clyde saved his arse that day. But he pushed the memory from his mind. It was different days, different times. And besides, in later years he paid Clyde good recompense, lining his pockets for standing around doing nothing more than show off his bulk. Any other boss would've put him on a club door for ten quid an hour tops and told him to be grateful.

He observed Clyde's lifeless face, mouth hanging open. Maybe he'd gone overboard, let his anger get the better of him there. But he pushed the notion aside before it bugged him. He hadn't got this far in the game to start letting regret cloud his vision, so why start now. Things are tough in this life, you live you die, shit happens.

Mike grabbed his jacket. The smell of blood and guts was beginning to turn his stomach. He headed for the door. He didn't want to see this place until it had been forensically cleaned and aired. Along the corridor, he felt the fatigue of a prolonged weekend. He needed to refresh. Shit was too fucked up round here for his liking.

'Deanna, I'm going to Pad No. 3 for some shut-eye. Tell nobody where I am and make sure I'm not disturbed.'

*

Going down the road for a morning paper, Quinn saw two men in a parked black Astra watching him. They'd been there yesterday too; same men, different car. It was loud and clear now, but to know the police had eyes on him changed everything. Concrete Kelly, with all his connections in high places, was already inside and if Quinn wasn't careful he'd be joining him.

He kicked himself. He should've kept his head down for six months, but he'd put himself about from virtually the word go. Perhaps the police had spotted him meeting with Kelly. Or maybe he'd been eyed on solo recces. More likely though, it was because a decade ago he'd shot one of their own, almost killed the bastard, and the filth had long memories. The worst thing he could do was stick his head in the sand. The cunts were throwing a spanner in the works.

On his way back from the shop he approached the car. The driver let the window down.

'Anything I can do for you, officer?' Quinn enquired.

The driver smiled, suppressing his surprise. He was a slick-looking bastard with gelled-back hair.

'Just keeping an eye, Sean. No harm in that is there. Anyway, how's life on the outside?'

'Good. Very good. Didn't know I needed protection though.'

The copper laughed. 'We've got better things to do than protect the likes of you, as you well know.'

Quinn smiled. He looked left and right. 'What's the big interest then?'

'That'd be telling wouldn't it.'

Quinn leaned down for a view of the other copper, a slob who was munching from a bag of doughnuts.

'You want some extra sauce on that, fatboy?'

The man almost choked and the driver put his hand up. 'Leave it, ignore him,' he told his mate. 'Now run along Sean, we're just doing our job. Orders from on high. Keep your nose clean and you'll see less of us.'

'Whatever you say. I'll leave you and doughboy to do whatever it is you're doing. Me, I've got places to go, people to see.'

The pair watched him walk across to his digs, go inside.

Dev turned to his associate. 'How did I do, Chris?'

'Fuck me, you do a copper impersonation pretty well. Good job the prick didn't come to my window though, the mouthy cunt, I might've lamped him one.' He wiped the sugar from his top.

'He bought it so it's all that matters.' Dev started the engine. 'We've seen enough. Typical lag, routine like clockwork. It's all set for Mike's men now. Let's get out of here.'

Quinn sat in his room. Involvement with Kelly had been a bad move. The bloke gets arrested then the police are outside his door. Who knows what tunes Kelly was singing to the bastards. Even if it was a coincidence it wasn't looking good. He'd have to get away for a while until the heat died down. A cousin in Manchester had offered him a job in his pub which he'd declined. Maybe he'd see if the offer still stood. Bernie and Phil owed him but that debt could be settled another time. Getting hauled back inside just wasn't worth it. If he'd almost opened Phil's face the other night, what else would he end up doing if he hung around?

He looked at the rolled-up fiver and the white crumbs on his bedside table. The powder would have to go. It was making him reckless. He was heading up north for definite. New start, new habits. Clear his head, get energised, then six months or so down the line he'd return a new man. Ready to collect.

26

The Crack Up

Evening and Bigz and Lil Killa were parked near the target's house, waiting for him to exit. It was fairly quiet, not too many passers-by. They'd been advised against a doorstep job as the house was multi-occupied and they could end up popping a stranger. The target left to go drinking most nights so it was best to positively identify, then get up behind him and bam, job done. The job had to be clean and professional. No fuck ups. Yesterday they'd agreed on Bigz doing the gunwork on this one, a face-saving move that he now regretted.

Bigz held the gun in his gloved hands, mask at the ready. He felt agitated, anxious almost. He wasn't in the mood for this shit tonight and hoped the target wouldn't show. Tomorrow would be better, or even next week. Or how about Lil just do the fucking thing and him take the wheel? Bigz had never done a planned hit before and was feeling the pressure. He tapped his fingers, annoyed at how relaxed Lil seemed to be, and finally announced he needed a leak - anything to stretch his legs for a minute. He was about to open the door when Lil said, 'Wait, here he is.'

The target stepped out and set off up the street.

'That definitely him?'

'One hundred percent. Go B, just get up behind and bang him.'

Suddenly a police siren sounded from a couple of streets away and Bigz froze.

'Abort, leave it,' Lil quickly said.

The siren faded and the target was away in the distance now. They watched him turn the corner towards the main drag.

'Shit,' Lil slammed the wheel. 'We've missed our chance.'

Bigz was quietly relieved. Now he'd be able to go home and hit the sack.

Lil started the engine. 'I'm not waiting another night, no way. Let's improvise, see where he's going. I bet he'll catch a bus down to that pub he drinks in. Let's see.'

Out on Burnt Oak Broadway they watched Quinn run for a southward bus, climb aboard.

'Bingo.'

They drove the straight five-miles down the A5 to Kilburn and found a parking space on a side-road opposite the pub. Within fifteen minutes Quinn entered the place.

'Right, there you go. Now we keep watch and wait,' Lil said, slouching low to settle in. 'Do him on his way out.'

'I'm not sure about this location,' Bigz said, searching for excuses. 'I'll have to cross the busy road, then get all the way back over here again. That could be tricky. And what about passers-by?'

'Traffic's slow. There's people here and there, but that shouldn't be a problem either. You're masked up, the car's re-plated, so rest easy.'

Bigz was silent. Why had he accepted triggerman duties when Lil was a trusted pro at this shit? He had a meeting first thing tomorrow morning at Stratford nick, which probably explained why he wasn't feeling his best right now. It was going to be his longest round of questioning yet, and they'd warned him they expected some solid info this time.

'And remember, finish him off with two good ones to the skull. You don't want him getting up and walking again, you know what I mean?'

Bigz nodded. Then he exhaled. 'But this could take hours. You know what these Irish guys are like, what if he stays in the pub knocking back ten pints?'

'Don't matter if he's there till the break of dawn. You've got to be patient with this shit. Chill. A good job takes time. Let's just keep our eyes on the door.'

Quinn walked in and sat at the bar. Tara saw him, turned away and continued stacking glasses. The gall of the man. She considered walking up and barring him on the spot, and definitely would if he dared utter one word to her. Two men along the bar sensed the tension and took their drinks to a table.

'Tara, listen,' Quinn said. 'I'm sorry about your old man.'

She came forward, eyes flashing. 'Get the fuck out of here you bastard.'

'Come on, don't be like that.'

'I said out.'

'I just want to say goodbye. I'm leaving. You won't see me round here anymore. I'm going up north, staying at my cousin's pub for a while. I'll be pulling pints just like you.'

'Go to hell.'

'When the time comes I'm sure I will be,' he laughed.

She served an old boy with a hearing aid. Quinn could tell she'd cooled. But only slightly.

'You still here?' she said, filing a nail.

He looked at her. 'Good while it lasted though, wasn't it?'

'I wish I'd never seen your face.'

'You've seen more than my face recently and you weren't complaining there.'

Tara leaned in, speaking quietly. 'My dad's stuck in front of the telly with stitches on his face. He hasn't left the house since you attacked him. You're an animal. I know all about you now. A decade ago you got put away, my dad and another mate didn't, and you're bitter about it. Well that's life, so you can just piss off.'

He laughed at her venom, shook his head. 'Fair play. One last pint and I'm gone.'

With a tut she poured him a Guinness, planted it down with no graces.

Bernie walked through the door but stopped when he saw Quinn. He'd come to call in on Phil, see how he was doing. But here the bastard was, again talking to Phil's daughter. He was taking the fucking piss. He was about to turn back when Quinn called him over.

'Come in Bernie, I won't bite you.'

Tara gave him a free pint. 'You deserve it - he doesn't.'

'How's it swinging Bern?' Quinn asked when she'd gone to serve some newcomers.

Bernie wasn't in the mood for niceties. 'Same old.' He stared ahead.

'Well one thing, you'll be happy to know I'm pissing off for a while.'

Bernie turned to him. 'Where are you going?'

'Up north.'

Bernie paused. 'Your cousins in Manchester?'

'Spot on. You remember Aidan? He's running his old man's pub now. Same place we used to stay in up there.'

Bernie recalled the nights almost two decades back when they'd spent some weekends hitting the clubs up there. Aidan was a lively little scally-type who ran around selling Es.

'You should see him now. He's built like a brick shithouse. I met him inside once up the country after not seeing the fucker for years. I'm just after talking to him on the phone earlier. He remembers you well. Said you were a right good laugh.'

Bernie nodded. 'He was a decent fella.' He didn't know what

more to say. He'd just paid a substantial sum to have Quinn wiped out and here they were reminiscing.

'You heard about Concrete Kelly yet?' Quinn asked.

'No, what's happened?'

'He's been nicked. He's in Belmarsh.' He studied Bernie's reaction after holding the news back for a fortnight. 'Guess you were right about the job not being a good idea.'

Bernie was worried now. Did the police know about the job? Conspiracy can land you years.

'What was Kelly nicked for?'

'Nothing to do with the graft, so you can relax. Some bent horse racing caper. He's looking at seven to ten I reckon, maybe more.'

'What if he does a deal, starts naming names?'

Quinn eyed him. 'Worried you might have to finally do some bird, Bern?'

Bernie didn't reply.

Tara came over wiping the bar. She ignored Sean.

'She's only allowing me the one,' he told Bernie. 'Then I'm barred.'

'I'm sure Phil's not feeling too good either,' Bernie said into his pint.

Perhaps he shouldn't have said that, but Quinn answered, 'No, I'm sure he's not.'

The conversation was stilted until Quinn placed down his empty glass.

'Well, that's me, I suppose.'

Bernie turned to him. 'Good luck.'

'Yeah, and you.' He stood, zipped up his jacket. 'But don't worry Bern, it's a temporary measure. We'll meet again, don't you forget that.'

'See you babe,' he called to Tara. 'Nice knowing you.'

She refused to turn. Quinn walked out and Bernie stared into his pint. He had a troublesome feeling. Should he tell Phil to call off the hit, or was Quinn just playing mind games? He'd have his drink then go upstairs and see what Phil had to say.

Meanwhile Tara stood vigorously polishing a glass, lips pursed. Good riddance to the bastard.

'Go, go, go!' Lil said.

Bigz woke up; he'd been dozing. Quickly he masked up, checked his gun and got out of the car. Quinn stood outside the pub thumbing his phone. There was a lull in the traffic as Bigz crossed towards him. Halfway over he raised his weapon and fired. Quinn jerked and Bigz fired another. He staggered and dropped to the deck. Bigz was approaching for the head shots when he heard an accelerating car. Suddenly he was thrown into the air with force.

Quinn had been hit in the chest and left wrist. He'd seen the gunman, knew it was a hit. Bernie and Phil, those conniving bastards. Then he'd watched a car purposely plough into the man, throw him out of view. Time slowed as the handgun appointed to kill him landed near the gutter, two metres from where he lay. Quinn crawled, gripped the piece and got to his feet. He staggered over to where the hitman lay injured on his back, moaning in the middle of the road. He heard panicked voices, someone screaming, a car horn sounding a long note. Faces peered down from a stalled bus as Quinn raised the gun. The man looked stunned, his flight and crash land something he hadn't bargained for. His hands were empty now, spine twisted, blood around his head. His mask hung to the side revealing his face. Quinn didn't know him; a hired gun for definite.

Bigz looked pained. 'Please, no.' Quinn blasted a hole in his chest. He fired again, centre forehead this time, and Bigz was motionless, dead.

Quinn looked around. Car lights and shop fronts blurred, the myriad sound of the street whirling in his ears. He was losing consciousness, the world slowing around him. Distant sirens sounded as he staggered back to the pavement. The gun dropped from his hand, blood coming up his throat. He fell and lay face-down, life force slipping away.

Stunned, Lil Killa fumbled to start the engine. He did a three-point turn and distanced himself from the scene. What the hell had he just witnessed? He'd heard of own goals with ricochets, but this was a whole new level. This was blasting lead into somebody all for them to rise like Lazarus, give you a taste of your own gun. But who would have factored a have-a-go hero flying in like a steamroller? Bigz hadn't been cut out for the job. He'd started firing too early, from too far a distance. Lil cursed himself for allowing Bigz to take the reins. If he himself had stepped up they'd be on their way now, assignment complete and a nice financial bonus to look forward to. Instead Bigz was dead, the status of the target uncertain, and Lil had the wrath of his lunatic boss to deal with.

Big Clyde's body was found in a wheelie bin beneath a rundown towerblock in Stratford. Word on the street was an increasingly unstable Hot Iron Mike had murdered his own minder on a whim, and people were not happy, including some of Mike's own henchmen. Clyde was a long-term member of Mike's security team and his reward for faithfully watching the don's back was to be stabbed and left out for the binmen like a piece of rubbish. Things were hotting up, a thirst for vengeance brewing.

Mike, none the wiser, woke up from a long sleep, his phone vibrating next to him. Answering it, an anonymous voice told him he was going to die. He shot up and told the man to go fuck himself. The caller laughed and the line went dead. Mike thought he was still dreaming until he remembered what he'd done to Big Clyde. Groaning he flopped back down on the bed wishing he could wake to a parallel universe where the incident had never happened. What the fuck had he wasted him for?

Everyone loved Clyde. Nobody had a bad word for the guy. Mike did his good turns for the hood, put his money where his mouth was, but Clyde took that community shit to another level. Recently Clyde had featured in an *Evening Standard* spread talking about his youth mentoring and hands-on charity work, helping kids get into sport and music, away from knives and crime. He'd had a photoshoot with the mayor and there was even talk of an upcoming MBE. The guy had been one hundred per cent reliable. He was going to be missed.

Mike phoned Deanna. She told him they'd found Clyde's body.

'The police got any leads?'

'The only lead is the gang of debtors from Stratford who he secretly owed a shitload of money to.'

'Good girl,' he smiled, glad he'd messaged her last night to get that rumour out there. 'You checked that with Serpico?' he asked, referring to their top inside man, a superintendent at Stoke Newington copshop.

'Of course.'

'Any other news?'

'Er...' She seemed a touch reluctant.

'Come on then, spit it out.'

'Somebody's been phoning the office. About Clyde. Saying stuff not very nice I'm afraid.'

'Like what?'

'Threats mainly, but I'm sure it's nothing to worry about. Security recognised the voice.'

'Who is it?'

'Clyde's cousin. A Tottenham man. Bloodstar, I think he's called.'

Mike's head pounded. He'd forgotten Clyde had a cousin in the Totty Man Dem. A war with Tottenham was the last thing he needed; troop morale was low and the attention would affect profits. However, Bloodstar was only mid-ranking and Mike was tight with their main man Pitbull Tony, he'd known him for years. Tony would never turn on Mike for such a trifle. But the fact was, someone had been telling tales.

'Tell me D, has there been a leak? Has someone put it out there that I killed Clyde?' He was suspicious of everyone now, including her.

'Not me boss, I promise you.'

He pounded his bedside table. 'How do I know that?'

'I swear down, it wasn't me.'

'Now you listen to me good. You better keep your eyes and ears peeled on this because if someone's been talking, I swear to God I'll be going full-blown Biblical.'

'Yes Mike, but I swear I…'

'Yes BOSS to you bitch, you hear me?'

She apologised.

Mike clutched his head and exhaled. He'd been hard on Deanna lately and needed to control himself, keep his inner circle onside or he risked his organisation crumbling like a house of cards. From now on the crack pipe was a no-no. It was bringing only grief.

'Look D, I'm just a little stressed at the moment, you understand what I'm saying?'

'Of course I do Mike, it's a difficult time. But the bad times will pass, they always do.'

'Get a message to Serpico. If he works his magic on this, diverts attention from me, he'll be getting a generous bonus.'

'I'll do that.'

'How are the security guys, Moses and Rib-Eye, they okay with everything?'

'They're fine. It's all good.'

'Expand on that – Clyde was a close friend of those two.'

'I know, but business is business. There's ups and downs, you roll with it. They understand that.'

He nodded. His secretary knew to say the right thing, but

hopefully those words were true. The pressure eased. Maybe he could ride this out and a few weeks from now it would all be history.

'I'm going to try and chill for a bit. Keep me posted on any developments.'

He needed some aspirin and headed for the bathroom cabinet. On the coffee table he saw a rolled-up fifty and a mound of coke. Fuck the aspirin, he needed a sharpener. He'd sunk low, been slipping, but he was on top of things now. He sat and considered the state of affairs.

With threats incoming, there had to be a snitch in the mix. Most likely in his own security team. Of the two remaining minders, he pinpointed the youngest man Rib-Eye as the culprit. The guy had an attitude. It was subtle, but he'd noticed it. A kind of arrogance. As if looking at Mike he thought: I could do what that mutha does and maybe one day I will.

He grabbed his phone. 'Deanna, tell Rib-Eye to call me asap.'

'Is everything okay Mike? You don't suspect he's the snitch, do you?'

'I can't answer that one D. But there's a traitor in our midst and hell or high water I'm gonna find him.'

Rib-Eye sat in the security room with Moses, an old G never short of a story that he loved taking his sweet old time to tell. Today Moses was recounting the time he'd fired a shotgun into the police line during the Broadwater Farm riots back in '85. He was three flights up blasting shots down into the uniformed throng. The police were jumping wild like a hive of bees. Rib-Eye was laughing along when his phone went. Deanna relayed the message.

'Me, are you sure?'

'He's not happy. He thinks you might've spread the word about Clyde.'

He jumped up. 'What the fuck? What would I do that for?'

'Calm down, he gave me an earful too. Just phone him and put him right on the matter.'

Rib-Eye hung up. He turned to Moses, who was shaking his head. 'Mike's out of control,' he said. 'He's turning on his own men wholesale now.'

Last night they'd dumped Clyde's body. Their workmate had caught Mike at a bad time and been unlucky. Neither approved but it was just one of those things. What happened at work stayed at work.

'If Mike's been grassed,' Moses said, 'it could only come from this building. So if we want to live another day it's in our interest to root out the culprit.'

Rib-Eye sat back down. Just then the cleaner passed by their open door, humming a tune as he wheeled a mop and pail along the corridor. Old Winston was an ancient Bajan whose temper would flare at anyone he saw dropping litter in or around the building. He took such pride in his work that he even once reprimanded Mike after he lobbed a Snickers wrapper towards the bin and missed. Mike laughed the lecture off, which made Winston pretty unique.

Ribs and Moses turned to each other in unison. Old Winston had been on the premises last night when they removed Clyde's body. They'd presumed he hadn't noticed anything, but maybe the old dude was sharper than they realised.

Rib-Eye shook his head. 'Nah, Winston wouldn't do that. He knows the score.'

Moses agreed. Then he raised an eyebrow and leaned forward. 'But if the worst comes to the worst...'

Rib-Eye looked puzzled, so Moses continued. 'What I'm saying is, if this becomes a life-or-death situation, we've got a scapegoat – right there. You understand me?'

'You mean blame it on Winston?'

'Only if absolutely necessary.'

It was a drastic measure but perhaps the man had a point. Sometimes you just have to pass the buck.

Moses closed the door and suggested he call Mike without delay.

Rib-Eye took out his phone and steeled himself. 'Hi boss, it's me,' he said, trying to sound upbeat. 'Deanna said you wanted a word.'

Mike launched into a tirade that whoever grassed him was getting chopped up and fed to the pigs. Go on, admit it, it was you, you scumbag piece of shit…

Rib-Eye's denials went unheard as Mike continued his rant. 'You and that motherfucker Moses think you can plot against me? I'll punish you so bad you'll regret you ever walked this earth...'

'No boss, this is crazy talk.'

'You calling me crazy? I'll crucify the fucking pair of you!'

Mike was relentless. There was no reasoning with him. Finally Rib-Eye turned to Moses. The older man solemnly nodded, giving him the go-ahead.

'It was Old Winston,' Rib-Eye announced. 'We heard him make a call.'

At last there was silence.

Deanna went downstairs to hear the latest. Opening the door she saw them on the floor zipping Old Winston into a body bag.

'Come in and shut the door,' Rib-Eye hissed.

'What are you two doing?'

'What does it look like? Winston snitched on Mike. He confessed, told us everything. We're just following orders now.'

Deanna wondered if they were being truthful. A confession was plausible I suppose because maybe Winston had finally lost the few marbles he had left. But more likely they were just using their heads, getting themselves out of the firing line.

'We did him with a pillow, now we're going to dump him

round the back where he leaves the rubbish. Make it look like a natural death.'

'Good thinking,' she nodded.

She returned to her desk and sat filing her nails with a sense of satisfaction. Mike's days on this earth were almost done. Thanks to a call she'd made earlier, the Tottenham boys would soon be paying his safe house a visit. She'd been lucratively rewarded - just like when she'd grassed Mike's garage info to an Essex firm. But more than money, it was a matter of self-respect. Boss or not, no man spoke to her the way Mike had been lately. No man.

27

London is Alive

Tottenham men Tony 'Pitbull' Johnson and Darryl 'Bloodstar' Lewis pulled up by one of the several anonymous locations across the borough where the Hackney bossman rested his head. The new privately-rented development had replaced a notorious council estate, its car park boasting a range of Audis, Range Rovers and Mercs, the complex popular with City professionals who only a few years ago would've run a mile from the Hackney hoodlands.

Mike was currently up there in flat 10 without so much as a single minder. Perhaps he thought he was indestructible. Who knows. But he'd been losing the plot recently, demanding bigger cuts, meddling in too many men's affairs, amassing enemies at an unsustainable rate. Even his closest lieutenants had grown tired of his ways, and on being informed of imminent action, many had agreed to turn a blind eye. But Mike's biggest crime was killing Bloodstar's cousin Clyde, a final straw that warranted only one penalty.

They swiped in and entered the block. The concierge had

been paid off, told to take a spliff break; the CCTV system awaiting repair. It was time to shake up the dynamic, make some history. Pitbull and Bloodstar were coming to deliver the news.

Mike sat in front of the TV clutching his crack pipe. He'd found a stash of rock and succumbed to the temptation. His eyes stared at the screen, his mind elsewhere. He was reeling back through the years. Recalling his rise up the criminal ladder. The ruthless dog-eat-dog violence that consolidated his rep.

He remembered early on when the Turks hired his team for a punishment job. A thief hung upside down in a warehouse near Manor House. He'd nicked a key of H and was being set as an example. It was the first time Mike had used a hot branding iron. His sadism that night sickened even his hardest men but earned him a catchy moniker that endured.

He recalled another time when he shot a rival behind a snooker club in Dalston. The man lay on the ground in a string vest, groaning from a neck wound. Mike pocketed his gun and walked up to him. He flicked out a knife, got down and cut open his vest. Inserting the blade into his skin, he sliced him open neck-down-to-his-groin like a pig. The man screamed and bled to death where he lay.

Whispers spread that Mike's act of butchery had included castration. That he'd stuffed the man's balls in his mouth and walked away laughing. He found that claim amusing and didn't deny it. Henceforth his name was spoken in hushed tones, igniting such fear that whenever the police tugged him, witnesses refused to snitch and he walked every time.

But Mike had more strings to his bow than brutal street thug. He worked hard and went on to become a successful entrepreneur, running a recording studio, record company, football team, fingers in every pie going, and his talents were spotted by respected kingpin Errol 'Dice' Daniels.

Mike became Dice's top associate and personal friend; Dice priming the younger man up to steer the ship when the day came to put his feet up and enjoy the fruits of his long career. With the don's throne awaiting him, Mike knew to keep the man sweet, but after four years of marking time his patience was running thin. He wanted the promotion fast-tracked. Blasting the kingpin out of existence would ensure a speedier process.

Dice never went anywhere without his minder Moses. But Mike uncovered a glitch in their security arrangements. Dice was balling a rival face's woman in Wood Green and rode solo on these jaunts, left his muscle at home. One rainy night Mike hid in an alley off Perth Road waiting for Dice to exit the house. When Dice appeared, Mike emerged with a Webley revolver. He motioned him back into the alley, wanted to enjoy this. He ordered his superior to his knees. Dice looked more disappointed than shocked. He wanted to know who put him up to this. You think I'm taking orders? Mike laughed. You're looking at the new bossman. Dice tried to pull his own gun and Mike shot him in the head. Dice lay spread out cold. Mike's promotion to top dog had just been granted. With a snigger he disappeared into the rainy night.

The doorbell sounded and Mike was jolted back to the present. He jumped to his feet, pulled his automatic. 'Who the fuck is it?'

'Hey Mike, it's me, Pitbull Tony. How you doing brother?'

Mike checked the spyhole and sighed in relief. It was his good Tottenham friend. Rival fiefdoms or not, CEOs stuck together. He returned the gun to his waistband and opened the door.

'Jesus, Tone, you surprised me there. Come in.'

Bloodstar stepped out from the side levelling a gun, silencer attached.

'Fuck you, Mike.'

He shot him in the face. Mike's cheek burst open, teeth and blood spraying, and he staggered back. Another bullet to the torso and he dropped. He lay clutching his chest, face scrunched in agony.

'Pussy motherfuckers,' he managed, before he took a final blast in the head.

His assassins stood gazing down at the scene. Hot Iron Mike lay sprawled in a mess of blood and gore, yet the don had never looked so peaceful. Mission accomplished the two men closed the door, walked downstairs and exited the building.

*

Terry and Dan took their stools at the jump, the barmaid presenting two pints. Terry pulled out a wad and told her to take one for herself and put a twenty in the charity mug. Life was rosy and it was looking to be a cracking summer. Earlier they'd been over to Basildon where they'd sold their stash of white for a good price. Paul Croxton hadn't wanted it but knew a friend who did.

'So,' Dan smiled, palate refreshed. 'How does it feel to be in the money Tel?'

'What can I say? I'm staggered, I really am.'

'Well you still haven't made your first million, but you're getting there.'

'Two hundred and thirty grand apiece? I couldn't be happier.'

'I told you something else would come up. It always does.'

'You're right there Dan, I'll tell you that.'

'So are you going to bring the family on holiday?'

'Definitely. Then when I come back I'll get a nice Range Rover. How about you?'

'Two weeks in Greece mate, then maybe get a Jag.' Dan took a sip of lager then turned to him. 'You told the missus yet?'

'No, but I will,' Terry said. 'All in good time.'

'What are you going to say, you won it on the nags?'

'That amount? Don't think so. But Stacey won't mind. She acts all prim and proper these days, but she won't ask. Never used to back in the day. Well, until I got banged up that last time. She grew up with naughtiness all around her. She knows the score.'

'That's the thing though isn't it. Don't get caught, but if you do don't expect tea and sympathy.'

Terry nodded. Only yesterday he'd been down B&Q for some bits and bobs to repair the patio when he noticed a streak of blood he'd missed in the boot of his car. Imagine if the police saw that. There he was, driving round for weeks on end with evidence that could have had him lifed off. He drove straight down to Big Al's scrapyard and had the motor destroyed.

'Before I get the Rover though I might have to hire something,' Tel mused. 'Or I could always use Stacey's Clio.'

'What about your own motor?' Dan asked.

'It's gone, I scrapped it.'

'Insurance job?'

'No, I just wanted rid. It was past it, gave me untold grief.'

Dan smiled. 'What you been up to Tel? Been out swinging your axe again?'

'Behave. I just fancied a change. I hardly need to count the pennies now, do I?'

'True. But don't spunk it all, that's all I can say. I've done that enough times myself to know. Invest it. I'm thinking of putting a lump into stocks and shares. Keep it legit. The market's good at the moment, you can't go wrong.'

'That might be a good idea.'

They sat in thought for a bit. Then Terry said, 'Thanks for counting me in Dan, I mean it. You could've kept that holdall all for yourself.'

'How long have we been mates? Don't be silly.'

Terry smiled wryly. 'Wonder how Andy and Rob are doing?'

'Don't worry about those two, they pull in a tidy profit legit with their plumbing firm. Think of yourself, it's your turn now.'

Terry nodded. It was true. It was about time he had some cash in his pocket. The only thing that niggled was the fact he'd made it from drugs. It wasn't junk or crack, but even so. The other day Stacey had found a wrap of coke in Leah's jacket and kicked up a right fuss. She got Terry to join in with the bollocking. All considering, he felt a little grubby. A few years ago Stacey's niece Melissa went from taking E's and coke at clubs to injecting H on the streets. The girl was skin and bones towards the end, but still rejected all help. Terry saw the damage at close range and it wasn't funny. He would've preferred the windfall to have come from a bank or some rich company, the kind of bastards who deserve it. But he was just being soppy. Unrealistic. Drugs was where the money was and it had been that way for years, even when he was running round with a balaclava and a shotgun. As Dan had told him, if they hadn't sold the stash, somebody else would've. Likely people with no morals at all. It's just the way it goes. Terry pushed the thought from his mind. It was a debate for another day. He was just glad to be flush.

Dan was paging through the *Daily Star.* A headline caught his eye.

CRIME LORD SHOT DEAD ON DOORSTEP. The shooting in Hackney was described as 'like a scene from a gangster film … Michael 'Hot Iron' Jacobs is thought to have been heavily involved in London's criminal underworld...

'Here, have you seen this?' Dan read the article aloud: '*This follows a double murder in North-west London on Wednesday night when two men died of gunshot wounds in a shootout believed to be a hit gone wrong.'*

Terry shook his head. 'There's so many killings these days it's hard to keep track.'

'Look at the state of this cunt,' Dan laughed, pointing to a mugshot of one of the victims, a thick-necked black man staring into the camera with an almost-comical grimace. Then he read about the other victim:

'*Sean Quinn was a recently released armed robber from*

Kilburn... Kilburn? I wouldn't be surprised if Concrete Kelly had something to do with this.'

Terry turned to the paper, interested now.

'Kelly gets himself locked up then people start dying,' Dan said. 'I'll have to talk to my sister about this.' He read on, then said, 'Look, this bloke was a hired gun. He shot Quinn as he left the pub, then a spirited member of the public ploughs his car into him. Gun goes flying, Quinn picks it up and shoots his assailant dead before dying himself. Luck of the Irish, eh?'

'What do you think it was all about?'

'Fuck knows. But it's good we never did that graft, that's for sure. Not with all this shit going on. In fact, we still better watch it.' Dan lowered his voice right down. 'Forget the filth, I'm talking about the real big boys out there. People dangerous to our health. Don't forget, we nicked someone's pension, or a group of people's, and they're obviously not too happy about it.'

'But they're never going to know who did it, are they?'

'Not if we keep shtum, no.'

'Well I'm not telling anyone.'

'Nor am I. But keep your ears open and watch out.'

Terry nodded.

'Anyway, that's by the by,' Dan said, not wanting to ruin their good cheer. He pushed the paper away. 'Onwards and upwards. It's time to enjoy the good life for a bit. Put the stress on hold. There's nothing a good wad of cash can't solve in this life mate, nothing.'

'Well said,' Terry agreed. When in doubt Dan's positivity was much needed. They clinked glasses. 'Let's drink to that.'

A few minutes later Terry's phone went. It was Stanley Dawson, the old boy he'd taken to Stansted Airport a while back. Stan asked if he could bring him on the same run this evening, around eight. He was sorry if it was short notice, his son had promised to take him, but he had work commitments.

'Of course I can,' Terry said. 'I'll be there eight sharp. No problem at all.'

When he hung up Dan asked who it was.

'A cab job, believe it or not.'

'I thought you were handing in your notice?'

'It's an old boy who knows Stacey's old man. I don't mind. I'll borrow her Clio.'

'Is he one of those *I knew the Krays* types?'

'He fucking did though, serious. The Krays, Nashes, Blundell brothers, you name it. He's no fantasist either.' Terry finished his pint. 'I suppose if I'm driving later I better switch onto lemonade.'

They sat having the craic for an hour, then Terry went home for a bite to eat and a word with Stacey. He hugged her in the kitchen.

'What's all this?' she said. 'What are you so happy about?'

'Nothing. I'm just happy I've got you.'

'Yeah, right. You on the funny pills?'

Later on his way to Woodford to pick up Stanley, he thought about how he'd broken the news to her. He'd said he'd come into some money, but before you start worrying, it was a one off.

She was shocked at first but ended up dancing around the room. Dan was right. Money solved everything.

He pulled up outside Stanley's house and went up the path to ring the bell. The old boy opened up and Terry took his suitcase.

'Nice to see you again Tel, how are things?'

'Sweet. Couldn't be better. You?'

'I'm off to the sun guv, can't complain.'

He put his case in the boot and the old boy smiled. 'No bodies in there this time is there?'

Terry stopped and turned to him.

'No mate. I did the Epping Forest run earlier. Six foot deep with a shovel, slung the fucker in and Bob's your uncle. Cleaned up the mess and you could eat your dinner out of this boot now.'

He let it down.

'You crack me up,' said the old gangster. He climbed into the car. 'That's what I like about you Tel. Always good for a laugh. And if you can't have a good old laugh in this life, what can you have?'

'You're not wrong there, Stan,' Terry smiled as they hit the road. 'You are not wrong there.'

Postscript

Thank you for reading my first novel. I hope you enjoyed it.

If so, please feel free to leave a review up on Amazon, even if it's only a line or two. Reviews are much appreciated.

Until next time…

Printed in Great Britain
by Amazon

26081515R00209